UNSUITABLE

Unsuitable

SUZY PARSONS

Quartet Books

FT

First published in 2008 by
Quartet Books Limited
A member of the Namara Group
27 Goodge Street, London W1T 2LD

Copyright © Suzy Parsons 2008

The right of Suzy Parsons to be identified
as the author of this work has been asserted
by her in accordance with the
Copyright, Designs and Patents Act, 1988

A catalogue record for this book
is available from the British Library

ISBN   978 0 7043 7129 3

Typeset by Antony Gray
Printed and bound in Great Britain by
T J International Ltd, Padstow, Cornwall

ACKNOWLEDGEMENTS

I would never have started writing this book if my husband, Jamie, had not told me I'd never finish it. And he may have been right had it not been for the following people, to whom I am deeply indebted: Judith Burnley, Alison Dean, Vee Lillis, Freddie Stockdale, Adrian Rowbotham, Lucy Fox, Jean Diamond and Marnie Rose, for their unfailing encouragement and support; my father, for his wise counsel as ever; my wonderful children, Annabel and Tom, for the joy they bring; and Alex, who understands not all stepmothers are wicked!

A special thank you to Patrick Stephansen and David Charters for introducing me to David Elliott, and to Naim Attallah at Quartet for having faith in a first-time author.

And my gratitude to Peter Mason, Maxine Kemp, Dimitri Hadjiminas, Catherine Hadjiminas, Helgi Johannsson, the nurses on the 4th floor at the Harley Street Clinic, Val, Karen and Caroline, Professor Trevor Powles and Clare Hambro, who were all there for me at a difficult time. I'll never be able to thank you enough.

TO MY MOTHER

1

I had to find a suitable husband before I was thirty, even if it did mean following what my mother had told me – on more than one occasion: 'Marriage is so difficult, darling, but if you must marry, make it easier by marrying someone of the same religion, background and colour and of the opposite sex. Then you argue about toothpaste tubes and not about Life.'

Bloody infuriating advice. Once again her words resounded in my head as the plane home accelerated down the runway.

'Mother,' I had explained patiently, 'all barriers between class, religion, race, even gender, are down. You can't say things like that in public.'

'Well it's not public, darling,' said my mother, irritably, 'I'm just saying it to you. I, of course, love all types of people.' She paused. 'Well, not lesbians,' at which she gave an involuntary shudder, adding inexplicably, 'all that hair. It's just . . . well you know what I'm trying to say, darling. Friends are fine, but it's trouble to marry someone different. You're attracted to them in the first place because they're exotic, not what you are used to, then that becomes the very reason the relationship falls apart.'

I couldn't bear it when she first expounded this theory – one of her many – and felt its horrible prophecy bear down on me when I left my old life behind. My exotic – if you can call Sweden exotic – life of four years in another country, living with a foreigner: a chocolate-box good-looking ski guide, Mats, whom I had followed down the slippery slopes all the way to Stockholm, where I married him. Rather rash, with the benefit of hindsight.

The seat-belt sign went off and I thought about being free and single again. I'd agonized for months, terrified of leaving, frightened of change, but I'd finally managed to get the strength to break away. Some people find deserting a way of life to launch into an uncertain future exciting. Not me.

I had no idea what I was going to do, but at least I'd be doing it in my own language. I was coming home to everything familiar. Except – as the adrenalin-induced high that had kept me going through the split-up started to seep away, the reality of what I was going to find hit me – there was no home to come back to.

Unbelievably, my parents, having swung like a nauseating pendulum between shall-we, shan't-we, were at long last divorced. When I got home my father would be off on one of his lecture tours or at a conference, my mother going round the world in order to 'discover herself' (although I rather suspected she was discovering her G-spot, if the postcards were anything to go by) and my brother still living in Japan. Even Bugger the cat had been rehoused. There would be nobody there. I'd left my Swedish life for a void and I felt sick.

I needed a shoulder to cry on and somewhere to live, so I turned to my best friend Bumble, whose cosy domesticity and down-to-earth motherliness, coupled with excessive amounts of vodka, food and Marlborough Lights, would make my ordered, serious and rather mundane life in Sweden seem far away. Bumble's favourite role in life is to nurture; people or animals, she adopts them all. Her husband, Gareth, is the most easy-going man on the planet. Each evening, when he returns from work, he never knows by how much his house will have expanded. Good food, good wine, good company and a good book are his staple requirements.

I toyed with the idea of taking up smoking again. In the appalling build-up to leaving, I'd sworn off nicotine – a desperate measure to prove to myself that if I had the will-power to stop smoking, which I liked, I could certainly leave Mats, whom I loathed. I shook my head. This was worse than choosing your A level subjects, much worse than choosing a career. There are no retakes in life.

So, here I was, twenty-eight years old, no family around, no money, no home and, although no one but Bumble knew, a divorcee – such an awful word and not what you want to be in your twenties. In your thirties it's better than being single, but in your twenties being a divorcee just makes you look impulsive and shallow, which I probably was, or rather had been.

As the plane touched down, my stomach knotted; it was only a two-hour flight, but it felt like a lifetime. I waited by the carousel as four years of meagre possessions slowly belched out from behind the plastic flaps. I loaded my trolley and looked at what I'd brought back with me – clothes and bed linen. No furniture, photos, crockery, cutlery, not even alimony – I couldn't bear to be beholden to someone. Just something to stand up in and something to lie down on. I wanted no reminders.

With a sigh I went through the appositely signed 'Nothing to Declare'.

'Polly!' yelled an excited small voice and I nearly tripped over as my small goddaughter, Minnie, grabbed my knees.

'Are you sad?' she asked, looking up at me with big, curious eyes. 'Mummy said you would be sad 'cos of Maps.'

'No, I'm not sad, sweetheart, I'm happy to be back.'

I looked up from her small blonde head across to Bumble. 'Thanks for picking me up, Bumble.' She enveloped me in a large hug.

'Never did like the fellow,' boomed a deep voice. 'Too tall, too blond, too good-looking and too damn good at skiing. You stick to us imperfect Brits from now on, old girl.'

I laughed as Gareth pushed out his tummy and rolled his large, kind eyes into an awful squint.

'Come on, where are those bags? Let's get you back to the menagerie we loosely call home. Bumble has fatted endless calves – she'll hate you being so thin by the way – William the Lodger, in huge anticipation of your new single status, has bought vat-loads of wine with which to ply you, hoping no doubt to render you susceptible to his extremely well-hidden charms. Pia the worryingly attractive au pair has promised not to speak your previous language, unless it's to complain about William's amorous advances, and the Jamaicans next door are planning a party to welcome you home. I'm sure you remember Troy, too tall, too black, too good-looking and too damn good at . . . '

'Gareth,' I interrupted his inane flow, 'stop! No more unsuitable men. I've come back to find a nice Englishman who wears a suit and works in the City. I shall then marry him and live in a house in the country with two children, a labrador, smock dresses, Pony Club, coffee mornings, toothpaste tubes. I'm going back to my roots. I'm never leaving England again and if,' I paused for breath as they looked at me in astonishment, 'if Plan A doesn't work, I shall put into action Plan B.'

'And what is Plan B?' asked Bumble curiously.

'I'm taking up carpentry.'

'Carpentry?' enquired Gareth. 'Is this something biblical?'

'No, I'll simply build a shelf to sit on for the rest of my sad single life!'

At which the enormity of what I'd done overwhelmed me, my bravado deserted me and I burst into tears.

'See,' said Minnie, 'Mummy said you'd be sad.'

2

I woke up the following morning feeling terrible. My head really hurt, my mouth felt like the cat-litter tray and my eyes seemed sort of stuck together. I wondered briefly if I'd caught conjunctivitis from the headrest of the plane and then realized I hadn't taken off my make-up – in fact, I appeared not to have taken off anything at all.

This meant two things: first I'd survived the night safe from William the Lodger's intentions, and secondly I must have been awfully drunk.

I opened one eye and saw a huge pink pig swaying in front of me. Feeling quite sick I opened the other one and saw I was in Minnie's room and her musical mobile farm was hanging over my head. I groaned as Bumble came in with a tray. On it was a glass of water, a cup of black coffee, two Alka-Seltzers and a packet of cigarettes. She perched herself on the end of my bed.

'Morning,' she said cheerfully, 'don't expect this treatment every day. Normally I don't get out of bed until at least eleven, but I make exceptions for hungover waifs and strays. Ciggie?'

'God no, I couldn't. I gave up.' I reached for the Alka-Seltzer.

'Could've fooled me! You must have had an entire packet last night. What with that and the Absolut vodka, I bet you feel really rough now.' Bumble looked far too perky and smug, I thought.

'Well, I expect you're used to it,' I muttered.

'Now, now,' she admonished, 'don't be bad-tempered. Have a bath and come downstairs. We can discuss your Plan A.' In a waft of cigarette smoke and benevolence she went out of the door.

I sipped on my fizzy mixture and wondered why I was in Minnie's room and where my suitcases were. After a while I went down to the bathroom and wallowed indulgently in a steamy hot fug, and then, wrapped in a huge white towel, I padded down to the kitchen.

'Bumble, why was I in Minnie's room? And where are my clothes?'

'Your suitcases are in your bedroom, which is on the third floor. However, last night you lurched into Minnie's room demanding a cuddle, talking wildly about sleeping with the innocent and waking to sweet baby breath. At which point, she not unsurprisingly woke up screaming on finding you lumbering into bed with her and ran into our room. Gareth, with all his Freudian theories and Electra complex concerns, couldn't cope, so he went to your room and I had to share my bed with a hysterical four-year-old. Ciggie?'

'No, thanks. Oh I am sorry, will the poor little thing ever speak to me again? And will Gareth? God, I feel awful. Was I terrible last night? My memory seems to be defying its job description.'

'Oh, shut up, Polly, you've just got the Nameless Dreads. They come with a hangover. You'll get used to them if you stick around here for a while. Of course you weren't terrible. Actually it was rather funny. I got a night off from Gareth's snoring, Minnie got to sleep with me, which she's normally only able to do when "Daddy is Away", and you kept us highly entertained with various renditions of Swedish schnapps songs. We drank an entire bottle of vodka singing those ridiculous ditties. I don't know how you remember them. The Scandies must be quite mad. Oh, and talking of memories, I have to remember to tell you your father rang at some ungodly hour this morning. Luckily Gareth was on his way to work so he could intercept the call and keep it brief. He wants you to call him; he's in Eastbourne for the week at some conference.'

'Right,' I said. 'I'll have another cup of coffee and brace myself.'

My father is very well-known, in the public eye and hence public property, along with his family. It's something I've lived with all my life and it has advantages and disadvantages. It was one of the reasons I went to live abroad, where giving my surname was not followed by the inevitable question of, 'Is your dad . . . ?' and being introduced as, 'This is Polly, her father is . . . ' Or the predictable, 'What's it like having a famous father?' (To which, by the way, the answer is, 'I don't know any different, so how can I tell you? Now please bugger off.') They say being an MP's wife is hard, well it's even harder for the children. Luckily the furore over his rather public divorce was yesterday's news and he was back centre stage, solo but with a lady in waiting. No more happy-family photocalls to disprove the rumours that the seams of my parents' marriage were straining like those of a pair of tight jeans over a very fat arse. He is minister for something or other, I forget what now.

The ringing of the telephone interrupted my thoughts.

'Polly, it's for you,' trilled Bumble. 'Julia at Recruitment Unlimited.'

'Who?' I asked puzzled

'Julia Rowse. You remember, we were at playschool together.'

Bumble had the most amazing knack of keeping in touch with absolutely everyone who had passed through her life. She put her hand over the receiver and hissed, 'I told her you were coming back and needed a job. Talk to her.' She shoved the phone into my hand.

Twenty minutes later I replaced the receiver and stormed into the kitchen. 'Bumble, I am going to kill you! How could you? I'm supposed to be wallowing in self-pity, bemoaning my lack of life, hanging around with you all day and doing nothing but watch soap-opera repeats. I am not supposed to be getting off my backside to go for job interviews. Tomorrow even! And I don't have a sensible skirt. It's not as if you work and yet here you are, soliciting for me. It's quite unbelievable . . . I've told her I can't type or do secretarial work and she won't listen. Says there are these City boys, running around in pinstripe suits in an empty office, who need organizing and I'm the best organizer she knows, which is a joke – I can't even keep my knicker drawer tidy. Their office isn't even in the City, it's in the West End. They're probably TV producers, long on hair, short on morals and not in Plan A category at all. I need to go shopping, my interview is at ten.'

I marched upstairs leaving Bumble smiling and looking rather pleased with herself in the kitchen.

Despite the fact this might not be the right job for putting Plan A into action, I realized I was going to need an appropriate wardrobe in order to look the part for any potential new job, so the rest of the day was spent trailing round Peter Jones and the King's Road. I fought the impulse to buy sexy short black skirts and figure-hugging tops and bought instead a sensible, knee-length navy-blue suit and a couple of crisp white shirts. I imagined myself to be very Miss Moneypenny. I couldn't bring myself to buy sensible shoes and bought some impractical high heels instead. I toyed with the idea of buying a pair of glasses so I could look intelligent when asked difficult questions (which would undoubtedly be often). Or I could take them off in the manner of a current television commercial and shake my hair loose at the end of a long day, to disconcert my new employers with the simmering sex appeal under my cool sophisticated veneer.

I then wasted ages trying on glasses, all of which I hated. I also realized that having spent a large amount of money on the type of clothes I'd never before worn and would be unlikely to use under any other circumstances, I may well have to take the job, whether I liked it or not. Assuming, that is, I was offered it.

Therefore, a degree keener, I arrived the following day at a huge white building which looked like a mini Sydney Opera House just behind the Ritz Hotel in Piccadilly. I was greeted by a surly-looking receptionist who momentarily dragged herself away from a magazine to snap, 'Yes?' aggressively at me. I felt rather nervous suddenly.

'I'm here to see Jonathon Lyle. My name's Polly.'

'K.' She picked up a phone and jabbed a button. 'Polly 'ere to see you.'

There was a pause and a loud sigh.

'K.' She managed a quick head-toss in the direction of the lift. 'Fifth floor.'

As I stepped out into a cavernous, empty room I was greeted by a firm handshake, a pair of piercing green eyes and a very curious accent indeed.

'Johnnie Lyle. Thank you for coming, let me take your coat. Tea? Coffee?'

I slipped off my decidedly unsuitable scarlet coat (the only one I had) to reveal my new Moneypenny outfit and followed a gloriously pert bottom down a corridor into what appeared to be the only room with any furniture: two chairs and a desk. Sipping on a cup of quite revolting coffee I sized up his potential.

I worked out quickly he was definitely not advertising or media. He was far too clean cut, with a generous mouth, nice lips and very even teeth. Dark brown hair cut in the way only very old-fashioned barbers called Mr Christianame can manage. Tailored suit, signet ring and beautiful hands, strong and masculine, with nice nails. About five foot eleven, not too tall, which was excellent. I always find the taller a man is, the more diluted he becomes. The one in front of me was all essence. The Gucci loafers added a bit of zing, and his Hermes tie was knotted in a way that made it fall in a rather jaunty fashion.

He was banging on about something or other – banks, mortgage companies, second mortgage companies (hallo?), money. What they did, I suppose. Every now and then I'd nod, smile or mumble something inane and then revert to my mental check list.

I did listen to bits and was slightly concerned there were currently only two men in the office. But I reasoned that if his partner, who was away skiing, had anything of the Plan A potential of this one, I'd be OK.

I was getting more interested in this job all the time. He asked me about myself. I embellished and reworked my past a bit and handed across a completely fabricated CV. However, I got the impression he wasn't really concentrating either and kept answering phones with his name and surname in a very abrupt manner.

Then he stood up and smiled at me. He had the most glorious, curly-wurly smile and his eyes crinkled at the corners. His rather stern profile softened and he looked like a naughty boy. Hardly daring to say anything more in case I flirted, I smiled back and held out my hand, saying it had been a pleasure to meet him and I hoped to hear from him soon. I turned to leave.

'Um, Polly,' he said behind me.

'Yes?' I turned, my stomach thumped a little, my heart beat a bit faster, he might be about to ask me out . . . 'Your coat.'

I blushed, how stupid. 'Thank you, Jonathon,' I said politely.

'I'll arrange for you to meet Hugo, and please, call me Johnnie, everyone does.' Another leg-weakening smile saw me to the lift. The doors closed and I leant against them with a big grin on my face.

3

I was so impatient to get back to Bumble's I grabbed a taxi to Fulham, which was an extravagance I could scarcely afford.

I burst through the door. 'Bumble! Bumble! Where are you?' I yelled, 'I've just met the man I am going to marry!'

'That is a huge disappointment to all men. Particularly me, as I have yet to succeed in tempting you to explore your sensual heights with the master of eroticism.'

The chiselled ebony features of Troy-from-next-door brushed my face with a kiss and his hands went round my waist as I stood in the untidy hallway. He was devastatingly good-looking and definitely not in my plan.

'Troy, how are you?' I hastily composed myself, removing his hands. 'Still seducing swathes of London? Isn't it time you settled down too? And what are you doing here anyway?'

His well-educated voice, with a seduction-defying hint of the Caribbean in the background, continued, 'Well I heard you were back and have left the cardboard-cut-out Swede. I would love to take you out for dinner.' His whole body oozed sexuality as he leaned towards me, his soft lips whispered into my ear, 'Time to introduce you to the BBC.'

I couldn't help but notice how the muscles in his arms tightened as he moved. His incredibly broad shoulders remained at perfect right angles to his head. He was, as usual, wearing black. Tight T-shirt and very tight jeans. He did have an extraordinary physique, tall, broad and lean. It was impossible not to let my eyes wander lower, below his flat, toned stomach. Troy's prowess with women and the reason for it were legendary. I looked up again hastily, I did not want to be his next victim.

'I can't, I really can't,' I squeaked rather inelegantly. 'You're not on the agenda and I mustn't be distracted from my goal.

I've renounced unsuitable men and you're about as unsuitable as they get. There must be hundreds of others you can go and play with. Anyway, I'm more of an ITV girl and,' I held up my hand to silence him, 'I don't want to know what BBC stands for. Where's Bumble?'

'She's gone shopping, we're all alone.'

He was like a black cobra, hypnotic. I didn't want to play the snake charmer and I certainly didn't feel comfortable being alone with him.

'So how did you get in?' I asked.

'Pia let me in,' he said with a slow smile.

'Pia! Brilliant idea, Troy, go plague Pia. Where is she?'

'She's upstairs,' he replied, lazily. The slow smile widened as he added, 'She's been plagued.'

'Ah, must be the reason she's on antibiotics,' I replied jokily, thinking it was amazing how two seconds ago he'd told me we were alone. Bloody men. Here was a marvellous example of what I was not going to fall for. Good-looking, charming, womanizing and utterly dishonest. This was why I was going to find a Suit. A nice, kind, honest, loyal man, who would not be lurking, ever-ready to pounce. My resolve strengthened.

'Troy, it's lovely to see you again, and to know your many talents have not deserted you, but we really can't have dinner. You're gorgeous, bad and, above all, unsuitable. I don't want to get involved with you.'

'I'm only talking about dinner and sex; I guarantee you'd have a wonderful time,' he replied, sounding rather hurt.

'That's my point, I'm on a diet from both.'

I wriggled past him and went upstairs. Dinner and sex indeed. He made it sound like coffee and mints.

Pia was standing on the landing, looking worried. 'Hasse gone?' she said in the sing-song accent all Scandinavians have, even in English.

'Yes, Pia, for the moment. Don't you like him?' I was curious.

'Oh Poh–lee, I thought he was liking me. Butti was terrrr–ible. Lof me and leaf me. I neffer, neffer want to see him again, he is making me wery sad, notatall lika Swedish boy, oh, sorre . . . ' She trailed off, looking embarrassed.

'It's OK,' I said, putting my arm round her. 'You're right, he's not like a nice Swedish boy, just the opposite in fact. At least now you know what you don't want. Which is good, because I think finding the right man is a process of elimination. You don't necessarily know what you want until you find out from experience what you don't want.' Which pretty much seemed to be how I had got where I was.

'I'm going to change out of these incredibly boring clothes and see if I can have my hair done before my next interview. Time to be blonde again.'

Pia looked at me with surprise.

'Butta why are you wanting to be blonde? I lof brown hair.'

'I hate having brown hair. It makes me feel serious, not glamorous at all. Plus, it's a well-known fact, Englishmen prefer blondes. Blondes get more attention and I need all the attention I can get because I've just met the most perfect man to marry.'

The front door downstairs opened as Bumble, laden with plastic bags, manoeuvred her way in. She'd picked up Minnie from nursery school. Minnie was clutching a very large piece of paper and had paint all over her.

'Hallo, Polly. Hallo, Pia. I'm home now,' she called.

I bounded down the stairs yelling, 'Bumble! Bumble! Guess what? I've just met Him, the man I am going to marry! Seriously, he's the one I had the interview with. I'm going to marry the boss! I can't believe it's this easy.'

At the bottom of the stairs I picked up Minnie and started swirling her around. 'Polly Lyle. Polly Lyle. Doesn't it sound great?' Minnie joined in the chorus.

'Oh stop it, you two,' snapped Bumble with uncharacteristic vigour. 'I'm quite exhausted, I've got PMT and currently cannot imagine why anyone would want to get married. Marooned at home all day, no one to interact with unless they are under three feet or homesick, lovesick or foreign.

Shopping at Sainsbury's not Joseph, having to think about some man's requirements on a daily basis – and I don't mean just his dietary requirements, being financially dependent on someone other than a parent, who then tells you what to do because he feels he can.' She paused for breath. 'Husbands loathe your girlfriends, particularly the single ones, who they think will lead you astray or undermine them. Unless of course they fancy them, in which case they'll flirt outrageously and then appear hurt and confused when you get cross, saying, "But I thought you wanted me to be nice to your friends." Oh and just wait for the glorious addition to your life that is in-laws. You don't just marry a person, you know, you marry an entire family tree. One's own lot are bad enough, but at least you've had all your life to understand them. And as for waking up every morning knowing exactly where you are, that it was the same place yesterday and will be the same tomorrow. Seriously, Polly, think carefully about this.' She dumped the shopping in the hallway and fumbled in her bags. 'Ciggie?'

I'd never heard Bumble quite so negative on the subject of marriage; it was a rather depressing picture and not one I wanted to dwell on. The alternative, however, eternal spinsterhood and having to work for a living, seemed far less attractive, even if it was filled with all my girlfriends.

'Troy was just here,' I said, changing the subject.

'I like Toy,' said Minnie, 'I'm going to marry Toy when I'm a big girl.'

'Oh no you're not!' said three voices in horrified unison.

Minnie was led away by Pia and I sat in the drawing-room and filled Bumble in on the morning's events.

The phone rang and she answered it. 'No, she's not here at the moment, can I take a message?'

She wrote something down, nodded a few times and after a while said goodbye and put the phone down.

'That,' she said, 'was no Englishman.'

'What do you mean? Who was it? Was that Him? Bumble, bloody hell, why didn't you let me speak? And of course he's

English, he's got a signet ring.'

'You are to meet a Hugo Windsor, who with his surname sounds a much better bet, at ten in the morning.' She carried on, ignoring me. 'He enjoyed meeting you so much, etc., etc. And would you wear your nice red coat. Flirt. He was far too charming, and anyway, I think he's Lloyd Grossman.' She added the last comment with a smile on her face.

'No!' I wailed, putting my hands over my ears. 'Bumble, you've ruined it! I knew it was a familiar accent, awringe not orange.' I paused for a moment, then rather defensively added, 'Still, it doesn't mean he's not English. He probably just does a lot of transatlantic travel.'

'If you say so,' said Bumble, settling down in a large squishy sofa and turning the television on. 'And it sounds as if he's got a stammer.'

'Well, he's probably nervous having to talk to an old bag like you,' I snapped ungraciously. 'I'm going to the hairdresser's to be a blonde again, then I shall have more fun.'

'If you say so,' repeated Bumble, smoothing down her rather shiny chestnut locks with a smug smile.

The following morning, back in Moneypenny clothes and with subtle blonde highlights, I felt much more buoyant. I even managed to smile at the surly receptionist. As I ascended the five floors to meet Hugo Windsor, I wondered whether he was related to the royal family. It was a very impressive surname. However, knowing how irritating it is to be quizzed on one's parentage I would most definitely not be asking him whether his grandmother liked corgis. The door opened once more into the empty office and standing in front of me this time was an extremely tall, thin man with very blond hair, blue eyes and a shy smile. I prayed he wasn't Swedish.

'Good-morning, allow me to introduce myself, I'm Hugo.' He spoke in an accent so plummy any doubts were immediately dispelled. He extended his hand rather languidly and I wasn't sure whether to shake it or curtsy.

He was very handsome and although I'd sworn off blonds

the prospect of working with these two boys looked like it might be fun. He towered over me, even in my high heels, as I followed him back into the same room as yesterday; the office remained as empty as ever.

'Well, as you can see, there's a lot to be done,' he said, waving a hand around in a general sort of way; I nodded, trying to ignore the ringing of telephones everywhere, 'and Johnnie says you're very highly qualified' (I began to question Johnnie's powers of observation) 'and ready to start immediately. So frankly that, coupled with the overriding fact we're desperate, means I'm very happy to go along with his suggestion and offer you the position, which I hope very much you will accept.' He reached for a phone. He was so well spoken and polite you could just tell he had been educated to within an inch of his life. He had the kind of manners my mother would kill for my brother to have.

'I would be delighted,' I replied in what I hoped was an equally posh voice. If nothing else, working here was going to get my vowels performing.

Hugo replaced the phone, which immediately started to ring again. He smiled, 'Well, marvellous. You can see we need help. I'm so very pleased, as will Johnnie be. Who, by the way, is sorry he can't be here today, but his wife has just had their second child.'

My heart stopped and then started beating again very fast. Second child? Oh my God, he was married! Hell's teeth. He didn't have a wedding ring on. Worse, he hadn't told me. Bloody hell. Now what? Plan A up in smoke. And I'd just accepted the job. Damn it all. I smiled at Hugo, 'Are you married as well?' I asked.

'Good grief no!' He laughed. 'Johnnie's the only one of our crowd to take the plunge, let alone start sprogging! So, where were we? Ah yes, would Monday suit?'

I grabbed a cab home again. Well, I was about to become employed and the salary was reasonable and this time I was bursting with unfortunate news.

'Bumble, Bumble, Bumble, where are you? I have good news and I have bad news.'

Bumble appeared from the kitchen with a large wooden spoon in her hand. 'And?'

'Well, the good news is I got the job and the bad news is the one I fancy is married.'

'Happily?' she enquired.

'Bumble! Not only married, but having his second child, so I expect blissfully happily married. Anyway, not the point. I would never go out with a married man. Happy or not, it's a disaster – self-destructive, soul-destroying, heartbreaking and ultimately leads nowhere. It's not even a moral thing, I'm ashamed to say. Just my survival instincts are way too strong and I've seen the casualties. Crikey, Troy's a better bet than a married man. And before you ask, the other one is really nice, but *a* he's blond and looks a bit like Mats, and *b* he didn't flirt with me at all. But I'd already accepted the job before I knew about the unobtainability of Johnnie. He was top of my list. Actually, the only person on my list.'

I paused for breath, before adding, 'But, I've been thinking, it might not be all bad. They're about my age and Johnnie appears to be the only married one in what I've decided is a group of friends who could turn out to be potentials. So I thought I'd stay for a while. The job seems OK, although I don't quite know what they want me to do. They're nice and I'm broke, so if nothing else I can look around from there. What do you think?'

'I think you should get out of that hideous outfit, then take over stirring this revolting low-fat sauce I'm trying to make and keep an eye on the dry-roasted potatoes while I go round the corner to the fat quack to get an injection in my backside, which will hopefully take my appetite away and give me legs like yours. William is in tonight, no doubt trailing some under-age nymphet. And anyway,' she paused dramatically, flourishing her final *non sequitur*, 'Gareth was married when I met him.'

'I know,' I replied, 'and even though he was separated from his wife when you met him and didn't have children, you still refer to her as the she-devil who impoverished your life. You leave the room if some of Gareth's "friends from before" mention her name. Cross yourself and the road to avoid her and are generally completely neurotic about her. I don't want to be like that and I don't want someone shop-soiled. Baggage, guilt and a large mortgage is what you end up with with a retread. Not for me. I'm going to find someone clean, fresh, unworn, a new Suit. I know he's out there somewhere. Now, give me the spoon and go and bend over for the doctor.'

4

Considering I'd been back only a few days I felt I'd achieved quite a lot. I'd unpacked – astonishing; got a job – even more astonishing; had my hair dyed – predictable; taken up smoking – inevitable; and turned down Troy – unbelievable.

Equally, there were a large number of things I still had to do before I started employment, one of which was to phone my father, who'd be worrying.

My parents were an interesting couple, well ex-couple. My mother used to be an actress; she gave up the stage to be a career prop for my father when he made it to the Cabinet. She was beautiful, talented and very theatrical. She made perfect little tea parties for my friends and told bedtime stories in a myriad of fantastical voices. She took the fact my brother and I had somehow grown into adults rather badly. Faced with empty-nest syndrome, she'd been unable to cope with my father. This wasn't surprising, it happens to loads of people, let alone a couple as disparate as my parents.

My father was practical, consumed by work, publicly and privately devoted to his children. It was he who drove us to school every morning and checked our homework at night. I know because there is much newspaper coverage to testify to this. Mother took scant interest in academia, in fact I don't think she ever went to a parents' evening throughout our entire childhood until she decided she fancied the headmaster at my last school.

I knew dad would want to know what was happening in my life – although I'd probably only get about halfway through before we'd start talking about him! He was frightfully nervous about my staying with Bumble because Gareth was a prominent journalist.

Anyone in the public eye knows the unscrupulous nature

of journalists – although this perhaps does them a slight injustice, because fame is hugely addictive and most people are in print because they wanted to be intially. You court fame and think you can handle it. Then you start to need it and realize too late you've created a monster and the tail is shaking you. Even worse, when the shaking stops, you miss it. I know they say the only thing worse than being talked about is not being talked about, but the depths to which people will go to fulfil the fame-crave is unedifyingly low. In politics you're not doing a good job unless you're quoted in the papers regularly, even misquotes are better than nothing. Ghastly.

I found my father at his hotel in Eastbourne.

'Darling, welcome home, how are you feeling?'

It was lovely to hear the familiar, modulated tones.

'Well, I'm OK, surprisingly. I thought I'd be depressed, mourning the death of my old life, instead I appear to be moving on rather faster than I anticipated. I have a job. I was going to marry my new boss, but sadly he's taken. Hopefully I'll find another nice man in a suit with whom I can have two point two children and domestic bliss. Sometimes I weaken and think I miss Mats, but it's a habit and once I get back into the swing of things here it'll be fine. I want to get on with my life and . . . '

He interrupted my babble. 'Quite right darling, I'm proud of you. You must be feeling very disorientated and I know how difficult it was for you to make your final decision. I just wish I was there with you now, not at this exhausting party conference.'

I could feel the thin façade of my bravery cracking beneath his gentle concern, so I quickly asked him what he was doing. He was back on familiar territory talking about himself. I eventually replaced the receiver, just as an arm curled around me, with a large glass of white wine on the end of it. It was William, the lecherous lodger, who planted a kiss on the back of my neck.

'Oh yes, please,' he said, nuzzling my neck, bedside smoothie manner to hand.

I had been forever at a loss to understand his quite astonishing success with women. Well, I say women, they were girls, some of them worryingly young. Known as the night-time nymphets, they were all from Essex, blonde and culled from the typing-pool at the same newspaper Gareth worked on.

William was a sports journalist. And he was most interested in indoor sports. He lived on the top floor of Bumble and Gareth's house in what was called the Blue Room – because it was that colour and so, no doubt, were the activities performed in there. No one else in the house ventured in. The excuse was the stairs were too treacherous to descend, so once up you never returned. Obviously the nymphs did leave, but it was generally a moonlight flit.

Very occasionally Bumble would meet one on the stairs and terrify her with a question such as, 'Hallo, who are you?' Like a startled bunny she would blink in the headlights of this scorching interviewer and remain silent, frozen to the spot. Realizing too many syllables were involved, Bumble would try again, 'Hi.' At which, the nymph would flee out of the front door.

'William,' I took the glass and turned around, 'how are you?'

'All the better for seeing you,' he replied in a *faux*-sexy voice, 'call me Willy.'

'I'd rather not,' I replied, prudishly.

'OK then, touch me willy.' He roared with laughter at his own joke – at least I hoped it was a joke!

'Really, William, is that your best chat-up line? No wonder your girlfriends are all so idiotic.'

He was oleaginous, you could virtually see the slippery little trail he left behind him as he walked. I marched into the kitchen where I knew I'd find Bumble cooking an enormous roast of something.

'Bumble, how can you live with that man? He's ridiculous.'

'Who, Gareth?' asked Bumble surprised. 'Oh no, you mean William. You get used to him. I think he's rather sweet.'

Bumble has to be the most tolerant person in the world. 'Well, I just love having people around – talking of which, I thought we'd have a little party on Saturday to welcome you home. You'll have Sunday to recover before starting work on Monday.'

'Great, Bumble. Where is Gareth by the way? I heard him come in ages ago.'

'Upstairs in the bath reading Proust. He'll be like a wrinkly white whale when he eventually emerges, having slopped at least a bucket of Floris-flavoured water all over the carpet, with my pink bath hat on, and a huge whisky all finished. It's how he relaxes at the end of a stressful day. Of course, the ceiling will come down eventually.' She continued to potter about the kitchen making mounds of food.

'I hope there are some more people coming for dinner, that's an enormous amount of food. I'm sure I've already put on weight since being here,' I said, feeling my tightening waistband.

Bumble opened her mouth as if to say something, then clearly thought better of it and instead handed me the knives and forks and told me to lay the table.

Life in Fulham continued in a gentle rhythm for the next few days, getting up late, watching endless soaps, playing with Minnie and eating vast quantities of delicious food every evening.

The party on Saturday night was the highlight of a very self-indulgent week. Flashbacks continued to haunt me. I'd dug out my old Swedish song-sheet and photocopied it for every guest, with English lyrics. I bought yet more Absolut vodka, including some flavoured ones, and prepared bowlfuls of prawns. The Swedes lead a generally quiet life, but they know how to party.

Kevina-Louise – a mad sobriquet for our friend Kevin – and his boyfriend of the week came clad, as usual, in exquisite clothes. Kevina was more of a girl than me and shrieked theatrically every time it was his turn to sing something, downing a tiny schnapps glass of vodka as a forfeit and then deciding to sing anyway. William had descended from the Blue Room with a very pretty but exhausted-looking nymphet, who perked up considerably after her seventh pepper vodka and sang noisily and out of tune.

Troy glittered dangerously in the corner, far too cool to sing and drinking alcohol with no visible effect. Various members of his large family, most of whom seemed to live on our street, filed in and out. They spent the evening trying out reggae versions of the songs, which was hilarious, and passing round rum and dodgy-looking cigarettes. Troy made me nervous, but I tried not to show it. Every time I turned to look at him I found his gaze directly on me and I felt instantly awkward and undressed. He didn't even glance at the nymphet, who was incredibly pretty and by the end of the evening had developed a personality.

Frank arrived, one of my best male buddies. He was from Huddersfield and as down-to-earth and placid as could be, except when he had had too much to drink, then he went wild. He was tall and cuddly, with dark blond straight hair and gentle brown eyes. He'd just finishing training to be a psychiatrist. His parents were monstrously rich and he had a new Aston Martin every year, which he drove very well, but fast. He also had a wicked sense of humour and a large group of lively, fun friends, who congregated almost every night in one of two pubs in Chelsea. He was the perfect safe date, because you could introduce him to your parents and he would charm them, in fact he could charm anyone. On a few occasions, when I'd been too pissed to drive, I'd ended up in bed with him. However, nothing ever happened. I wasn't sure if he was waiting to be forcefully seduced or if he just didn't fancy me, and I didn't want to find out because he was much nicer as a sort of brother you found attractive, without the complications of incest.

Women loved him because he really listened to what they

said. He never seemed to have a regular girlfriend, but was always surrounded by females. He enveloped me in an enormous hug.

'Miss P. Welcome home. Now I have it on good authority you're looking for a suitable husband and I have just the man for you.'

I could sense the hand of Bumble behind this.

'My word, Frank,' I replied, laughing, 'word travels fast. Please, set it up, but make sure he's single, English and available.'

'Tick to all three and some.'

'Handsome or "and some"?' I asked.

'That too, just wait – call me early next week and we'll meet. You won't be disappointed.' With a deep chuckle he disappeared into the growing crowd. I was rather excited.

More and more people turned up, Bumble having for-gotten how many she'd invited had clearly overbooked, but typically, there was more than enough food and drink to go round.

When the dancing started in the drawing-room, Troy came up to me and wordlessly wrapped me in his arms. He danced slowly and rhythmically, despite the fact it was quite a fast tune. Perhaps it was the vodka, but I allowed myself to relax into his arms and move with him. I could feel the heat of his strong body against mine and felt my stomach turn over in the way only laxatives or lust can engender. It was heaven being this close to such an attractive man. I closed my eyes as he bent his face next to mine and felt his breath flutter in my hair. His soft lips brushed my ear and he whispered, 'Doesn't this feel good?'

I couldn't pull away.

'Do you know how I feel about you?' He continued, his hands stroking my back, fingers curling round the nape of my neck, playing with my hair. 'Have you any idea how long I've waited for you? I have such fantasies. We would be wonderful together.'

This soft mantra went on, flattering and wooing me, and I could sense my resolve weakening. He put his mouth on mine and pressed down, not insistently, but slowly and seductively, making me lean into him. Kissing is so important. How a man kisses will probably tell you everything you need to know about him in bed. It was one of my yardsticks. And thumbs – you can generally tell not only the size but the actual shape of a man's penis by his thumb. Watch how quickly most men hide their hands under the table if you throw that into the conversation! Troy had enormous hands, with long, long fingers . . .

I turned my face away and caught sight of Pia, who had just appeared in the doorway. She was staring at Troy.

'Troy. I can't do this. I mean I can, and with worrying ease. You're an amazing kisser, but you're a heartbreaker. I'll fall for you and you won't be there to catch me. You must let me go.'

I pulled myself away and felt very cold out of his embrace. My head was spinning. He looked at me with such an un-fathomable expression, I couldn't work out what he was thinking. He walked over to Pia, whispered something in her ear and then continued out into the night, the door closing softly behind him.

Pia came over to me.

'What did he say to you?' I asked.

'He said he is missing me and if I am wanting to see him I can go to his house in fife minutes. He is waiting. He is saying he lof me. What can I do?'

I was thunderstruck by such quick work.

'What can you do? What can you do?' I repeated myself in shrill fury. 'You can leave him well alone, like me. He'll break your heart all over again – it's what he does, on a practically professional basis. He is not good news. He is bad, bad, bad, despite all the lovely, lovely words. Go and dance with Frank, he needs to be distracted.'

I pushed her reluctantly on to Frank and busied myself leaping around with Kevina, trying to forget just how lustful

I'd been feeling a few minutes ago. It had been a close shave and I resolved to watch myself more closely in future.

As I dragged myself off to bed much later on I realized Pia had vanished and presumed she'd succumbed. I could hardly blame her. Troy was gorgeous, but he was not what my delicate heart could cope with at present.

5

On Monday morning I walked rather stiffly down the street because my legs, jacked up in high heels, still ached from all the dancing on Saturday. I knew it had been bad when I woke on Sunday and found I'd put on my sunglasses already, something I did only on the direst of occasions. At least I was in my own bedroom this time. I popped another extra-strong mint into my mouth and swung through the doors of the huge white building which looked like a vast sailing ship in full blow.

'Good-morning,' I said, smiling broadly to surly-puss at reception. 'My first day!'

'Yeah, an' my last,' she snapped back at me. 'An' all I can say is good luck. I can't wait to get aht. Right pair of stuck-up tossers, those two.'

Excellent, I thought to myself, what a lovely start.

As the lift doors opened, I was greeted by the sound of telephones ringing all over and the sight of Johnnie standing in front of me.

'Ah, Polly, good, you're here. The first thing I want you to do is sort out this reception area. Put in some sort of mini-switchboard thing, what we have at the moment is archaic. The ghastly witch on the switch downstairs has handed in her notice; get someone to replace her, preferably one who speaks with a decent accent. Find some furniture for the office – desks, chairs, sofas, word processors; we've only got one very old typewriter here at the moment. We need art for the walls, food and drink, fridge to put them in, here's a list, must dash.'

Whereupon he stepped into the lift I'd just vacated.

'Good-morning to you too,' I muttered, thinking it was a pretty weird way to greet a new employee. Fatherhood obviously energized him. I couldn't find a chair but after walking round the large echoing expanse located a phone which wasn't ringing and a *Yellow Pages*. I sat on the floor and studied the long list with its loopy writing.

I had absolutely no idea what kind of furniture they would like, not a clue about switchboards, didn't know what a word processor was and wondered if it was related to a food processor. I was horrified at the prospect of putting art on the walls, convinced my taste for modern art was not theirs; they probably wanted hunting prints. Food and fridge I could manage and a new receptionist was easy. I rang Julia.

'Julia,' I began, 'I've just started at this bizarre place – do not expect many thanks. I've been abandoned very unceremoniously by Johnnie, whom I'm already beginning to go off. His people-skills suck. What is a word processor and where do I get one? I have to buy a switchboard for heaven's sake and the receptionist downstairs has just quit. There are no chairs to sit down on, so I am on the floor, which, if you could see how tight my skirt is, would bring forth from you gasps of admiration, I'm practically a contortionist. Who are these people?'

'Polly, I'm sorry, she's the third receptionist in two weeks; those young men are quite impossible. It's why I sent you. You're perfectly qualified.'

'What can you mean? I don't have any qualifications at all!' I spluttered, feeling rather duped.

'Precisely, except the one thing they need, you can organize. You see, you rang me. I'll send you a new receptionist, please be nice to her; they don't require a huge amount of maintenance, but good-morning, goodbye and an occasional thank-you work wonders. You might suggest it to your new employers. I'll tell her to report to you and avoid conversation as much as possible with the other two. You can be a buffer – how's that for a job description?'

She also told me where to find all the other items I needed. I didn't know whether to be amused or annoyed.

By about lunchtime I was feeling hungry. I was still alone

and curious to know what happened on the three floors below. I walked down one flight of stairs and could see lots of people through the glass doors. I pushed them open and for a moment there was normal office babble – then silence as everyone turned to look at me. I nervously introduced myself, still silence.

'Um, the boys have gone out and I wondered if you could tell me where to buy a sandwich?'

A tall, round Indian man with a jolly face walked over to me and held out his hand. 'Hallo,' he said. 'My name is Rohan. I run the computer department. Many apologies for the silence, it's just unusual for anyone from the top floor to descend to this level, let alone talk to us. We're one of the many companies bought by the Americans, same as downstairs. I'll show you round if you like and on the basis you eat sandwiches like a regular person and don't spend every lunch at the Caprice like our new wonderboys, I'll take you to lunch afterwards.'

The chatter resumed and Rohan introduced me to everyone. I tried to understand who did what. I did at least learn the wonderboys (I immediately adopted Rohan's term) ran the UK end of an American company that did Mergers and Acquisitions – or Murders and Inquisitions as Rohan called them.

This gobbledegook was City-speak for buying companies who had no idea they were for sale, sorting them out – i.e., firing half the staff – then selling them, or parts of them, to another company, who had no idea they needed them. All of this was performed in the utmost secrecy. The staff in the building were very jittery because they didn't know who would be first for the firing squad, hence the silence when I arrived. Sitting on a chair for the first time all day with a spritzer and a sandwich, I grilled Rohan for more information.

'What is the American connection?' I asked.

'Well, Johnnie used to work for some English bank and got poached to set this up. He is a Yank, or rather half-Yank, himself.' (He was crossed off my list permanently. Rude,

35

married and foreign! However, it did explain the strange accent.) 'Hugo used to work in the States but wanted to come back to the UK. This situation is all very recent and nobody really knows what's going on, they don't talk to the likes of us, we're far too junior and none of us went to public school. Then there's a couple of old guys called Bill Shark and Freddie Thomson who come over from head office in New York every now and then. Funny characters, one tall and loud and the other a mute shrimp. They're busy putting together a securitization of the mortgage portfolio.'

'English, please,' I interrupted.

'Well, if you really want to know, which I suppose would be useful for you, here's how it works. People apply to us for a mortgage. We lend the money and therefore own the mortgage. We then take the mortgage and sell it to another company, along with a number of other mortgages, so it's all wrapped up as a package.'

'Does that mean someone else is lending the money then?' It seemed very complicated. 'Why would they do that?'

'Because our company takes a fee for selling the package and some of these mortgages are pretty dodgy, so you put those in with some good ones and try and bury them.'

'Is this legal?' I was worried I was about to become involved with some money-laundering outfit; my father would have a fit.

'Of course it is. Everyone is scrambling over themselves to do this. Property is booming and these packages look good on the books. My job is to get the mixture of good and bad.'

'But why would you have bad ones in the first place?'

'Money, of course,' laughed Rohan; 'the more risk, the higher the interest.'

More people trickled into the pub and I had a very jolly time. I got back to the office to find Johnnie returned and demanding to know where I'd been. I told him, rather annoyed at being questioned, particularly as I felt it was an essentially work-related lunch – at least now I had a vague idea what they did.

'Who's Rohan? Why were you so long?' barked Johnnie.

'He runs all the computers and I wasn't long, it was my lunch hour, I presumed I had one. Anyway, I needed to sit down.'

Johnnie looked at me for a moment, complete astonishment on his face, then seemed to compose himself and asked if I'd done all the tasks on his list. I ran through the rather impressive list of all the things I'd arranged, adding that British Telecom would be arriving on Friday with the new mini switchboard.

'Why can't the telephones be sorted out before?' he asked, not even congratulating me on the mammoth feat I thought I'd just pulled off in doing everything else.

'Well, it was quite a struggle to get them here on Friday actually,' I replied rather huffily.

'Art?' he barked at me.

Really he was impossibly rude

'There's a woman coming on Thursday morning to show you a selection of what's available and at the same time you can tell her what you like. Now unless you have a new list, I ought to go and stock up the fridge and buy some coffee and tea.'

He then proceeded to tell me what to buy. He didn't like this and he didn't like that. Talk about fussy.

'Where's Hugo?' I asked, hoping for a bit of relief from this man.

'Hugo is having a problem with his car at the moment, he's at the garage. It's a Porsche and very temperamental. I told him to get a BMW, the new 7 series is quite remarkable. Now,' he said abruptly, changing the subject and his tone of voice, which had gone quite soft when talking about cars. 'I have to make some phone calls.'

He marched into his office and even his pert backside failed to impress me. It's amazing how quickly you can go off a person.

I was about to leave at the end of my first, long day when Hugo, who had arrived back looking pained, called me into

37

the large room the boys shared. Johnnie was pacing up and down muttering quietly into his handset, Hugo was standing up.

'Ah, Polly, I just wanted to thank you for all you've done today,' he said, 'and so does Johnnie. Johnnie?' He called over to his colleague, who looked rather irritated at being interrupted and nodded at me.

'Well, thank you,' I replied, in what I hoped was a conciliatory voice, but Hugo obviously noted a tone of dissatisfaction.

He ran his hands through his blond hair in a distracted manner, although it almost immediately fell down over his forehead again. He directed his blue eyes at me and lowered his voice conspiratorily, 'Don't worry about Johnnie, he's got a lot on his plate at the moment, his bark is much worse than his bite. I'm sure you two will get along just fine.'

I sincerely doubted that.

6

I arrived early at work the next day to meet the new 'witch on the switch', settle her in and make sure all the furniture and equipment were delivered safely.

A bouncy brunette with a large open face and a big smile rushed hurriedly through the massive doors of the building.

'Hi, I'm Jayne with a y,' she announced breathlessly in an accent which was clearly not going to be up to Johnnie's exacting standards, but did at least leave the glass panels in the doors intact. 'Sorry to keep you waiting, I'm not used to this posh area of London and didn't know how long it would take me from Dagenham.'

I held out my hand and introduced myself. I pointed out the incredibly complicated machine that worked the existing switchboard, which she instantly knew what to do with, and then took her to the third floor to introduce her to the other people I'd got to know, who were all a lot more friendly today and welcomed her warmly.

'Has she met the wonderboys yet?' asked jolly Rohan, smiling at me as he came over to us.

'Well no, not yet,' I replied.

'Thought you'd leave that little treat to last, did you? Well with a bit of luck they'll pay as much attention to her as they do us.' He walked off down the corridor as Jayne turned to me and asked who the wonderboys were. I tried to explain, saying they were very busy and erred on the abrupt side – a massive understatement in the case of Johnnie, but never mind. It was to be hoped she wouldn't have to deal with them too much.

'No probs. I'll go and have a butchers at the switchboard and work out everyone's extensions. I'll call you if I need anything.' With another lovely smile she bounced away. I thought anyone arriving at the office would be very happy to be greeted by such warm, uncomplicated niceness and went upstairs to phone Julia to thank her.

The boys hadn't arrived, but had left copious instructions as to how I should fill my time, what their movements were and that they were not to be disturbed unless in dire emergency, what to do with the furniture, where to place the phones, and on and on, as if anyone else were quite incapable of decision making. Dumping the reams of paper, I spent the rest of the morning happily playing 'house' in the office, directing large sweaty men carrying furniture and equipment in and out of the rapidly filling floor space.

The telephones rang incessantly, but at least now Jayne put them through saying, 'Call for Johnnie, Polly,' or, 'Call for Hugo, Polly,' and I wrote endless messages for the boys. There was one very persistent female who wanted to speak to Johnnie. She refused to give her name, but must have called at least six times during the morning.

She would begin with the same rather imperious question before I had time to speak. 'Is he there?'

Patiently I'd explain he still hadn't returned, but if she left her name, I'd ask him to call her.

'I'll call back,' she would reply and hang up.

She had a cut-glass Sloane Ranger accent and I imagined she was smart girls' boarding school and had been Finished Off in Switzerland, learning how to cook, arrange flowers, get in and out of sports cars and look decorative at SW7 drinks parties. She was so arrogant I assumed she was his wife and thought they must be made for each other. Their children would be ghastly.

The phone rang again and once more the familiar voice asked if *he* was there, adding a *now* at the end, as if I were deliberately keeping her from him. I was getting seriously irritated and was just about to reply when the lift doors opened and the boys stepped out. I put my hand over the receiver. 'Johnnie, a call for you. I don't know who it is, I think it may be your wife.'

He looked startled. 'Er, p–put it through to my office,' he said and walked off.

After much ringing at the other end of the corridor, I realized I'd put the call through to the wrong office, and not knowing how to retrieve the call, had to, infuriatingly, ask Johnnie to take it in the other room. He strode down the corridor very unamused and shut the door loudly behind him.

'Sorry,' I said to Hugo, who was still standing there, 'I'm just getting used to the phones. Did you meet the new receptionist, Jayne?'

'Um, er, no,' said Hugo, looking rather embarrassed.

'Well, you were probably in a hurry. I'll ask her to come up later,' I said, as he walked into his office. I prayed they liked their desks – they had cost more than my month's salary.

The door at the end of the corridor opened and Johnnie strode out; you couldn't really call it walking, not the way his arms swung.

'Polly, that was not my wife, my wife is B–Belinda. She rarely calls. That was a – ' he paused, obviously searching for a description (I could have offered him one) – 'er, friend. See to it you always put her straight through.' He spoke tersely, looking directly at me with his jaw set.

'Well, I will, when you are here.' I replied, rather frostily. 'And does this, er, friend have a name?' I asked.

'Yes, she does.' He glared and then turned his back on me and marched into his office!

I decided she was probably some spy from another company they were about to take over, and planned at a later date to question Hugo, who was far more approachable.

I went into the office and said I'd like to bring the new receptionist up to meet them; she was called Jayne, with a y.

'Why?' asked Johnnie.

'Well it's how she spells it,' I replied.

'No, W–H–Y?' he said, letter by letter. 'Why do you want to introduce her to us? I don't give a d–damn how she spells her name.'

I couldn't believe how appalling he was. I drew a breath and said coldly, 'A receptionist is the first person anyone calling speaks to, or meets when they come to the office. The initial impression is very important. This is a nice girl and an excellent receptionist. She's the fourth in two weeks, which says a great deal about your man-management skills. If you wish her to remain the exception and stay, may I suggest you offer a vestige of courtesy and welcome her. If you want to keep your staff, conversing with them occasionally helps.'

I marched out of the office, amazed I'd just delivered such a pompous lecture. It was very out of character for me but I was so cross I wasn't even gratified by the astounded looks on their faces. I thought they'd probably fire me for being rude, but brought Jayne up to meet them anyway and they both managed a smile, a handshake and some words of welcome.

'They're nice,' said Jayne as she left.

'Yes, they are,' I lied, thinking at least one person could be happily deluded; she was unlikely to have too much to do with them anyway. It was I who had that happy task.

I managed to be very busy for the rest of the day sorting out the office, and at five o'clock was rather surprised to be called into their room. Probably to be sacked I thought to myself, pushing open the door.

Hugo was sitting down talking into his telephone so quietly it was impossible to hear anything he said. Johnnie was at his desk. 'Polly, can you take some notes for me?' He looked up from a scarily tidy area in front of him, 'Here's a pad.'

He handed me a spiral note-pad and a pencil. I drew up a chair in front of his desk and he proceeded to dictate a letter to me. I started to write some of it down, but he was going too fast, on and on without stopping. I let my pencil hover over the pad, thinking how ridiculous to expect someone to keep up at such a speed.

'Er, are you getting any of this?' he asked.

'No, of course not, you're going way too fast,' I snapped.

'Can't you do shorthand?' he queried, surprised.

'No,' I replied rather indignantly.

'Can you type?' he gazed at me in the same disbelieving, rather irritated manner

'A bit,' I said. 'Slowly,' I added helpfully.

'Well, what kind of secretary are you?' he asked in astonishment.

'I'm not a secretary,' I replied indignantly. 'I don't know what you think I am, but clearly you need a secretary. I shall hire one for you tomorrow.'

I flounced out of the office, pausing outside the door briefly to overhear Johnnie say to Hugo, 'God, that girl is mind-blowingly irritating.'

The feeling was quite mutual, I thought darkly to myself. I couldn't remember when I'd met a man I disliked more. I decided before I completely lost my temper with him I would have to resign. Before I was fired, obviously.

7

I returned home to Bumble and soaked in a hot bath, which seemed the best way to cool off. Afterwards I rang Frank, who arranged to collect me and introduce his mystery man.

Wrapped in my more usual outfit of leopard-print leggings and high black boots and around a glass of white wine in the Nag's Head, I began to feel much better and regaled most of the pub with stories about the two men I worked for. They found it particularly amusing that Johnnie and Hugo signed everything with all of their initials, of which there were quite a few. In fact most people were referred to by initials. Weird. Some sort of City code no doubt.

'Well, they are Very Important People. VIPs in fact,' I said, with mock seriousness.

'Not enough initials, got to be at least four,' chuckled Frank.

I noticed a new face in the crowd.

'Who's the man over there?' I asked casually.

'Spot on Miss P, he's the one,' he replied with a smile. 'His name's Henry, he hangs out here quite regularly. In property or surveying or something. Very rich, very single, very up-market. Father's got a title of some sort, slightly eccentric but nice. I'll introduce you, but I warn you, he drinks like a fish and drives too fast.'

This particular irony seemed lost on Frank, who was a demon behind the wheel on occasions. He called Henry over to sit with us. He was about my height, which is a reasonable height for a man, but can be an issue, depending on the man.

My first serious boyfriend was shorter than me and used to make me walk in the gutter. It was only because he was captain of rugby and cricket and seriously cute that I put up with such behaviour. My next boyfriend was really tall so I could wear heels again. However, tall men, apart from not being quite as feisty or funny as shorter men, tend to be rather vain about their height, resting their laurels on it, as it were. As if just being tall and good-looking was enough. So, apart from my recent Scandinavian aberration, I've stuck with same-height men and worn my heels (which has proved to be quite a useful ploy, because the moment they ask you how tall you are, you can be sure they're interested).

Henry was of average build, a nice, regular face with brown hair and eyes. He was wearing faded cords and a check shirt. A Barbour hung over the back of his chair and he looked as though he'd come straight off a large estate in the country. He spoke with the kind of accent which makes me feel as though I should rush off for elocution lessons.

'Frank, old bean, how are you?' Henry settled himself down with us. I wasn't too sure about the old bean bit, but . . .

'Fine,' replied Frank with a smile. 'Let me introduce you to Polly, recently returned from Sweden, newly single, successfully employed and a great teller of jokes if you get her pissed enough. Polly, Henry.'

We politely shook hands. I was feeling desperately socially inadequate.

The trouble with being from a political family is you lie in a social no man's land. You're assumed to embrace your parents' allegiances, and if your views are different, you have to keep quiet about it. I'd mixed with everyone and felt I belonged nowhere. Some people's lives are structured from birth, others are just a flimsy show to win votes. When I'm with a person like Henry I wish I'd gone to some smart Sloaney school and that my mother was called Henrietta, my friends were called Annabel, Alexandra or Charlotte and I went back to 'the house in the country' for weekends. I'd always compensated for what I perceived to be my lack of breeding by being funny, and I hoped I was amusing Henry. He seemed too good to be true.

At the end of a very happy evening Frank drove me home

and said with a satisfied smile on his face, 'Good result, Polly. Henry asked me for your phone number.'

'And, and, and . . . did you give it to him?' I replied rather excitedly.

'No, of course not, you dummy. I can't have you looking available. I said I'd have to check with you first. To interest a man, show no interest. At the moment he's a bit intrigued. Keep it like that. He's got loads of girls chasing him, so be cool. You had a rough old time with Mats, so don't rush, you need a break. After all, still eighteen months to go to the big three-oh. Plenty of time to find Mr Right!'

He ducked as I tried to hit him. 'Lord Right, if you please.'

He continued, 'Henry's a nice chap, but I don't know him really well. If you are keen, bide your time. Men love to chase and unobtainability is catnip for chaps. No fee for the advice, just a ringside seat at the wedding, OK?'

I laughed, it was fun to be thinking about the future without utter despair. I asked Frank to explain the rules of entanglement from a male viewpoint.

He thought for a moment and then said, 'I shall tell him you don't want to give him your phone number. Wait.' He held up one hand as I opened my mouth. 'This will spur him on. He's interested, obviously, but he's playing the field. Don't rush straight ahead. Next time you see him, be the same – charming, funny. No mention of telephones. He'll ask again, unless he is a real pudding, in which case, he's no use to you. There's no hurry and you need to make it perfectly obvious you have a full life and are not some sad cow waiting for phone calls. Which reminds me, although you must know this, if he tells you he's going to phone at a certain time, either be out or don't pick up. And above all, don't phone him. Wait until he phones again. Always remember, if you really want to catch a man, you can. It *is* in your control. The female of the species is the stronger in the wild, the so-called civilized lot should not be the exception. Snivelly, insecure, clingy females are about as attractive to a man as slugs. Play the game.'

I thought about the role I was already playing and decided I had room for at least one more, so I nodded. 'Thanks, darling. Where do you get all this wisdom from? And why hasn't some girl played the game successfully with you yet? I do hope there isn't an antidote by the way.'

Frank replied rather quietly, 'The only antidote is when you are already besotted with someone else. Then you're immune.'

Was this a chink in the normally impenetrable armour around his private life? 'Frankie, you're so secretive! Who are you besotted with? What's her name?'

He was even quieter in his response. 'No one at the moment. I'm still waiting . . . and hoping.'

He seemed to be getting rather depressed, so I changed tack and said jauntily, 'Well, with all this advice you've been giving me and my greater understanding of the male psyche, I expect I shall soon be all sorted out with my suitable man, and then I'll concentrate on finding you the perfect partner. OK?'

His car drew up outside Bumble and Gareth's house and he stopped the engine. He turned to look at me, his rather chubby face serious. 'I doubt they exist, and if they did, I cannot imagine how I could ever be with them. But, thank you, friendship is the foundation to life and I cherish my friends. Without them life would be unbearable.'

He was obviously going through one of his northern glooms, so I put my arms around him and said, 'Listen, you are one of the loveliest men around, kind and generous and with the best friends in the world who would do anything for you. There's a girl out there who'll spur you into action one day. The trouble is you're so bloody rich, you suspect every woman is after your wallet and not your willy. Having too much money can be a curse sometimes. But cheer up, you're not thirty yet either and you don't have a biological time-clock yelling, 'Reproduce!' at you. Enjoy your freedom while you can. And believe me, the loneliest place in the world is when you are with the wrong person. I should know, I've been there.'

Frank looked at me gently. 'Was it awful? Mats appeared to

be such a nice guy and he was so good-looking. Life and soul of the party.'

I looked back at him. How do you explain to someone what it's like to live with a person who appears so wonderful in public and yet can be so morose, depressed and angry privately. How difficult it is to live with someone who erodes your self-confidence and makes you feel stupid and inadequate just because their own demons make them that way. I used to dread being alone with him. We'd be out at a party, he'd be lovely, funny, smiling, having a good time, but in the car on the way home he'd be silent for a while. Then he would start complaining about how awful the party had been, how he loathed and despised the people there, and as for me, how could I have said what I said, did what I did, worn what I'd worn, on and on. I'd subsequently say something which would irritate him more and he'd get angry. I'm scared of anger, I wasn't brought up with it. He'd slam fists into dashboards, yell I was driving like an idiot, calling me all sorts of names. It was horrible.

It got to the point where I couldn't drive, couldn't cook, didn't dare open my mouth for fear of the haranguing I'd receive later. I became a mouse. I totally understand how people can get trapped in abusive relationships. He didn't hit me, but emotional and verbal abuse are just as soul destroying. Even though you're really unhappy, you stick with what you know and are fearful to make any decision. Incapable of making a decision in fact. You don't think anyone else could possibly want a useless creature like you and what's even more unbelievable is your pathetic gratitude on the rare occasions they are nice to you. It's a terrifying, never-ending cycle. And you think you don't have the strength to leave.

I smiled at Frank, 'Another time, I think, but I've learnt two things. One, a woman should be the better looking in a relationship and, two, there's a man in Sweden to whom I owe an unrepayable debt of gratitude.'

He laughed with me.

I wasn't quite ready yet to explain how bad it had been without feeling I was somehow showing myself to be weak. I hadn't really been able to tell my parents what had been going on; my father had never liked Mats and my pride couldn't admit I'd made a mistake. On the other hand, my mother loved Mats, his being her dream type of man to look at, and I didn't want to shatter her illusions so soon after her own painful experience of divorce.

'Who was this other man?' asked Frank curiously, 'you haven't mentioned him before.'

'It's a very long story and I'll tell you one day. He's someone who gave me back my self-confidence, which in turn gave me back my life. But we need a couple of hours and I have to go to bed. I need all my reserves of strength to cope with this new job. Shall I see you at the end of the week at the pub? I don't want to keep Henry waiting too long!' I added with a smile.

'I'll try and find out if he's going to be there,' replied Frank, 'he usually goes to the country at weekends.'

Of course he does, I thought to myself and then, because I didn't want Frank to think Henry was the only reason I was going, I replied brightly, 'No problem; it would be lovely to see just you. I'm going to search my address book and see if I have any single girlfriends for you.'

I kissed him on both cheeks and gave him a hug and let myself into the house.

8

I struggled through the rest of the week on my own without being fired, which was amazing, and without murdering Johnnie, which was extraordinary.

The following Monday, Julia produced a secretary and I didn't think there would be many complaints from the wonder-boys about this one, certainly not about her looks anyway.

Samantha was a cross between a petite Marilyn Monroe and a Siamese kitten. Her platinum-blonde hair was cut so that it fell seductively over one of her piercingly blue eyes, which were rimmed with heavy black mascara. Her red lipstick outlined a pert, pouty mouth and her nose descended in a straight line down her heart-shaped face. She was dressed demurely but sexily and held out a small hand like a soft paw to greet me.

'Hoi, I'm Samantha. Are you Polly?' she asked in such a broad Antipodean accent I was startled. It was so at odds with her appearance. I'd expected a gentle purr.

'Er, yes,' I replied, still taking stock of this dazzling vision in front of me and feeling tall, formal and elephantine beside her. 'Welcome to Big Stone Enterprises. I'll take you upstairs.'

I introduced her to Jayne and as we ascended I hoped to myself she had good secretarial skills, as mine had already proved to be so lacklustre.

'Samantha, you can type, can't you?' I ventured, 'and do shorthand?'

'Oh yeah, no worries. I can do it all, I'm pretty fast and really efficient.' She added, 'I'm saving up enough money to go travelling next year, so I've got to be good, haven't I? Unless of course, I manage to snare some hunky, rich Brit.' She giggled.

Each day the lift door opened on to a slightly less empty office. I explained everything was still in the process of being set up, which was what I was trying to do, and the boys needed a secretary. I pointed her in the direction of a desk next to mine, which was graced with an awesome machine called a word processor. It was less of a typewriter, more of a control panel for a satellite rocket, and I still didn't know how to turn it on.

'Can you work this thing?' I asked hopefully.

'Yeah, no worries, it's quite a new model, but they're all pretty much the same.'

I was hugely relieved I didn't have to explain it to her. I took her in to the boys, who typically had been at their desks since six-thirty a.m., and introduced them to Samantha. Their reaction was extraordinary. One look at her and they leapt to their feet, striding over in a race to shake her hand.

Johnnie smoothed a hand over his hair, adjusted his tie and cleared his throat, 'S–Samantha, welcome, how very nice to meet you. I'm Johnnie Lyle.' He spoke in the tone of voice normally reserved for his BMW 7 series. He shook her hand gently.

Hugo put his hand out and she took it.

'Ah, hallo Samantha, I'm Hugo Windsor, it's ah, a great pleasure to have you here.' I could have sworn Hugo had gone a bit pink: he looked rather endearing. 'I do hope you'll be happy and if there are any questions, don't hesitate to ah, ask me.'

'Or me,' interrupted Johnnie, clearly not wishing to be left out.

I felt rather peeved. No one had greeted me so attentively.

'Would you like a cup of tea, or coffee?' asked Hugo solicitously.

Samantha smiled back with a mischievous smile, clearly used to the impact she had on men and looking even more like a cat.

'Oh no, it's fine thanks. I'll just go and learn the ropes with Polly here and if there's something you need me to do, just call.'

We left the office and walked down to the small kitchen and

I busied myself making coffee and getting to know Samantha a bit better. There was something about her which unsettled me. It was probably her obvious effect on men. But she tried hard to be friends with me, so I brushed away my reservations and suggested we go to the pub for a drink after work.

'Do the boys always work this late?' asked Samantha, looking at her watch. It was six-thirty p.m.

'Yes,' I replied, 'and they are always in before seven. They can't have much time for a social life. Although Johnnie's such a pain I doubt he'd have anyone to socialize with anyway.'

'I thought Hugo was rather cute,' she said, glancing at me sideways as if to gauge my reaction. 'Is he married?'

'I don't think so,' I replied. 'I haven't been here very long myself. Johnnie is, with two children, but I don't know if Hugo even has a girlfriend. No doubt we'll find out soon enough. I'm longing to see Johnnie's wife, she must be some sort of saint to put up with him. Or perhaps a lunatic?'

Samantha laughed. 'He doesn't seem so bad . . . he's very good-looking.'

'Hmmph!' I snorted. 'If you like that sort of thing.'

'Well, whatever. I prefer Hugo anyway. Do you think he's related to the royal family? I wonder how long it'll take for me to wangle a date with him?' She looked rather excited at the prospect. It turned out Samantha was from New Zealand, and as she said, New Zealanders are very direct. When they want something, they go for it. I decided office life was definitely going to be interesting with Sexy Samantha around.

'Well, go gently with him, he looks rather unprepared for someone like you!' I laughed with her. Some of the people from down below trickled into the pub and the quick drink turned into quite a long evening.

The next few days passed quickly; it was nice to have someone to talk to in the office as the boys were often out. Whenever they came back, Samantha would make a beeline for their office with cups of tea or coffee, lingering over Hugo's desk. She would flirt with him outrageously, managing to make the question 'Is there anything you want me to do?' sound like an indecent proposal, and Hugo would flush pink and hand her mounds of letters to type.

It was Friday afternoon, when Samantha replaced the telephone receiver with a bang. 'Jeez, who *is* that woman?' she asked in an exasperated fashion.

'Who?' I enquired, slightly distracted. I was busy trying to find a new night guard for the building, and while juggling two phone calls was directing a very bad-tempered builder to the places we wanted pictures hung.

'Never gives her name, just says is *he* there?' said Samantha.

'Oh her. I don't know, but she's bloody irritating. Treats me like some office junior,' I replied.

'Well, I'm going to tell her next time that I'm not putting her through until I have her name. Cow. Do you think it's his wife?'

'No, his wife is called Belinda and to my certain knowledge hasn't rung here so far. Talking of wives, how are you progressing with our Hugo?'

'Slowly, but I think surely,' she giggled. 'Underneath his tall, cool, blond exterior, he's rather shy – it's sweet. But he's quite a challenge and I haven't had one of those for a while.'

How wonderful to be so confident of your power over men, I mused, then a thought struck me. 'Samantha, are you busy tonight? I'm going out with my great friend Frank, who's lining me up with one of his friends, but he really needs to meet someone new himself and you'd be perfect. He's lovely, one of my best friends. He can distract you from Hugo and you can stay at my place, well, Bumble's place; it's a huge house in Fulham with loads of room. Say yes,' I entreated.

'Yeah, why not, I'm game,' she replied without much hesitation.

And so later on we both wandered into the Nag's Head and I introduced her to everyone, including Frank. I was delighted to see Henry there. Samantha was on fine form, having recovered from the shock of seeing me in my more usual clothing.

'Poll!' she shrieked, 'just as well you don't wear those clothes to the office, the boys'd have a fit!' I hadn't explained Plan A to her, so muttered something about sensible office dressing.

Samantha got on famously with everyone, as I knew she would. She was so pretty I was rather nervous having her around Henry, but I pulled myself together, remembering the words of a good friend of mine who says 'every girl should have one dangerous friend'. I suppose it keeps you on your toes. After a long session at the pub we all repaired rather drunkenly to a tiny Chinese restaurant in Soho. At the end of the meal we read each other's fortune cookies. I strategically placed myself next to Henry and grabbed the little piece of paper as it fell to his plate.

'Oh no,' I exclaimed in mock horror, 'I can't read it!'

'What does it say? It can't be so bad,' asked Henry, curiously.

'It says here a small dark stranger will be entering your life.' I looked crestfallen.

Henry laughed, 'No doubt our diminutive waitress is about to arrive with the bill. Let me have it.' He reached over for the piece of paper and looked at it quickly. 'It doesn't say anything of the sort, you naughty girl. It says, "Rays of sunshine cast long shadows." Load of old bunkum.'

'Well,' said Frank, 'Polly's a ray of sunshine and she's so bloody tall, she casts a very long shadow. I think it's quite appropriate, Henry.' He winked at me.

'So, Ray, how Fah can you cast your shadow on Me?' punned Henry.

'Keep me vertical and I can cast my shadow on you for as long as you like,' I replied with smile.

'And horizontal?' He was following right along.

'Hmm . . . ' I thought fast, 'then it would be night. No sun, therefore no rays, no shadows, just moonlight.'

'Very romantic, moonlight. We should go and explore it

one night next week. May I now be allowed your telephone number?' He had an amused smile on his face.

'Of course you may,' I replied, pleased. 'Now I've met you again and read your fortune cookie, I feel we are so much better acquainted.' I was trying hard to forget Frank's advice about being out when he rang and could have predicted his next sentence when he said, 'Good, I'll call you.'

God, I hate that! When exactly? What day precisely? I want to know, now. But no, I have to play it cool and tell Bumble if some gorgeous-sounding man phones for me to say I am out. Damn, damn, damn.

Samantha and I tottered back to Fulham, comparing notes on the evening, and I was dismayed Frank hadn't made any kind of approach to Samantha.

'Well, what do you expect?' she said rather huffily. 'He's gay.'

'He most certainly is not,' I replied, indignant on behalf of my friend. 'He's had loads of girlfriends.' Which wasn't quite true, but I felt I needed to stick up for him.

'Yeah, well if he had sex with any of them I'd be surprised – and, anyway, I bet they were all ugly,' she laughed.

'Samantha, you're outrageous, you meet one man who doesn't fall all over you so you decide he's gay. Maybe you're not his type, but more probably, he's just being an Englishman.'

I was quite cross. No one could ever have thought of Frank as gay. He was from Huddersfield for heaven's sake! No. I decided Samantha was miffed at not being leapt on by Hugo and was taking it out on Frank. 'You didn't say Hugo was gay and he hasn't asked you out,' I added.

'Yet,' she replied confidently.

'You're quite impossible. Anyway, here we are, Altonative Towers, playground for grown-ups. Watch out for lecherous lodgers, anguished au pairs, cute children, huge amounts of food, being quizzed by Bumble on every aspect of your life and given a lecture on literature by Gareth. However, as it's quite late, all that can wait until tomorrow.'

We crept into the unusually silent house and fell into bed.

Samantha stayed the weekend and Bumble, naturally, immediately welcomed Samantha into the ample bosom of her house and spent most of the weekend trying to fatten her up, a heartless and cruel habit of hers she put down to caring and I secretly knew was revenge on all females who were thinner than her!

I enjoyed relating the Henry progress to the household, and having bonded rather rapidly with Samantha, told her about the Plan. She thought it hilarious, if slightly cock-eyed.

'When I want a man, I just go for it.' She was stating the already perfectly obvious.

'I'm just trying to be a little more subtle about it,' I explained, 'to make sure it's the right one this time. Anyway, it's easier for you, looking like you do.'

'Oh, give me a break, Poll. Looked in the mirror recently?' she asked with typical Kiwi bluntness.

I laughed, 'Sorry, I must stop being self-deprecating. Spend four years with someone who knocks the stuffing out of you and look what happens.'

'So why do you stay with the wonderboys when they're not on your list?' she asked. 'Aren't you just wasting time? Especially when I think Henry might just fit the bill.'

'Well, I nearly left, just before you arrived. Johnnie was driving me round the bend, barking orders at everyone, not just me. Those poor people from downstairs are all terrified of him. Marching around the place like some sort of despotic mini-Hitler. So I went in to see Hugo when he was on his own and said I loathed Johnnie's attitude, was treated like a dogs-body, didn't need the grief and was going to leave at the end of the week.'

'Thanks for telling me!' said Samantha. 'You could have left me there all by myself. What happened?'

'Well, Hugo all but begged me to stay. Said Johnnie needed someone to stand up to him; I was really good for the company (untrue but nice) and would increasing my salary help? I

56

replied it might, but only if it was by a huge amount, and low and behold, he agreed! I was so stunned, I could only thank him and promise to stay on. He actually suggested I take Johnnie out for a drink and tell him what I thought. Everyone around him just gets steamrollered. He also said it amused him greatly to see Johnnie flummoxed by someone, that that alone was worth at least half the raise! So I'm still there; to amuse Hugo and give Johnnie grief. Besides, I'd never be paid this amount anywhere else. So if I am not going to find my husband in the office, at least I can afford to go out and look for him.'

'Well, I think it's quite a good idea,' said Samantha, rather thoughtfully.

'What is?' I asked

'Taking Johnnie out and telling him how he behaves. He probably doesn't have a clue.'

'I'd rather die, thank you – unless I could put ground glass in his drink. Why don't you do it?'

'No, it wouldn't be the same from me. First, I'm a Kiwi, and secondly, he wouldn't take me seriously. Probably on account of too much lipstick. You, on the other hand, are tall, and at the office you dress,' she paused to consider her words, 'appallingly. Like some bank manager's wife. He'd listen to you.'

Isn't life funny? There I had been thinking how wonderful to look like Samantha, not realizing she felt no one went beyond what she looked like. How disappointing to think appearances are taken so literally. Being tall means you have stature and wearing sensible clothes means people take you seriously. Are appearances deceptive or are we? Either way, I wasn't going to have a heart to heart with Mr J. J. B. Lyle.

9

The following week at work was fascinating.

On Monday morning Johnnie informed us the two directors from New York were arriving the next day for a week and the office had to be immaculate and our dress code (big glare at Samantha) must be 'serious'.

I was then called in by Johnnie who proceeded to give me a long, terse list of orders: arrange hotel, limos, theatre, dinners, presents, you name it, for the entire duration of these men's stay. On top of which Samantha and I had to attend the dinner on Friday! No request, just a statement. I was intrigued by the prospect of spending out-of-office time with Johnnie and Hugo and wondered if they developed personalities after dark. But also rather irritated at having to give up my own time for two old men who, if only because they lived in New York, sounded particularly uninteresting. I could imagine the conversation would revolve around deals, banks and mortgages. Scintillating stuff. I decided at least we would eat at a venue of my choice and duly booked Green's Champagne and Oyster Bar.

'What do I have to wear?' I asked Johnnie rather sniffily.

'Wear?' he asked, as if it was the most irrelevant question he'd ever heard. 'Whatever you wear when you go out for d–dinner.'

Fine, I thought, so I shall. And marched out of the office.

I had a very happy day with a limitless budget organizing the week for the Americans, whom, on reflection, I decided I was now looking forward to meeting because they seemed to make the wonderboys rather nervous.

It was with some surprise, when the lift door slid open on Tuesday morning, that we found ourselves confronted with Little and Large. Two more disparate men you would be unlikely to meet. Freddie Thompson was tiny, with a cat-like, almost oriental face, and the thickest, straightest snow-white hair I had ever seen. He had pale, waxy skin and cold grey eyes. When he spoke his mouth scarcely opened, but he stared at people with an unnerving intensity which made them feel they wanted to put on more clothes. He was probably in his late fifties. Bill Shark, on the other hand, was very tall and raven haired, with a florid complexion and piercing, bright blue eyes. He had a handsome if slightly dissipated round face and a ready, ironic smile played around his mouth. He must have been late forties.

We didn't see much of them for the first few days as they were closeted with the wonderboys in the office. Samantha had never made quite so many cups of coffee and was called in frequently. I spent my time ensuring the copious arrangements ran strictly to schedule, as Johnnie issued orders with the rapid-fire intensity of a machine gun and about as much grace.

Henry had rung on Wednesday, and on being told I was out, said he would phone back. I was glad to be distracted at work so I was incapable of thinking about telephones all day. I hate this initial stage; it's so annoying having to play games, but being busy made it easier.

The hotel I had booked for the Americans, 47 Park Street, turned out to be quite a find and they thanked me frequently for all my various arrangements. I began to suspect they were flirting with me, which was rather gratifying as the wonder-boys treated me as the Office It.

Friday evening came and I still hadn't heard from Henry, which was annoying. I was also having a complete fashion crisis upstairs and had only Minnie to be my guide. She was dressed in my office suit and looked rather like one of the dwarves in a Disney film. She insisted on handing me hideous garments from her dressing-up box, which consisted principally of her mother's fashion disasters over many years. After resisting her kind offer to do my make-up, I raced out of the house dressed in a rather tight, short black dress with very high black boots and a completely mad jacket Minnie had found, which amused me greatly.

On arriving early, as instructed, I sat at the bar on my own sipping a glass of champagne. I wasn't sure I'd ever been early for anything and experienced a vague feeling of jet-lag. I wondered what was expected of us. Was this a formal office dinner where we would be quizzed on the finer points of the company? I did hope not; Rohan's explanation, whilst succinct, wasn't exactly City-speak. Or were we office candy? I wasn't hugely keen on that prospect either.

Johnnie and Hugo arrived first, and looked rather startled when they saw me. They were both still dressed in their office suits.

'Ah, where is the rest of your dress?' enquired Hugo, with a rare touch of humour. I think.

'Johnnie told me to wear what I usually wear,' I replied, 'so I did.'

'Evidently,' said Johnnie rather oddly, and then proceeded to ignore me and order a bottle of champagne.

Samantha came in next, demurely dressed for once and in marked contrast to me, perhaps also wondering what was expected of her. The four of us were rather awkward and overly polite, as if the change from an office environment to a social one had shifted the balance of the relationship – but no one seemed quite sure where to. Finally, Bill and Freddie came through the doors and the atmosphere lightened. More bottles of champagne were ordered and we repaired to our table. Bill's capacity for drink was enormous and he grew louder by the minute, his accent becoming increasingly strong. Freddie remained inscrutable and the boys were unctuously polite and seemed rather nervous.

After a couple of drinks, the devil in me came out and I threw caution to the wind and started telling a few of my more *risqué* jokes. (I am incapable of telling a joke sober.) As the jokes became ruder, I could see Johnnie and Hugo visibly tense to see the reaction, and when gales of laughter came from Bill and smiles from Freddie, their shoulders would relax and they'd join in. I decided Bill was rather attractive and was pleased when Johnnie suggested we go on to Annabel's.

It was a slightly inebriated party that staggered down the narrow steps to the cavernous club. I had to do a very quick recce to work out where the ladies was, but had read enough *Tatlers* to know the name of the venerable lady who guarded the cloakroom.

'Mabel, how lovely to see you again,' I said in my best posh-pissed voice. Despite having never seen me in her life, she smiled and said, 'Welcome back, madam!'

Samantha, who had been rather quiet all evening, said, 'I didn't know you came here.'

'I don't,' I hissed. 'I mastered the art of faking it years ago! Are you OK?' I asked her.

'Yeah fine, but Hugo's a hard fish to catch,' she replied, while applying a vivid scarlet to her lips.

'Well get him up on the dance floor then,' I said, peering into the mirror, madly trying to powder down my rather flushed face. I gave up and snapped my compact shut. 'Right, follow me, I don't have a clue where I am going, but look purposeful, no one will know.'

We found the men sitting with yet another bottle of champagne. Johnnie stood up. For one horrible moment I thought he was going to ask me to dance.

'Right now, Polly, I have to go. G–got to get back to the country. I've told John the barman you can sign the bill on my behalf. Whatever Bill and Freddie want, just order. I'll see you on Monday.'

Whereupon he spun around and he and his pert little derrière marched out of the club!

Samantha purred up to Hugo and took him on to the dance floor and I was left with the two Americans. Bill, who was now pretty drunk, asked me to dance.

He guided me unsteadily to the dance floor, where we found

Hugo and Samantha. Hugo looked extremely nervous and she looked predatory. I laughed.

'What are you laughing at, darlin'?' asked Bill, as he slipped an arm around my waist, more for support than technique.

'Samantha is moving in on Hugo and he looks terrified!' I replied unguardedly, and tried to prevent his foot landing on mine.

Bill laughed, 'I wish her luck, I always thought he was gay! Not like Jump-me-Johnnie.'

'Jump-me-Johnnie?' I queried.

'Darlin', the man's got a girl in every town and a libido the size of the Empire State Building. If he's going home to his wife now, I'll eat my boots.'

'Really?' I was amazed any girl would want him. Then I added rather lamely, 'But he's married.'

'Never stopped any man I know. Why, don't say you're interested too?' he asked, as he inelegantly twirled me around the floor.

'God no! I can't bear him!' I exclaimed, rather indiscreetly on reflection. Must be all the champagne, must shut up. It was terribly hard to concentrate on staying upright for both of us and have a conversation, particularly one this interesting. But I felt I had better redress the balance. Bill was, after all, Johnnie's boss, and I didn't wish to appear unprofessional, so I added, 'I mean he's very good at his job, it's just he's not really my type.'

It was Bill's turn to laugh. 'Honey, I couldn't imagine a girl like you would be interested in him. And by the way, I much prefer your out-of-office clothing. Oh God, here comes Thompson, I guess he wants a dance too. Can't keep you to myself all evening.'

He lurched off, and I was rather disappointed to be handed on to Freddie, over whom I seriously towered. Dancing with him was bizarre, as he moved expertly but very slowly, while silently staring at me. It was unnerving, particularly as he was pressing himself very close to me, and, unless I was imagining things, his lack of stature was not at all proportionate!

I escaped after two dances and went to find Bill. I sat down beside him and he poured me yet another glass of champagne. My head was spinning a bit and I decided he really was very attractive. I was even beginning to like his accent.

'So,' I began, 'do you like London?' and then thought what an incredibly stupid question it was.

'Like it more now, darlin',' he replied rather slurrily, adding, 'I'm going antique-hunting tomorrow, do you want to come with me?'

I was rather pleased. 'I'd love to,' I smiled, then I looked around, 'Where's Hugo?'

'Disproved my gay theory and taken Samantha home. Foxy lady that one, make no mistake.' Bill hiccuped rather loudly.

'No!' I gasped, 'how incredible, she's been after him since day one. I don't think he's gay at all, by the way, he's taking a girlfriend to the dinner tomorrow.'

'God, not another dinner,' groaned Bill, 'where are we going?'

'You're going to the Waterside Inn, which is fabulous and I'm sure you'll enjoy it,' I replied.

'Aren't you coming too?' asked Freddie, who had just rejoined us.

I explained it was strictly wives and girlfriends.

Bill leapt to his feet, 'You must come with us! OK? I insist. It'll be much more fun.' He swayed to and fro.

'Well,' I started doubtfully, 'I'm not really invited.'

'I AM INVITING YOU! I AM THE BOSS!' yelled Bill.

'Fine, fine,' I said hastily, looking round nervously. I didn't want my first trip to Annabel's to be my last. 'I'll come, thank you.'

'Great,' added Freddie quietly, getting to his feet as well. 'Shall we go?'

I sorted out the bill with the rather handsome barman John, which involved merely signing my name, which I thought was incredibly cool. I then went up the stairs and out into the night to join Bill and Freddie, who appeared to be having a row. As I ascended I could hear them arguing, but couldn't get the gist of it. By the time I reached them, Bill had stormed off, leaving me with Freddie.

'Is there a problem?' I asked, wondering what on earth was going on.

'No,' said Freddie evenly, 'Bill gets a bit over-excited on occasions. He's walking back to the hotel. Do you want to come back for a night-cap?'

I really did not. He unsettled me – apart from being about as tall as Ronnie Corbett. And I was disappointed Bill had deserted me.

'No, it's fine, thank you, I'd better get home. Was Bill serious about dinner tomorrow?' It was going to be riveting to see the boys' faces if I turned up, besides I'd be fascinated to meet the wife and girlfriend.

'Sure, call me at the hotel tomorrow and we can pick you up in our car. Good-night then.' He turned and walked into the night, leaving me completely on my own in a jacuzzi of whirling thoughts.

10

I woke late on Saturday morning with a large headache. I must stop all this drinking, I thought to myself as I reached for the sunglasses under my pillow. I wandered downstairs to be met by Bumble holding a glass of the fizzy stuff.

'Drink this, you old stop-out. You'll either be sick or feel better.'

'Great,' I mumbled, taking a tentative sip. 'Eugh!'

'So, low-down on last night please,' demanded Bumble. You got back really late. Ciggie?'

I shook my head – which wasn't wise – and related the events of the evening to her, adding, 'I must phone Samantha and see what happened.'

'What are you going to do about the antique-hunting with Bill?' asked Bumble.

'Oh, bugger, I don't know. If I didn't fancy him, I'd just phone the hotel. It's quite ridiculous – the moment you get interested in someone, your instincts go all blurry. Or maybe I'm just generally blurry. But he is my employer, sort of, so maybe it would be rude, as a member of his staff, not to follow up. What do you think? I can't, not with this hangover.'

'Well, you've nothing to lose really. He's going back on Monday and he's absolutely not Plan A material. Don't even think about fancying him. But as you're seeing him tonight you could phone on the pretext of finding out the arrangements and see if he mentions anything.'

'Good idea, thanks. I'll phone Samantha first though.'

She was in a frightfully bad mood.

'Jeez, Poll, what is wrong with these English blokes. I can't bear all this behaving-like-a-gent business. I have this unbelievable thought, maybe he doesn't fancy me! The shock of it. You want to know what happened? Absolutely bloody nothing. I must be losing my touch. I am sooa depressed.' Her accent was heightened in her misery.

'Did he kiss you on the cheek good-night?' I hardly dared ask.

'Nooooooa!' she wailed down the phone, which I had to hold away from my ear.

'Well, it's really weird,' I said, musing. 'You know what, I bet he really, really fancies you and just doesn't know what to do. Probably never met anyone like you before and is a bit intimidated. Listen, we'll plan a campaign next week. We can call it Plan C. No more Kiwi tactics, let's go with English rules. Now listen, don't get depressed, go and look at your glorious reflection in the mirror to cheer yourself up and I'll see you on Monday.'

I decided not to tell her about going to dinner tonight as it would depress her more.

The next call I made was to 47 Park Street. 'Mr Shark's room, please.' My stomach churned a little and I wondered if the Alka-Seltzer was choosing an inopportune time to work its magic.

'Mornin' darlin',' said a rather croaky drawl. 'I was hoping you'd call.'

Phew, right decision.

'You left me,' I said with *faux* indignation.

'Well, I thought Thompson was going to make a move on you, and I didn't want to be in the way,' he replied inscrutably.

I thought it was a bit of a weird reply, if not a little insulting, and wasn't sure how to take it. He was either very insecure, or he was testing me. As I wasn't up to playing games, I replied honestly, 'Well, I would have much preferred to have been left with you. Are we going antique-shopping today?'

'Sure,' he said, and I could sense I'd said the right thing. 'I'll come and pick you up in an hour; we can shop and have lunch afterwards if you like. Give me your address.'

I was really quite excited. I was also feeling a little smug, being paid attention by the big boss of the company, when the other two were *a* clearly in awe of him and *b* clearly oblivious to me. So with a slightly lighter head I went upstairs to change.

There was a knock on my door and William the Lodger came in.

'Are you undressed?' he asked, hopefully.

'No, I am not, luckily,' I replied crossly. 'What do you want? Can I have no privacy?'

'Not in this house. Some plummy-sounding man rang for you last night, can't remember what he wanted, said you were out. OK?'

Damn – Henry . . . twice I'd been out. I wondered if he'd phone again. Whilst the whole unobtainability business was understandable in theory, I didn't want to go overboard and seem completely indifferent. I was getting side-tracked by older, foreign men, who, while very nice, still ranked high on the Unsuitable list. However, it was only to fill in a Saturday when I had nothing better to do . . .

A rather large, black, shiny Mercedes slid to a gentle halt outside the door and I was impressed to see a man in uniform open the door to let Bill out. He walked purposefully up to the door and rang the bell.

As I descended the stairs, Bumble said, 'Careful now, don't let all this go to your head. He isn't part of the plan.'

'I know, I know,' I replied rather crossly, as she echoed my own thoughts. 'It's just work.'

'Right,' said Bumble unconvinced. 'Well, try and have a good time then.'

There is something about the smell of new leather in very expensive cars which is unique and immediately makes you feel you are in luxury. As we purred along Bill and I chatted about his house in New York and his love of English antiques. I'd lived in London all my life – with a few notable absences – but had never once set foot along the nether regions of King's Road and all the shops there. I felt there was a certain irony in an American telling me about things English and the best shops to find them, but I soon discovered Bill had an encyclopaedic knowledge of just about everything in life. I could see why he was so successful and found myself mesmerized by his mind.

He was incredibly good company, and we laughed and joked for the entire morning. I'd never had an older boyfriend and was beginning to like the feeling of security being with an older man engendered. I didn't think I had an Electra complex, but maybe Freud was right and it's deep seated in all of us. It was intriguing.

As we sat over lunch in a little Italian restaurant, we discussed art, theatre, life, even religion and money, and I found myself hanging on his every word. He had an opinion on everything. He was also very, very funny and told the rudest jokes, which I did my best to try and remember.

'So darlin',' he finally intoned, 'what in the hell is a girl like you doing with those two boys?'

'What do you mean?' I asked, not sure how to answer.

'They must be terrified of you. Not some – what do you call them over here? – Sloane Ranger, whom they would have grown up with. One of those girls who can whisk up a soufflé, wipe up dribble and rub down a labrador all in one go. You appear to have a couple of brain cells, what are you doing with them?'

I was immensely flattered and didn't quite know what to say. I was also rather disheartened by his description of a life I was currently aspiring to. Obviously refraining from telling him about the Plan, I explained how I had ended up at the company more by default than anything else, and was sure any minute now they'd fire me as I had no real qualifications to do anything, particularly as Johnnie seemed to have a serious aversion to me. (I wasn't being completely naïve, I knew Bill ran the group and I also knew I was going to have to get some sort of job description sooner or later. Samantha was so efficient I was fast becoming redundant.)

'We need to put you to better use.' He paused and his face took on a serious aspect. 'I have an idea. Let me talk to Thompson, but if he agrees, which he will, I'll tell the boys on

Monday what you're gonna do. Get another girl in before Lyle tries to turn you into his secretary.'

I couldn't imagine a more appalling prospect.

Then he ruined it by adding, 'Make sure she's a babe as well.'

After downing a couple of rather alarming flaming sambuccas, I was deposited back at Altonative Towers with time to recover before the evening ahead.

I managed to create the usual chaos, not only in my bedroom, but in every other one in the house, having yet another huge fashion crisis. My wardrobe simply did not allow for all these smart evenings out and I ended up in William the Lodger's dinner jacket, Gareth's dress shirt, a pair of Bumble's black trousers and my own high black boots. I felt like I had just been spewed out of the Red Cross Charity Shop and I was really grateful for my one Sloaney accessory, the ubiquitous Hermes scarf, which I'd pinched off my mother a few years ago.

The look on Johnnie and Hugo's faces when I arrived at the table with Bill and Freddie was hilarious. Johnnie appeared furious; Hugo stunned.

'Thought we'd bring Polly along,' said Bill, completely aware of the stir he was causing.

Johnnie recovered his composure quickly. 'Of course, what a lovely idea. Polly, let me introduce you to my wife B–Belinda, and Hugo's girlfriend, Jenny.'

I tried so hard not to stare. Jenny was small with a very pretty but serious face, devoid of any make-up. She looked very sporty and rather boyish, with short brown hair. I guessed she'd be happier in cords and a woolly jumper or leaping about a squash court. I could still see the marks of her ski-goggles round her eyes, white in contrast with her tanned face.

Belinda was a complete revelation. I don't know what I'd been expecting, probably someone rather cool, stuck up and sophisticated, able to cope with Johnnie's extraordinary forcefulness. But facing me was a fresh-faced, floral-frocked attractive county girl, with an open smile and a gentle voice. Her blonde hair was cut sensibly and she had sensible shoes to match. I was amazed and momentarily lost the power of speech as I contemplated the incongruity of this coupling. Perhaps Johnnie had a side to him I had yet to uncover, maybe he was a gentle country boy in wellies at the weekend, but I had no idea how a girl who seemed so typically 'nice' was ever going to keep up with him. However, she seemed charming, if a little guarded with me. Her conversation centred around her new baby, who I was stunned to discover had been brought along too, with a nanny, and deposited in a nearby private room, so Belinda could disappear and breast-feed, which she did twice during dinner.

Clearly Bill thought this kind of behaviour quite bizarre, but agreed with me privately it was infinitely preferable to doing it at the table. I thought it pretty stoic of her to come out to what she probably thought was a dull business dinner when she had a tiny baby. Johnnie kept on looking at me in a very curious way and I realized that if I was annoying him now he was going to go potty when Bill and Freddie announced their new plans for me.

Dinner was much quieter than last night, everyone on best behaviour, particularly me. I marvelled at the delicious food and wine and the setting in which it was served, thinking I could get used to this life . . . Michel Roux came up to us on a couple of occasions and his pretty Australian wife, Robyn, sat and had drinks with us at the end of the evening. They seemed to know Johnnie very well.

Bill had placed me between himself and Johnnie, who was trying to be charming. Clearly my relationship with his two bosses was keeping him on his toes and he made sure the conversation flowed. I discovered a little more about him. He had spent his early childhood in the States, his father being American, and then returned to London where, curiously, he had lived quite close to me – it turned out we had taken the same bus to school, although unsurprisingly, given his ridiculous dawn rises, we had never met. I then discovered he had dated one of my friends from school – I could hardly wait to tell her what a lucky break she'd had – and finally it turned out he had gone to the same school, same house, as my father. It was an odd series of coincidences and I tried to remember the name of the book, *The Celestine Prophesy* (it came to me at last), which said there was no such thing as coincidence in life. I found him to be a more pleasant dinner companion than I could have envisaged. The only time I had to stifle a giggle was when I asked how he and Belinda had met and, in all seriousness, he replied, 'at the Pony Club'!

Bill was great and had a talent for telling long, anecdotal stories which made everyone laugh. Belinda kept apologizing for getting up and leaving the table and then apologized for returning and she and Johnnie went quite early. Hugo, also a member of Annabel's, suggested we have a nightcap there. There are certain habits I aspired to acquire.

As I descended the stairs and headed for the ladies with Jenny, I pondered the irony. Last night here, with Samantha desperate for Hugo, and tonight standing in front of the same mirror, with the girl who was already with him and about as opposite to Samantha as you could get. No wonder Hugo wasn't interested; if this was his type, Samantha was the equivalent of a Martian. I resolved to tell her to tone down the make-up and lipstick as a first measure.

This time I could greet Mabel and see recognition on her face, very amusing.

Hugo took me off for a dance, which was rather surprising. 'Thank you for being discreet about last night,' he said.

'Well, there wasn't much to be indiscreet about. I don't hold with cross-pollinating and last night you were on business,' I replied carefully, thinking I was going to have to be a master tactician with Samantha as well.

'I'm glad you're getting on so well with Bill and Freddie,' said Hugo evenly, changing the subject. 'They're clever men who have been very successful. It's nice for them to have a distraction when they're over in England.'

I wasn't so sure about being described as a distraction, but decided it was just as well I'd kept quiet about my day with Bill. It occurred to me my omissions were becoming greater than my admissions.

Bill then cut in and started dancing with me. 'Do you want to go for lunch in Oxford tomorrow, darlin'?'

I loved his accent. He exuded power and intellect and it was exciting to be with him. Because of his obvious capacity for drink, he was still quite upright, and I thought it would be fun to go, so I said I'd love to, but added, 'However, I think I may have to head home now, it's been a long weekend already.'

'I'll get the car to take you back,' he said. 'I'd better stay in case they start talking about you and me!' He had a large smile on his face. 'I'll pick you up around eleven.'

I said my goodbyes and fell into the back seat of the large black Mercedes with a contented smile on my face.

11

'I must not fall for Unsuitable Men, I must not fall for Unsuitable Men.' I muttered my mantra repeatedly as I dressed on Sunday morning. 'This is just business. This is just business.' I paused for a moment, trying to find a clean bra. 'He's going back to America tomorrow. He's going back to America . . . '

'What are you banging on about?' asked Bumble coming into the bedroom.

'I'm off with Bill again today and I'm just psyching myself up not to fall for him,' I replied.

'Well, in my experience,' began Bumble, rather pompously I thought considering she'd been with Gareth for ever, 'the unexpected always happens and the inevitable never does. I think you have already fallen for this man. Ciggie?'

'No thanks and I haven't fallen for him,' I replied. 'This is work. And, I will have you know, I'm being promoted tomorrow, so I have to be nice to the boss. OK?'

'Delude yourself all you like,' she replied airily, waving her cigarette around in the air, 'I know what I'm talking about. I have great objectivity.'

'Well, I object to your objectivity and I'm not falling for anyone who leaves to go and live on the other side of the world. I've done that once before. But I admit I like his company and he is very attractive. He could be married for all I know about him – you see, we haven't even got on to a personal level.'

I realized as I said this I would immediately have to find out these salient details. 'So don't worry, I'm in control. And if Henry phones, ask for his number and say I'll call him back. He's someone worth pursuing. And listen, what the hell do I wear for lunch in the country?'

'Oxford is hardly the country. The town is about as sub-urban as they come, full of commuting husbands and ex-London mothers discussing their children's education. The dons are debauched, the restaurateurs priggish and the shopping consists of woolly jumpers with farmyard animals cavorting across your chest or thermal knickers. Wear what you would wear to the West End which is what they all wish they were wearing.' With that damning picture she walked out of the bedroom and I finished dressing.

We had another great day.

I also learned some personal details, like he was still married to his wife, but they had been separated for ten years – an arrangement which I suspected suited him as he was not at all keen to remarry. He had one doted-on daughter who was the main female in his life. He loved work, parties and drinking. He knew tons of people but had few close friends and appeared to trust no one. He was hugely patriotic and when not dressed up in a suit went to what I suspected was his enormous farm somewhere outside New York where he pottered around in jeans, cooked on the BBQ, walked in his woods, planted things, rode his horses or played with boats on his lake. He was really, really rich. I was definitely not falling for him.

He behaved impeccably the entire time, and on dropping me off after our day out, merely kissed me on the cheek and said he'd see me tomorrow.

'So, how did it go?' enquired Bumble before I'd even got through the front door.

'Fine, he's a perfect gentleman, just a lovely lunch and a walk around Woodstock then home,' I replied, irritated by the inquisition.

'How very disappointing for you.' She smiled and I got quite a bit crosser.

'Not at all,' I countered, 'it shows he thinks of me merely as a nice colleague. A distraction if you will' (Hugo's words were re-used). 'I don't think he's interested in me in any other way, which is fine, because I don't want to get involved in complicated situations.' I stared at her for a moment in the hallway, then relented, 'Oh, bugger it, Bumble, I don't have a clue what I think and I can't fathom him at all. I do like him, but he's my boss and he's going away. He only kissed me on the cheek and if he did make a pass I don't think I'd know what to do with it. So altogether, I think I shall put this down as a nice blip on my path to Mr Right.'

'Do you seriously believe Mr Right, the one and only, actually exists?' asked Bumble curiously.

I thought for a moment before replying.

'To be really honest, I believe Mr Right Timing exists. A dozen potential Mr Rights may have already passed through my life, but if a whole number of circumstances don't coincide, it doesn't happen.'

I followed Bumble into the sittiing-room, where she poured us both a glass of wine and I turned down the offer of a cigarette.

'But what about Mats then? You even married him,' said Bumble.

Ouch! My big secret!

I try to forget about the fact I had married Mats. Bumble and Gareth had been the only witnesses at the ceremony, as she was rather uncomfortably reminding me.

'Bumble, you know the only reason I married him was to get a work permit. No one knows, not my father, not my brother, none of my friends, except you and Gareth, oh and of course my mother. But she just guessed in that uncanny, mother-psychic way of hers. As far as I'm concerned it was not marriage. We lived together, but I was not married in my mind. I never thought Mats was "the one". He was just "the one for now". When I get married properly, it will be very different.'

'Well, you've blown your chances of the full white shebang in church, because even if you don't consider it a marriage "in your mind", as you so quaintly put it, legally it was and one day you will have to explain it to Mr Right Timing,' said Bumble, exercising her great 'objectivity'.

'Yes, well I shall cross that bridge when and if I come to it,' I replied, a bit snappy. 'Anyway, I don't regret doing it because it showed me very clearly what I don't want. No doubt one day I shall be grateful to him for propelling me back home with a serious agenda. It has helped me to resist, for example, the charms of yet another foreign Unsuitable, see?'

'Well, maybe you're right. I like the Mr Right Timing idea, but I'm just not sure you can calculatedly set out to get the person you've decided is suitable for you via all this game-playing. Don't you want the person to know you for you, who and what you are?'

'Well, of course I do, just not in the first five minutes of acquaintance. It's like,' I struggled for an analogy, 'a bottle of wine. You choose the one with the colour and taste you want and then sip it gently, you don't knock it all back in one go.'

'You'll be bloody disappointed if the bottle you chose said Chablis on the outside and it's some cheap German plonk inside,' replied Bumble, delighted to be able to continue the theme and ruin it.

'OK, God you are irritating, I can't think of anything better at the moment. And I'm sure you're wrong. I'll find exactly what I'm looking for,' I added, probably more to convince myself than anyone else.

Bumble got up from the sofa, cigarette and drink in hand. 'Whatever. Be careful what you wish for, you might just get it. I'm going to see about dinner. Sunday roast as usual – we're fourteen, I think.'

I rose to join her in the kitchen, continuing to talk on the way. 'All I can say is watch this space. I've given myself nearly two years to find someone suitable. I've put myself in an environment where it should happen and along the way I'm meeting all sorts of interesting people. I'm also furthering my career. Tomorrow, I'll have a job title and promotion. See? I can't be doing completely the wrong thing.'

Bumble looked at me, 'No I don't think you are doing the wrong thing at all, I just think life is full of surprises and I know I'm repeating myself, but truly, it's generally what you don't expect that happens. I also believe it's only when you're fulfilled as an individual, someone comes along to complement you. If you need a man to make your life complete, then by definition you're incomplete and, therefore, who'd want you? If you're fulfilled the addition of a man merely enhances your situation and you're a much more attractive, whole person. So although it might not be the way you planned, by having this good job in an interesting environment, you may just end up with what you want.'

I thought about this long and hard as I scrubbed the potatoes.

12

I arrived at the office early on Monday, wondering what was going to happen. The more I thought about it, the more I really wanted this new job.

The men were there already and Johnnie called me in to join them. He explained Bill had outlined his idea for me to organize the relocation of the companies downstairs. It was quite a big job and I started to worry I might not be able to manage it, but having no qualifications had never stopped me before and at least there were friendly faces in the companies. I was also going to have to employ a secretary, for Johnnie. Hugo had nabbed Samantha.

'So,' said Johnnie. 'Congratulations. I'm sure you'll do an excellent job. You will still report to me and if you have any questions, I would really prefer you to ask rather than screw it up.'

Charming, I thought, just when I thought I might have broken through. I managed a polite reply. I wasn't quite sure what this job was kitting me out for, but at least it didn't involve typing or making coffee, only one of which I was any good at.

I got back on to the phone to Julia Rowse and explained we needed yet another secretary; one, I added, who needed to be resilient as she would be working for Johnnie.

I replaced the receiver and looked up to see Bill and Freddie emerge from the big office with their bags packed. They came over to me to say goodbye.

'Good luck,' said Freddie, with the same inscrutable look on his face, 'it was nice to meet you.' He held out his hand, which I shook.

'Thanks for making the trip so enjoyable,' said Bill. He didn't hold out his hand. 'See you next time we're over.'

It was rather an anticlimax, although I wasn't sure what I'd been expecting. I was very glad I hadn't allowed myself to get involved with Bill. I had my new job and Henry to pursue and I needed to focus.

Samantha arrived in the office and I carefully told her about the weekend's events. She was so keen to hear details of Hugo's girlfriend she scarcely minded she hadn't been invited to the dinner and was really nice about my promotion.

'Soooooy,' she dipthong'd in the way only Antipodeans can, 'what was she like? What's the competition? Was she gorgeous?'

I dragged her off to the coffee machine and told her my plan for her.

She shrieked, 'If you think for one minute I'm not going to wear make-up you can take a hike right now! Do you know what I look like without it? It's an evil sight. I might tone down the scarlet lipstick for a bit of pink, but no eyes, are you insane? No foundation? Nobody in their right mind wants to see what lies beneath!'

It was amazing she was so insecure.

'Tomorrow night, we'll go to the pub round the corner and plan your campaign for Hugo. In the meantime, I have a ton of work to do.'

I busied myself for the next few hours and when I looked at my watch towards the end of the day I was surprised to see it was nearly six.

Johnnie came over to my desk, 'Um, Polly, I have a friend arriving shortly. As the receptionist has gone home now, would you let her in if I'm on the phone?' He was being oddly polite.

'Of course, Johnnie,' I replied, gripped to see who would be arriving. He strode back into his office and shut the door. My telephone rang a short while after, indicating someone was at the door, and before even checking to see if Johnnie was busy, I raced down to the reception to let this friend in. I stopped in my tracks at the entrance. Standing impatiently outside, tossing her long ebony hair, was a stunning-looking girl. Well, actually, not a girl, an African Princess. All long limbs and big eyes and soft skin. Immaculately and expensively dressed, completely coordinated down to her long red talons. I knew, before I opened the door, she loathed me. I was terrified of her.

'Oh, hallo,' she said, in a familiar, haughty voice, dismissing me with a cursory glance of disdain, 'I've come to see Johnnie.'

'Yes, I know,' I replied slowly. 'I've come to get you, he's on the phone. I'll take you upstairs.'

'That's all right,' she replied, 'I know the way.'

She promptly took her over-extended limbs, and strode towards the lift in front of me, got in the moment the doors opened and, before I had a chance, pressed the button to ascend, leaving me marooned in the reception area, absolutely fuming.

Stomping up the stairs, I was madly trying to work out who on earth she could be. At least now the mystery of who kept phoning was solved; she didn't look like any business executive I'd ever seen and I quelled the nauseating thought that Johnnie was having an affair. It wasn't that I was overly moralistic or judgemental; after all, I wasn't married to him, thank God. Clearly this disgustingly gorgeous, terrifying creature would be irresistible to all men and Belinda had seemed a bit of a mouse. I supposed it was the fact she had such young babies, or maybe that was the reason; anyway, I couldn't imagine Johnnie had met this one at the Pony Club – more like on safari. She reminded me of Bagheera in *The Jungle Book*. A pantheress.

As I reached the office I could hear flirty laughter, followed by soft voices and then, alarmingly, silence. I made a large noise opening the door. Johnnie was at his desk and on his knee with a snake-like arm wrapped round his shoulders sat the Pantheress, who gratifyingly nearly fell to the floor as Johnnie leapt to his feet upon seeing me.

She looked pure daggers for a moment, then regained her

cool composure. 'Hmm,' she said, I swear it sounded like a growl. 'It's you. I thought you were on your way out.'

'No,' I replied levelly, while keeping my eyes fixed on Johnnie, who looked really strange. I couldn't work out if he was proud or embarrassed to be caught with her. 'Can I get you both a drink?' I asked sweetly.

He cleared his throat and said they were just going to go out for one and would I wait till Hugo returned before locking up.

'How super, darling,' she said in her purry, husky voice, headlamp eyes fixed adoringly on him. 'Are you taking me somewhere lovely, again?'

I'm sure she added the 'again' just to prove this was not a first date. Johnnie looked highly uncomfortable; the 'darling' practically sent him into orbit. Never before had I witnessed such possessive behaviour, particularly over somebody else's property. I half expected her to pee on him, like a dog marking its territory. Clearly they were as impatient to go as I was to get rid of them and in lightning time I was alone.

Shortly after they had gone, Hugo walked through the door. I leapt to my feet and followed him into his office, bursting with childish curiosity.

'Hugo . . . ?' I began tentatively. 'Can I ask you something?'

'Yah, of course,' he replied rather absent-mindedly. 'Ah, has Johnnie gone?'

'Yes, he left a while ago, with . . . ' I paused. I wasn't sure what I was going to say next, or whether it was any of my business or even if I should ask, but what the hell. 'Er, he left with a girl, the one who phones all the time. A sort of terrifying Uber-Creature from some exotic country.'

'Ah,' he said, non-committally. 'Complicated.'

There was a huge pause.

'Well?' I said expectantly.

'Do you assume people will just, ah, tell you everything?' he asked, with a smile on his face.

I was surprised by such an obvious question. Everyone

always told me everything, and I consider myself brilliant at keeping secrets. I nodded.

'I thought so,' Hugo sighed. 'Let's go out for a drink.'

'Well as long as it is as far away as possible from them,' I said. 'She was so buffed-up, glossy and sleek, I felt like an unpolished, inky fifth-former. I even found myself checking to see if my shoes were scuffed. I mean, how ridiculous.'

'It's all right,' said Hugo sympathetically. 'It's how she makes most people feel. Well, girls anyway. Men are just bewitched by her. Currently, Johnnie is her target.'

As we sat at the bar of the Caprice, Hugo gave me a few more fascinating details. Her name was Theodora, or Dora to her friends. (Except I bet she didn't have friends, just slaves.) Her father was the exiled ruler of some far-flung African country, with pots and pots of money, probably dodgy, no one dared ask. Dora was his indulged only daughter in a family full of grossly overweight boys. As the apple of daddy's eye she wanted for nothing and therefore lusted after the unobtainable, particularly men. Not that they remained so for long as every single one of them would fall at her Manolo Blahnik-shod feet. Johnnie was presenting the ultimate challenge.

Johnnie was a very bright but quite insecure boy from a ruthlessly upper-middle-class family. He'd followed the not unusual route of marrying his parents' best friend's daughter, contracting into the solid social continuity of rural England. However, meteoric success in the City can change a person quite profoundly, and suddenly the girl next door seemed rather dull compared with the bright sparks flying round the pavements.

'There are always two sides to a story,' continued Hugo, 'and I don't think Belinda has helped the situation by having two children in such quick succession and basing herself solely in the country while Johnnie works up here during the week.

'The fact remains, men need constant support (and a great

deal of ego boosting) when they're making their way up the success ladder. After the adrenalin rush of big business and all the deal-doing testosterone swishing round the body, staying alone Monday to Thursday night isn't a hugely appealing option.

'Deep down I don't think Johnnie wants to be unfaithful. In many ways marriage has stabilized him. Fundamentally most men like being married, especially on terms they like. But where women are concerned, he's weak and very susceptible to flattery and home-alone syndrome is as dangerous to a marriage as empty-nest syndrome can be many years later,' added Hugo.

I mused that men are like house plants, you have to nurture them. The only low maintenance type are cacti, and who wants those little pricks? I was quite surprised at Hugo's wise take on life, and asked him how he felt about the situation.

'Dreadful,' he replied. 'And like all men I'm just pretending it isn't happening. I feel rather disloyal, but I'm sure once the baby has grown up a bit and Belinda stops being quite so involved with the children and turns her attention back to Johnnie, it'll be tickety-boo again. Dora will tire of him soon enough, and quite frankly, until she does, I defy any man to resist those charms. She's a Venus flytrap in female form.'

13

As I was lolling in my bath back at Altonative Towers, mulling over the last few day's events, there was a hammering on the door and Bumble's voice telling me Henry was on the phone. I sped down the stairs. At last. Someone Suitable.

'Henry,' I controlled my breathlessness and tried to sound calm. 'I'm sorry to have been out so often.'

'Never mind, I have you now. Would you like to have dinner this week, say Thursday?'

'I'd love to.' I smiled down the phone and realized I was excited at the prospect. I'd been so involved at work, I hadn't really had time to think about my Plan. Which made me realize Bumble was right, it's very important to have a life when you are seriously husband-hunting.

We arranged when and where, and then I raced into the kitchen, where Bumble was surrounded by steaming, delicious-smelling pots, to tell her the good news. I also told her about the Johnnie/Dora situation. She was her usual philosophical self.

'What can you expect? Hugo's right. If you leave a successful man to his own devices, he turns to vices.'

'Very funny.'

'But true, I am not a believer in giving a man too much rope, they usually end up hanging you. A wife has to be a very clever prison warder if she wants to keep her man. Look how difficult it is to find a good one. They're all snapped up. But unless they're taken care of, there are far too many predatory women out there who do not have your high and mighty ideals about pinching someone else's husband.'

'I didn't say it was a moral thing, Bumble, I said it was self-preservation. They might have children and the idea of being a stepmother is about as appealing as a sackful of slugs. She's

84

welcome to him. I have better, bigger and single fish to fry. Roll on Thursday.'

The following morning I had to sit down with Johnnie and not look worried while he outlined my role in the relocation of the two companies downstairs to Milton Keynes. I couldn't imagine how the personnel were going to react to it! Piccadilly to Milton Keynes – like going from heaven to hell. I sincerely hoped it wasn't my job to give them the happy news. I also wondered how I was going to get backwards and forwards and decided I would have to invest in a car. My salary, which kept rocketing up at a very amusing rate, could cope with the additional expense and the whole project, including reorganizing the remaining offices here, was going to take at least nine months. What with supervising the building and decorating, buying in furniture and equipment and arranging security, I was going to have to stay on my toes to juggle all the balls. I spent the rest of the day with Rohan sorting out details from his end and desperately trying to cover my ignorance about computers and systems. There was good news from Julia, who'd found an apparently great girl called Miranda to start tomorrow.

I repaired to the pub with Samantha at the end of what seemed like a very short day.

'So,' I started, clutching a spritzer, 'we need to plan your mode of attack on Hugo. It's quite clear he doesn't like flashy girls, more the sporty intellectual type.' I started to giggle. 'Soooo like you, Sam. I'm just not sure this will work, you are completely the opposite of what he appears to be comfortable with.'

'Excuse me!' she exclaimed. 'Who's kidding whom here? I'm not the one wearing the schoolmistress kit to work to snare some eligible man. Anyway, don't they say opposites attract?' she demanded rather indignantly. 'He doesn't even look sporty. Not compared to the Kiwi boys I know; they really know how to fill their pants.'

I laughed at a description so sure to find our Englishmen

puny by comparison, and Samantha reluctantly started to laugh as well. 'You have to understand, Poll, I know he finds me attractive, he's just scared. I'll tone down the make-up a bit, but I can't have a complete personality lobotomy' (she pronounced it labahdamy). 'Gotta take someone for what they are.' I didn't like to say Hugo probably thought she was a tart, albeit a very nice one!

'Anyways,' she continued, oblivious, 'I'm gonna join a gym and look for someone to play squash with there.'

The word squash sent us into fits of laughter, and after a couple more spritzers I tottered home with a bundle of car magazines under my arm and the *Evening Standard*. Without either my father or my brother around, who both had an encyclopaedic knowledge of cars, I was going to have to rely on the dubious talents of the occupants of Altonative Towers, of whom only Bumble possessed a licence. The boys were too fond of the famous Fleet Street tradition, getting absolutely rat-arsed at lunch and topping up again in the evenings, to have managed to hold on to theirs. But they could probably tell me which car made the best minicab. As I fiddled with the keys to let myself in through the front door I dropped the magazines.

'Bugger,' I said loudly.

A tall dark shadow appeared at my side. 'It would be my pleasure,' said Troy languidly, leaning his head over the fence from next door.

'Oh disgusting, Troy, and don't creep up on me. I'm just having a bit of trouble getting the key in the lock.'

'Ah, let me try, I am an expert at putting things in small holes.'

'I really don't want to think about it! Does even a normal household cavity have to relate to some human orifice for you, Troy? I know all about black men and size discrimination.'

'It's the reason white men are so threatened by us.'

'Oh, don't be ridiculous, nothing is that simple,' I snapped.

'Trust me, Polly, when the white men landed in Africa, we

86

were all naked. The first thing they did to us was put us in clothes. You know why? Because they didn't want their impressionable wives to see us and find their husbands lacking.'

'It cannot be all about size – what about technique?' I found myself being dragged into a conversation I really didn't have time for but which was, none the less, rather interesting in my slightly pissed haze.

'Combined, you would never be with a white man again,' Troy replied confidently.

'Exactly, and I want to be,' I replied firmly. 'Stop trying to mess me about. You Jamaicans, monster trouser snakes and voodoo men the lot of you!'

Troy started to laugh and put one long leg after the other over the fence and opened the front door for me. Then he bent to pick up the magazines. 'Buying a car?'

'No, a boat, durr-brain. Yes, of course I'm buying a car. Not that I have a clue where to start.'

'I can help. I'm an expert. Seriously, why don't you get out of your awful office clothes, which I can't believe you wear, and I'll take you out for dinner and advise you.' He looked intently at me. 'No funny business. I do know about cars. My brother runs a car dealership in the West End, and my other two brothers are mechanics, although one's in prison for car theft.'

I hesitated. I did need help, but Troy? Oh, what the hell, I thought, someone had to help me buy a car. It might as well be him and maybe he'd leave the seduction bit alone.

'Give me ten minutes and I'll be ready, thanks.'

I raced upstairs and pulled on some jeans and a T-shirt, gulping down some water to try to reduce the effects of the alcohol.

'And where are you off to in such a hurry?' asked Bumble, appearing at the doorway with a large glass in one hand and the inevitable cigarette in the other.

'Don't say a word, but Troy has offered to help me buy a car and is taking me out to dinner to discuss it. It's all perfectly above board.' Even as I said it, I realized it sounded pretty lame.

'Hmm,' said Bumble. 'Be careful. You know his reputation. I'm so pleased I'm happily married.'

She could be really infuriating.

'Listen, underneath all the simmering sex talk, there's probably a very nice person, with whom it will be perfectly possible to be friends. I intend to find that person, while he finds me a car.' I flounced past her and down the stairs.

As good as his word, Troy behaved impeccably, and I was very careful not to drink too much more. Booze goes straight to my groin and I didn't want to end up feeling all squirmy around Troy of all people!

He was a very interesting man. Although I'd met him innumerable times at Bumble and Gareth's I'd never really talked to him. It was better than his usual sexual banter. I was surprised what a good time I had and how much I liked him. He was very interesting and was also very funny, and by the end of the evening I was tired out from listening and laughing. We had yet to decide on cars, as I pointed out as we walked home.

'I'm sorry,' he said. 'I enjoyed talking to you so much, I forgot the main purpose of the evening. Come round tomorrow and I'll have spoken to my brothers.'

'Well, under normal circumstances I wouldn't set foot over your threshold, but you have been something of a revelation tonight, so thank you, I will. But could we make it Friday?' He nodded. 'And thank you for dinner by the way, it was delicious, I've never eaten Lebanese food before.'

'Well, I can cook it better myself, of course, but it was good enough. Remember, it's sleep-alone food. After all those beans your duvet will be flying.'

I laughed, 'Who would have thought Troy Clarke, serial seducer, would be advocating chastity.' Wrong thing to say.

'Oh, don't worry, I haven't given up on you yet, I'm just

biding my time and lending a helping hand in the meantime.' He stopped walking and looked very seriously at me for a moment. 'Underneath this exterior I'm a very insecure person. But there's something about you. I want you to get to know me and I want to get to know more about you. Find out how your head works. Sex is of no interest to me without the mind being invited along to the party. Yes, I give pleasure to many women. It's what they want from me. But I have to feel something, emotionally, really to trust that person, to go the whole way myself. I'm quite happy to spend all day just stroking you, caressing you, mere physical sex is not enough. A truly fulfilling sexual experience is sensual, passionate, mind engaging. Encompassing every centimetre of your body, every pore.' I stared at him, transfixed by this monologue which I would no doubt be analysing for days to come. He shook his head, 'Maybe one day, but enough for tonight, little one.'

I shivered, so few people could call me little, and I always feel small and protected when they do, particularly when they are as huge as Troy. However, I couldn't let my guard down completely. 'Excuse me, I believe I'm older than you, Troy, and wiser. If not taller.'

'Your age is immaterial to me, don't ever mention it again, it has no bearing and it must never be an issue for you. You will be attracted to people who are older than you, so why not people younger?'

I thought of Bill, who must have been at least fifteen years older than me, and nodded. 'You're right. It's just convention, and men seem to age better than women. But there can't be anything much sadder to look at than some old crone hanging on to the unwrinkled arm of her toyboy lover. What would he see in her other than flabby underarms and saggy tits. Older men are still attractive.'

'First, you're not so old, and secondly, why can't I say as a man, older women are attractive? Saggy tits and all. I've had women twenty years older than me who've been some of my best sexual experiences. Anyway, have you ever seen what the penis of a sixty-year-old man looks like? No, I didn't think so. Well let's just say I would take saggy tits any time.'

'Eugh, enough! I'll stick to someone my own age. Thank you again for dinner, I had a really good time and I'll pop by on Friday.' I leant up to kiss him good-night on the cheek, but he moved his head and I ended up on his lips, generous cushion lips, which I had tried hard not to look at most of the evening and of which, as a result, I knew every contour.

'Oops, sorry,' I said, drawing back hastily.

'Don't be. Good-night, Polly, sweet dreams.' He let himself into his house and quietly shut the door behind him.

My poor head was spinning as I climbed into bed. What with Bill and Troy I was very pleased I had someone like Henry to focus on. I seemed always to be attracted to completely the wrong type. I had this vision of what I wanted and what my future would be and it felt like my plans kept on being sabotaged. I was glad, despite all the odds, I actually enjoyed my job. If I had too much time to think about everything, I would start obsessing on all the wrong people.

14

I was in the office quite early the next morning to meet the new secretary. Samantha had already arrived, presumably trying to make a good impression on Hugo. I noticed she had toned her look down considerably since our chat yesterday. I turned to walk down the corridor to make some coffee when the lift doors opened and out bounced a small blonde figure with the tiniest tip-tilt nose I'd ever seen and the roundest, deepest blue eyes, leaving Samantha's in the shade. She looked like an adorable Pekinese, except not so hairy. Even more irritating, she was incredibly pretty, despite appearing to be wearing no make-up.

'Hi, everyone, I'm Miranda, but call me Merry, everyone does.' Like Samantha's, her voice also belied her appearance, it was smokey, low and sexy. Her vowels were cut-glass. Great, I thought, another bloody Sloane running around. The boys would love her and I was destined to remain the Office It.

I held out my hand, 'Hi, I'm Polly. I'm the sort of general factotum here, and this is Samantha, who works for Hugo. You're going to be working for Johnnie, for which you will require nerves of steel and an imperviousness to dictatorial manners bordering on rude, but I'm sure you'll cope. If you can't, let me know and I'll attempt to sort him out for you.' I smiled. 'Don't let me put you off, it's quite fun here really. The wonderboys are out right now.'

Of course, at that moment once again the lift doors slid apart and out they stepped, looking like Tweedledum and Tweedledee in their perfectly tailored suits, sharp haircuts and shiny faces. They were looking rather serious until their eyes alighted on Merry. I made the introductions and I could tell they were both rather excited to have her in the office and I almost felt sorry for Samantha.

'Merry, come into my room and we can run through a few things,' said Johnnie, adding, 'Um Polly, make us some coffee.'

I don't mind making coffee, but the way he asked, well demanded, really annoyed me and I stomped off down the corridor thinking not only did he still treat me as the Office It, but general dogsbody as well. I was really pleased I was going to be out of the office more. As I brought the coffee in, I could see Johnnie laughing with Merry. It struck me he was flirting with her and I was amazed, what with a wife and a Dora, he had the inclination, let alone the energy. But it was clearly what he was doing and she didn't seem to mind one bit. In fact she was lapping it up. I rather grumpily returned to my desk and buried my head in a pile of papers.

Merry popped her head round the corner. 'Johnnie's charming, Polly, and don't worry – I can handle him.' As she smiled one of her eyes crinkled into a sexy wink and she let out the dirtiest, gravelliest chuckle I'd ever heard. 'Takes one to know one.'

At five-thirty I wandered out to the girls and asked whether they'd like to have a drink later. Merry looked at her watch, '*OhmyGod!*' she exclaimed. 'I'd love to, but I have three drinks parties this evening and I'm late for the first already. Must dash, perhaps tomorrow.' I opened my mouth to say that really she wasn't due to leave until six, but she'd sped off.

'Well,' I said to Samantha, 'she was something else!'

Samantha looked irritated and said, 'You cannot imagine how many personal phone calls she received in the course of one day, Poll, it was unbelievable. I think I know all her social engagements for the next year. And Johnnie never said a thing. I reckon he really fancies her. Lucky she's just got engaged.'

'Samantha, don't be naughty.' I paused. I hadn't told her about Dora and some perverse sense of loyalty stopped me. 'You know Johnnie's married.'

'Take it from me, they're the worst or rather the easiest,' she laughed. 'Do you want a drink this evening?'

'Well, I have a date with Henry tomorrow, so I need my beauty sleep, but I suppose we could have a quick one.'

We repaired to the pub.

Thursday morning was sunny and cold and I was excited about seeing Henry. Once again I was in the office early, as were the boys. They were talking in their room. I could just about hear Johnnie's voice; Hugo possessed an amazing ability to be able to speak so quietly on the phone, only his interlocutor could hear. They stopped the moment they saw me.

'Just talking about the new secretary, Polly,' said Johnnie rather over-cheerily. 'Great find, well done.'

I nearly dropped to the floor at such unexpected praise. He must really fancy her.

'Thank you. I'm making some coffee, would you like some?'

They both nodded and I wandered out as they resumed their discussion.

'Fantastic tits,' were the only two audible words I heard.

Merry managed to appear in the office only half an hour late, breathlessly apologetic, apparently the tube had been delayed; Johnnie was irritatingly charming about it. I would have received a filthy look at such an hour. The phone interrupted my dark thoughts. I handed it to Merry. 'For you,' I said, and went into my office.

The phone rang ceaselessly all day, mainly for Merry.

As Samantha said, she appeared to have more in her social calendar than the Queen and even juggled two phones at a time. Without our wanting to know the details of her life, we found them impossible to miss; most centred around her recent return from India where she'd gone in order to drive her then suitor mad with missing her and eager to make a proposal of marriage. Clearly the strategy had paid off and by the end of the day I knew the venue, date and time of her engagement party, the names of her seemingly countless friends, and that her current dilemma was finding a ring. That she actually managed to do all Johnnie's work rather efficiently at the same time was yet more annoying. She was, however, so bubbly and bright, it was impossible not to like her. I even found myself telling her about my dinner date.

'Oh Henry,' she said. 'I've known him for years. Quite a catch, good for you. You must tell me all tomorrow. By the way, when you get to a certain stage, he goes mad if you lick his nipples!' With another of her naughty grinwinks and a filthy laugh she sauntered out of the office, leaving me inelegantly open-mouthed.

I'd invested in a smart little black trouser suit for dinner, which was very flattering and understated. I decided not to go the leggings/miniskirt route as this was, after all, sort of business as far as I was concerned.

'How do I look, Bumble?' I yelled from the top of the stairs. She emerged from the kitchen, wooden spoon in hand. 'Hmm,' she pondered. ' "Official". Let your hair down, I mean literally, it'll make you less formal.'

I let my rather unruly, but at least blonde, hair fall to my shoulders.

'Better,' she said. 'Happy hunting.'

She turned round and went back into the kitchen and I went into the bathroom just as the doorbell rang.

'I'm on the loo,' I yelled. 'Someone answer the door.'

Minnie raced to answer it. What she was doing up at such a late hour I had no idea, but Pia had gone off somewhere and Bumble was rather flexible on bedtime, particularly if it interrupted the cooking.

Henry stood in the doorway in a checked shirt, brightly coloured baggy cords and a sort of battered tweedy jacket. All very Hooray.

'Hallo. Who are you?' Minnie said, looking up at Henry quizzically. 'Have you come to see my mummy?'

'Well, I . . . er . . . ' Henry looked aghast, clearly believing Minnie to be mine. 'I don't know. Is your mummy Polly?' he queried, rather desperately. I was frantically trying to zip my trousers up and of course the zip kept getting stuck. Unable to

94

relieve his plight, I could hear it all through the door.

'Sort of,' the little minx continued. 'She's only just come back to live with me you know, so I don't remember her very well, but I like having her back. Come in, do you want a vodka? I know how to pour it, daddy showed me.'

'Daddy?' There was real confusion in his voice now. 'Your daddy lives here too?'

'Uh huh,' she enthused. 'And Uncle William. He's in lust with mummy, but she ignores it. He lives in a big blue room at the top of the house and I'm not allowed there 'cos daddy says it will . . . ' her little brow creased, 'corrogate me.'

I all but fell down the stairs. 'The word is corrupt, Minnie. And it's too late in your case. Hallo, Henry, I see you've met my naughty goddaughter.'

Henry regained his composure a little and turned to the small innocent child in front of him, who had a mischievous smile on her face. 'I thought you said your mummy was Polly.'

'I said she sort of was,' replied the child calmly; 'she's my godmummy. My mummy is in the kitchen.'

Henry roared with laughter and I was happy to see he had a good sense of humour. Essential in a man, particularly one who is going to have to wake up with me every morning for the rest of his life.

'Shall we go, my dear?'

He offered an arm and then bent low to Minnie. 'Very nice to meet you, young lady, thank you for nearly giving me a heart attack.' He turned to me. 'It was rather close to home – my last girlfriend was a single mother, bloody nightmare.' He shuddered dramatically and shut the front door behind me.

We had a very nice dinner in a little Italian restaurant in Pimlico and I realized Frank was right when he said Henry was a prodigious drinker. He also appeared to have a rather weak bladder as he kept leaping up to go to the loo. He didn't change dramatically in person, but his eyes became a little wild and his speech, while not slurred, became very fast and, on occasions, incomprehensible. And his hair started to stand on end. Despite talking quite a lot about himself, he was funny. His dark-brown eyes shone in the dark and I thought he was very good-looking. I hadn't quite got to the stomach-churning, unable-to-eat stage with him and so was able to retain a vestige of detachment, which I was pleased about. I told him stories of my office; at the mention of Merry, he laughed.

'What a girl, bloody funny. Great shot, you know.' (As if!) I hoped it wasn't an important criterion for him, as the only time I had held a rifle was at a fairground on Hampstead Heath.

'She's certainly stirred the office up, my two bosses have their tongues hanging out and our telephone bill must have trebled. She's getting engaged and I've never known such a flurry of activity.'

'Expert husband hunter, not sure how I escaped her un-scathed. Probably the fact I've known her all my life and our mothers plotted too ferociously.'

We then got around to the dreaded subject, my family.

'What does your pa do?' asked Henry, in a semi-interested fashion.

'Well, he's sort of an MP,' I replied.

'Rarely?' he said, 'what sort of MP?'

'The usual. Kind of in the government at the moment.' I cringed with embarrassment as I told him who he was.

'Oh yar! I know who you mean,' exclaimed Henry. 'Smooth chappie, what's his name? Bloody funny, bloody funny. Well, well.' Naturally he was fascinated. 'What's it like, having a high-profile father? Lots of perks eh?'

Arghh! Not again . . .

'What does your father do?' I asked, trying to redirect the spotlight.

'My father?' He looked astonished at the question. 'Well, he's at home most of the time, looking after the estate. Goes up to the House every now and then, bit like yours in some ways, but mainly he just pootles around. Doesn't understand why I want to work in London, but I love the bright lights and the buzz up here. Plenty of time to fester away in deepest darkest Gloucestershire when I eventually decide to settle down.'

I asked him where his father's house was and it turned out it wasn't too far from my father's.

'Yar, you rarely must come over next time you're staying with your pa,' said Henry. 'Come for dinner one Saturday, let me know when you're next down.'

I thought things were coming along nicely.

Henry leant over the table and took one of my hands. 'Hmm, what small hands you have for someone so tall. How tall are you by the way?'

Bingo! He was interested . . .

'Five foot ten without heels,' I replied, trying to contain my smile. I regained my hand and composure.

'How about a nightcap at Annabel's?' asked Henry.

'Oh yar' (I had quickly picked up on the yar in place of yes), 'I'd love to.' I really could get used to this, I thought, I mean 'rarely' used to it.

Henry called for the bill and we left. I wasn't mad about his driving after a couple of bottles of wine, but threw caution to the wind as I once again descended the steep steps into the nightclub.

'Good-evening, madam.' John the barman greeted me with a smile.

'Good-evening, madam.' Chris, the *maître d'*, shook my hand.

I said hallo to both of them and turned to Henry, remarking on what good memories people here had.

'Not rarely,' said Henry, dampening my spirits somewhat. 'They call every female madam. Safer that way.'

Henry turned out to be rather a good dancer and when the slower numbers started, he moved in closer. I was good, didn't lean into him or rest my head on his shoulder (or my hand on his bottom). I stayed uncharacteristically cool, despite far too many vodkas. It was about three a.m. when I eventually hit Altonative Towers, rather unsteadily, having received a hand on my thigh in the car and two kisses on each cheek as a goodbye, but only because I turned my head. I leant down through the passenger window from the pavement.

'Thank you for a lovely evening.' I knew I was showing a glimpse of cleavage.

'I had a rarely good time, Polly, thank you. We must do it again, I'll call you.'

He sped off into the night.

Bugger! Yet another, 'I'll call you.' When? I don't mind, but tell me. Name a day, a week, two, then I'll know at least. I must be really insecure, but limboland drives me nuts. Lucky I'm not head over heels about him – when you are, it's torture. It must be some horrible male thing. Maybe they don't think. Perhaps they don't care. Could it be playing cool? An inability to plan? To hell with it! I'm going to busy myself in work and avoid the phone.

15

I rang Frank the next morning, nursing a sore head and a very weary body.

'How did it go?' he asked immediately.

'How do you know why I am phoning?' I asked indignantly.

'I have my sources. Well?'

'It was good, I had a lot of fun. He is eminently suitable, attractive, funny and lives close to daddy. All a bit too good to be true. I think I could really like him.'

'Great,' replied Frank. 'Do you want to come out tonight to discuss further strategies?'

'Oh, Frank, I can't. My head is throbbing, I have to have an early night. You were right, he can certainly knock back the booze. Oh and I have to go and sort out my new car purchase.'

'A new car now, you do move fast. What about Sunday lunch? I'll cook.'

We agreed, and as I replaced the receiver, Merry sauntered in.

'Well?' she asked.

'Well, I haven't got to the nipple-licking stage if that's what you want to know,' I replied, thinking how incredibly un-private my private life was.

'Quite right too, keep him dangling for a while. I had to use every card available to ensnare my Michael. I have more tips, one of which is to have a spare in the background, so I wondered if you'd like to come to supper in a couple of weeks. I have lots of single men lurking and now I'm off the market I find myself in the enviable position of being able to matchmake for my discards.'

'Well,' I said, not sure about a bevy of discards, 'are they worth having?'

'Of course, silly, I've always been strategic. My mother was quite insistent, you can lower your knickers, but never your standards.' I laughed as she continued, 'Anyway, they're only to distract you and make sure you don't sit around waiting for the phone to ring. A girl's gotta keep her options open right up till the last minute.' She had all the confidence of a girl who'd got her man.

'Well, I'd love to, thank you.'

'Good, I'll sort out a date with Michael. Now, I have to get on. I'm having the most awful trouble finding a ring. We've been to about three jewellers and I can't find anything I like. By which I mean, of course, anything that is large enough without Michael thinking it is either too common or too expensive.'

Johnnie popped his head round my door. 'Oh, Merry, I couldn't help overhearing your dilemma. I have a great friend who works in the diamond world, and I wonder if perhaps you and Michael would like to see some stones? I'd be happy to arrange it for you.'

What a creep I thought to myself.

'Oh, Johnnie, you are a darling, thank you so much.' Merry skipped out of the office behind Johnnie in a happy discussion about sapphires and diamonds.

I spent the rest of the day fighting the impulse to eat everything that passed under my nose. Hangovers give me the most incredible appetite and I end up feeling sicker than before if I give in to the craving for carbohydrate.

So it was with a rather delicate head I knocked on Troy's door, with my car magazines tucked under my arm.

He was expecting me and smiled, 'Come in.'

He looked divine and dangerous.

'Am I safe?' I asked, half joking as I stood on the doorstep.

'Only if you want to be,' he replied, not joking at all. He led me into the drawing-room of a terraced house identical to Bumble and Gareth's on the outside and completely different internally. The walls were a sunny yellow, covered in large, brightly coloured paintings. Landscapes, women with baskets on their heads at the market, men sitting on the shady deck of a clapboard house with children playing in the garden. They were vibrant, alive and like nothing I'd seen before. Scattered around the room were beautiful wooden carvings, ebony heads and various primitive, but none the less effective-looking, weapons. Bob Marley was playing softly in the background.

'Wow!' I exclaimed. 'Those paintings are incredible.'

'They're all by Jamaican artists, and some of them I can't bear to sell. But even sitting on the walls here, they increase in value. This one here is my favourite, a Lester.'

I remembered Troy did something in the art business. 'I don't blame you, they're lovely; in fact the whole room is lovely.'

'Do you want to see round the rest of the house?' asked Troy.

'Would we be disturbing anyone?' I ventured, partly to find out if we were alone. Troy often had various transient members of his family staying.

'We're all alone, but don't worry, I won't lay a finger on you until you ask.'

I thought this was extremely arrogant of him and was about to say so, until I watched his bottom ascend the staircase and I realized, actually, he was just being realistic. What is it about black bottoms? They are just more rounded and defined than those of any other race. I knew it was especially true of the Hottentots, who had such large bottoms they used to put their children on them like a seat. Over the generations as their lifestyle changed, their bottoms must have got smaller, but I think most black people still have a residue of Hottentot Bot. Lucky them.

The rest of the house was filled with more beautiful paintings and artefacts. Troy clearly had a very good eye and Gareth had reliably informed me he was pretty successful.

We went downstairs to the living-room and spent what seemed like ages looking at innumerable car magazines and discussing the various opinions of his brothers. I stifled a yawn.

'Late night?' enquired Troy.

'Rather.'

'With anyone interesting?'

'Well, a possibility, but very early stages.' I described Henry to Troy, who leaned back in his chair regarding me sceptically.

'You'll be bored. He sounds like a labrador man.'

'A what?' I asked.

'Oh you know, all waggy tail and adoration.'

'He's not at all, in fact he's just what I'm looking for. I couldn't possibly be bored. I'm not looking for a roller-coaster ride of emotions, I want some lovely man, with a good job, who is responsible, caring, adores me and will not cheat. I don't want mind games to keep me in someone's thrall. I want to be able to bask in reciprocated affection and my first purchase upon marriage will be a labrador, so there.'

'I shall watch your progress with interest, but you'll be bored with some county chap, mark my words. But, look here, we're getting distracted – have we decided on the car? I would recommend this Peugeot, it's on interest-free credit, small but solid, and you can get it tomorrow from the garage.'

I was so bored at the thought of talking about cars again, I immediately agreed.

'Good,' said Troy; 'so now that's done . . . ' he leant over and gently stroked my hair and rubbed the back of my neck, 'how about something to eat?'

'Er, what?' I muttered, in a bit of a daze. The effect of having my neck rubbed while still being a bit hung-over was making me feel very distracted.

'Dinner.' Troy got up and went into the kitchen. 'Give me five minutes. I'm just going to prove to you I can cook better than any restaurant.'

God, he was arrogant, I thought to myself. I wondered if it was anything to do with having a huge thingy, which kind of went before you, giving you confidence. Like girls with really amazing boobs and swingy hair. I tore myself away from thoughts of his anatomy with some difficulty and decided to go into the kitchen following the wonderful smells.

'Something smells really good,' I said. 'What is it?'

'Rice and peas, kallaloo and curry goat,' said Troy, turning to me with a smile.

'What!' I exclaimed. 'Have you gone mad? Do you think I'm going to eat goat? I have a hangover. I'm in a very delicate digestive state and I don't want to feel worse. What kind of food is that anyway?'

'Jamaican speciality. And this is recommended for hangovers, just try it. Here.' He handed me a small glass of clear liquid. 'Take a sip. I'm nearly ready.'

I took a tiny sip and felt something like firewater hit my lips, then my tongue and finally the back of my throat as I swallowed. My eyes watered and my head spun.

'Ahh!' I managed to squeak. 'My vocal chords, what's happened to them? And my lips, what have you done with my lips? I can't feel anything! Hell's teeth, what did you give me?'

'Relax, little one. I told you, a tiny sip of real Jamaican white rum is the best hangover cure. It's a cure for most things.'

My oral sensations were beginning to return and my mouth now felt pleasantly warm, even my head was feeling clearer. But I wasn't going to give up too easily.

'Very clever,' I muttered. 'Probably the only thing to do is to rip out someone's taste buds, before you give them goat to eat.'

'Have another sip, you'll feel even better.' Troy continued to stir what was admittedly a rather nice-smelling pot.

I tentatively took another sip, hot hot hot, but easier to drink. I took another sip.

'OK, enough,' said Troy, removing the glass. 'It's very strong.'

I was beginning to feel warm all over.

'Hungry?' asked Troy, taking two steaming plates over to the table, lighting candles and handing me a glass of red wine. 'Take a seat.'

I cautiously took a small forkful of the curry. To my amazement it was delicious, in fact it was all delicious, the wine, Troy. . . . oh bugger! I didn't mean to think that. I caught him looking at me with an amused expression on his face.

'Did I mention the rum is an aphrodisiac as well?' he had a wicked smile.

'Troy Clarke, how dare you try and take advantage of me in such a defenceless, weakened position? You ply me with delicious food and wine and candlelight and now you tell me I've had some voodoo drink to make me feel all hot and squirmy.'

'And are you feeling "all hot and squirmy"?' he leant closer.

I was and it was most disconcerting.

He removed the glass from my hand and pulled me towards him.

'I thought so.'

And then he kissed me. But really kissed me. He was soooo good. This is going to ruin me for ever, I thought, as I pulled away hastily.

'Stop, please,' I said. 'I can't do this.'

He looked at me in surprise.

'I'm really serious, Troy, please; I find you incredibly attractive, but really, you're not what I want. I want to settle down, have kids, be with someone stable and have a proper relationship. It's not what you want and I can't just have sex with you while I continue my search. I have some weird inbuilt mechanism, if I sleep with someone I wake up the next morning and I'm in love with them. It's a pain and, believe me, over the years I've really tried to cure myself, but I failed. I have to accept I don't do casual sex, it just doesn't work for me. And I can't go around falling in love with you. However much you may like me, I know I'd be one of many and you're not looking to get settled. Please, can we just be friends, I don't know how long I can resist you and I can't avoid you, as you live next door. You have to stop.'

I felt so wet (not like that) in front of this incredibly attractive man, but I knew he was all wrong for me. I've taken the path and I know where it leads. I was trying very hard to make my head not my groin rule me. Troy was almost disbelieving.

'Whatever you say, if it's what you want. But it will be hard.'

'I'm sure and I'd rather not think about that either.' I laughed, and the tension between us started to relax. I reached back for my wine glass. 'Do you have a compulsion to try it on with everyone?'

'I'll tell you a story,' he said, 'if you want to hear it. But it's not pretty.'

'Carry on,' I said, wondering what was coming.

'I was abused as a child.'

I held my wine glass tight and tried hard not to look shocked; I just nodded with what I hoped was an understanding expression.

'It affects you. Obviously. It started when I was young and carried on until I was big enough to stop it. But it leaves its mark, in many ways. Your relations fuck you up, then subsequently you fuck up all relationships. You assume sex is what people want from you because obviously that's all you are good for. A service provider.'

I was struggling for words. 'But what about all the stuff you said before? Sex having to be in the mind, not just the physical act, the all-encompassing picture, it sounded so . . .' I tried to think of a word, 'normal,' I ended lamely.

'I said I had to trust someone, they had to get to know me. I don't want to be a sex object, but if I am going to be, then I'll make sure I'm the best around. It's not much of a legacy, but it's all I have. What I said to you was I wanted you to get to know me. So . . .' he paused. 'Now you know.'

I fought the horrid thought that this must be the ultimate chat-up line. 'I was abused, be nice to me.' Then I looked at Troy's serious face and pushed the thought right out of my mind. No one would make it up, not even Troy. I went over to him and gave him a hug.

'I'm so sorry,' I said.

'It's life. Shit happens.'

'Well, yes, but you know, some things are shittier than others. Who was it who abused you?'

'Do we have to talk about it?' He stared into the contents of his glass, seemingly unable to look at me.

'No, of course not,' I replied, feeling helpless in an area I knew nothing about. I didn't really know what to say. 'I'm just so shocked. Did any of your family know? What about your mother? Couldn't you tell her?'

'My father drank and hit my mum, she had her own problems. My older brothers left home as soon as they could.'

'Do you think they were abused as well?'

'I never asked,' he said flatly.

'Meaning you think they were?'

'Meaning I didn't ask.'

'Sorry, it's just quite a lot to take in. When you see them now, what do you talk about?'

'Cars, generally,' he smiled. 'And my mother's health.'

'What about your mother's health?' I asked.

'Well, since my father walked out on her, she's become really depressed and agoraphobic. Never leaves the house.'

'At least she doesn't get beaten any more.' I tried to sound positive, faced with this welter of depressing facts.

'She misses my dad. Funny isn't it?'

'Only funny peculiar,' I replied.

'Come on, let's eat, the goat's getting cold.' He changed the subject abruptly.

I wondered how he could possibly have an appetite but it seemed unimpaired; in fact he helped himself to the rest of my plate as I had unsurprisingly completely lost the desire to eat. I was shocked and upset for him – what an awful child-hood! He appeared so successful and confident. But those experiences cast long shadows over the rest of your life and not repeating the cycle is only part of the daily struggle .

'Who else knows, Troy?' I asked gently, putting my hand on his.

'Just my wife,' he said, without raising his head from the plate.

I snatched my hand away as if stung and barely managed

to squeak, 'Your what? Suddenly you have a wife? Where?'

'She lives with my son in Sussex.'

There was a silence, before I started to laugh.

'Troy, you are amazing. One minute trying to seduce me, the next you're telling me your life history, which frankly has the aphrodisiac properties of bowel surgery, and now you tell me you're married, with a child. I hardly dare ask if there are any more skeletons in your closet. God, my life is boring compared to yours.'

'We're separated. I see my son Owen every week, but I found being tied to one woman difficult. I thought she'd understand, but she didn't, what can I say?' His head was still bent over his food so I couldn't tell what his mood was.

'Ahh, the old fidelity issue, always a bit of a stumbling block for us girls, you know. As I said, no matter what this liberated age has brought women in terms of sexual freedom, I think we still haven't quite mastered the art of sex without feeling.'

Troy looked up indignantly at me. 'What do you mean? I have feelings for the women I have sex with! What I don't understand is why it has any bearing on my feelings for someone else. Those are separate. Feelings aren't like a single cake that you divide up between people; everyone has their own cake.' He shook his head uncomprehendingly. 'Women!' he muttered.

'Well, it's an interesting theory, but it's going to take a lot of work to convert a woman to it.'

'Listen, you love animals don't you?'

I nodded.

'Well, you have a cat and one day you see an adorable little kitten for sale and you buy it. Do you love your old cat less? No, you just find more love in you for both cats.'

'Yes, but the old cat might not like this new kitten in its life. We were talking about how the other person feels, not how you feel.'

'Really,' he paused, his wicked smile back in place, 'I thought we were talking about pussies.'

16

Merry sauntered into the office a mere forty-five minutes late on Monday morning.

'Super weekend everybody?' she trilled joyously. 'Mine was just wonderful. Look at my whopper!' She extended her left hand to show an enormous sapphire, surrounded by diamonds.

'Isn't it fab?' she said, holding her hand out in front of her face to admire it. I thought my Michael was going to pass out when I put this one in front of him, but Johnnie's friend was soo kind and got us such a good deal, even my Michael couldn't complain. What a rock! It's al–most vulgar, but not quite. My friends are green with envy, sooo gratifying.'

And after thirty minutes of exuberant babble about her bauble and her weekend in the country, during which she managed to make coffee for all of us, type ten letters and juggle many phone calls, I was even more convinced someone like 'her Michael' was the type of man I required.

Having recovered from Friday's extraordinary revelations, which I hadn't shared with anyone, I spent the weekend quietly. I bought the car, had lunch with Frank and watched endless, mindless telly. I felt well-rested, if rather fat and ready for the onslaught of my new job. An hour with Johnnie, cooped up in my new little purchase on the way to Milton Keynes, started to erode my good mood. I felt rather sorry for the poor people who were being 'relocated' from the salubrious environment of St James's to the provinces, but Johnnie pointed out, in his most sensitive manner, they were lucky to have a job at all. One of the millions of things I had to do – he kept handing me large pieces of paper covered in his loopy handwriting with yet more instructions – was to work out each person's new route to work. His only comment on my new baby – 'What exactly is this car?' – had done nothing to endear him to me.

On arrival, I was faced with a vast, dilapidated, empty shell of an office. 'How long before the staff move up here?' I tentatively asked him.

'Four months,' he replied curtly.

'Grief!' I exclaimed. 'Do you think you've given me enough time?'

'Why? Can't you do it?' he challenged.

'Of course I can,' I snapped, annoyed.

'Well, B–Bill seems to think you can, so here's your chance to prove him right.'

The tone of his voice gave me the distinct impression he had not been my greatest supporter in this new role. Our return journey was silent.

I don't think I'd ever worked quite so hard or such long hours before. I didn't even have time to chat with the girls. The good news was by Friday I could see a chink of light winking at the end of the very long tunnel, the bad news was working late meant I had to witness two glorious visitations by the Pantheress, who continued to treat me with the utmost disdain. My only compensation was I knew Johnnie had taken another woman out for dinner that week as well. My rosy picture of living in the country with a commuting husband, two children and a labrador was fading fast. I suppose if your husband had something resembling moral fibre it would help.

My thoughts returned to Henry, whom I'd gone out with on Thursday. A trip to the movies and another Chinese meal afterwards. He'd been terrific company, although his alcohol consumption was at a record level. Too much sake later we had ended up kissing under a lamp-post in Soho, much to the amusement of a very voluble prostitute, who yelled ribald encouragement to us from a window above.

On Friday night Samantha came home with me as her increasing lack of success with Hugo was beginning to get her down and I thought Bumble would probably have some pearls on the subject. Privately I was beginning to think she was on to something of a non-starter, particularly as her idea of 'toned-down' involved putting on more 'natural-looking' make-up!

'So how's your Plan shaping up?' she asked as we emerged from my car outside the house.

'Well, touch wood, I think it's OK so far. I'm having dinner with Henry again next week and he actually told me when he'd call, which is a huge improvement. I like him, but I'm just keeping it li – ' I didn't have time to finish my sentence because she grabbed my arm.

'Who is *that*?' she hissed, turning her head away from the front door. Sitting on his porch, reading a book, was Troy.

'That is Troy, our next-door neighbour. I was rather hoping we might avoid him, but too late.' I could see him getting up from his chair as we spoke, except this wasn't really getting up, it was more like uncoiling.

'Why avoid him? He's *gorgeous*! God I wish I had more make-up on!'

She was still whispering but turned round as I said, 'Hi, Troy, how are you? This is Samantha, we work together.'

As she extended her little kitten paw of a hand and peeped up coyly from under the thick fringe of blonde hair, I watched Troy literally lick his lips; I recognized that look on his face of old. Discretion being the better part of most things I decided to let them get on with it – although judging by the way her hand lingered in his, I realized there was no way I was going to be able to stop her.

'Can I invite you two ladies in for a drink? A little white rum perhaps?' His smile was broad, showing his white teeth off to maximum effect.

'I think I'll pass, thanks,' I said. Samantha turned to me with a very peculiar look on her face. It was obvious she wanted to stay. 'But you go, Sam. I'll call you when Bumble's got dinner ready.'

It was one thing to have shifted the balance of my relationship with Troy to 'just friends', but quite another to have to witness the seduction of a replacement quite so soon. I opened the front door and was greeted by my goddaughter in the most extraordinary garb. She was draped in a huge flag, with pink fairy wings attached, black, red, yellow and green stripes were painted over her face, she wore a long black wig and was waving a toy cigarette at me.

'Minnie, what on earth are you doing?' I asked.

'I'm a Rastafairy and this is my can-jar,' she announced proudly, waving the cigarette at me.

'You've been playing with Toy, haven't you?' I said, dubious of the merit of his telling a three-year-old about the joys of ganja, local dope of Jamaica.

'Uh huh,' she nodded. 'I'm going back now.'

'No, stay with me. He's got someone else to play with at the moment.' I steered her back into the kitchen where, inevitably, Bumble was cooking.

'Who's in the lion's den now?' she enquired, while idly stirring a pot, smoking a cigarette and drinking wine.

'I'm afraid Samatha got lured in, he's plying her with white rum as we speak. I doubt very much she'll be back in time for dinner.'

'Well, she looks like a girl who can take care of herself,' said Bumble nonchalantly. 'How about you, how do you feel about it?' She gave me a very direct look.

'I beg your pardon, what on earth do you mean?' I feigned indignation.

'Oh, come on now. I've known you all my life. Despite your protestations, I detect a stirring in his direction.' Bumble was far too perceptive.

'Well, maybe, but it doesn't mean I'm going to do anything about it. I'm being sensible, we sorted it all out.'

But it did feel slightly odd having Samantha next door with Troy after our own, albeit very different, type of intimacy. With so much emotional baggage, Troy couldn't help but remain a serial seducer. I wondered if he'd ever find some incredible woman who could deal with all those demons and with whom he could find peace. Whether it would be possible for him to settle for just one partner. The idea one can find in someone else a soulmate and friend, someone to laugh with, over and above just the physical side, is surely what we all want? God I was beginning to sound like my mother.

Bumble must have read my thoughts. 'Another postcard from your mother,' she said. 'She's with a man in Penang!'

'Oh no,' I groaned, 'what is she up to now?'

I poured myself a drink, wandered over to the hall table and read with some alarm that my mother would be returning in a couple of months with some man in tow. This was going to be ghastly, as my mother's current taste in men was appalling. They all irritated me beyond belief because they were, to quote Troy, labrador men. Overly devoted, bouncing with enthusiasm, soppy eyes and a bit too biddable. Marvellous qualities, in a dog.

'She's coming back with the new man,' I yelled unnecessarily to Bumble, who had already read it.

'How exciting! I love your mother.' Bumble came into view holding two enormous glasses of wine, 'Here,' she said, 'drink this. Ciggie?'

I shook my head.

'By the way,' she lowered her voice conspiratorially, 'William has the latest nymphet upstairs as we speak and I'm convinced I should have asked for a passport before I let her in – she looks really young, even by his standards. Do you think I should offer her wine with dinner?'

I laughed, 'I never cease to be amazed anyone could possibly want to do anything with William, except give him a thoroughly good wash.'

'Some people find the dishevelled look rather attractive,' said Bumble, 'and he's clever and charming when he wants to be.'

'But so lascivious and leery. I can't imagine what those young girls see in him when they could be having fun with someone their own age.'

'They have a good time.' She lowered her voice. 'He's supposed to be a–mazing in bed. What he lacks in youth he makes up for in experience.'

I found the whole thing very strange, although I had to remind myself Bill was considerably older than me and that seemed acceptable. I changed the subject. 'When's dinner? Have I got time for a bath?'

'Yes, it won't be for ages, I'll round everyone up later. Will you take Minnie up with you and try and get her out of her ridiculous costume.'

'Now, Bumble,' I said. 'Rastafairyism is a very serious religion, don't knock it.'

About three hours later we all sat down to a very late dinner. Having spectacularly resisted my efforts to get her to go to bed, Minnie was tucked up on the sofa watching television, pretend-smoking her cigarette. William and a very youthful nymphet, Troy and a rather flushed Samantha, Gareth, Bumble, Kevina with new, gorgeous-looking boyfriend, Frank and I had just sat down to eat when there was a knock on the front door and a male voice said, 'Police, open up!'

Bumble got up with her usual calm. 'Just coming,' she said and turned to Gareth, 'Typical police, got the wrong house again. I told you they were dealing down at the end of the road.'

She had barely opened the front door, when an irate man with a scarlet face and hair askew barged through it yelling, 'Where is she?'

Standing behind him were two policeman, one of whom stepped forward, 'Mrs Knowles?' he enquired.

'Mrs Smith,' Bumble replied, irritatedly – she hated her surname. 'Look, I think the people you want are down the street, that's where . . . '

Before she could finish he interrupted her. 'Mrs Smith, we believe the person we're looking for is right here.'

There was a bit of a commotion going on inside and both policemen walked past Bumble, who hurried behind them in a bewildered state, insisting they were in the wrong house and demanding to know who the wild-haired, red-faced man was. Just then William fled out into the hallway and up the stairs,

'Get that man immediately,' said the policeman, turning to his colleague, who ran up the stairs in pursuit of William.

Minnie appeared sleepily in the doorway. 'Mummy, what's happening?'

The red-faced man emerged, struggling with William's nymphet. 'You're coming home with me, young lady. Ow! Stop it,' he yelled as she bit him on the hand.

Everyone else at the dining-table got up, and I looked around for Samantha, but she seemed to have disappeared.

'Where's Sam?' I hissed to Troy.

'Gone out of the back over to my house,' he whispered. 'She doesn't have a work permit and the sight of the police panicked her a bit.'

Oh fantastic, I thought, I've employed an illegal immigrant. Johnnie will kill me.

The nymphet's screams were getting louder,

'Be gentle with her,' said Troy to the man. 'What do you think you're doing?'

'And who might you be, sir?' asked the policeman in a cool and patient voice.

'Another of them pedi-whatsits probably,' said the red-faced man, beside himself.

'I beg your pardon?' said Troy icily, drawing himself up to his full height and looking like he might strike out at any minute.

The red-faced man turned to him and snarled, 'You know, one of them blokes wot likes doing it to kids.'

It suddenly dawned on me that since William's nymphet was clearly a bit short on years this irate man must be her father. I hoped fervently he wouldn't say anything more to Troy, who was looking thunderous.

'I am most certainly not.' I'd never heard him sound quite so venomous. I thought he was going to attack the father. On so many levels, this would have been a particularly sensitive subject for him.

'Now, sir,' said the policeman, perhaps sensing trouble, 'please stay calm.'

'Stay calm?' Troy turned to look at him, his voice stony. 'Do you know what this man is accusing me of? I have never, ever, laid a finger on a child.'

'You play with me, Toy,' piped up Minnie at a singularly inopportune moment. 'Here,' she waddled up to him still swathed in her flag and offered him her cigarette, 'canjar to stop the stwess.'

'I'll have that, thank you,' said the policeman reaching for the cigarette.

'It's fake you idiot,' I snapped at the policeman, rather unwisely as he turned to me with a very angry look on his face.

'I am not an idiot, madam. Please do not insult me.'

'Baby, darling!' Kevina appeared in the hallway, 'tell the nasty man to stop being mean to you or else . . . '

'Or else what?' asked the policeman, calmly.

The atmosphere in the room was suddenly colder.

'Or else I may have to grab you myself!' tittered Kevina's boyfriend, his arm snaking round the policeman's middle. 'It's so exciting, these big, burly men in uniform! I might just faint.'

'I think,' said the policeman coldly, 'this will be better dealt with at the station.'

That appeared to be Gareth's cue. 'I'm sorry, officer. This is getting beyond a joke.'

'And who might you be?' snapped the policeman, who was becoming increasingly irritated.

'Gareth Smith. I live here with my wife and child and these,' he waved his arm airily about him, 'are my friends.'

'Got him,' called the second policeman, descending the stairs holding tightly on to William; 'this one is Mr Knowles.'

'He your friend too?' the policeman asked Gareth.

'Mr Knowles lives here too,' said Gareth. 'He's an associate of mine.'

'I would like to ask all of you to accompany us to the station,' said the policeman, a hard note entering his voice, 'to assist in further enquiries.'

'On what grounds?' Frank appeared.

'And you might be?' the policeman turned to look at Frank.

'My name is Dr Frank Hobday. I am a psychiatrist. Now what on earth is going on?'

'Don't tell me, these are your patients.' The policeman looked across at his colleague and they both smirked. 'Well, I'm running out of mine.' The policeman pulled out his pen, then paused before checking off his list on his fingers. 'Let's see, what have we potentially got? Running a house of ill-repute, unlawful sex with minors, dealing in marijuana, abuse of children – ' I thought Troy was going to pass out – 'I think we've got enough to sort out at the station.'

'Please,' said Frank in a very calm, measured tone, 'let's look at this objectively. First of all, I think you should delete the dealing bit. Take a closer look at what you have in your hand.' The policeman looked at Minnie's toy cigarette and threw it to the floor in an extravagant gesture. 'This gentleman, whom the small child refers to as her toy, is called Troy,' he indicated the simmering cauldron of fury that was Troy, 'who to my certain knowledge has never laid an untoward finger on this child and I am speaking in my professional capacity. Finally,' he turned to the now weeping nymphet, 'how old are you?'

'Fourteen,' came the reply, between large sniffs.

There was an audible gasp from all of us and William looked as though he might faint.

'And did you tell Mr Knowles how old you were?' asked Frank gently, his training in dealing with nutters being put to fantastically effective use, I thought.

'No,' came an even quieter reply. 'I told him I was eighteen.'

'And has Mr Knowles done anything illegal with you, or something you are uncomfortable with?'

'Nooooh!' she wailed. 'We was just watching a video, honest, 'e didn't even kiss me. Worst luck . . . '

'That's enough!' roared her father. 'You're coming home with me, young lady, and you . . . ' he paused ominously, 'you are *grounded*!'

The policeman looked wearily around him at the chaotic scene. 'All right, sergeant, just take their names.'

17

MINISTER'S DAUGHTER IN DRUG SWOOP. Bumble dumped a large wad of Sunday newspapers on my bed with the headlines glaring at me. 'You'd better read these; Gareth's gone potty, he's on the phone trying to find out who leaked it to the press. He's convinced it's one of the policemen.'

'Oh my God,' I groaned, as I flicked through the papers. 'Don't they have anything better to do? I can hardly believe they print this rubbish – there's no story. After all, none of us were actually arrested. And hell's teeth, look at the awful picture of me! It must have been taken when I was about fifteen and really fat.' The repercussions would be hellish. My father was going to kill me. My squeaky clean image at work was going to be shot. And what the hell was Henry going to think? Buggeration, my new image was about to become seriously damaged and I thought I'd been doing so well. Bloody typical!

I didn't suppose any of the others were particularly pleased at the articles either, as we all featured, although none quite as prominently as me. Damn the bloody press on occasions. I pulled the sheet over my head, despairing.

'Listen,' said Bumble, 'just weather the storm. If you read the article, it doesn't say much and it's pretty accurately reported, so you can't sue. It just says what happened, a series of mistakes. If anything, the police look more stupid than anyone else. It'll all blow over in a couple of days. It's a non-story, just a headline. You're going to have to shrug it off because if you take it seriously, so will other people. There's no story – OK? Tomorrow's fish and chips, etc.'

She could be very forceful at times and, of course, she was right. But then she didn't have to take the inevitable, furious phone call from my father. Media coverage for him was something to be ruthlessly controlled, he stormed, and as for smoking and drugs when he was Health Minister, ahh . . . it was just too dreadful. Not to mention politically embarrassing. I could hardly get a word in to explain that it had all been a misunderstanding, and that quite frankly if he hadn't been so well known, no one would have written about me in the first place. I knew he cared about me, but did his bloody job have to come before everything? After much explaining and apologizing he calmed down and I agreed to see him for lunch the following Sunday.

Most of my other friends who rang seemed to think it was pretty funny. But I didn't hear a word from Henry, which I thought was ominous. We all gave William the Lodger a very hard time about his choice of girlfriends. After all, it was only luck nothing untoward had happened, miraculously due to his restraint, not hers. There's nothing like escaping a rape charge, particularly with a minor, to cool the libido and he swore repeated oaths vowing to change his ways!

I was, however, dreading going into work. Arriving very early, in order to get there before the girls, I found Johnnie and Hugo already at their desks.

'Nice weekend?' asked Johnnie, without a trace of a smile.

'Er, OK,' I said hesitantly.

'Not too stoned to come into work then?' asked Hugo, innocently.

'Er, I . . . '

At which point, to my complete surprise, they both became helpless with laughter. 'I'm sorry, Polly,' said Johnnie, wiping tears of mirth from his eyes, 'we couldn't resist.'

I was extremely put out. I'd been fretting for twenty-four hours about what I was going to have to say to them, and here they were, wetting themselves with laughter at my expense!

'We had no idea who your father was,' said Hugo.

'No,' said Johnnie. 'Fascinating. D–do tell him any time he feels like popping in he's more than welcome.'

I was amazed. You can never tell with this fame thing;

advantages and disadvantages every time. The wonderboys are being nice to me and want to meet my illustrious father and I'm annoyed they're being nice to me because I have a illustrious father.

Next thing was to sort out Samantha and her work permit. I hadn't seen her for the rest of the weekend, but it didn't take much imagination to work out where she was; just the enormous smile on her face when she came in said it all.

'Jeez, Poll, what a weekend! Troy is just amazing.' She shut the door to my office and sat down, desperate to talk.

'Listen, I'm dying to hear all about it' (I wasn't), 'but I've got to talk to you about your work permit, or rather lack of it.' I sounded like the office crone.

'No worries, all sorted. Troy has a friend who works in some immigration department – he's always bringing over Jamaican relatives. He had a word with him on Sunday, and my papers are as good as done. He's sorting it all out today. Don't say anything to the boys and by the end of the week I'll be legit! Amazing isn't it? Friends in high places.'

As far as I was concerned Troy's friend was in a low place, but I merely smiled and said, 'Good.' At least it was one fewer thing to think about.

'Ah yeah, it was a lucky break all right. Imagine if I'd ended up in the papers as well, just because of you,' she laughed. 'And I did enjoy thanking him a lot!'

She looked like the cat that got the cream. 'You can forget Hugo for a while, I think Troy really likes me; we're going to have some fun together. He's sooo cool and talk about filling his pants!'

I held my hands to my ears and told her to save it for later. I felt a curious sense of divided emotions and decided to follow my mother's advice: if the words don't come easily to you, say nothing.

I didn't hear from Henry until the Tuesday morning. We were due to have dinner later and I'd been sitting on my hands to stop myself picking up the phone. He said there'd been a slight change of plan and would I go to dinner at his house as he had a few other friends coming over. He didn't mention the article in the paper and I wondered if he'd missed it or was just being polite. Either way I was thrilled to be going to his house. As I said, rather smugly to Bumble, meeting your 'potential's' friends is the next relationship rung.

'I just hope you like them,' said Bumble.

'Of course I'll like them. Why wouldn't I? Henry is the perfect gentleman, his father has a title of some sort, he's funny, rich, employed, good-looking and a home-owner. He has everything going for him, why on earth would he have awful friends? More like, what will they think of me?'

I was more nervous about meeting them than I was prepared to admit, even to Bumble.

'Under normal circumstances, I would say just be yourself and they'll love you. But if you are still persisting in this new image of yours, I can only say good luck and please will you not dress like a bank manager's wife.' (Now I knew where Samantha had got the expression.) 'I'm so glad I'm not single any more.' She relented a bit at the sight of my crestfallen face. 'You'll be fine, don't worry.' I wished she'd be more consistent, one minute lambasting the state of marriage and the next, making dating sound only marginally preferable to guerrilla warfare.

A number of clothing crises later I settled for a white blouse, pearl necklace, black trousers and Bumble's patent pumps with bows on (eugh – flatties!). Bumble assured me I could almost pass as a Sloane Ranger!

I knocked on the door of Henry's house with more than a little trepidation. The door was flung open and Henry greeted me effusively. Much more so than usual. With his arm still around me he ushered me into the room and I let out a mental sigh of relief as I saw the other girls were in almost identical clothes to me. The only real feature distinguishing us was I just hadn't been able to bring myself to wear a velvet headband. The boys, too, were uniformly clad: cords,

Thomas Pink shirts, suitably frayed at the collars, Church's lace-ups, gold signet rings twinkling on little fingers of left hands. The men did something in the City and talked incessantly about insurance and Lloyd's – not the bank. The girls also worked in the City, two cooked directors' lunches, the other was a secretary, or rather a PA, as she described herself. They talked non-stop about whom they knew, shrieking noisily each time they discovered a common thread, or rather, a well-bred thread. It was like being with dogs in Hyde Park, a form of social bottom-sniffing to find out with whom you were dealing.

'Be prepared, Henry's a terrible cook,' said the chap on my right as we sat down for dinner. And it was indeed a rather curious affair, consisting of long uncut baguettes, whole tomatoes with sprigs of basil strewn over them, a plate of rather dirty carrots, a large ham, a bowl of very undercooked baked potatoes, jars of home-made pickles with silver spoons in them and a pack of butter still in its wrapper. It was, however, served with the most delicious red wine out of extremely old crystal decanters in matching heavy crystal glasses. The chipped crockery was incongruous against huge, ornate silver candlesticks and the two odd-looking birds with ruffled feathers who seemed to be having some sort of frozen courtship dance on the table.

'That's not fair, Harry,' yelled Henry across me, frightfully animated. 'It's just cook didn't make me enough tuck for the week. The old parents are away, so I had to improvise a bit.'

'Completely spoiled you are,' tittered one of the girls opposite me, adding in a flirty voice, 'I'll come and cook for you, Henry.'

I kept rather quiet as my culinary skills were second only to my secretarial abilities.

'Well, I would have asked Polly to come and help, but she was too busy getting arrested over the weekend!' Henry bellowed with laughter. Oh marvellous, I thought, here we go. So he had read it.

'Say what, old chap?' said one of the other men, as the girls looked at me in fascinated horror.

'Rarely, chaps, don't you read your headlines? Our Miss P here was arrested for dealing; all over the Sunday papers it was.' He was finding this very funny.

'Well, you obviously only look at headlines, Henry,' I replied in what I hoped was a faintly aloof voice. 'Because if you had read on you would have seen it was all a big mistake.'

But of course the damage was done. Having been quietly ignored, I was now a minor celebrity, by virtue of my parentage, of course, and my headline-making ability.

'Ooh!' squeaked one of the girls. 'What's it like having a father in politics, are you frightfully clever?'

I smiled back. 'Well, you know, um . . . ' I never know what to bloody say.

'I've seen him on TV, where's his constituency?' asked one of the boys.

'Is he Prime Minister?' asked one of the girls excitedly.

'Er, no, Health Minister,' I replied sweetly, refilling my glass.

'Course he is, silly me,' said one of the other chaps, his complexion by now nearly as florid as his shirt. 'Seen him on the telly!'

Oh God, I hated this.

'On the telly?' squeaked another of the girls. 'Is he famous? Have you met Chris Tarrant?'

'Dash it all, Penelope,' yelled one of the men, 'you know who he is, don't you? Michael Parkinson. That's your pa, right? Sat next to him in a restaurant once.'

'No,' I replied wearily.

'Who?' asked one of the girls.

'Isn't he dead?' asked another.

'You might mean Cecil Parkinson, and no, he's not my father and he's not dead. But he was on Michael Parkinson's show recently.'

I was cringing with embarrassment.

'Eeau,' replied the girl. 'What channel is it on?'

'BBC, I think,' I said. 'Oh look, pudding!' I tried to steer the conversation back to matters in hand as Henry plonked two enormous bars of Cadbury's Dairy Milk, still in their wrappers, on the table.

After everyone had gone, Henry and I had a nightcap.

'What are you doing thish weekend?' slurred Henry, who seemed very drunk. We were lying on the sofa having a rather long good-night kiss.

'Well, I'm going to my father's for lunch on Sunday, but I have no definite plans,' I replied carefully.

'Fatashtic! Come and stay with me on Saturday and you can pop over to him next day.'

This was progress indeed. Meet-the-parents time.

'How lovely, Henry. Thank you.' I was trying to keep the excitement out of my voice.

I thought this would be a good moment to leave, while the heat of the moment was still there, as it were. 'Thank you for a fun dinner party.'

'Do you really have to go?' said Henry, wrapping a rather wobbly arm around me.

'Yes, work tomorrow.' (Play hard to get tonight.) 'I'll see you at the weekend.' I removed his arm and kissed him on the cheek.

It was all I could do to stop myself skipping back to my car. The Plan was working well!

At work the following morning, I saw Merry arrive, only an hour late. 'Merry,' I hissed at her. 'Come here quickly!'

'Oh! I am soooo sorry I'm late,' she started to say.

'I don't care. Listen, Henry's invited my to his house this weekend!' I was so excited.

'Brilliant darling.' She sat down, all efficiency. 'Now, you haven't slept with him yet, have you?'

'Of course not!' I exclaimed. 'Are you mad?'

'Well, don't this weekend either, is my advice. When I was hooking my Michael I never bestowed upon him anything more than an enticing snog – oh, and I think one quick grope just to get him really going – and then I buggered off to India and waited three months. It was agony.'

Crikey, what self-restraint, I thought.

'Literally, as it happened. I got the worst case of Dehli Belly and was laid up for six weeks. He was calling all the time and I was bedridden and delirious, quite unable to talk. Drove him absolutely crazy; then he heard I'd been ill, so he flew out to see me. I was so thin and vulnerable-looking when he arrived he popped the question then and there! Couldn't have worked out better if I'd planned it.'

She looked extremely pleased with herself.

'Well done! I think I might just forgo the tummy-bug thing though, it seems a bit drastic. OK, so I won't sleep with him over the weekend. You're sure he won't go off me and think I'm not interested?'

'He won't go off you, silly. He'll get keener. He can get any girl he wants and they all say yes. After the weekend you rarely *must* come to supper. I know I've been saying it for *ages*, but it's *such* a social whirl this engagement lark, I'm finding it *utterly* exhausting. But I will organize it, I promise you, a bit of competition is the best challenge. Now, let's plan the wardrobe.'

'Good-morning girls,' Johnnie appeared at the door. 'Working hard are we?'

'Johnnie, good-morning,' twinkled Merry at his rather stern face. 'Just discussing some very important work-related issues. I'll be right with you.'

He smiled at her, then turned to me all stern again.

'Shouldn't you be in Milton Keynes?' he snapped.

'I was just on my way.' I sometimes wondered if he disliked me as much as he appeared to, and whether the fact I'd received a couple of phone calls from Bill at the office was the only reason he continued to employ me.

'Poll,' Samantha came up to me as I was just about to get into the lift, 'I have to talk to you. I'm just having the most wonderful time with Troy. I've never met anyone so romantic; he – '

'Sam,' I said hurriedly, 'I have to go to Milton bloody Keynes. Johnnie's like a bear with a sore head at me. Can we talk later? I'm really sorry.'

Things seemed to be moving swiftly with her and Troy and I wondered where it would all lead. She was completely smitten and who could blame her? I knew only too well how charming he could be and his seduction technique was virtually irresistible. I was sure under other circumstances even I would have succumbed. Even I, who was I kidding? I determinedly put my head back into work mode and set off for Milton Keynes in my gorgeous little car.

18

With the mid-morning sun streaming through the open top of my car, I sped down to Gloucestershire the following Saturday. I had no idea what to expect. All Merry had said was the house was quite old and on the large side, so take something warm for the evening. Dress casually for the day, but smart for dinner. I had a large box of chocolates for his parents in the boot and was clad in a pair of jeans and a stripey shirt I'd borrowed from William the Lodger, who was being extremely nice to everyone at the moment. My stomach fluttered as I turned down the little lane signposted to The Swellings. This countryside was so graphic, I thought to myself, having passed Lower Assenden and the Slaughters. There was also Old Sodham, which made me laugh. Not to mention Crackpot, Bottoms, Maggots End and Pant.

I peered at my handwriting on the piece of paper where I'd scribbled down the directions. Second left, entrance on right. I looked at the enormous, heavy wrought-iron gates in front of me, which were firmly shut. All around there was a high stone wall, so I got out of the car to see if there was some sort of bell I could ring. I peered through and saw a little cottage just inside.

'Hallo?' I said quite loudly. 'Is anyone there?'

Nothing.

'Hallo!' I shouted a bit louder and then louder again; still nothing.

I walked back to the car, thinking I was going to have to find a phone box and call Henry at home, when a grumpy voice behind me said, 'Hold your horses, I'm coming, I'm coming.'

I turned around to see a very rickety old man in rather tatty clothes trudging slowly over to the gates. He put an enormous key in the lock and pulled one of them back. One allowed room enough for my car to drive in.

'Thank you very much,' I said. 'Can you tell me where the main house is, please?'

He cupped a hand to his ear, 'Eh?' he said.

I repeated my question and he just looked blankly at me. He was either very slow or very deaf, so I all but shouted, 'Where is the main house?'

'All right, all right, I'm not deaf, just follow the road down, can't miss it.'

He turned around and started the tortuous process of shutting the gate again.

'Thank you,' I said cheerily, into silence. I drove on. And on. And on. After about three or four minutes I thought I must be in the wrong place and the mad old man at the gate just didn't hear me properly, despite his protestations as to the effectiveness of his hearing. All I could see around me was parkland with the occasional deer grazing – until, startled at the noise of my car, it would dart off into the trees out of sight.

Then suddenly, looming up before me, I came upon the most enormous, imposing, dark stone house. A vast sort of urn thing with revolting-looking carved reptiles climbing over it, twisting round each other in all manner of positions, stood in the centre of a large turning circle in front of the main door. Great pillars held up the porch and terrifying gargoyles stuck their tongues out at each corner of the house. At least I hoped they were tongues. It was reassuring to see relatively normal lions snarling on either side of the door.

I made a note to throttle Merry when I got back; to describe this house as 'on the large side' was as inaccurate as describing the Atlantic Ocean as a 'big lake'.

The huge doors opened and a smartly dressed man, who I assumed was Henry's father, appeared. I still didn't know what to call them; Frank didn't have a clue and Merry delighted in telling me they had a title which I would find out soon enough and then falling about with laughter.

I held out my hand and started to introduce myself.

'May I take your bag, madam?' asked the man tonelessly.

'Oh, er what? Yes, thank you.' I recovered quickly, realizing my mistake. Where was bloody Henry?

'His lordship is waiting for you in the Venetian Drawing-room. John will take you there.'

A young boy in an over-large suit appeared through a door.

'John, please take our guest through, thank you.'

He turned back to me and said, 'I'll arrange for your luggage to be taken to your room. Perkins will unpack and press your clothes.'

My head was spinning. His lordship? Must be Henry's father. Where on earth was I? I hated the idea someone was going to go through my suitcase. I desperately tried to remember what I'd flung in and how clean it was. I felt my face go all hot as I thought of a particularly unattractive bra, which gave me a good shape under clothes, but was absolutely not for public display. I was mentally cursing everyone, particularly myself. Yet, of course, at the same time I was very excited. No wonder Henry had so many women chasing him. I will not get carried away, I will not get carried away, I muttered to myself silently, willing on a calm I certainly didn't feel.

I followed young John down an endless corridor with enormous portraits and tapestries hanging on the walls and delicate little gilded chairs and tables scattered under vast windows. We finally reached our destination and he ushered me through.

Henry jumped up from the sofa. 'Polly, you made it. Thank you, John, you may go.'

'M'lord,' he said, closing the doors.

'What on earth is going on, Henry?' I demanded before he even had time to open his mouth. 'Who the hell are you? Have you rented this creepy old house just for the weekend to impress me, because I would like to point out, I am singularly unimpressed.'

This was a big lie of course.

Henry threw back his head and laughed loudly. 'God, you are funny. You really don't have a clue do you?'

'No,' I replied rather crossly. 'Are you going to enlighten me or is this *Twenty Questions*?'

'Let's have a drink before lunch.'

He walked over to a table groaning with decanters and poured two large vodka and tonics.

'Thank you,' I said, accepting the glass offered to me but adding rather sarcastically, 'Surely you have someone to do that for you?'

'Well, actually, I've given all the live-in staff the weekend off as my parents are away. I thought it would be cosier.'

He grinned rather strangely at me.

The idea this house could ever be described as cosy was very funny; however, the prospect of being alone in it was not.

'Watson, whom you met you at the front door, lives at the lodge with his family; you presumably met his father at the gate.'

I nodded.

'Watson senior, yes. Deaf as a post,' said Henry. 'His family has worked for generations for my family; he used to be my father's butler. Watson is his son. John, Watson obviously, is his son. Perkins is Watson's wife.'

'Which Watson?' I was getting confused.

'And cook, is the elder Watson's wife.'

I think he was having fun confusing me.

'Take a seat,' he said. 'Lunch will be about an hour, I'll fill you in. No pun intended.' He laughed hysterically again. He seemed rather agitated.

A couple of vodka and tonics later, I was sitting in a dining-room with more antiques in it than Christie's could easily supply, with, as it transpired, one of England's most eligible bachelors, the son of one of England's premier noble families. No wonder he had so many girls chasing him, and lucky old me to be with him now! It was ironic, I mused, to think that the shadow of parental fame in which I lived was as nothing compared to this.

To my amazement the old man from the gates was doddering about the room on butler duty. He was very bent and he looked as though he had shrunk in size as his morning suit hung off every wasted limb. He served us with very shaky hands and I was convinced either food or wine was going to end up in my lap on more than one occasion.

Henry leant over to me and said, in a conspiratorial but quite unnecessary whisper, considering the old man's aural faculties, 'I let him come and butle for me when I'm on my own. He's much more discreet than Watson, who relays everything to my father.'

From this I surmised my visit to his house fell into a dubious category, which was rather annoying. I held on firmly to my glass as old man Watson slopped yet more delicious wine into it, leaving a large inky red stain on the tablecloth. Henry did not seem particularly relaxed and kept popping out of the room, leaving me twiddling one of the many forks on the table in front of me, avoiding eye contact with the ancient retainer. My head was feeling a bit fuzzy, not only from taking in my surroundings, but also from the amount I'd already drunk.

I thought I'd need a siesta later on if I was going to be on form for the party Henry had apparently planned for tonight. He'd been rather vague about it, just saying some local friends would be coming. I expected I was going to be the only untitled person there. Henry walked back into the room again, came up behind my chair and, putting his hands under my jumper, grabbed my boobs. He twisted his head down and round and started to kiss me. I was slightly taken aback, not only because Watson senior was in the room, although he had immediately turned around, but because this was a bit more intimate than Henry had been before and I wondered if he was planning to sleep with me later on. I also wondered if I was going to be able to refuse.

The intoxicating mixture of alcohol and stately homes was

fast eroding my resolve. I mean, I had fancied Henry before I knew who he really was and it had been ages since I'd been to bed with anyone . . . no, I shook my head, I was not going to give in.

I tried to think of Merry and her advice and knew to sleep with Henry would be disastrous. I still had to keep him keen. Anyway, the amount he was drinking he'd probably never be able to get it up, or at least not be able to come which would be really depressing. I mean, it's bad enough having to concentrate on one's own orgasm, without worrying about someone else's!

'Er hem.' There was a discreet cough at which Henry looked up. 'Would you like coffee to be served, m'lord?' asked the old man in a croaky voice, looking directly at Henry.

'Thank you, Watson, in the Yellow Parlour, please.' His hands were still firmly clamped round each boob and I felt most uncomfortable, particularly as Watson then turned to me and asked if I took milk or cream.

'Come on, let's go,' said Henry, abruptly getting up. He poured himself an enormous brandy and weaved down another long corridor waving his arms at various extremely unattractive people on the walls, who all had big, black, starey eyes and were relatives of some sort. They must be awfully inbred, I reflected. They all look the same. I decided it was about time Henry's family added some new, mongrel blood-line, like mine. I giggled.

'What's funny?' asked Henry.

I started to laugh even more because, with his hair a bit rumpled, his face flushed and his dark eyes lit up by alcohol, he was the image of one of his relatives about five canvases ago.

'Oh, er nothing,' I said, regaining my composure a little. 'I was just wondering how on earth I was going to find my way around this enormous place. I don't even know where I'm sleeping yet.'

'Plenty of time. Come and have some coffee.'

Henry opened double doors into another breathtakingly beautiful room where the smell of some rather welcome coffee greeted us. Old Watson handed me a rattling cup and saucer.

'How did he get here so fast?' I asked; even though we'd dawdled on our way, looking at the paintings, it had still been a fast trot compared with Watson's uncertain gait.

'The house is full of back passages and short cuts. I don't know them all myself,' said Henry.

He motioned for me to come and sit beside him on the sofa where the sun's rays streaming through the windows were bathing the fabric in a golden yellow glow. Putting his cup down, he started to kiss me again. He really was a good kisser when he put his mind to it and wasn't jumping up and down. He was getting more persistent and began to undo the buttons of my shirt, his breathing becoming heavier. I felt very relaxed and in the hazy, horny stage you can reach after a long boozy lunch. The sun was making me feel warm and I shut my eyes. He started to kiss my neck and was moving down to my breasts when suddenly he sort of snarled and bit me, hard.

'Ouch!' I yelled. 'That hurt!' I put my hand to the place and rubbed. I could see teeth marks!

'Come on, you love it,' he said, pinning me to the sofa.

'No. I don't love it at all. I am not into pain, stop it at once.' I saw his head descend worryingly to my breasts again. 'I'll kick you,' I threatened, 'where it hurts.'

'Oh, goody-goody. Will you spank me too? I'm such a naughty boy.' He looked very excited at the prospect.

'Henry, I think you've had far too much to drink to feel any pain at the moment. Why don't we go for a walk, it's a beautiful day. When you sober up I might be able to inflict pain so you can feel it.'

I thought if I let him think I might be into 'punishing' him later I'd at least be able to get him off me now.

It seemed to do the trick and he jumped up. 'Come on then, let's go.' He held out his hand and pulled me up, all smiles and sweetness. Talk about a mercurial personality. I wondered if there was any way to limit his alcohol consumption tonight in the hope Wolf-Boy didn't re-emerge!

We went across the manicured lawns, around the box-hedge-bordered beds, through the wild-flower gardens and then down a steep hill where the lawn slipped away into a beautiful valley where wild lilies grew by the side of a wide stream. An ancient weeping willow grew on one side, its branches almost reaching the other bank. Some old, frayed ropes hung down off various higher branches, imitating the delicate green tendrils that touched the running water below. It was peaceful and romantic. I hesitated for a moment, trying to decide if it was safe to lie down beside Henry, but he looked very calm now, lying on his back, staring up at the sky with a blade of grass in his mouth.

'I used to play down here with my sisters,' he said.

I was happy to learn more about his family, so asked what they did.

'One's married, lives in Dallas with some oil baron, all twang and no wang. Dreadful man, even wore his stetson to dinner one night; thought the parents would have a fit; tons of money but no class.' Henry's tone of voice didn't indicate whether he was being serious or not.

'My other sister is in and out of institutions – she's barking, every kind of legal disorder you can name, eating, depression, paranoia, cutting herself, you know. One minute she's the size of a small plantation and jolly as hell, next thing you see, there's more flesh on a slice of bacon and she's as miserable as sin, saying how fat she is. Tried to top herself countless times.'

His voice continued to be quite emotionless. 'Very pretty girl. Never could quite work her out though. And my baby sister died a number of years ago.'

'Oh, how sad.' I reached over and put my hand on his. 'I'm so sorry, how did she die?'

'She drowned. Just over there.' He leant up on one elbow and pointed to the stream in front of us.

'We were playing with those ropes and she fell in. One rope was still attached to her foot and it got caught under one of the roots of the tree, kept her down. We all thought she was mucking about and had swum underwater to get home before us. It was ages before we realized what had happened.'

I thought I was going to be sick. The gentle scene in front of me was no longer peaceful, but an insidious, menacing death-trap place. I shuddered. And Henry was talking so matter-of-factly about it.

'How can you still come back here?' I asked.

'I like it, it's peaceful. Sometimes I come down at night; they say when the river is full and laps against the bank, it's her last gasps for breath. Weird isn't it?' Henry was spooking me once again.

'Henry, I think I'd like to go, I'm very susceptible to atmospheres and this place is now very creepy for me. Can we go somewhere – nice; you know, someplace where no one died?'

Henry started to do his manic laugh again.

'You've come to the wrong house if you want to find some-where somebody didn't die. There isn't a room where a foul deed didn't take place. When the folks are feeling a bit strapped, they hire the house out for a small fortune to a company that organizes murder-mystery weekends. Half the people who come get so scared they can't even hack the whole weekend.'

Oh wonderful, I thought. Here I am, in what turns out to be one of the spookiest old houses in England, scared witless at the mere thought of a ghost, let alone a massive infestation of them, with a man whose personality makes Mr Hyde look like a regular sort of bloke. I was definitely going to have to sleep with the lights on tonight. I sincerely hoped Henry wasn't planning on doing any corridor-creeping later on because I'd probably scream the house down if my door opened! I wasn't sure who I was more worried about, the living or the dead. I was going to have serious words with Merry on Monday.

'Come on you,' said Henry, getting up. 'I'll give you a tour of the house, but,' he looked at what I assumed to be my terrified face, 'I'll omit the gory bits.'

It was pretty spectacular, I had to confess, even with a few nasty facts thrown in. Plus, Henry was back to his usual self now; the effects of our lunch seemed to have worn off. I was beginning to feel sleepy and said I thought I might have a little nap before dinner.

'Good idea.' He wrapped an arm around me.

'I meant to sleep, Henry, you naughty boy.' Instantly regretting the last two words, although he didn't seem to pick up on them, I lightly removed his arm. Under other circumstances it might have been rather nice, the afternoon being my absolute favourite time.

'All right, all right. You don't know where your room is, I'll get old Watson to take you. Everyone else has gone home now except cook, who's just putting the finishing touches to the buffet for tonight.'

I followed Watson's tottering form down the long corridor and went into my room and saw all my clothes had been pressed and either hung up or put in drawers, including my horrid bra. Oh well, it could have been worse, at least I'd remembered to pack underwear. I slipped under the covers and within minutes had fallen asleep.

It was dusk when I woke and still feeling quite sleepy I thought I'd have a bath. I wandered into the adjoining room and turned the taps on. After a huge shudder the taps trickled into life and a rather bubbly, light-brown liquid began to fill the tub. I pulled the plug out and let it run for a while hoping it might clear up, but it didn't. Not wishing to lose any more hot water I looked around for something nice and smelly to transform the tea-like liquid which was slowly rising up the sides but couldn't find anything, so I regretfully put in a bit of my scent. If it didn't look nice it may as well smell nice. I'd just got into the bath when the door burst open. Henry appeared with armfuls of lilies and a manic look on his face. Oh hell. Wolf-Boy was back . . .

'Henry!' I squeaked, trying unsuccessfully to cover myself up, 'What are you doing?'

'Flowersh,' he slurred, 'flowersh for you. Just picked 'em.'

Whereupon he started to throw them at me, one by one, where I lay in the bath. He hadn't done a good job in picking them as some still had their roots attached, so lumps of earth landed in the water as well, turning it an even darker colour.

He must have been drinking again.

I thought of the sister who was in and out of institutions and wondered if the whole family had a problem of one sort or another. I was particularly unhappy to realize these were the lilies which had been growing by the stream where his sister had drowned.

'Henry, have you been drinking?' I asked.

'Nope, not a drip.' He started to laugh his weird laugh and I began to feel very uncomfortable. I didn't want to get out of the bath as my towel was right over on the other side of the room and I wasn't keen to parade naked in front of Henry, although his eyes were now so wild and staring I wasn't sure he'd focus properly anyway. However, my bath was filling up rapidly with flowers and mud and, to my revulsion, worms and bugs. This was really too much. I couldn't just sit there. God knows where the worms might end up!

'You are the Lady of the Lake – no, no, retract, you are Ophelia.' Henry started to quote rather garbled Shakespeare at me and dance around the room, his hair askew, still throwing endless bloody lilies at me. I was not having a happy time at all and decided rather than suffocate in flowers or go the way of Ophelia, I was going to have to get out of the bath.

'Henry, I'm getting out of this tub now, will you please turn your back?'

'Oooh, baby is a prude is she?' he put on a funny little voice. 'Don't be scaredy, Hensie-wensie won't peek. Let's play grandma's footsteps. I'll turn around and count to ten.'

He covered his face with his hands and let the remaining flowers fall to the ground

'One . . . two . . . three . . . '

I hopped out of the bath and ran over to grab the towel. I looked at my legs which were all streaky with mud.

'. . . four . . . five . . . and TEN!' he yelled and turned around, grabbing the end of my towel.

'Henry! Let go!' I pulled the towel back to me.

He was quite strong, but then suddenly let go and I nearly fell over backwards.

'Boo!' He jumped at me putting both his hands up by his face.

I yelled, 'Stop it! It's not funny,' quite unnerved by this strange behaviour and the almost unrecognizable man in front of me. 'Let me get dressed and I'll come down for dinner. What time are the other people arriving?' Henry started to dance around the room again.

'Arriving and arriven, some here, some there.'

I didn't have a clue what he was talking about.

'Don't bother to dress, you look lovely just as you are!' He came over to me again and started to pull at the towel.

'Henry, no, stop it. I'll be down in ten minutes, OK? Now go on, shoo!'

I put on a very calm voice and just about managed to get him out of my room while still keeping my towel on.

I shut the door and leant against it, thankful to see it had a lock and key. What on earth had I let myself in for? His personality changes were really quite dramatic and there were times when he scared me a little. I was pleased there were some other people coming for dinner, hoping for safety in numbers. If the worst came to the worst I could always leave, I had my car right outside. What a ridiculous situation. I looked down at my body and wondered how I was going to get clean. I rubbed my legs but succeeded only in making them a more even tan colour. I reached for the tin of talcum powder I'd brought with me and shook it generously over myself. It was the best I could do.

With some trepidation I opened my door a little later and

walked along to the main staircase. Loud throbbing music started to reach my ears. Then the sound of voices. Quite a lot of voices it seemed. I looked down the staircase to see piles and piles of fruit had been placed at the bottom and were creeping upwards. Great ferns trembled, their delicate fronds jittering to the thud of music. Henry was obviously having quite a party. I followed the noise as it got louder and opened the door into the drawing-room I'd first been in.

I gasped. The room was lit only by vast candles, giving off a soft muted light. The loud orchestral chamber music nearly deafened me. More overflowing mounds of fruit lay on the tables. Two enormous white borzois padded around, huge spiked collars circling their necks. There must have been about fifty people in the room. Some were standing up, but only just, swaying to the music, and others were sprawled over the various sofas and armchairs. There were couples in various stages of undress writhing around on the floor and the overpowering smell of dope curled its way up my nostrils.

'Ah, Polly, welcome!' Henry weaved up to me, his arms wrapped round two fantastically huge-breasted girls, neither of whom had tops on.

'Meet Mandy and Mitsie. Girls, say hallo nicely to Polly.'

The girls reached out for me with long, red-taloned hands. I stepped back, not at all keen to get too close.

'Er, I'll just get a drink, I'll be back in a second.'

I was shaking and my heart beat very fast as I tried to turn away but Henry took hold of my wrist hard and hissed, 'Now now, you're my guest, you can't be a party pooper.'

He looked horrible. His shirt was half off and he had scratch marks on his chest. Welts of lipstick covered his mouth and face. He looked like one of the gargoyles adorning his house. I was getting quite panicky and pulled away from him.

I turned round and nearly fell over a virtually naked couple, who appeared to be having sex on the floor. I needed a drink fast. I went over to the sideboard and with a shaky hand poured myself a huge vodka. I looked up to see Watson senior tottering around, navigating bodies, with a tiny silver object in his hand. I peered closer; it looked like a miniature dustpan and brush and he was going over the surfaces gently brushing them and then pouring the dust into a little plastic bag. I looked around me and saw bowls full of white powder, which had spilled over. And then realization dawned. God, how stupid I'd been. Cocaine. No wonder Henry had such mood swings, it wasn't only booze, but drugs. What a fool.

It might have been funny, certainly ironic, if only I hadn't been stranded with a whole load of doped-up strangers, in this vast, isolated, not to mention probably haunted house, with women prowling round the room like cats on heat. This time, I thought, the living were definitely scarier than the dead.

More and more people were coming into the room. I jumped as I felt a hand on my shoulder. I turned around and found myself looking into the glassy eyes of Mandy or Mitsie.

She mumbled, 'Do you like girls?'

I was beginning to feel really sick and predatory females were very scary. The room was like a snake pit. I tried to hide myself in a corner as I watched with horrified fascination what was developing into a full-on orgy unfold in front of my eyes. It appeared I was not nearly as broad-minded as I thought. But there again, if this was sophistication, they could keep it.

I was dumbstruck by Henry. Was being up for this a prerequisite for an aspiring girlfriend? If he thought this was my kind of scene I'd clearly been giving off very misleading signals.

I looked round and saw him lying underneath the other bosom-enhanced girl. I felt sick. It was perfectly obvious what they were doing. Thank God I hadn't slept with him! I was also fanatical about germs and despite my dirty bath felt I was a lot less grubby than this lot.

A body from the floor got hold of my ankle. I found it repellent being touched by a complete stranger, particularly when I couldn't see what gender they were. Where had these people come from? Were they Henry's friends? Outwardly respectable people getting high and horny on a Saturday night? Obviously some of the girls were the hired help, as it were. No wonder he gave the staff the weekend off! I looked at the big clock on the wall, it was only eight-thirty! This could go on for hours . . .

I couldn't bear it a moment longer and ran back to my room trying to decide what to do. I had the shock of my life when I opened the door and found old Watson there, on his hands and knees. Oh no! Not him a pervert as well!

I took a closer look. He was sweeping up the talcum powder I'd left on the carpet with that little silver dustpan and brush of his. For the first time in the evening I started to laugh.

'Watson!' I managed to shout. 'You're wasting your time, it's talcum powder. For heaven's sake don't mix it in with the other stuff.'

He got up slowly, his face flushed with the effort – either that or he'd been sampling the contents of his little dustpan, which in this house wouldn't have surprised me.

'Thank you, madam,' he said solemnly.

I made a decision.

'Watson, would you be very kind and tell his lordship' (my voice was heavy with irony) 'I've decided to spend the night at my father's house. I'm afraid I'm not this kind of party animal.'

'Very good, madam.'

His voice was expressionless. He looked at me with his bleary eyes for a moment and then said, very quietly, 'Good for you, madam.'

Then he turned around and hobbled out of the room, leaving me in silence.

19

It hadn't taken me too long to pack and find my car; the gates were open and I sped away as fast as I could, longing to get to my father's house. In the morning, dad was very surprised to find me curled up asleep in one of the guest rooms. He made coffee and listened as I told him the story. His first advice was to keep quiet about the whole thing. Henry's lifestyle was his own affair and we both knew how easy it is for people's private lives to become public. Kiss and tell was not an attractive scene. My father, with whom I've always shared most confidences, was sympathetic, but also shocked. He'd met Henry's father on a few occasions and I made him promise not to say anything to him. At which he replied rather huffily that the idea of his approaching a peer of the realm and discussing the orgies that took place at his house was not one that appealed to him! Shame though, he added, because while I would always be his princess, another title would have been nice!

We ended up laughing and our talk left me in a much better frame of mind. In fact by Monday, I'd managed to regain my equilibrium and, more importantly, my sense of humour. It was one of life's more interesting experiences and a good lesson in how deceptive appearances can be.

However, the downside was back to square one in terms of the Plan. The irony that someone so outwardly suitable had turned out to be just the reverse was not lost on me, but even so, the situation was so extreme I refused to be daunted. I would just have to see what Merry's dinner party was going to be like, if it ever happened.

She, of course, was all agog to hear the details, even managing to arrive on time at the office!

'Well?' she burst through my door. 'What happened?'

I paused before replying.

'I don't really think he's my type after all – despite the fact he turns out to be practically the most eligible bachelor on the planet, and thank you very much for telling me. Rather large house indeed! Have you actually been there?' I decided to avoid the details and instead give her a hard time.

She giggled. 'Just didn't want to make you too keen, darling. Anyway what do you mean he's not your type?'

'He's barking and the house is haunted. I couldn't live with either.'

It was a glorious understatement.

'Barking?' she looked at me curiously, her cornflower-blue eyes full of surmise. 'What on earth are you saying? Of *course* he's barking, he's a *lord* for heaven's sake. They're *all* mad, you don't nab a title without a teeny-weeny downside.'

'There's nothing teeny-weeny about his mood swings, they make a menopausal woman look serene. He's lovely, but I have absolutely decided we will remain just good friends, as they say.'

I had no intention of ever seeing him again, but I didn't want to inflame her curiosity further.

'Well, if you ask me, you're the barking one, letting such a big fish slip away. But it is strange,' she said.

'What is?' I asked.

'You're at least the third girl I know who's returned from a weekend at his house and been distinctly evasive about what happened.'

I wasn't in the least surprised. But I suppose if you were desperate enough to snare a man, especially one with a title, perhaps you would go along with his sexual proclivities. I know girls will do a lot of wild things to please their man and I often wonder just how comfortable with it they really are. Men seem to like pushing sexual boundaries, looking for a new thrill. Whereas girls tend to prefer polishing the same apple over and over until it really shines.

'I'm not being evasive. I just got to know him a bit better and realized we were not really compatible. As I said, nice guy, but not for me.' I changed the subject. 'Anyway, I'm pinning my hopes on your dinner party. When is it going to be?'

'Ah, I have at last compared diaries with my Michael. Miles away, I'm afraid, two weeks from tomorrow. Is that OK?'

I couldn't imagine I was doing anything so far in advance. I nodded, adding, 'I hope you have some eligibles lined up.'

'Absolutely,' she smiled. 'Two in fact. You can take your pick.'

'Not cast-offs of yours, I hope?' I enquired.

'Good Lord no! Well, not publicly anyway,' she laughed. 'I'm practically a married woman now. I have no past!' And still laughing she sauntered out of my office.

I hoped I wasn't going to be grilled any further but of course Samantha was next to come bouncing in.

'Well?' she demanded. 'How did it gooa?'

'Funny, I was only asked the same thing a minute ago. Fine but not going anywhere.'

'Why not? I thought he was perfect, stately home, title and all.' She looked puzzled.

'Grief, did everyone know who he was except me?' It was really irritating.

'I was sworn to secrecy by Merry. She decided it would be much more fun for you to find out by yourself. She thought he'd be pleased if you didn't know who he was and liked him just for himself.'

Which was a shame, because that was not an option.

'Despite who he is, he's not ready to settle down so there's no point in my wasting my time.' I was keen to change the subject. 'Anyway, how about your life? What's going on with Troy?'

'Oh Poll . . . ' her eyes went all gooey. 'I don't know where to begin. He's not at all what I expected. He's just wonderful. The most romantic, interesting man I've ever met. It's like he gets into your soul. I'm telling him things I don't tell anyone. He just has this zest for life. On Saturday we drove to a remote spot he knows in the country, so beautiful. He loves nature and said he wanted me to touch life; it's like he's waking me up to the world around me. I asked him why he was doing this and he said he wanted me to get to know him; there was something different about me, something he could relate to; that he was really quite a shy, insecure person.'

Familiar words I thought to myself, darkly.

'And as for the sex! I've never had a lover like him and I doubt I ever will again. Forget the fact he has the most enormous you-know-what I've ever seen – and New Zealand boys are not wimps in that department, so you can imagine' (I was trying hard not to). 'He says sex can only be fulfilling if it is mind and body combined. What was it he said?' She screwed up her face for a moment and I waited, anticipating the rest. 'Yea. He had to really trust someone emotionally and get to know them before it did anything for him. Just the physical was not enough for him. I've never felt this way about someone before, it's scary. But do you know, I think, even though it's only been a little while, well, I think he might be falling for me too.'

Torn between anger at myself for so nearly falling for the same lines, I was furious at Troy for using them on Samantha – and presumably every other girl he was seducing. I was also relieved I hadn't succumbed myself, but concerned for Samantha. Buried way down, much as I didn't want to acknowledge it, I felt some strange stirrings of jealousy too. It was extremely confusing.

'Just be careful, Sam,' was all I felt able to say.

'Oh *you*, Polly. Just because your weekend didn't turn out, doesn't mean every man is bad. You're just jealous.'

'Hey, not fair!' I exclaimed, hurt. 'I was the one who introduced you and I'm happy you're having a good time. I only said be careful. Anyway I don't think all men are bad. It's just . . .'

She didn't give me time to finish my sentence. 'Right, whatever you say, but don't patronize me. I know all about you and him.'

'There was no me and him, Samantha.' What on earth had Troy said? 'What do you mean?'

'Oh I see,' said Samantha, her hands crossed in front of her defiantly, 'so you never tried to seduce him then?'

Oh, here we go again, I thought. Men are such complete arses. I was furious with Troy.

'No, I did not, quite the reverse if anything,' I snapped, knowing my words would fall on ears that only heard what they chose.

I should be used to it; even before I lost my virginity, boys were bragging about shagging me. Well, not me, the Minister's daughter. It was definitely one of the downsides to being in the public eye by proxy. If I had shagged the number of people who had claimed I had, I wouldn't have had time to get out of bed!

Samantha got up abruptly from the chair she was sitting on, 'I've got some work to do.' She turned and left the office.

Bugger, I thought, she's mad at me because she thinks I'm jealous. So even if I did tell her those were well-rehearsed lines, she wouldn't believe me. Urghh, men!

The phone rang and interrupted my thunderous thoughts.

'Hallo?' I snapped

'Well that sure ain't the most professional telephone manner I've heard. What happened to you this morning, darlin'? ' Bill Shark's gentle drawl came down the line.

'Oh, sorry Bill, nothing at all. How are you? Isn't it the middle of the night in the States?'

'Sure is. But it's mornin' for me.'

'I'm sorry? What do you mean?' I was being a bit slow.

'I just arrived in London. Do you want to have dinner with me tonight?'

I felt my stomach leap a little. 'Oh! I'd love to. You're just what I need.'

'Having a bad time? Those boys of mine not treating you right?' he asked.

'Oh no, they're fine, I just had a rather weird weekend. I'll tell you about it later. Are you coming into the office?'

He said he was coming in the following day, and not to mention this phone call. I was really happy to hear from him and we made the arrangements to meet.

It couldn't have been better timing as I was feeling rather deflated after my weekend and irritated Samantha was angry with me. Johnnie came strutting into my office in the afternoon enquiring how everything was going and proceeded to check every detail, cross questioning me even on trivialities; he was a complete control freak. I wondered what on earth was the point of asking someone to do something and then going over how it had been done. It was very undermining. When he announced Bill was coming into the office tomorrow, it was all I could do not to say I already knew. The staff downstairs were now rather looking forward to going to Milton Keynes as it was a way of avoiding Johnnie and his meddlesome ways.

'What are you planning on doing with the space downstairs when the two companies move?' I asked Johnnie.

'Your next task, once you finish this. I want you to rent or preferably lease those floors for as much as possible. It's prime real estate. I want a lot of money for it. But it has to be a blue-chip company, no flaky fly-by-night advertising agencies or scruffy media people.'

I thought the riff-raff would have been infinitely preferable, or at least fun. But then, I wouldn't find a husband, so blue chip it would have to be. Johnnie was so pompous I couldn't resist winding him up a bit.

'As we're so close to Piccadilly, have you thought about renting it out as a brothel? It would make you much more money.'

He looked at me in astonishment. 'Are you quite mad? A brothel?'

'It was a joke, Johnnie. Heavens, where's your sense of humour?' I resisted the temptation to suggest putting his Pantheress in as the madame.

'I fail to see anything remotely amusing. Do I have to remind you this is a serious, multi-million-dollar company and you are paid very highly to do a sensible job.'

He was quite the most exasperating man I'd ever met. I couldn't imagine what his idea of fun was. Luckily he spun on his heel and walked out, nearly colliding with Hugo.

'What was all that about?' Hugo asked in his usual calm fashion. It was such a shame he looked so like Mats; he must have some Scandinavian blood somewhere, no one in England is a natural blond.

'Oh, I just tried to lighten Johnnie up a bit with something he appears to be completely unfamiliar with called humour. But as usual, I failed dismally,' I replied.

'Ah, well, he has a lot on his plate at the moment,' said Hugo. 'There's a huge amount to do and he's a perfectionist, you see.' (Didn't take a clairvoyant.) 'Don't let him rattle your cage. Despite what you may think, he has a very high opinion of you.' (This I found truly difficult to believe.) 'I told you before, take him out for a drink and talk to him.' Ever the peacemaker.

'Well, maybe I will, if I get really mad at him. But I can't think what we'd talk about, we have absolutely nothing in common.'

'You'd be surprised. There's a lot more to him than meets the eye. But anyway, that wasn't the reason I came in.'

He brushed his floppy hair off his forehead with one hand and handed me an envelope with the other. Must be danger money to stay, I thought.

'It's my thirtieth birthday next month and the parents are holding a party for me and I'd like to invite you. And Samantha and Miranda, of course.'

'Hugo, that's so kind, thank you.'

It was ages since I'd been to a big party and the thought of all the eligible men who might be there was fabulous.

At about five o'clock my phone rang; it was Henry.

'What happened to you on Saturday?' he asked, all innocence.

'Henry, I'm sorry, but it wasn't really my scene.' I wondered why I was the one apologizing.

'I realize, which is why I'm phoning. I wanted to say sorry to you. Things got way out of hand, nothing like that's ever happened before, but one of my friends brought these girls . . . ' he went into a long rambling excuse, which I cut short.

'It's fine, don't worry. I've put it down to experience. Not one I'd care to repeat, however.'

'So,' he paused, 'can we have dinner this week?'

I thought for a moment, before replying. 'Henry, it's a nice thought, but you know, it isn't just the party. I think you and I are too different.' I didn't mention the drugs, but I think he got the idea.

'A one off, I told you, none of it's my scene. Please, give me one more chance. I rarely like you, we had fun.'

I thought of old Watson with the little silver dustpan and brush and doubted it was the first time he'd ever used it – and I remembered his parting words.

'Henry, thank you, but no. I'm sure I'll see you around with Frank, but let's keep it light for a while.'

'Well, have it your way,' he said rather huffily, before adding, 'I won't give up though, I have my family motto to live up to.'

'Which is what?' I asked, despite myself.

'You'll find out.' He laughed and put the phone down.

I sat back, thinking. He was going to have to change a lot of his ways if he was serious in pursuing me and I doubted it could be done, but it was gratifying he wanted to try.

I raced home to get changed. Bang on time, the big black Mercedes slid to a noiseless halt outside the door. When I came downstairs, Bill was in the drawing-room looking incredibly elegant, in the way successful middle-aged men can. He was having a drink with Bumble, Gareth and Troy; they were all laughing. Minnie came bounding up to me, brandishing a fluffy pink pig. 'Look what this Bill gave me! It snorts, listen.' She proceeded to wind the toy up and it walked, grunting, over the drawing-room floor. It was very funny.

'Looks like my ex,' I said ruefully, 'after too many aquavits.'

'Hey, darlin',' Bill came over and kissed me. God, he was attractive.

'I see you've met my friends.' I turned to Troy. 'What are you doing here?'

'You know me and cars,' he replied, looking me straight in the eye. 'Always interested to see who's doing the driving.'

I was still angry with him. Samantha hadn't spoken to me all day and here he was again, getting in my life. I didn't feel like being nice to him but I was going to have to ask him not tell her that Bill was taking me out. It was so irritating to have him involved. When you start cross-pollinating your social life, you always seem to end up with some difficult hybrid situation to deal with.

'Ready to leave?' I asked Bill, keen to go.

'Sure.' He put his glass on the table and then bent down to pick up Minnie and twirl her round in the air. She shrieked with enjoyment.

'Goodbye, little princess, enjoy the pig.'

Bumble sidled up to me and hissed in my ear, 'Polly, he's great. We all really like him.'

'Oh! I see, just because he's nice to your daughter, you're suddenly a pushover.' Although I had to admit it was pretty clever to bring a toy for Minnie, particularly as I didn't remember telling him about her.

'And flowers for me,' Bumble added smugly, pointing to a huge bouquet sitting on the dining-room table.

'He's too old, he lives in New York, he's hugely successful, what on earth do we have in common?' I was having a hard time convincing myself, let alone her.

'Hmm,' said Bumble in her irritating fashion.

'Listen, will you tell Troy not to mention this to Samantha. The office doesn't know he's here yet.'

Even as I said it I could see her smile broaden. I held up my hand. 'Just don't say anything more, OK?'

'No problem,' she said, still smiling.

Bill's hotel had arranged tickets to a musical and then dinner at Joe Allen, a really theatrical restaurant in Covent Garden, where I'd gone on many occasions with my parents. Being full of actors it was one of my mother's favourite places.

'Did you choose this restaurant?' I asked.

'Course, darlin', thought it might appeal to your theatrical background.'

I was deeply impressed by his attention to detail, how on earth could he remember my mother had been an actress. I tried to stop thinking all the girly thoughts like, Is he serious? Does he really like me? Do I like him? (Duh!) Why me? God, I hate oestrogen. Another one of my mother's mottos came to mind: 'Darling, you don't need to listen to what people say; look at what they do. That will tell you all you need to know. Words are too easy.'

'Dollar for them,' came his voice, interrupting my reverie.

'Oh nothing. I was just thinking what a lovely time I was having and what great company you are.'

'Feelin's entirely mutual I assure you.'

He reached out for my hand and gently started stroking the palm and my wrist. I shivered.

'Cold?' he looked up at me with a smile.

'No, no.' I didn't want to say he'd just given me goose-bumps up and down my spine. 'It's, er, just a bit tickly,' I ended lamely. 'Oh look, here's the waiter with the menu; I highly recommend the black-bean soup.' I withdrew my hand and wondered how I was going to be able to eat anything at all, it felt like my stomach was turning around and upside down in an alarming fashion.

'So you want me to sleep alone tonight?' he chuckled – what is it about men and beans?

My heart started to beat a little faster.

'Safest place for you, I expect,' I replied lightly, trying to infuse a bit of humour into the hurdy-gurdy of wild thoughts in my brain.

'Really?' He looked intently at me.

Oh God, he was definitely flirting. I did *not* want to fall for him. He lived on the other side of the flipping ocean. I'd sworn I wouldn't go out with a foreigner again. Why could I never get a single, normal, English boyfriend?

'Really,' I said. More firmly than I felt.

He withdrew his hand. 'Let's order then.'

I felt a sharp stab of disappointment.

We fell into an awkward silence for a moment or two until he asked about my weekend. I ended up telling him practically everything about it, except Henry's name, and once again found myself laughing.

'Well,' said Bill, wiping away tears of mirth, 'you've made it sound very amusing, but it can't have been much fun. If it had happened to my daughter,' his face turned serious – I knew he doted on his daughter – 'I'd kill the guy.'

'Well, you know, I escaped unscathed. It's good to learn things are not always what they appear.'

'You should apply that reasoning to other situations,' said Bill in a sort of hidden-message kind of way.

'What do you mean?'

I pushed away my virtually uneaten steak, curious.

'You want to find a nice, suitable, single young Englishman to settle down with.'

I wondered if I had a neon sign over my forehead announcing my intentions.

'But suitability comes in all manner of shapes, not necessarily the one you've decided. Compatibility is more important. Life never works out the way you think it will and the only thing you can plan for is the unexpected.'

He was certainly right about that. I was having a huge internal struggle and after a moment or two decided to be honest; after all, playing a part hadn't got me very far to date. I took a big breath.

'Bill, I am trying to resist you, for all manner of reasons, not least of which is you're married. I've just come out of a bad relationship and I don't want to fall for someone I can't have. You don't even live here.'

'That's just geography. I'm married on paper only. I haven't lived with my wife for ten years, you know that. It suits me just fine because I use it as an excuse not to settle down with anyone. But you're rushing, deciding every potential relationship has to end in marriage. Try dating a bit first. You might be surprised what you come across in unlikely places. You're being too narrow-minded.'

I resented the last comment and replied indignantly that I most certainly was not.

'You're judging everyone by your desired standards and it's not fair. You're not giving a whole heap of the population a chance.'

'By which you mean you?' I asked, curiously.

'I've told you, I don't have it in the front of my mind I want to settle down. If I find the right person I will. But I'm still looking and looking can be fun.' He stared at me intently, making me involuntarily shiver again. He continued softly, 'Look, let's just see what happens, OK? You call the shots. I'm here now, just have some fun. Not hungry?' he looked at my plate.

'I, er . . . '

He laughed, pointing to his own still full plate. 'Me neither, let's go.'

'Well you're a mad fool if you let him get away.' Bumble did nothing to improve my mood when I got back and slumped on a sofa.

'Oh, don't start, Bumble. I'm so confused. I'm terrified of falling for him for so many reasons, but he makes me go quite weak at the knees. I can't eat around him, a sure sign I've got it bad.' I hugged a comforting cushion to me.

Bumble looked at me, seriously.

'He's right, you know; you should put aside this stupid Plan of yours and just enjoy yourself, let it evolve. When are you seeing him again?' she asked.

'I don't know!' I wailed miserably.

'Don't be silly,' she snapped. 'He'll be in the office tomorrow.'

'Yes, but it's different. We won't be able to talk and Johnnie will be strutting around like a demented Dalek organizing everything. I won't have a chance to speak to him.'

The thought of the day ahead was getting to me already.

'I'm sure he'll speak to you. Now go to bed and get some beauty sleep; you can't look like a wreck tomorrow. And perhaps you can hoist your awful skirt up a bit, try making yourself look a bit more glam around the place. The office-drone look does nothing for you.'

20

Sometimes I didn't want to be right. Work was dreadful. Johnnie was impossible, Hugo was very quiet, I could have sworn Bill was flirting with Samantha, and to make matters worse, I had to confirm the evening plans for the boys, so I knew I wouldn't be seeing Bill. Only Merry hummed around the place as cheerful as ever. Just as I was about to call it a day, Johnnie came marching into my office and told me I had to take Bill to the offices in Milton Keynes tomorrow. Bill was standing behind him and as I looked up he winked at me, an amused look on his face.

When we got there the following morning, the place was in complete chaos. There was rubble everywhere, wires poking out at all angles, broken panes of glass and not a workman in sight. In fact the only evidence workmen had been there at all was innumerable issues of the *Sun* lying around, open of course at page three, enormous bosoms thrusting through the dust. There wasn't even a phone to pick up and shriek down. I eventually found a telephone kiosk that wasn't vandalized and tracked down the site manager.

'Yeah, sorry, love,' the patronizing voice of the builder said casually to me. 'Yeah, 'ad to take a couple of the boys to another job what we was running a bit late on. Don't you worry your pretty little 'ead about it.'

I was momentarily panic-struck and speechless, what on earth was Johnnie going to say? – other than gloat over the fact I was obviously not up to the job, as he'd suspected. In a little over three months the offices were supposed to be up and running.

'Yeah, well, like I said, be back in a coupla days,' he repeated, as though it was no big deal.

'Hey, darlin', let me have that.' Bill took the phone from my hand and proceeded to give the builder the biggest bollocking I have ever heard and then handed back the receiver.

'Yeah, well, like I said, the men will be there this arftanoon. Sorry about that, miss. It'll all be done in time for yer move.' The builder was sounding ultra grovelley.

I managed to thank him before turning to Bill, half furious, half grateful. 'This bloody world! Why is it a man can get a builder to jump through hoops and women are merely boob jobs on the floor of a building site? Thank you, but, God, I'm cross.'

He smiled at me. 'Life's just not fair. Accept it and you have an outside chance of drawing a few lucky cards.'

He moved closer and whispered, 'Carpe diem.'

'What?' I asked, Latin not being one of my languages.

'Seize the day. In this case, seize the dame.'

He pulled me out of the battered telephone booth, put both arms around me, causing me to drop the receiver, and proceeded to kiss me with such passion I couldn't breathe!

'Wow!' was the best I could muster when I eventually came up for oxygen. 'That was unexpected, and in such a romantic environment!'

'Just couldn't help myself. I've waited a long time.'

He looked at me intently, as if he was trying to read my mind. Which would have been impossible, such were the confusing thoughts racing around in my head. Then he kissed me again.

We must have looked very funny, pressed up against a telephone kiosk in such a barren place, but I didn't care. All sensible thought deserted me as this immaculately dressed, gorgeous-smelling, unbelievably attractive man let rip in the mouth-to-mouth department.

'Lunch?' he asked, after what seemed like far too short a time.

I hesitated before mumbling something about getting back to the office, at which he laughed.

'You're with me. You can do what you want.'

'Do you really think we're going to get something to eat here?' I gestured around me.

'Well,' he paused. 'I was thinking we might go back to London. My plane leaves this evening.'

I felt a stab of enormous disappointment when I learned he was leaving so soon. I hadn't realized his trip was going to be this short. The geography sucked.

'Let's go to London then,' I said more brightly than I felt.

We got back into his car, and despite the presence of the driver, he proceeded to kiss me again. He was an excellent kisser. I could have sworn the route the driver took back was much more convoluted because every time we turned a corner I slid across the leather farther on to Bill's lap, which he didn't seem to mind at all. Finally, I was sliding so far down the seat I was virtually on the floor. Bill pulled me up and asked if I wanted to eat at 47 Park Street.

I wondered if he knew the hotel didn't have a restaurant.

'They own Le Gavroche, we could eat there. Unless you'd like room service . . . ?' My nerves were jangling all over the place and it felt like I had the entire New Zealand rugby team in my stomach doing the Hukka. I must have looked terrified because he continued, 'We'll have a drink in the bar and then decide. Now, where was I?' He kissed me all the way to London. The poor driver.

Sitting in the bar, gulping down Krug, I wrestled with my thoughts. I was so nervous my hands were shaking. He was not in my Plan. But, my Plan wasn't working. What if I fell in love with him after sex? I know myself and I didn't want to start obsessing over someone who was so far out of reach. He was still married and yet had been single to all intents and purposes for ten years. His daughter and work were his priorities. Until now he had used them as excuses for not getting involved. Oh bugger it, I eventually reasoned, why not?

'You know,' I started slowly, 'one of my favourite meals is club sandwich, with fries. Does room service run to that?'

It was done, the first step into the abyss.

He put his hand on mine, which I was gratified to notice was shaking a bit as well. 'Sweetheart, they serve the best here.' He had such a gorgeous smile. 'Let's go, we can order upstairs.'

He took the champagne bottle and holding out his hand led me into the lift.

As the doors shut, he pinned me against the wall and started kissing me again, holding tight on to the back of my hair with his free hand. My legs buckled a little and he pulled me closer to him, releasing me only when we got to his floor.

He opened the door into his enormous suite and let me pass in front of him. I looked around, uncertain where to go, and opted for the living area. He followed me and went over to the drinks cabinet to find two fresh glasses, which he filled with the champagne, silently handing me one. Dutch courage, although why it's Dutch I have no idea. I needed Anglo-American courage.

'Cheers.' He raised his glass to me and I took another huge swig of champagne. 'Come over here, you don't need to be scared.'

I walked over to him. He gently took off my coat, which fell into a heap on the floor, removed my jacket and began to undo my shirt buttons. Miraculously, I was wearing a decent bra! He expertly removed it and I stood in front of him, naked from the waist up, shivering with nerves.

He ran a finger across my chest making me shiver and then bent down and kissed my neck. It was delicious. I took a final, huge swig of champagne and put my glass down. I raised my hands to his shoulders and pulled off his jacket. I fumbled clumsily with his tie, which I managed to tighten into a hard knot before eventually releasing it. Then I carefully undid his shirt, revealing a silver-haired, tanned chest.

'Let's go into the bedroom,' he said, not taking his eyes off my breasts. He held out his hand and led me into the next room.

Silently, he removed the rest of my clothes and then took

off his. He was in remarkable condition for a man of his age, tanned and toned. It was so long since I'd been to bed with anyone, well, a couple of months at least, and the first time with someone is sooooo nerve-wracking, especially when it's with someone you didn't expect it to be.

'Wow!' It was my turn to exclaim, 'you're in great shape for an old man!' I laughed in my nervousness.

'I'm burgundy, better with age.' It was a dreadful cliché, but he was right.

He pushed me on to the bed and I lay, pinned underneath him. And it was amazing. Leg-tremblingly, jaw-lockingly, scarily, A–mazing. He was gentle and tender and took so much time; like each part of my anatomy was a precious object. There was none of the haste of a younger man, eager to prove his virility, with little thought for his partner's satisfaction. A female's anatomy is much more complex than a man's, requiring an attention to detail many ignore. It's not just about shoving your willy in and out and expecting us to be grateful, admiring even. No, it happens in our heads, hopefully our hearts and, most importantly, involves that microscopic piece of body tissue we females know as the clitoris, a nether-region detail so unfamiliar to many males they either ignore it, or think it's only used by lesbians.

I lay in the glorious, tired and very happy after-glow of a good sexual experience, willing myself not to fall for this man.

'I'm hungry,' I said, 'can we eat?'

'Thought I already had.' He smiled at me, giving me a dirty wink and then leant across for the phone.

This was the life, I thought to myself as I wriggled around on the bed, in this beautiful room, beside this gorgeous man.

'So, darlin',' Bill turned to look at me, 'you OK?'

'More than. You were a revelation. My first older man.' I smiled at him. 'You've ruined me for ever.'

He looked frightfully pleased.

'I loved every minute of it. I knew I would the moment I set eyes on you.'

'Do you mean you had every intention of seducing me?' I asked, indignantly.

'Eventually, just didn't think it would be this good. Ah,' he said as there was a knock on the door, 'lunch. That was quick.'

It was such fun, eating, drinking and laughing in bed. It was only the knowledge he was leaving in a few hours' time that kept me reasonably grounded. I managed to restrain myself from asking when I would see him again, which was the only bit of restraint I did manage, as he rolled over, pushing the plates aside, and started kissing me again, sliding a warm hand between my thighs.

It was dusk when I woke up, my head against his shoulder, a leg straddling his. 'Oh my God! The boys will be wondering what on earth happened to me.'

'Don't worry,' he said, 'I called while you were sleeping. Said we were sorting some things out on site and you would be in tomorrow.'

'Thank you. I'm glad there are some advantages to sleeping with the boss,' I mumbled, wondering if my mascara had run and I looked awful.

'Well, if it's any consolation, I broke a rule too. I never mix business and pleasure, but you are a delightful exception.'

He got up and went into the bathroom and I realized he was getting ready to leave. I thought it was time I too was up and dressed.

'What time's your plane?' I asked through the shut bathroom door, once I had repaired my face and hair to a degree that didn't look totally 'shagged in'.

'I've got a car coming in half an hour.' He emerged wet, with a fluffy white towel wrapped round his waist. He was so attractive. 'Do you want some coffee?'

'No thanks, I'd better get going.' I found it hard to leave, but thought I should be the first one to do so – didn't want to look limpet-like. 'Thank you, I had a wonderful time.'

'Feelin''s entirely mutual. Now, I'm going to be travelling

around the States, so I won't be over in London for a while, but I'll be in touch.'

He came over and gave me a kiss on both cheeks and then, as if on second thoughts, pulled me to him and hugged me.

'Bye,' I said, sounding much more cheerful than I felt, thinking how strange it was now. Had I made the most awful mistake? God knows when I was going to see him again . . . I slowly shut the bedroom door behind me.

'Look, it was about time you had sex with someone,' said Bumble, pouring me a large vodka, 'I was beginning to think you might have become hermetically sealed.'

'Bumble!' I exclaimed, 'it's only been a couple of months. You don't moss over in such a short time. I was convinced my mother had, you know, but judging from the sound of her postcards, she found a man with a large pickaxe.'

'Shut up, that's disgusting,' said Bumble, wrinkling her nose. 'What do you mean only a couple of months. I thought you said you and Mats never had sex.'

She looked expectantly at me.

'Um, well. I may not have been having sex with Mats, but I did have a little fling just before I left Sweden. I mean, I would have gone mad with Mats, he had the sex drive of a panda in captivity – and you know how often they mate.'

It was astonishing really, not to mention extremely demoralizing. My boyfriend before Mats had been Italian, and his sexual appetite was so voracious I had to resort to head-aches! To go from him to someone whose idea of an active sex life was about every three months had been very difficult. I mean, I was in my twenties and, at a rough calculation, a year with Mats was the sexual equivalent of a day with Carlo!

'Oooh!' squeaked Bumble, 'tell me more.'

I sighed, realizing I was going to have to tell the story sometime. 'His name was Steffan. He was a darling man. Do you really want to hear this?' I asked her.

'Well anything's better than having to listen to you

mooning on about Bill.' She giggled. 'Come on, tell me.'

'Well,' I started slowly, 'as you know, along with all the other issues with Mats, there was this lack-of-sex thing. It was pretty dreadful really. There's a saying, "A good sex life takes up five per cent of your time and a bad sex life takes up ninety-five per cent of your time." Well, believe me, a non-existent sex life takes up a hundred per cent of your time. I was feeling really bad about myself, convinced there must be something wrong with me. And Mats was awful. Any time I suggested we might have sex, he said he was tired and I was oversexed, always so desperate, and finally, to cap it all, I had "no finesse in bed". That was it really, to be told I had "no finesse". I was convinced I had to be the worst lay in the world. Anyway, at a party one night I must have been looking a bit down, and one of Mats's friends, Steffan, came over to chat. He asked me what was wrong, and probably because I was a bit pissed, I blurted it all out, ending up with the 'and I'm rotten in bed' bit. Instead of finding me pathetic, Steffan hit the roof, saying it was an awful thing to label someone, etc., etc., even managing to make me laugh, which was quite astonishing. To cut a long story short, we had lunch a couple of days later and he said he was quite sure I wasn't bad in bed, but had just lost all my self-confidence. Major understatement! And if I would like, it would be his pleasure to give me lessons. According to him, no one is bad in bed, but some need a bit of help. It was definitely one of the more bizarre offers I've had. And although he was nice looking, tall and funny, I hadn't really thought about fancying him before. In fact, I'm not sure I did even then, but the Swedes are very practical about sex. They start doing it at such an early age, I think by the time they're in their twenties it's become a bit mundane for them. All moving in with each other and nesting in their early teens, like little middle-aged couples. Anyway, Steffan claimed to be something of an expert in the bedroom department and I decided I needed all the help I could get. Bumble, your ash is about to fall.' I shoved an ashtray under her untouched but smoking cigarette. Bumble was clearly riveted by all I was saying, her face a hilarious mixture of incredulity and fascination.

'So, the next day I went to his flat, nervous as hell, to begin my lessons. Stop it!' I threw a cushion at her as she started to laugh. 'I'm being serious. He greeted me with a glass of wine, which was pretty generous considering how expensive booze was in Sweden, and said he'd run a bath for me. There was a divine smell coming from the bathroom and he told me to go and soak in the bath, drink my wine and when I was ready he'd wash me. That was a first! He'd put candles all around the room and some sort of seductive Latin-type music was playing gently in the background. I slipped into the bath and told him he could come in. He had a bathrobe on, which in fact he kept on as he sat on the bath ledge behind me and started squeezing water out of a sponge over my neck and shoulders. It was lovely, and then he started to massage me, which was heaven. I turned round to him after what seemed like an age and asked him what he wanted me to do. "Just relax and enjoy it. I want you to do nothing at all. This is about you. Most important lesson in sex is to think about yourself. Everyone gets it wrong. Women need to learn to be selfish, to say, 'Do this, that does nothing for me, more, less, left a bit, right a bit.' Men don't come with the right navigation equipment and we need guiding. We think we know it all, but every woman is different. What works for one, doesn't necessarily for another. Today, we are going to start with the basics, touch, kiss, stroke." Did I tell you by the way, that all of this was in Swedish? It was very sexy.'

'Show off,' muttered Bumble. 'Carry on, I'm gripped.'

'So, I get out of the bath and he dries me. He's still in his robe and I'm completely naked, still a bit shy. Shy and dry. He took me into the bedroom and started to rub body cream all over me and I went off into a trance again. Then he began to get a bit more intimate, for want of a better description, and I panicked, thinking "orgasm pressure". It had been so long since I'd had one, I wasn't sure I was capable any more.

' "Relax," he said. "We have all afternoon, you don't need to rush. Just lie back and enjoy it. Don't think about me, just think about you and your body." And he carried on, kissing, stroking – well, I've no idea what else he was doing down there, but it was wonderful. It took a while, but the boy was persistent and extremely talented. I'd never thought about sex like that. I'd always thought it was about pleasing the other person. It's completely different when you do it for you, Steffan's theory being that a woman is much better in bed if she puts her own satisfaction first. After all, it's easy for a man, couple of shoves and they're away, well, most of the time. I was so relieved that everything was in working order, I cried. Anyway, I digress. He then goes out and brings me back a cup of coffee and sits on the edge of the bed and lights a cigarette for me! I hadn't smoked in bed for years, there's something so decadent about it. I told him it had been amazing and thanked him. "Don't thank me, we've only just begun. I enjoyed it too. How that Mats can say you lack finesse . . . " he looked so angry, it was sweet. And I really was beginning to feel better about myself. I asked him how he had learnt such talents. "Do you remember Kerstin? My ex-girlfriend? Well, she was older than me and more experienced. She taught me some and then we learnt a lot together. Sex is a continual process. To say you have to work at it makes it sound onerous, but you can't just keep to the same old routines, it becomes boring. And boring sex is unfulfilling sex and you end up not fancying the person any more."

'I realized, sadly, that that was precisely where Mats and I were. And so it started. I'd see him perhaps two or three times a week and each time we'd do something different. I found myself telling him what I liked, asking him what he liked. He'd take me out to lunch sometimes and we'd delay sex, just to increase the anticipation. Other times, he'd choose an unusual place to do it and we must have tried every position possible. Above all we had fun. Of course, the greatest irony of all, now I wasn't interested in Mats any more, was that he became interested in me. That's just typical in life isn't it?' I paused for a moment to reflect on this particular condundrum. 'We must give off completely different pheromones when we're not attracted to someone. Shame it isn't something you could learn to do, or take in pill form, just to give that impression. How much easier it would be to catch a man!'

'So what happened in the end?' asked Bumble. 'Why aren't you still with this paragon? He sounds like one in a million.'

'Well, that of course was the eventual problem. Stockholm is a small town and although we'd managed to keep our affair secret for a couple of months, it was only a matter of time before we were going to be found out. I'd decided I was going to leave Mats and I didn't want to stay in Sweden. I wasn't in love with Steffan. Of course I loved him, who wouldn't love a man who could do that to you? But not enough to stay in the country. People think love is all you need, but it's not. It's a good foundation, but I didn't want to put down my roots in Sweden. I wanted to get home. I'd lived in Sweden long enough to know no matter whom I was with, however lovely, it was not where I wanted my life to be. Not the place I wanted to bring up my children. When you have the frenzy of first infatuation, love, lust, whatever, you believe you'd live anywhere. But once you're actually going to spend the rest of your life with someone, reality creeps in. It's the add-on factors – friends, families, lifestyles, cultures, religions, you name it – they all have an input. You can't remain an emotional island. Finally, and this wasn't a deciding factor, there was the almighty great scandal that would ensue once people found out what had been going on. Mats could be very frightening at times, it didn't bear thinking about. So I'm back here. Steffan is over there. He was quite cut up about my leaving. The professor had become very fond of his pupil. But he understood. He was, still is, a wonderful man and some lucky woman will benefit from him, but not me. He changed my life and I will for ever owe him.'

'Well,' said Bumble, getting up with a very peculiar look on her face, 'Gareth's in for the shock of his life tonight!'

21

The boys were extremely nice to me when I arrived at work the next day, which was very worrying. I hoped some unseen builder hadn't reported me snogging Bill in a phone booth.

Johnnie called me into their office. 'Um, Polly. B–Bill called just as he was leaving.'

Oh shit, I thought. I hoped I wasn't turning red, because my cooling system seemed to be failing.

'He said that you gave a great performance yesterday' (I was definitely over-heating!) 'with the builders, who I gather had been off site but now seem to be back on track. So, congratulations, if we manage to keep on schedule I'll be extremely happy.' He gave me a rare smile, adding, 'Thank you.'

'I'm glad you're pleased,' I said, overwhelmed. 'I expect I'll have to spend a bit more time there, to make sure they actually do turn up.'

'Yes, of course. Oh and one more thing. I . . . um, I was d–due to have lunch with someone today and they've just cancelled. Would you like to join me instead?'

I nearly fell to the floor. I looked across at Hugo, who's head was buried in papers, but I could see he was smiling and deliberately avoiding looking at me.

'I, er, yes, thanks.'

'Right, then.' He resumed his abrupt manner. 'Twelve-thirty at the Caprice.'

I managed to return to my office without bursting out laughing. What a joke. Suddenly Johnnie's being nice to me? Just after I'd spent yesterday afternoon shagging his boss? He wouldn't be so quick to take me out to lunch if he knew that!

In fact, he'd be horrified. I was feeling a bit strange, day-after blues or something. The whole episode seemed slightly unreal. I decided that the only way to treat it was as a one-night stand, or rather a one-day stand. I may see him again, I may hear from him and, equally, I may not. I would not let it divert me from my path to finding a suitable husband. It had been just a very nice little stroll down a lane, but it was time to go back on the motorway again. Plus, I had a lot of work to do, which would occupy the rest of my time.

Johnnie was obviously very well known at the Caprice, which wasn't so surprising considering he ate there almost every day. Jesus, the unbelievably suave *maître d'* ushered us with great reverence to two seats at the bar, where side by side we ate delicious food – how anyone can make fishcakes and burgers that exotic beats me – and shared a bottle of Sancerre. Johnnie was surprisingly good company out of the office and I gradually began to relax a little, due in some part to the wine.

'Don't give me any more to drink, Johnnie, I've got to go to glorious Milton Keynes this afternoon with Rohan.'

'Why are you taking Rohan?' he asked, curiously.

'Oh, we have to meet the electrician to discuss something horribly technical to do with computer points and systems which only he can sort out. He's very clever.'

Johnnie looked serious.

'They're a funny lot down there,' he said; 'silent almost to the point of rudeness, unhelpful and demotivated.'

I paused, collecting my thoughts, wondering if this was the moment to say something. Definitely too much wine, because I opened my mouth.

'Johnnie, please don't take offence at what I'm going to say, but they're like that because you've never really bothered to talk to them. They have no idea what's going to happen to them. They're worried about their jobs and some of them have families to support. They find you completely unapproachable, which, to be honest, is not surprising. You know, sometimes you do behave as if you exist on another planet. In fact,' I said, drawing in a breath, 'you can be a complete arse sometimes.'

He gave me a very direct look, which was extremely disconcerting. I thought I might have gone too far.

'I was wondering what Hugo had up his sleeve when he suggested I take you out to lunch. I didn't realize it would be so – anatomical.'

So, Hugo was behind this! I was mildly irritated to think it hadn't been Johnnie's idea.

'So, what do you suggest I do?' he asked, not appearing to be too put out by my frankness.

I said trying to be nice to the people who worked for him would be a start.

He looked amazed. 'Polly, I come from a background of investment banking; people are so highly paid, they don't mind how badly they're treated. Even secretaries are paid a fortune. We're in an economic boom, there's no room for this cuddly environment of yours.'

I made a mental note to put in for a pay rise and continued on my reckless theme. 'But these people are not in investment banking, they work in a small company which is owned by an investment bank. None of them are paid anything like that. You have to treat them differently, make them feel part of a team. If they like you, they'll work better. Not everyone is motivated by fear and greed. Try pride and interest. Listen, if you've got the time, why don't you come to the new offices this afternoon with Rohan? He's a really nice man. Without him and his systems there wouldn't be a company.'

'Right then,' he said with conviction, 'I will. The only condition is we take my car, I hate being driven and that little thing of yours is quite ridiculous.'

'Johnnie, you still have a long way to go in terms of people skills. I love that car.' I was really annoyed; we couldn't all afford a massive BMW.

'Sorry,' he said, chastened, 'thank you for t–telling me off.'

What an interesting turn of events. I wondered if he was one of those men who liked being told off, eugh! Or wanted to be spanked – or worse, whipped by a big, fat dominatrix! I tried hard to get the picture out of my head and to compose my thoughts.

Rohan's face was very funny when he saw Johnnie was going to drive us. 'Thought it was time that I learnt more about what you did, Rohan,' said Johnnie, politely, 'and perhaps there are some things you might be able to explain to me. Polly says there isn't anything about the companies you don't know.'

It was all a bit hard to take in, this suddenly oozily charming Johnnie. Rohan was eating out of his hand within minutes. It was amazing that someone who could be so objectionable could be so nice when they tried.

As we returned to the office at the end of the day, Johnnie told Rohan to talk to the staff about the plans for the future.

Emerging from a reverie in the back of the car – the sight of the telephone kiosk had me drifting back to the afternoon in 47 Park Street! – I said, 'Johnnie, why don't *you* tell them? Have a little drinks party or something next Friday evening; I can organize it for you and you can explain what's happening in a less formal style. That way they might not be so worried about their future. Or so wary of you,' I added.

'All right, Polly. Good idea. That all right with you, Rohan?'

'Fine, er, yes, Johnnie.' Rohan turned to look at me and winked. 'How the hell did you manage that?' was the first thing he said to me after Johnnie had disappeared into his office.

'Well, I don't know really. I had a couple of glasses of wine and just sort of blurted out that he needed to be more approachable. I don't know how long it'll last, but at least he's trying.'

'He's quite a nice sort of bloke underneath all that tailoring,' said Rohan.

'Hmmm,' I said, remembering only too well how appalling he could be and not convinced of the new model yet. 'Let's see how it goes. But it's certainly an improvement and I'm going to enjoy organizing this little soirée. So, how many people?'

The time flew, and the following week was finished off by what turned out to be a rip-roaringly successful party, even if I do say so. Johnnie was charm personified, Hugo attentive and looking as though anything anyone said to him was the most fascinating piece of information he'd ever heard. Samantha, who was speaking to me again, came along; even Merry sacrificed a drinks party to put in an appearance. It was all good, except I hadn't heard a word from Bill.

'He'll call,' said Frank, later that evening, as we sat in the pub, 'eventually. He's a busy man and he told you that he was travelling a lot.'

'There's always time to pick up a phone, I don't care what men say. I really, really hate not hearing from someone. I don't want hundreds of calls a day, but just one would be nice. Otherwise, I feel like I must have been a lousy lay, or a really boring person they can't wait to get rid of.'

'Polly, this is a ridiculous lapse in self-esteem. You're being quite absurd. I love you. Everyone loves you.' (He had had a bit to drink and was exaggerating.) 'Even that mad git in your office seems to like you, so stop being silly. He's one man and not one you want anyway. You got laid, end of story. Don't romanticize everything.'

'I'm a girl, it's what we do,' I protested.

'You're right on that score,' Frank said ruefully, 'probably why I never go out with them. Frightened of all that "Oh why don't you love me?" business.'

'Is that why you never have a steady girlfriend?' I asked him, curious. 'Because you don't want to get involved? You must have felt something for a girl once? Did you get your heart broken and resolve never to get involved again?'

Frank laughed. 'You girls! It's never that simple. I'm just not interested.'

(Oh help, maybe Samantha was right and he *was* gay.)

'But, Frankie, what do you do for sex?'

I was venturing into uncharted terrain, not even sure I wanted the answer.

'Hookers.' He hiccuped – we had drunk a lot.

'I beg your pardon?' I wasn't sure I had heard right.

'I said *hookers!*'

'Shhh! Frank, everyone will hear you.' I looked around to see if anyone had. 'Why? Where do you find them? You don't just pick them up on street corners, do you?'

'Don't be ridiculous. I use an agency. Bloody expensive, but fan-bloody-tastic girls.' He hiccuped again.

'I don't understand. You're gorgeous, clever, funny, you drive an amazing car, you could get anyone you want and not have to pay for it.'

'No complications. That's what I pay for. No bloody compli-bloody-cations. I don't have to talk to them, wine or dine them, listen to their problems and, above all, I don't have to question their motives. They do what I say and then go away. They even take credit cards. I have my friends and I have my hookers. Two separate entities. I like it that way.'

I was nonplussed. I'd known Frank for years and had never so much as suspected – but then, why would I? 'Does everyone know?' I asked, wondering if I'd been spectacularly slow in not guessing.

'No, silly. Just you. I thought you'd understand, not react like some outraged adolescent.' He looked a bit bleak and disappointed.

'I'm not reacting like an outraged adolescent, that's not fair. It's just not exactly – ' I paused, not wanting to say 'normal' because for all I knew it might be, 'usual.'

'Polly, you'd be very surprised at just how busy these girls are. I'm not alone. Loads of businessmen use them for all the same reasons. Lots of married men, happy but bored at home, who don't want the complications of an affair to rock their little world. They're not going to get pregnant, they're not after your money, they just want to get paid for doing a job. Some of them are so good it makes the idea of going to bed with an amateur quite unappealing frankly.'

'Well, don't ever tell that to a girl you do want to get into the sack, she'll be inhibited for ever! Even me, and I've had some lessons.'

He looked up, curious. 'Ah ha! So, tell me. I think I might like this story.' He had a smile back on his face now.

Once again, I found myself telling the Steffan story.

At the end and another couple of vodkas later, he said, 'So you see. What you did wasn't very different.'

'I think it is entirely different!' I squeaked. 'For a start I didn't pay him. And secondly, I really liked him.'

'Are you saying I don't like some of the girls? Well, you'd be wrong, I even have regulars.'

It was all very confusing. I tried to explain that my time with Steffan had been with a view to having a better relationship – self-improvement or something. I didn't do it with the specific intention of *not* having relationships with other people.

'Frankie, darling, you're as rich as Croesus and think that's why a girl would want you. On top of which you're terrified some girl might get pregnant just to use you as a meal ticket. You have heard of condoms, haven't you?'

'Yes, and I use them,' he said.

'Good. Well, I think you hide from emotional attachment.'

'Don't psychobabble me, you have no idea what you're talking about.' He sounded irritated.

'Well, you should know what I'm talking about. After all, you're the shrink.'

'No, I'm a psychiatrist, we hand out drugs not ridiculous hand-holding sympathy drivel.'

'Ouch,' I replied. 'You really are in denial.'

'Bloody hell, woman. This is just my point. Why does every-thing have to centre on emotions. I have feelings. It's quite simple, I just don't want complications. If some wonderful person comes along and takes my breath away, then fabulous. In the meantime let me get on with my life as I wish to and don't judge me by your Mills and Boon-type standards.'

'OK. OK. You've made your point. I've never read a single Mills and Boon by the way. I'm a woman and, therefore, according to your definition, incapable of understanding. I hope one day you will meet some wonderful woman whom you trust enough to have a relationship with that does not involve currency.'

'Don't kid yourself, Polly. All relationships with women involve money, it's just some are more open about it than others.'

'I think you're very cynical.'

'Maybe. But that's my experience. Come on you, time to go home.'

We got rather unsteadily out of the pub and tottered over to his car.

'New model again?' I said, as I slipped into the newest looking Aston Martin I'd ever seen.

'Gorgeous, isn't it?' he said with pride, screeching out of the little lane and into Hyde Park Corner. 'Want to see how fast it goes?'

Without waiting for an answer, he put his foot on the accelerator and my head was thrown back against the headrest as he zipped on to Park Lane, going at what felt like a hundred miles an hour.

'Slow down!' I pleaded. 'You'll get caught.'

'Not in this, I won't!' He laughed and went even faster. Thank God there wasn't much traffic, nor any police. He nipped in and out of the other cars and carried on down Edgware Road, turning abruptly right at some lights, hurling me against the window. I grabbed my seat-belt, checking it was fastened. Frank wasn't even wearing his! Sharp left again and another screech of burning rubber and left again on to the Marylebone Flyover. I swear we were doing a hundred and fifty miles an hour. I was terrified. I love cars and speed, but this was a nightmare. I pleaded with him to slow down, I was beginning to feel really scared.

'OK, OK,' he said, reluctantly reducing his speed to a moderate hundred. 'We'll turn off at Hammersmith and get you home.'

'You're mad, Frank, what on earth would have happened if the police had caught you?'

'You don't listen, typical woman. They can't catch me.'

'Yes well. I think you're potty, you may be a very good driver and this car is amazing, but don't do that again, at least not with me. And will you wear your blasted seat-belt?' I leant over and clicked it into place, my hands still shaking a little.

I was relieved to step over the threshold of Altonative Towers in one piece. I could hear the noise of the Aston Martin receding down the road, Frank with his foot back on the throttle, and I wondered who or what he was racing from.

22

'Good *grief!*' shrieked Merry when she opened the door of Michael's small house in the Kings Road. 'I've never seen you in clothes like *that* before!'

I wasn't in my most outrageous get-up, but clearly the change from my office outfit was different enough.

'Yes, well, that's just my work wardrobe,' I muttered.

'But you look a *million* times better. I never realized you had legs. Throw those other clothes away *immediately*! Now, come inside and meet everyone.'

She led me into the drawing-room and over to a clean-cut, bespectacled but attractive man in his mid-thirties. 'Polly, this is my Michael. Michael, Polly.' I held out my hand. I had been hoping to meet the famous Michael for the first time at Merry's long-promised dinner party.

'Ah, hallo,' he said in clipped tones. 'How verry nice to meet you at last. I've heard so much about you from Miranda.'

Merry continued to haul me around the room. 'And this is Bella, and Araminta, two of my *greatest* friends, and Bella's husband Tom. And these two are George and Haldo.' She turned to give me an extremely unsubtle wink. 'Boys, say hallo to Polly.'

'Hallo, Polly,' they said in unison. They were pretty indistinguishable, in the compulsory Hooray kit of alarming coloured cords, open-necked shirts and loud jumpers. Their gold signet rings flashed at me. They both had what my mother would describe as 'ruddy complexions'. I couldn't work out if it was the country air they'd recently vacated or the booze.

'Can I get you something to drink?' asked one of them, as Merry disappeared to busy herself in the kitchen.

'White wine, please,' I said gratefully. I was finding it rather daunting, being at a dinner party with a group of people who all seemed to know each other.

'Tell me,' said George or Haldo. 'What do you do?'

I groaned inwardly, back to social bottom-sniffing again.

We managed to make polite conversation until we were led into the dining-room. It was really quite grown up, matching plates and cutlery, nice glasses. I wondered what they could possibly put on their wedding list.

Everyone drank a huge amount: my glass was constantly refilled, refusals completely ignored. After what seemed like endless discussions about engagement rings, parties and wedding preparations, we then covered equally foreign territory to me, shooting, stalking and fishing. I was struggling to add anything to the conversation, until at last we got on to something I could do.

'Do you ski?' asked George (I had now worked out which one was which).

'I do, I spent a couple of seasons in France.'

'Rarely?' drawled one of the girls, 'where were you?'

'At Les Arcs and Meribel.'

'Oh! I *love* Meribel,' said Merry. 'Michael, are we going skiing this year?'

He looked nonplussed for a moment. 'Er, well, do you think there's enough time? What with the engagement party and the wedding?' He looked like a man completely taken over by events.

'Of *course*! I'll start looking tomorrow. You are *so* kind darling.'

I don't think Michael had realized he'd said yes.

'Were you cooking out there?' the other girl asked me.

'Actually, no.' (I loved this bit!) 'I was a ski guide.'

'Rarely?' she looked astonished. 'You must be a frightfully good skier.'

'Well, not really, certainly not at the beginning.'

'So why did you go?' someone else asked.

I could see I was going to have to tell the whole unlikely story.

While completely unappealing to me, winter ski jobs are popular, and you're considered to have landed the best if you're a rep. I ended up in France by default and not design. I'd spent the previous year working for a travel company in Capri, where I'd virtually grown up and where I had my passionate romance with Carlo, a local boy I'd known since my late teens, who was utterly gorgeous. Right at the last minute the company had some problem with a rep in Les Arcs and sent me as a replacement. Despite my protestations that I couldn't ski and my bags were all packed with skimpy bikinis and strappy sandles to return to Italy, on the flimsiest of grounds (I spoke French) I was told if I wanted to stay employed it was on my skis, or on my bike.

I seriously didn't want to go. I hate the cold, had never skied and was not going to be able to see my divine Italian.

I arrived, shivering, at the resort, which was all white and like a sort of lunar landscape. It was very modern, very high at eighteen hundred metres – I also suffer from vertigo – and of course nobody believed I couldn't ski. All the other reps were seasoned performers and it was an impossible concept to them that someone would not want to be in the snow.

A couple of the girls took pity on me and kitted me out correctly, before I died of hypothermia. 'No such thing as bad weather, just bad dressing,' was an oft repeated mantra, as I struggled into layers and layers of clothes. Huge great clumpy things adorned my feet, both on and off the slope. I looked and felt like a Yeti. I had ten days before my first clients arrived to learn to ski. I remain convinced nothing is more tiring than learning to ski. Certainly, nothing is so physically damaging. I was covered in bruises, stiff, sore, cold and, even worse, having spent so long in Italy, I found my French had completely deserted me and I kept calling everyone 'Signor' instead of 'Monsieur' and saying 'Si' instead of 'Oui'. It was appalling.

I'd been there a week and the first night I went out with some of the girls I met Mats. He was working for a Swedish company. To say he looked like a picture on the lid of a Christmas biscuit tin, would not have been doing him justice. He was the best-looking man I had ever seen. Even Carlo didn't quite compare. Tall, tanned and very blond, he had brilliant blue eyes, a huge smile (with perfect teeth) and spoke fluent English with an American accent. He was also incredibly arrogant and appeared completely uninterested in all the other reps, who'd been vying for his attention since day one. I'd heard about this Adonis-like creature, who was also rumoured to be the best skier in the whole resort – which naturally is the accolade to have – but had yet to meet him. Too busy falling down. Anyway, we were sitting in the bar, when up he strolls. There was a collective sigh from everyone as he sat down.

'So,' he said. 'Who's this chick that can't ski?'

The girls looked blank.

'Come on,' he continued. 'There's a story going round about some girl here, keeps talking Italian, supposed to be a ski guide but has never been on skis before. I know the Brits are bad skiers, but I have a beer on it just being a wind-up. British fake-modesty and all.'

It was quite true, all the reps seemed to play this game of 'oh I don't ski very well' in order to show off immensely the next day.

Still the girls, loyally, said nothing.

Reluctantly, I piped up, 'Ah, well, that would be me.'

'Right,' he said. 'I gotta earn that beer. Come skiing with me tomorrow.'

Immediately two things happened. First, every girl I was sitting with changed from friend to foe, as they had all been dying to go skiing with Mats, and secondly, I was filled with such a horror at the thought of even having to share a ski-lift with this man, I just stared gormlessly at him with my mouth open.

There was a huge pause.

'Are you asking me, or telling me?' I composed myself and sounded more belligerent than I felt. He threw his head back and roared with laughter.

'Well, at least you have a bit of spirit. I'll see you at nine-thirty tomorrow by the main chair-lift. What's your name, by the way?' He got up to go.

'Polly, and I can't ski!' I wailed.

'Yeah, right.' He turned his back on us and walked away. It struck me later he hadn't even bothered to introduce himself. He assumed we'd all know who he was.

'It's not my fault, don't look at me like that. I don't even like him. He's scary. You go skiing with him tomorrow,' I babbled to the girls, adding, 'please.'

But they had no sympathy.

In Les Arcs they had a method of teaching called Ski Evolutif, which meant you started on very small skis and progressed to longer ones the more proficient you became. Needless to say, I was still on baby skis when I turned up the following morning at the main chair-lift, which I had hitherto never been near! Despite my dread, I had to admit to myself he looked glorious in his red ski-suit, like Father Christmas's son.

'I knew you could ski,' said Mats, as I just managed to avoid colliding with him.

'What do you mean?' I asked indignantly.

'You've got trick skis on, I know what you're doing.'

'They're not trick skis, they're the Ski Evolutif skis,' I protested.

But because all Swedes are virtually born with skis on their feet Mats wouldn't have any reason to know about someone needing to learn to ski. As a result, he didn't have a clue about this new method.

'Yeah, right.' He completely ignored my comments and continued, 'Come on, get on the next chair with me.'

I'd only just had the lesson 'getting on and off the chair lift' so could at least manage to hop on with a little more grace than usual. But the lift went on and on *and on*. Higher and higher we climbed.

'Mats,' I said, anxiously, 'where are we going?'

'Right to the top.'

'But, it's a black run. I'll never get down. I've only ever been on a green run before.' I was panicking.

'Yeah, right,' he said with a smile.

'Will you stop "yeah righting" me. This is not funny.' I was getting furious with him but he wouldn't listen to me. I was also slightly hysterical, I'd never been so high and thought I was going to pass out every time I looked down. I gripped the bar in front of me tighter, staring straight ahead.

After what seemed like for ever in silence, we arrived at the top of the most terrifying mountain I'd ever been on.

He pushed the bar away just before we had to jump off. I appeared to have lost all sensation in my bottom and I wondered if my legs would work. I started praying, over and over again. Please God, don't let me fall down. Please God, keep me upright when I get out of the chair. Please God, let this be a horrible dream.

Somehow I managed it. Thank you, God.

'Race you to the bottom,' he called out to me over his shoulder, pushed on his poles and with a *whoosh!* was off. I was marooned at the top of this Everest-like peak, entirely alone. It was terrifying. Well, I guessed the only way back was down.

I started off tentatively. What lay ahead bore no resemblance to any of the smooth, wide, gentle slopes I'd been on. There were mounds, lumps, craters, black bits, rocks. I had no idea how to get down. The only clear areas of path were about two inches wide and appeared to be sheer drops. I navigated a little bit and then sat down with a bump. I really couldn't do it. Mats was a little red speck in the distance below. I got up again and negotiated a little more and then fell on to a huge lumpy thing, covered in snow. I was getting a bit breathless with fear. I looked around, I couldn't even seen Mats now. I sat on my bottom and slid down for a while, until the *piste* looked a little less menacing. I got back up on the skis. This is ridiculous, I thought. I must be able to do better. I'd been on skis five days now, I couldn't have learned nothing! Pushing my poles into the snow with determination, I put my legs together and decided to go for it. And it was fine. For about thirty seconds. And then one of the huge white lumpy things came out of nowhere at me, I swerved to avoid it and fell off the *piste*. And I didn't stop falling; first my skis came off, then I lost a pole, then the other one. My goggles filled with snow and came off. Over and over I turned. I'm going to die, I know, I am going to die and I shall come back from the dead and *kill* that bastard Mats. I managed to cover my head with my arms as I fell farther and farther down. Eventually I stopped. I was not only covered in snow, I had snow in my boots, in my sleeves, down my neck. I hardly dared move in case I'd broken something. I raised my head. Where the hell was I? I couldn't even hear the clank of a ski-lift. Oh fantastic. I sat up. I could move my upper body; my arms were sore, but functioning. My head hurt where it had been knocked. I wriggled my toes in a snow-filled boot. Yes, working. Not paralysed. Just bloody freezing. And I was marooned!

Whoosh! There was a sudden noise beside me as yet more snow got flung in my face. 'I have never seen anything so funny in all my life!' Mats was standing above me, holding his sides with laughter. 'You really can't ski, can you?' He could hardly stand up straight.

'You could have killed me, you irresponsible bastard! What kind of ski guide are you? I told you I couldn't ski and what do you do? Brilliant, take me to the top of some impassable, impossible rock face and desert me. I've probably broken a leg under all this snow. Or I've got concussion, my head hurts dreadfully – and all you can do is laugh. And I've lost my skis, poles, gloves, not to mention my dignity. Piss off and leave me alone. I'm going to wait for some nice person to rescue me. You're the last person I ever want to see again.'

'I'm sorry.' He managed to look a tiny bit chastened through his smile. 'How many fingers am I holding up?'

'Two fingers, most appropriate.'

'Come on, I'll help you up. I don't think you're concussed, you're too stroppy. We can walk to the nearest chair, it's not too far. I know the slopes like the back of my hand. That is, if you can walk.' He held out his hand and pulled me up. My legs, though wobbly, seemed to function. Certainly better than with skis on the end of them.

Slowly we navigated our way to a chair-lift and I sank, exhausted, on the seat.

Halfway down to the resort, he said, 'Let's get off here, if you can manage it. I at least owe you a drink, but maybe you should eat something as well. It's good for shock.'

'Yes, well, the biggest shock is you being nice now,' I muttered, 'and what about my skis and poles and other things?'

'I'll arrange for one of the *pisteurs* to get them for you, I can pretty much work out where they are. Now, have a hot chocolate with brandy and a croissant. You'll feel much better.'

He was right, after two hot chocolates with lots of brandy, I felt much better! I even decided I quite liked Mats, who was very funny and charming, not to mention, drop-dead gorgeous.

'I think I need to make this up to you,' he said.

'I agree, I'm thinking of a penance as we speak.'

'Did you just say penis?' exclaimed Mats incredulously. 'Wow, you British girls . . . '

'You bloody dirty Swedes, more like; the last thing I'm thinking of is a penis, you idiot. I said penance, you know, act of contrition – oh forget it. I'm never going to ski again.'

'That's a real shame, I think you're the worst skier I've ever seen in my life. Don't rob us of the spectacle so soon.'

'I did try to tell you, but oh no, you wouldn't listen.'

'How about I teach you to ski?' he asked.

Oh fantastic, I thought. Not only will I have no girlfriends, I'll have no legs if I have to go to the top of a black run again.

'I think your methods are a little advanced for me,' I said. 'Anyway, can you teach?'

'Of course I can,' he leant forward, conspiratorially, 'and don't tell anyone else, but I'm the best skier in the resort.' He looked very pleased with himself.

'It still doesn't make you a good teacher. In fact, you'd be bored out of your mind,' I retorted.

'No, I like a challenge. What do you say? Do we have a deal?'

It was impossible to refuse. And that was how I learnt to ski.

All this made for a rather long anecdote, and having told it, I looked at the faces around the dining-room

'What a story,' said George.

'What a way to learn to ski,' sighed one of the girls, wistfully.

'What happened to him?' asked Merry.

'Even longer story, which I won't bore you with, I've talked enough. But we ended up going out, of course. Italian boyfriend disappeared off the scene in a major and amazed strop. I went to live with Mats in Sweden. Came back here a few months ago.'

There was a lot of editing.

'Sweden's loss is our gain,' George raised his glass to me.

'Thank you.'

At about midnight, I said I really had to go and George offered to give me a lift home.

He stumbled as we left the house and I realized he was quite drunk.

'Are you all right to drive?' I asked nervously.

'Absolutely fine,' he replied very firmly.

I was a bit doubtful, but it was only a short journey back. He drove, badly, to Earl's Court.

'George, what are we doing here?' I looked at the unfamiliar surroundings.

'Thought you might like to come in for a nightcap.' He glanced expectantly at me.

Good grief! I was stunned. Why on earth would he think I would want to go up for a 'nightcap'? Must be all the talk of living in Sweden; clearly he thinks I'm an easy lay.

'No, thank you,' I replied, coldly. 'I'd like to go home.'

'Hold on.' He swerved the car abruptly to the side of the road, opened the car door and was violently sick.

I hate vomit! I hate people being sick more than anything I know. I struggled with the passenger-door lock, desperate to get out.

'Sorry about that,' he said, wiping his mouth, adding quite unnecessarily, 'Bit too much to drink.'

'Clearly,' I replied, trying not to look at him.

'So, do you want to come up?' he asked again.

It was ridiculous. 'No, I don't. I'm going to get a taxi home.'

'How about a little kiss then?'

I couldn't believe my ears. 'No way! Are you insane?'

I really couldn't open the blasted door and the smell was becoming overpowering. I thought I might be ill any minute.

'Ah, I know what you Swedish girls are like.'

He tried to grab me, but I had managed to open the door and fled into the night.

23

'I am, really I am.'

I sat with Bumble at the end of the week, drinking a large vodka, lime and soda, puffing on a cigarette.

'You are what?' she asked idly.

'I'm going to have to put Plan B into action. Take up carpentry and build my shelf. Plan A is absolutely not working. These last couple of months have been a disaster.'

'Not entirely. What about Bill?'

'He doesn't live here. It took him ten days to phone me. I don't know when I'm going to see him again. He's lovely, but unobtainable. It's perfectly obvious I'm doomed to be a spinster. I must get a cat immediately.'

Bumble chuckled. 'Well, at least he rang.'

'Yes, I know. And he was really nice on the phone, but he's not coming over for ages. I just never meet any nice Englishmen. Where are they all hiding?'

'What about George? He might be nice when he's sober,' said Bumble, mischievously.

'Oh! P–leeeze. That was the worst ever. Besides, he seems to think I'm some sort of Swedish tart. Merry thought it was hysterical; apparently he rang the next day and said what a nice girl I was, quite omitting to tell her he virtually threw up all over me! Wanted my phone number. Bloody cheek.'

'You never know, you might meet some more eligible men at her wedding. Which reminds me, when is Julia's hen night?'

'Oh God, I'd completely forgotten. It's next Friday. I can't think why she's invited me, I hardly know her. And I hate hen nights. All those hysterical women, do I have to go?'

'Of course you do,' said Bumble, firmly. 'She's one of my oldest friends and she's getting married.'

'It still doesn't explain why I have to go,' I replied.

'Well, I think she's very grateful for all the money you've made her; and anyway, I can't possibly go on my own, I'm terrified. A room full of people talking about sex all the time! It's bad enough living here. I need moral support so you have to come. Now hurry up, I've got to get dinner ready. Your mother's arriving any minute. Gareth phoned from the airport and said he'd tracked her down. He thinks she might be a bit pissed.' She giggled.

'Oh no!' I groaned. My mother had clearly not got over her fear of flying.

A little while later the front door opened. 'Darling!' came the familiar voice. 'Where's my darling daughter?'

My mother stood in the hallway, with Gareth behind, laden with bags. She raced, unsteadily, towards me.

'How is my beautiful baby? I've missed you sooooo much! Darling Bumble, how lovely of you to send darling Gareth to collect me, I really didn't want to spend my first night alone, particularly as I haven't seen my darling Polly.'

We were dripping in darlings. She enveloped me in a fug of brandy fumes, covering me with kisses.

'Still don't like flying, mother?' I enquired, amused.

'What do you mean?' She pulled herself up and regarded me haughtily, 'I only had a couple of glasses of wine.'

'No brandy then?'

'Well, darling, that doesn't count, purely medicinal. Settles the stomach. Oh, Gareth darling, would you take my cases upstairs for me? Thank you so much.'

She turned back to me. 'Isn't he lovely? Now, where's Melanie? I brought her a monkey from Malaysia.'

'Melanie?' I wasn't sure whom she meant.

'No, darling, Bumble's daughter, what's her name?'

'Minnie, mummy.'

'That's right, knew it began with an M. Where is she? Coooeeey, Minnieeee, where are you? Now where's the monkey? Oh, upstairs with Gareth, silly me. I'll go and get it.

Maybe Gareth can tell me where she is, as you two clearly have no idea.' She tottered perilously upstairs.

Bumble was laughing. 'I do love your mother. She's such fun!'

'Well, she has her moments, certainly,' I replied.

We sat down for supper about half an hour later.

'I do so much prefer you blonde, darling,' said my mother, looking across the table at me, 'couldn't bear you with brown hair, so dingy. I was thinking of going blonde myself. What do you think? Now I've lost so much weight I thought it might suit me?'

'Well, I . . . ' I couldn't imagine my dark-haired mother as a blonde; I found it rather disconcerting, 'maybe . . . '

'Just look at my trousers, falling off me.' She stood up and pulled at the waistband of her, admittedly very loose-fitting, trousers. She turned sideways. 'And look, no tummy!'

'Fantastic, mother. Very impressive. What did you do, eat a worm?' I was uncomfortably aware I must have put on about half a stone since I'd been living with Bumble.

'Now, now. Don't be jealous,' cooed my mother, 'it's called the Divorce Revenge Diet!'

'I remember it well,' I muttered. 'Hope you keep the weight off. I didn't.'

'Oh, darling.' My mother sat down with a bump. 'I am so sorry, I forgot. How *is* poor Mats?'

'Poor Mats?! Mummy, I have no idea, I haven't spoken to him for months. I'm sure he's fine, running around with his ex-girlfriend, I gather.'

'He must be missing you – oh yes, please, Gareth darling, I'd love some more of that delicious wine.' She took a sip and put on her crystal-ball, mystic voice. 'You can never go back, you know.'

'Mummy, I have no intention of going back,' I snapped.

'Not you, him. You can't reheat yesterday's dinner – although, darling Bumble, this food is so delicious we could make an exception – once the vase has broken, you can't use it again.'

Her analogies were flowing confusingly fast and I could sense another of her little maxims coming.

'What do you mean, Hermione?' asked Bumble, who hung on my mother's every word.

'A relationship is like a beautiful vase, with flowers in.'

I groaned inwardly, her voice had gone completely Gypsy Rose Lee.

'When the relationship breaks down, imagine it's the vase. You can glue it back together, you can do it so well you can't even see the cracks, but . . . ' she paused dramatically, 'you can never use it as a vase again. It's changed irrevocably. No strength to hold water, only paper flowers. Same as relationships, it's never the same again. No, no. When you break up with someone, there should be no going back. I wouldn't go back to my ex. Not ever! I am so much *happier* now.' Her voice resumed its normal tone, 'Oh, thank you, Gareth. I get so thirsty when I talk, must be the jet lag. Now, let me tell you about my trip.'

She entertained us with her stories for the rest of the evening. Looking at her talking away, I couldn't deny she looked incredible. Tanned and slim, her face animated, her hands waving about expressively, rings glinting. Not only beautiful, but funny, she had us all in stitches, giving voices to the characters she had met on the way, of which there were a myriad. She really had gone round the world, as opposed to round the bend.

'And then I met this lovely man in Penang.' She paused for a moment, expecting a reaction.

'Yes, mother. I gathered from your postcards. What was he like?' I asked.

'Well, you'll meet him, darling. He's coming to England next week. I'm quite sure you'll loathe him.' She turned to Bumble, 'She doesn't like my male friends, darling, Can't think why.'

Which was not fair really, it was just her men friends to date had consisted of love-struck wimps, entranced by her, suffering from some kind of deluded, unrequited love. Mother adored having her admirers, but never *did* anything with them.

'Mummy, if any of them were real men, I might like them. But they're so wet!'

My mother turned to me and said, 'Well, you won't be able to describe this one as wet. He's completely broken the mould. He's big and tough and from Yorkshire. He even has a Northern accent, and you know I normally I can't bear that.'

She could be an astonishing snob on occasions.

'Well, I bet you didn't shag him,' I muttered, half to myself, half hoping she hadn't.

'Polly!' said Bumble, outraged. 'You can't say that to your mother.'

'Actually,' said my mother, in a very proud voice, 'I did!'

'Good Lord!' said Gareth, as I dropped my knife and jaw simultaneously.

'I don't see why you should be so surprised,' said my mother, sounding rather put out, 'it's perfectly possible at my age, you know.'

'Yes, thank you, mother,' I said hastily, 'please, spare us the details.'

It was distinctly disconcerting, the idea of my mother having sex. I'd only just got used to the thought of my father with another woman.

Bumble giggled and said, 'Well, I hope we all meet him, Hermione. I'm sure he must be lovely if you like him.'

'Creep,' I hissed at her.

'Well, darlings. Enough excitement for one night, I must go to bed. I'm quite exhausted. Good-night everyone, it's so lovely to be here. Thank you, Bumble darling – and, Polly darling,' she came over to me and gave me a huge hug, 'it's wonderful to have you home again.'

And with that she wandered unsteadily towards the stairs.

24

Having spent the weekend with mother, settling her back into her little house in the Cotswolds, I returned to work rested and ready for action. The atmosphere at work was changing. Johnnie managed to ask if I'd had a nice weekend – although that was as far as his pleasantries to me extended – and people from the offices downstairs kept popping up to see the wonderboys, without looking like they were heading for the guillotine; some even emerged from meetings with smiles on their faces. I had a quick lunch with Rohan, who told me with some satisfaction that everyone was working with much more enthusiasm and looking forward to the move.

'Amazing what a little communication and consideration can achieve,' he remarked.

'Well, long may it last,' I replied. 'Johnnie hasn't had a complete personality makeover, but he's trying.'

'And you're looking a little less formal, if I may say so,' continued Rohan. 'I like the new look.'

As I could no longer squeeze into my original Moneypenny suits, I'd been reluctantly forced to go up a size – deeply annoying, I loathed Bumble – but decided if I had to buy more clothes, they could be a little more my style.

'Thank you. I decided the office-drone look did very little for me.' I pulled down the hem of my much shorter skirt. 'Not too short?'

'Not at all, the wonderboys must be enjoying your legs.'

'Oh don't be ridiculous, Rohan, they hardly notice me. I am officially the Office It.'

'Think of it as a compliment, means they are taking you seriously.' He smiled at me.

'Maybe. Is it really too much to ask a man to take you seriously even if you are wearing a short skirt?'

'Probably,' said Rohan.

'Well, it's pathetic. Anyway, I'm extremely pleased the boys don't fancy me.'

'Oh, really?' Rohan looked at me quizzically, raising one eyebrow.

'Yes, of course,' I replied crossly. 'Why?'

'Only . . . I think Johnnie likes you.'

I thought Rohan had completely lost his mind and told him so. Johnnie might be trying, but he was still a Martian as far as I was concerned. On top of which, I doubted he had time in his busy personal schedule to consider liking anyone else since the ghastly Pantheress was still making flouncy visits to the office, after hours. And when she wasn't, he was taking all sorts of other women out. I got up to go back to Milton Keynes.

'Be careful in that skirt, those builders may not take you seriously,' Rohan laughed.

'Rohan, compared to what they look at, I'm in a nun's habit. Anyway, I have no intention of being nice to them, I'm employing Johnnie's former tactic of inspiring fear and greed.'

I was so busy the week flew by, interrupted only by a very brief phone call from Bill, who was doing something weird called a 'road show' round the States, the purpose of which was to raise money for the company from investors, but which sounded more like fun dinners in the evenings with a whole load of boozy bankers. I was cheered slightly when he said he would be over in a couple of months to do the same in the UK. Particularly as it appeared I was going to have to organize it, which meant I'd be seeing a lot more of him. Oh well, it was better than no one, even if he did live so far away.

On Friday, it was the dreaded hen night for Julia. Bumble and I went to her house to collect her. The dress code for the evening was 'skirts, bare legs, no knickers'.

Bumble was most put out. 'Disgusting,' she muttered, wearing her longest possible skirt, 'why on earth can't we wear pants? I'm regretting this already.'

I was feeling distinctly draughty between my thighs.

Julia was looking stunning. Being a recruitment consultant, or whatever she was, clearly paid well, as she was designer clad. Tonight she was in the most micro of mini skirts, her long, thin legs tottering on stilettos.

'It's my greyhound skirt,' she explained with a naughty smile. 'Only an inch away from the hare!'

We were at the house of her sister-in-law, who'd organized the party. There was loud music blaring and a gaggle of girls, most of whom I didn't know; even Bumble was hard pushed to find a familiar face. First it was party games (horrors!). We were all blindfolded and had to identify various icky substances – from pubic hair to egg yolks – before attempting to guess the length of a dildo, the cup size of a bra and the weight of one of those balls you put inside yourself! Losers had to drink a shot of vodka, and as we all drank more vodka, it became noisier.

'Right everyone, dinner time,' somebody said. We took off our blindfolds and went into the dining-room. Trestle tables had been arranged to form a large square, with a gap in the centre. Our napkins were knickers – new, thank goodness – which we weren't allowed to wear, but could take home if we wanted to. We'd all been given tiny vibrators with our names on – I thought Bumble would pass out with shock. Each plate had a picture of a *Karma Sutra* position on it and the glasses were engraved with various animals up to no good whatsoever. Unsurprisingly, the menu was themed to be rude, each course looking remarkably like some body part, and we finished off with a gigantic chocolate penis, which was very life-like indeed. I was extremely thankful it wasn't the real thing – it made me think of Troy. Who, incidentally, was still hot and heavy with Samantha.

I was sitting between Bumble and a lovely girl called Chloe, who used to go out with Julia's brother. She'd recently got married to some merchant banker and was busy trying to get pregnant. He sounded like the perfect Suit and I wondered if he had any friends. Chloe was taller and blonder than me and full of fun, giggling through dinner at the tricks of the conjurer – an astonishingly clever woman, who I later discovered was a man! I wondered if she'd conjured away her bits, but as she had a very deep voice, I rather suspected not.

Suddenly, all the lights went out and a male voice boomed, 'And now, ladies, be prepared for . . . Eddie the Eagle!'

The lights went on and a standing in the centre was a cloaked and masked man. It was the inevitable male stripper. The girls got very noisy indeed as he gyrated suggestively past us all, slowly removing layer after layer and showing off the enormous eagle tattooed all over his back in amazing, vibrant colours. He was at last down to the briefest thong-type garment, which left nothing to the imagination – except we didn't have to imagine anything because, as quick as a flash, he removed it to reveal a willy so big and erect it rivalled the chocolate cake! There was an audible gasp from the audience, followed by whoops of I don't know what – amazement, shock and delight, disbelief even? I'd certainly never seen anything like it. Eddie then produced a large bottle of baby oil, and grabbing the nearest girl, pulled her out of her seat and into the ring with him. He then poured the baby oil into her hands and told her to rub it in, all over his chest. It was difficult for the poor girl to get close to him, what with his great stiffy rearing up between them. But she managed. The forfeit for not doing this, as he went round the room to each girl, was to remain in your seat, while Eddie disappeared between your legs to apply baby oil! Now I knew why we weren't allowed to put on underwear. I thought Bumble was going to have a coronary – she was very shy when it came to things too ribald and was puce in the face when it was her turn.

'Polly! Help! What am I going to do?' She looked plaintively at me.

'Well, choose whichever you think is the lesser of the two evils, and kill Julia tomorrow – this was her idea apparently.'

Unfortunately, Eddie seemed to sense a good victim in

Bumble and donned his black cape again. Bumble reluctantly went over to him, hissing to me, 'I don't even let Gareth do the other thing, ugh!'

Eddie enveloped her in his cloak. He looked like an enormous, pregnant bat, about to give birth to Bumble's bottom. We had no idea what was going on, but Bumble's muffled shrieks hinted she may not have been having her most favourite time.

'Ooh, I hope he does that to me too,' whispered a very excited-looking Chloe.

'Tut tut,' I said, jokingly, 'and you so newly married too.'

Bumble emerged, looking very dishevelled and a bit oily herself. She had a strange look on her face, and drank an entire glass of wine in virtually one gulp.

Now it was my turn. Eddie had still got his cloak on, and the bulging of the folds was a clear indication his impressive hard-on was also still in place. As Bumble appeared incapable of speech, I had no idea what was going to happen next. The cloak was dramatically flung back and I was pressed up against his by now very slippery body. I momentarily wondered if baby oil would wash out of clothes and then got distracted by that enormous, broom-handle willy of his. As I was a bit taller than Eddie, it was alarmingly close to going between my legs, and in my knickerless state, I had to make very sure I stayed upright, without 'impaling' myself! The girls all yelled and shrieked and the music got louder as Eddie poured baby oil liberally all over himself. He then took hold of both my hands and placed them on his massive erection. It was so hard, it felt like concrete; I even wondered if it was real. He then started to rub my hands up and down and it was unmistakably real! I was amazed he didn't faint, with all that blood pumping it up. After the initial shock, I realized this was not really erotic at all. I suppose it might have been something to do with the detached look in his eyes and the knowledge that this was just a job to him. But it was not like being under the covers with someone you fancy. I returned to my seat next to Bumble, as a very excited Chloe leapt up, willingly.

'That's what I had to do!' said Bumble, still stunned by the whole experience, 'but at least no one could see me! My God, where's Chloe disappeared to?'

'Same place, I expect,' I replied, 'it's not such a big deal.'

'Not a big deal!' she exclaimed. 'I'm sending Gareth to a doctor immediately!'

'Oh God, Bumble, don't be silly; going to bed with something that size wouldn't be sex, it would be surgery.' We both fell silent, contemplating the thought, as a rather flushed Chloe emerged.

'Well, it was an experience,' said Bumble, as we lay on the sofas back in Altonative Towers, at the end of the evening, 'but not one I'd care to repeat.' She raised her head from the armrest and looked curiously at me. 'Where did those girls disappear to afterwards?'

'Well . . . ' I said, 'I overhead someone saying they were going up to get a more personal service. Apparently Eddie isn't averse to a bit of extra curricular. Not surprisingly with that thing of his. I heard someone say he was a famous porn star. Did you see the tattoos on his willy?'

Bumble shuddered at the memory. 'If you remember, I was under the bloody cloak. I couldn't see anything, thank God.'

'Well, I saw. He has two animals tattooed on his foreskin and when you rub it up and down, they, you know, mate. It was quite fascinating.'

'Good God,' said William the Lodger, who came in, his arm draped round Pia.

'Eeffning effreyone,' sing-sang Pia, looking dreamily at William.

'What have you two been up to?' he asked, curious.

'What have you two been up to more like?' I was surprised to see them together, as Pia had always made a point of avoiding William.

'Same sort of thing as you two from the sounds of it,' said

William with a lascivious smile on his face, squeezing Pia's bottom.

'I seriously doubt that,' said Bumble, looking mildly irritated. 'William, could I have a word in private with you.'

She dragged him off to the kitchen.

'Pia?' I turned to her and asked her in Swedish what on earth she was doing with William.

'Nej! Jag glömmde att du talade svenska!' She proceeded to gabble away in Swedish, telling me how nice he was, how he treated her so well that he was fixing her broken heart after Troy.

'Well, I hope you are having fun this time. How old are you, by the way?'

'Nineteen,' she said.

At least that was one problem out of the way, I thought to myself as Bumble and William re-emerged.

'Come on, *älskling*,' said William, emphasizing his use of the Swedish word for darling. 'We're going out dancing.'

After the front door closed I asked Bumble what she'd said to William.

'I just told him Pia is the best au pair I've had for ages and I don't want him to muck about with her. She's here for another six months and William doesn't usually go more than six nights with the same woman, so I don't want her mooning around with a broken heart, again. It was bad enough with Troy. Anyway, he's promised he'll be good. Where is Troy by the way? I haven't seen him for ages.'

'With Samantha. She's all starry-eyed about him. Come on you, let's get to bed, I'm exhausted. Everyone's got a partner except me, it's too depressing.'

25

Two weeks later the doorbell at Altonative Towers rang: it was
Samantha, in floods of tears.

'Sam!' I exclaimed, 'what's the matter? Come in.'

'Oh, Polly, it's Troy, you were right all along. He's such a
bastard.'

'What's going on?' enquired Bumble, coming out from the
kitchen, spoon in hand.

'It's Samantha, something's happened with her and Troy,' I
replied.

'I'll get the vodka and the glasses, you get the fags and the
Kleenex. Meet you in the kitchen,' said Bumble, in a military
fashion.

I led the weeping Samantha into the kitchen and sat down
with her at the table.

'So? What happened?' I asked.

She buried her head in her hands for a moment, then
looked up. 'It's been so amazing for all these weeks. He was
just lovely, romantic, sexy, talking of the future, and all along,
it seems, he was *married*!'

She started sobbing again.

Bumble came in with a bottle of Absolut, three glasses and
a purposeful air.

'Here,' she said, handing Samantha a glass, 'drink this.
Ciggie?'

I grabbed one and took a swig from the other proffered
glass. I nearly spat it out.

'Hell's teeth, Bumble! That's practically neat vodka!'

'Medicinal, as your mother would say. Drink up, Samantha.
What were you saying?'

'She's just found out Troy's married,' I replied.

'Is he?' said Bumble. 'I never knew that.'

'Well, I did,' I said, as Samantha raised her head, looking at me in horror, 'but he said he was separated.'

'He may be se–se–separated,' sobbed Samantha, 'but it d–d–doesn't seem to stop him ha–ha–having sex with her.' She blew her nose, noisily.

'Blimey,' I said, 'that's a bit sophisticated.'

'And he has at least one other girlfriend he's been seeing all the time he's been with me. I'm now suspicious of every female in his address book. Oh God, I've been such a *wally*!'

'No, you haven't, Samantha. He's very plausible. But it's what he does, he's a serial seducer. I'm so sorry for you. But at least at the time it was fabulous, remember?'

She nodded.

'And it's not as if you thought it would be a long-term prospect, is it?'

She looked up at me, aghast. 'You don't get it do you? *I loved him!*' she yelled at us.

'Loved whom? What's going on here?' Gareth walked into the room, a great white towel wrapped round him, cigarette in one hand, large vodka in the other.

'Troy, Gareth. What are you doing here? This is girls' talk.'

Bumble got up to push him out of the room, but he was having none of it.

'Ah, Troy, the old devil. Up to his old tricks again? What a chap!'

He sat down at the table.

'I should've listened to you, Polly. I should've known better,' wailed Samantha.

'Ah,' interjected Gareth, ' "The intellect is always fooled by the heart." '

'What did you say?' She looked puzzled.

'I didn't, de la Rochefoucauld did,' said Gareth.

'Who?' said Samantha, thoroughly confused.

'French count, lots of maxims,' I said. 'Dead. Not helpful, Gareth.'

'Duke, actually. Anyway,' he turned to Samantha, 'he also

said, "One is never as fortunate or as unfortunate as one imagines," so buck up, old girl, you'll feel better tomorrow.'

'Gareth, I really think you ought to go and put some clothes on. I don't see that your ridiculous quotes and bare white legs are helping at all. Go on, run along.' Bumble shooed him out of the door.

'Sorry about him, Samantha,' she continued. 'The trouble with Troy, I mean one of the many troubles with Troy, is secretly most men admire him and wish they could get away with what he does.'

'Don't know about secretly,' I pointed out. 'Sam, have another drink.'

We filled her glass and slowly her sobs subsided to an occasional sniff.

'How did you find out?' I asked her after a while.

'It wasn't pretty, but,' she paused, 'I shall get revenge.' She waved a little book at us.

'What's that?' asked Bumble, curiously.

'Ah ha! It's his address book. I stole it. I'm going to phone all the girls in this book and tell them what he's been doing. See if there are any other "overlaps".' She looked momentarily happy.

'I say!' Gareth came bursting back into the kitchen, 'you can't do that. It's just not on. Poor chap, man's worst nightmare.'

'Gareth!' Bumble leapt to her feet, 'I've told you before to stop listening outside the door. Bugger off *immediately*!' She almost managed to sound cross as she shooed him out once more, flapping a tea towel at him. He retreated hastily, muttering, 'Women!' under his breath.

'How did you get his address book?' I asked, amazed.

'I was at his house earlier this evening. Then *she* arrived, let herself in, own key and all. He tried to brazen it out, but it didn't work. It was obvious she knows he has other women, but she seemed a bit pissed off with him so she says, "Oh, and which one is this then, Monday or Friday? I know it can't be

Wednesday because that was me." I was standing there like a lemon, thinking what the f . . . is going on? I wasn't upset just then, more like bloody shocked and as mad as hell. I said I needed to go the bathroom, but I went to his office, upstairs. I didn't know what I was going to do, but I found this book lying on the desk, so I grabbed it and ran out of the house, straight round here. It was only after I realized he wasn't making any attempt to follow me – I know it's not far – that I started to cry. And now I can't stop.' She burst into tears again.

'Oh, Samantha, stop crying, sweetie. He's not worth it.' I tried to soothe her. 'He's a hopeless case. Just try and remember that. You're better off without him. It's like a disease, he just can't help it. I'm sure if you went back and said you'd be Tuesday, he'd be thrilled. I bet you if you went over right now, he'd be all hurt and saying he didn't undestand. He thinks monogamy is a board game, certainly a bored game. It's wrong for him to pretend to be all love and flowers, misleading you like that. But don't forget, he's very clever and I'd bet if you go over it, you'd probably find he never said anything concrete and it was your own mind that was running with the love-for-ever theme. When you're infatuated with someone, they don't need to do much to fan your fantasy flames. You could have interpreted all sorts of things incorrectly, just because you wanted them to be your way.'

'Very wise all of a sudden, aren't we?' said Bumble, unused to me being the one giving out practical advice.

'Easy to be wise when you don't have a man to mess your head up. It's all I've got now, theory.'

'But he said he loved me.' Samantha started wailing again.

'And I'm sure he does, in his own way. But we all love differently. It's finding the person who loves you the way you want them to which is tricky.' I must remember that, I thought to myself.

'Listen, I preferred you in revenge mode,' said Bumble, clearly anxious to get a word in. 'You don't want to be someone's Tuesday girl. Come on, open up the book, let's find Monday and Friday.' She looked rather excited.

'Bumble Smith, I thought you liked Troy!' I exclaimed.

'I do, but I'm with the sisterhood on this one. Let's nail the bastard.'

After about two hours and countless calls, we'd discovered there weren't enough days in the week to accommodate all the girls.

'Wow, you've got to give him credit for stamina,' I said, amazed.

'I feel sick to my stomach,' said Samantha quietly. She was clearly shocked by the legions of women he had been concurrently shagging.

'And it certainly explains one thing,' she continued. 'That's obviously why he never came.'

'I beg your pardon?' said Bumble incredulously. 'What on earth do you mean?'

'Just that. Never, in all those weeks. I thought it was pretty weird, but he said it was because he liked always to be ready. Now I know what for. Servicing all those other girls.'

Bumble and I were still too stunned to say anything.

I wondered if it was anything to do with being abused as a child. Perhaps if you felt yourself to be a service provider, you couldn't enjoy it, or felt guilty about enjoying it. Certainly you would need to be 'ever-ready'. What a complicated, conflicted man. I felt sorry for him.

'Anyway, some of these girls have agreed to meet me for a drink next week. We're going to plan our revenge.'

The reactions of the various women had been interesting. Some had been very upset, some found it amusing, some had been complicit, others were angry. There were a few who obviously didn't care.

'I think it must be time for supper, poor Gareth will be starving,' said Bumble, getting up from the table. 'Samantha, you will stay, won't you?'

'Thanks, Bumble, I'd love to, you're so kind. Thank you

both, I do feel a bit better.' She looked shattered but was calmer at least.

'We'd better get some beauty sleep tonight. It's Hugo's party tomorrow. Hopefully, there'll be lots of distractions for you there.'

'And you too. Don't forget Plan A,' said Samantha.

'I'm just about giving up. I've never had so little action on the man front. But you're right, tomorrow night should be full of Old Etonians and bankers and Suits galore. Maybe it will be fun.'

26

On Saturday afternoon, Samantha and I drove down in my little car to Hugo's parents' home in the country. We were staying in a small guest-house near the party and arrived early to get ready. Samantha was in fighting form, deciding this was to be her final attempt to crack Hugo, and had bought a dress which would have tempted a saint.

'Wow, Sam, that's a hell of a dress!' I said, when she showed me her little black number in our room; 'it doesn't leave anything to the imagination. You're going to cause quite a stir! This is the country remember.'

She laughed. 'I have every intention of causing a stir in Hugo's pants. If this doesn't show him what he's missing, nothing will. And if he doesn't respond, then he's gay.' She started to apply some very red lipstick.

'Samantha, you cannot say that every man who doesn't fancy you is gay, it's not fair to gays for a start.'

'Polly, they don't have to be gay, I just feel better telling myself they are!'

I laughed with her, there were clearly a lot of 'gay' men in my life.

'Listen, he'll probably be here with his girlfriend, so be careful.'

'Don't be such a fusspot, from what you said about her, I don't think she'll be much competition. Come on, get dressed,' she continued, impatiently, 'we can go downstairs and have a drink before we leave for the party.'

We went down into the little floral-swathed sitting-room and were greeted by the couple who ran the guest-house. Standing in front of the fireplace was a very tall, very, very good-looking man, all dressed up in his black tie.

'Girls, let me introduce you to another guest, who's also

going to the party. Steven Hunter, Polly and Samantha,' said the woman who was the lady of the house.

We shook hands with the gorgeous-looking man.

I was sure Samantha must have been having the same thoughts as me, this one was a definite possibility!

'Now, ladies, would you like a drink?'

We both requested a large vodka, lime juice and soda.

'Soooa,' said Samantha, tilting her head coquettishly on one side, 'who's friend are you? Johnnie's or Hugo's?'

'Both actually,' replied Steven, with a strong American accent, 'I used to work with them in the City. I'm now at an American company that set up in London a few years ago called Goldman Sachs.' He paused, as though he expected recognition, either for himself or his company. He drew a blank.

'Are you American?' I asked, mentally deducting a few points from his potential on account of being foreign.

'Well, I was born in the States, but I've lived in London for the last fifteen years.'

OK, I gave him back a few points, based in London and the use of 'I' indicating he wasn't married.

'What about you two?' He turned to Samantha, 'You don't sound English.'

He was definitely flirting with us.

'I'm a Kiwi, Polly's English, we both live in London as well. I work for Hugo and Polly's the bossy boots who runs the office.'

'Well, they're lucky guys to have you two around all day, but I guess I'm the luckiest guy, sharing a house with you charming ladies.' He was laying it on with a shovel.

Samantha had her naughty catface on and kept licking her lips and looking at him from under her long black lashes.

'Oy!' I hissed to her, when he briefly left the room, 'you're supposed to be after Hugo.'

'Shut up, I know, but I thought a bit of competition might make him jealous. Anyway, he likes you too, let's see who gets him first.'

She giggled and I exhaled sharply; how on earth could

I compete with her? Particularly in the dress she had on. I was a lot more covered up, although my dress was quite a striking red.

'Ladies, shall we go.'

Steven came back into the room and linking arms took us to the waiting taxi.

'Everyone sure is going to be looking at me when I make my entrance with you two on my arms. I do hope we're sitting near each other, I can hardly bear to be parted from either of you.'

He was dripping with flattery. He was probably a little too charming – but who cared?

We walked into a huge, white marquee, where lots of smart-looking people were milling around, drinking champagne. A band played in the background. Just as I was wondering if I'd know anyone, Merry came rushing up breathlessly. 'Hallooo, girls, such a *super* party. So many old friends here, just wonder-ful. I never realized Hugo and I knew so many of the same people.'

I thought it would be a very remote place in the world indeed where Merry didn't actually know someone, or at least someone who knew someone she knew.

'And *halloo*,' she lowered her voice, '*who* are *you?*'

'Merry, this is Steven Hunter, he's a friend of the boys and staying in the same guest-house as us. Steven, Miranda, another employee.'

'Wow, those boys just get luckier and luckier,' drawled Steven, eyeing her up and down. But she was too distracted to notice.

'Now, where's my Michael gone?' she looked around the room. 'Ah! There he is, chatting to some blonde. Better go and keep my eye on him – haven't got him up the aisle yet!' She gave us a wink and one of her dirty chuckles and dis-appeared in the crowd.

Hugo came up to us and his eyes nearly popped out of their sockets when he saw Samantha's dress. 'Ah, hallo! I see you've met Steven. You both look, erm, very ah . . . nice tonight.' He couldn't take his eyes off Samantha's cleavage, which was hardly surprising. 'Have you got a drink?'

'Oh no, Hugo, we haven't,' simpered Samantha. 'Shall we go and get one?'

Hugo looked rather flustered as Samatha steered him towards the bar.

'May I escort you to the bar?' said Steven, guiding me purposefully towards the drinks.

'Hallo, Polly, Steven, how are you both?' Johnnie and Belinda came up to us. 'You've met B–Belinda before.'

We all shook hands.

Belinda was looking very nice this evening, no baby in tow.

'How's the baby?' I asked her politely.

'Fine, thank you very much. I've left him with the nanny for the first time.' She didn't look madly happy at the arrangement. Always a tough one, putting your husband before your baby.

'He'll be fine, darling,' said Johnnie, rather irritatedly, adding, 'you need to get out more.' He turned to me. 'That's a very nice dress, Polly. I like red.'

'Thank you,' I said. 'Wait till you see Samantha's.'

'I have, if you can call it a dress.' He sounded disapproving. 'Anyway, better move on, we need to sit down for dinner in a minute and I haven't found our table yet.'

They disappeared into the crowd.

Steven and I went over to the board displaying the table plan; he was delighted to find he was sitting between Samantha and me. 'Some guys have all the luck,' he said, squeezing my arm meaningfully.

Samantha was already sitting down when we arrived, looking a bit stony-faced.

'Hi, what's up?' I asked her quietly.

'Bloody Hugo, dumps me at the bar the second his mousey girlfriend arrives. Beats me what on earth he sees in her.' She sounded as fed up as she looked.

'Well, she's probably gay too.' I succeeded in making her

smile and she perked up considerably when she saw Steven.

'Oh hallo, Steven, come and sit down with me.' She patted the chair beside her.

On my left was a very shiny, chinless-wonder type. He did work in the City, and I suppose he was a Suit, but he was incredibly boring and not attractive at all; even I couldn't have considered him as Plan A material. Subsequently, I spent most of the evening chatting to Steven, when he wasn't chatting up Samantha.

The band started to play and Steven took me up for a dance. I was pleased to be asked first, although I didn't like to point-score. I don't believe in competition between women as there are very few men worth losing a girlfriend over. After one dance I told him to ask Samantha.

'Well, only if you insist,' he said, 'I was really enjoying myself. Johnnie was right, it's a fantastic dress. You are way and above the most attractive woman in the room tonight.' He planted a little kiss on my hand.

'Thank you very much,' I replied, surprised.

'And I love your hair.' He fingered a strand. 'Blonde, mmmm.' I thought he was a bit too heavy on the charm offensive.

I sat down at our table and prayed the chinless wonder wouldn't ask me to dance, but he did. Clammy hands, no rhythm and, worst of all, crooked teeth. Eugh.

I returned to the table as quickly as I could, only to be whisked off by Merry's Michael moments later, an altogether much better dancer and a lot more fun.

Samantha and Steven returned to the table and he promptly took me out to dance again, I was getting a little hot.

'After the party, you should come and have a little nightcap with me,' Steven whispered in my ear.

'I, er, well, thank you, but I'm sharing a room with Samantha,' I said rather lamely, thinking, That was a bit quick!

'Sneak out after she's gone to sleep, I'll wait up,' he said, grinning at me.

'OK, maybe. Let's see how late it is,' I said, fobbing him off more than anything.

We had a couple more dances, then he whizzed Samantha on to the floor again. He must have been the busiest dancer there.

They started to play Chris de Burgh's 'Lady in Red'.

Someone came up behind my chair. 'Would you like to d–dance?' I nearly dropped my glass, it was Johnnie!

'Oh!' I was appalled. The idea of dancing with him horrified me. 'Er, thanks.' I got up unsteadily, but clearly not on account of the champagne; it was just sheer trepidation.

He led me on to the dance floor. Crikey, it was a slow song, he was going to have to touch me! It was really weird and I was quite disconcerted. He was the same height as me and I found myself looking into very green eyes fringed by dark lashes. I hadn't noticed his eyelashes before . . . He was also a very good dancer.

'You wore a red coat to your interview,' he reminded me.

'I, er, yes, I did.' What was going on?

'I like you in red.' He looked at me.

'Er, yes, you said so before.'

I was thoroughly confused and told myself he was just being polite to an employee in an out-of-office kind of a way.

'No, I said I liked red before.'

OK, he was definitely giving me some hidden message here and I was flummoxed. Then I reminded myself this was the man who had a wife and two babies, a horrible scary girlfriend and loads of other women as well. It was probably compulsive in him to be nice to women in a social context, in his blood or something. He must have had too much to drink. This was definitely not about me. This was just about being polite to the person you were dancing with. He probably felt it was a duty dance.

'Thank you, I enjoyed that.' He led me back to my chair. 'I'll see you in the office on Monday.'

'Are you going already?' I looked at my watch, it was eleven forty-five.

'Yes, I like going to bed early. Good-night.' He turned and walked away.

There was something in the way he said he liked going to bed early which gave me the distinct impression he did not go to sleep early. Oh well, lucky Belinda, at least she had him to herself tonight.

'What was all that about?' Samantha flopped down on the chair beside me.

'What?' I asked, distractedly.

'You and Johnnie, on the dance floor. You couldn't take your eyes off each other.'

'Don't be silly, Sam. He was just being polite. Because we're the same height it might have appeared we were looking at each other.' I was irritated.

'Yeah, and I've got a koala up my bum. He fancies you.' She looked round for something to drink.

'You're completely mad. He doesn't. And I don't. He'll be back to his ghastly self on Monday, don't even think any more about it. I'm certainly not.' I lit a cigarette in defiance.

'Well, he didn't dance with anyone else, not even his wife,' said Samantha, 'so don't tell me I'm mad, except mad with rage. I am, as of this evening, officially dumping Hugo. He hasn't even asked me to dance.'

'Go and dance with Steven then, you seem to be getting on well with him.' I saw him in the distance, making his way back to our table.

She giggled. 'Horny bastard, asked me back to his room for a nightcap!'

'No!' I exclaimed. 'He asked me too! What a bugger!'

'Said I was the most attractive girl in the room,' added Samantha.

'Snap! Did he say the hair thing?'

'About loving blonde hair? Yes. Did he kiss you on the hand?'

'Yes.' I started to laugh. 'I can't believe it. Talk about keeping your options open. But really, using the same lines. Are all men the same?' (I thought of Troy) 'You know, I'm coming round to your Kiwi tactics, we should teach him a lesson.'

Samantha smiled broadly. 'Brilliant, he's such a creep. Let's play him along, get him all hot and bothered and we'll plot later.'

For the next hour, Steven must have thought he'd died and gone to heaven as Samantha and I flirted, flattered and encouraged him up the garden path. It was very funny, or at least we thought so. We dirty danced with him, we put our hands on his bottom, we looked him in the eye when we danced, we shared our drinks, we lit cigarettes for him, you name it, we behaved as though we were game on! He was loving every minute and had a very unchaste look in his eye as he kissed each of us chastely good-night outside our bedroom door.

'Did you find out where his room is?' I asked Samantha, as we lay on our beds.

'Yup, it's straight down the corridor, three along.'

'But you didn't say you'd go?' I asked.

'No, stupid, I just said I might,' she replied.

'Same as me, good. He'll be lying there wondering whether one of us will turn up, and if one does which one will it be. God, the man must be mad. Right, so here's what we do. Let's leave it half an hour, give him time to really fret. Then you *and* I will go down to his room and get into bed with him!'

'Naked,' added Samantha.

'Naked? Oh bloody hell, Sam, not sure I can do that.' Trust her to up the ante! 'I'll settle for topless, it's too weird for me to be naked in bed with you and another man.'

'Why? Have you never been with a girl?' she looked at me in astonishment. 'Or had a threesome?'

'No!' I squeaked, rather nervously, thinking my original, probably rather silly, plan was heading in a direction I wasn't hugely comfortable with. Maybe I should just send Sam in on her own.

'You Poms are so square. Two girls and a man, it's amazing.'

'Sam, you're lucky I've had about fifteen glasses of champagne too many, because otherwise I'd be turning into my mother. Sapphic is definitely not my scene.'

'Stupid, I'm not a lesbo.' Samantha looked amazed. 'It's just sex. Blimey, Poll, where's the minibar, I'm going to broaden your horizons a bit.'

I wasn't at all sure I wanted them broadened, but she was on a mission. I was now dreading going into Steven's room. She handed me a glass of neat vodka and told me to knock it back – this at least I could do after my time in Sweden.

'You have to understand that Kiwi and Ozzie men aren't exactly in touch with their feminine side. Most guys think they're doing a girl a huge favour by having sex with her. Yeah right. Their technique's learned on the rugby pitch – you don't so much get a caress, more a tackle. Foreplay? Forget it. Tits? The bigger the better, just for leering at and squeezing, like that blasted ball. Go down on someone? Grosses them out, they'd probably only do it with a gum-shield on. It's about scoring: a goal is an ejaculation. They want to score as many times as possible. It's not exactly a turn on; in fact the only guy I've ever had an orgasm with is Troy.'

'Really?' I exclaimed. 'You never had an orgasm before?'

'Not from a man,' Sam smiled.

I tried very hard not to be my mother. 'Oh, I see,' I said, in what I hoped was a voice that didn't portray panic.

'No you don't, silly. Now you think I'm some kind of bulldyke. I've never gone to bed with a woman alone. I couldn't fall in love with a woman, I like guys. Why d'you think I left home? To find a different type of man, a Brit, Italian, Frenchman, someone who knows about sex. Who doesn't think it's weak to pleasure a woman. Someone that understands it isn't about how big or how many times.'

'Why don't you just tell the guy what to do?' I thought back to Steffan. Sam clearly needed some lessons from him.

Sam looked at me in astonishment. 'You just don't get it. These are Antipodean men. You can't challenge their virility.

It's all they've got. So rather than die of sexual frustration, I came up with a solution until I had the money to leave. Add in another girl. That way, everyone's happy.'

Despite myself, I was curious. 'How did you know what to do?'

'Ha! See, Miss Polly Prudey Pants. Thought you might like to know more.'

'Sam, I'm not a prude, I just haven't needed the services of another woman. I can see it must be most frustrating to be burning up in bed with no release.'

'Now you're getting the picture. Look, with sex you get to the stage where you're so horny, you're, like, gender non-specific. If the guy you're in bed with hasn't done it for you, then roll over to the girl and let her take care of you, and vice versa. The guys think we're doing it for them, but in fact we're doing it for each other. It's kind of an unwritten sisterhood. Now see, the first time was a bit intimidating, but after a while it's, like, really normal. I'm going to take my clothes off so you can get used to the idea.'

I didn't really want to get used to the idea, but Sam had already whipped her kit off and was cavorting around naked in front of me.

'Poll, I'm not trying to seduce you, OK? Don't panic. It's just a body, like yours, no stiffy that's all.'

I looked at her – might have been the vodka, but her body didn't look quite right.

'Sam,' I asked, tentatively, 'can I ask you something?'

'I know what you're going to ask, they're *great* aren't they?' She cupped her rather large tits and stroked them as if they were pets.

'Ah right,' I found myself getting ridiculously English. Other than Henry's memorable, or rather mammarable party, I'd never seen anyone else's boobs quite this close. At boarding school everyone disrobed under a duvet or performed some Houdini-like movement with bra straps.

'Want to feel them?' she proffered a prosthetic.

'No, no,' I yelped. 'Not quite ready for that yet.'

'Oh go on, you can touch them. I don't mind. It's not like I can feel anything there. You kinda lose sensitivity once you've got the implants in. Physically and metaphorically. They're not exactly yours any more.'

Her tits were getting way too close to my face for comfort. It didn't matter she felt emotionally detached from them, they were still another girl's boobies to me, even though they did look, upon closer inspection, alarmingly . . . full. 'Where's the vodka, Sam? *My* cup is definitely not overflowing.'

She poured me another glass. Heavens, I thought to myself, I mustn't get too pissed, God knows what might happen . . .

'Sam, you don't have any plans to, er . . . seduce me tonight, because I have to tell you now, I'm really not up for it. I'd prefer you went to Steven's on your own.'

'Poll, you're insane. But I did think if you lost a few inhibitions we could have a bit more fun with him. Torture him some. If you trust me not to overstep the mark, I think we can drive this man demented.'

'Why are you so mad at him? Or is it men in general?' I asked.

'Bit of both. I found out our flirty Steven's married!'

Dear God, another one! Married men are the scum of the earth.

'He has some very high-powered banker wife who's in the States on a business trip and, wait for this, pregnant! He's a shocker! So, this is what we do. I'll put my knickers back on, as I can see you're stupid about complete nudity; you get your top off. We go into his room and hop in either side, say we couldn't sleep, so we thought we'd spend the night with him on the understanding he doesn't touch us. What do you say.'

'Well . . . ' I was a bit off this plan now.

'Look, and I won't touch you.'

'How comforting you felt the need to reassure me. Come on, I'm rising to the challenge. Let's get this over with; if nothing else I have to prove I'm not a complete wimp.'

I knocked back my final vodka and felt some reckless courage return. We opened our bedroom door, checked there was no one else in the corridor, and then raced down to Steven's room. Sam knocked on the door.

'Come in,' he said, huskily.

'We're coming!' we shrieked and burst in. We headed straight for the bed and hopped in either side of him.

'Dear God in heaven, what on earth are you both doing here?' He sounded shocked and delighted.

'Well, you did ask us both, so we thought it would be rude for one of us to stay behind,' purred Samantha.

'And we couldn't sleep, so we thought we'd sleep here. Hope you don't mind. Good-night, Steven.' I planted a kiss on his cheek and turned my back to him.

'Yeah, good-night, Steve, sweet dreams.' Samantha kissed his other cheek and turned her back on him too.

'Do you mean, you're going to sleep, just like that?' exclaimed Steven.

'Oh, did I forget something?' said Samantha, sitting up in bed, boobs to the fore. 'Of course, I didn't kiss Polly good-night; come here, girl.'

Terrified, but by now drunkenly excited, I sat up and leaned across Steven's chest.

Sam pulled my face to hers. 'Don't panic,' she whispered, 'this is nice.'

She placed her lips gently on mine. I could feel her tongue tip and in an almost involuntary reaction, opened my mouth. Her tongue went in gently. Weird. I was having my first girl snog. It felt rather good, different, softer. I was enjoying it. I relaxed a bit. There was a moan from under us. We broke apart and looked at Steven. He had an agonized look on his face.

'Girls, closer, let me join in.'

'Oh dear, Steven, don't be silly, we're just saying good-night. You can't do anything. You can't even touch,' I said in a silky voice.

'We're doing you a favour really, because this way you won't be unfaithful to your wife, will you?' said Samantha, as she bent closer to his ear, a boob brushing his rather hairy chest. I tried really hard not to laugh at his horrified face.

'My . . . wife . . . ' he stammered

'Yes, I know, I'm sure she doesn't appreciate you. But unlike you, we do have some standards, even if they are slipping a bit.'

In a moment of extreme bravery I put my hand around Sam's breast which was resting on Steven's chest and raised her up a bit. (She was right, it didn't feel strange, just not very boob-like.) I tentatively put my hand round the other, she moaned. Oof, I wasn't sure about that, I really hoped it was for show.

'One last kiss then?' I volunteered – I did hope I wasn't becoming a lesbian so soon.

'Mmm, OK then.'

Two little slippery tongues later, and much sighing from Steven below, we parted.

'So go to sleep, Steven, like a good boy. And no touching!' I said, removing a hand that was trying to feel a breast.

'Yeah, no touching, you creep,' said Samantha, more forcibly, obviously removing the other hand.

'But, but, I'll never get to sleep with you two beside me!' he wailed pathetically, a rather impressive hard-on making a priapic tent of the sheet. I was quite tempted for a minute, then realized I must be very pissed.

'You should have thought of that before asking us in. Now go to sleep!' I put on a school-mistressy voice.

And then we both put our heads on our pillows, turned our backs to him and fell fast asleep!

27

Back at the office on Monday, everyone was in a good mood. Hugo's party seemed to have broken the ice between 'us' and 'them'. Even Johnnie had improved, slightly. He still strode up and down the corridors in a purposeful way, barking orders at people, but at least he now added a please or a smile, and on a rare occasion, both.

Samantha was getting very hooked on her revenge-on-Troy evening with the other girls.

I'd been a little worried about seeing her in the office, but it was as though nothing had happened. It really was much simpler with girls. I still wasn't about to become a lesbian, although I suppose it did give me Plan C! Sam's campaign started with five of them meeting in Green's on Tuesday to compare diaries. I declined an invitation to attend; luckily I hadn't been one of his 'victims' – although it had been a near miss – and I was also feeling a degree of internal conflict; normally I'd adhere to the 'all men are bastards' theory, but I thought I knew Troy well enough to believe he wasn't deliberately being bad.

On Wednesday, Samantha came into work with a very satisfied look on her face.

'Morning, Sam,' I said. 'You look happy.'

'Ooh!' she beamed, settling herself down on a chair in my office, 'we had such fun last night.'

Apparently she and the girls had had a wonderfully vindictive time getting hammered in Green's, comparing diaries and discovering all sorts of cross-overs. One had to give Troy credit for running quite such a large stable. However, they didn't see it that way. They went round to his house and daubed lipstick and nail polish all over his car, punctured the tyres and ended up throwing a brick through his window.

They were lucky not to have been caught and I was really glad I hadn't been with them. Hell hath no fury like five drunken women scorned.

I spent a lot of time dashing between London and Milton Keynes and was happy to see the revolting builders seemed to have responded to my more savage approach and the new offices were taking shape. Next I had to plan the interiors; it was like being a housewife, except, of course, I was being paid to do it. The only other development was that Johnnie asked me out for lunch on the Friday, unprompted by Hugo. It was rather strange in that he was beguilingly charming and rather good company.

'Told you he fancied you,' hurrumphed Samantha.

'He absolutely doesn't,' I replied. 'We only talked about work. He's just being nice because, well, I don't know why, but I'd be amazed if you were right. Anyway, he's married.' (Not that it seemed to hinder him or any other married man.)

'He did manage to see the funny side of the restaurant-booking thing though, which gives me some hope for him.'

To amuse myself at the office when Johnnie was being particularly foul, I used to make his lunch reservations in the wrong name. The thought of him saying in his pompous restaurant voice, 'I have a reservation in the name of Lyle, Jonathon Lyle,' when I had him booked in as 'Mr Bile' or 'Mr Liar' or 'Master Johnnie', kept me chuckling for hours. I have moments of incredible maturity.

'You didn't tell him, did you?' asked Samantha, amazed. 'You see, you are getting on well.'

'I did. I wanted to see if he had any sense of humour at all. Transpires he does, occasionally.'

'Well, watch this space is all I can say.' She left my office.

The next couple of weeks were a flurry of activity, with the wonderboys on the UK bit of this roadshow thing. It culminated in the arrival of Bill and Freddie.

I was getting very nervous about seeing Bill again, not knowing how things would be and trying to be cool. I was organizing the 'closing dinner' which was quite a palaver. Not only was the venue discussed endlessly, but the menu was changed, the wines tested, the seating rearranged and the corporate gifts everyone was expected to receive had to be specifically engraved in time.

I had a phone call from Bill towards the end of the week, just prior to their arrival.

'Hey, darlin', whatya doin' this weekend?' His transatlantic drawl sent shivers down my spine.

'Nothing specific,' I replied. 'Why?'

'Wondered if you'd like to spend it with me. Thought I could take you someplace nice in the country.'

'Ooh!' I nearly squeaked, 'how lovely.'

'I'll pick you up on Friday night and whisk you off. Don't pack too much.' He chuckled down the phone.

'Ahhh! Bumble! What do I wear? What do I wear?' I was having a major fashion crisis on the phone to Bumble.

'Oh for God's sake, stop fussing. You probably won't get out of bed, let alone leave the hotel. Nothing for night – do you have any decent underwear by the way? That's crucial. Then just a pair of jeans and a white shirt for the day: it's a killer look, no man can resist it. Something smartish for dinner on both nights. Where's he taking you by the way?'

'The Lygon Arms, in Broadway.'

'It's a heavenly place,' sighed Bumble. 'I spent the first night of my honeymoon there. On second thoughts, maybe you'd better wear something a bit more smartish on Saturday night.'

'Oh hell, Bumble, I'm really nervous. I think I'd better go and buy a decent pair of pants. What colour?'

'White and lacy, much sexier than black, which is too obvious – and definitely not red. Try and make sure they match the bra.'

I went out in my lunch hour and spent a fortune on underwear. Just hope he appreciates it, I thought to myself as I checked the bill again, disbelievingly.

A uniformed chauffeur driving a big black Mercedes pulled

up outside Altonative Towers on Friday and out sprang Bill. He looked divine. All slick and business-suited and successful. He had yet more flowers for Bumble (anyone would think she was my mother!), a toy for Minnie and a magnum of Krug for everyone in the house.

He kissed me on the cheek, saying, 'You look lovely, darlin'.'

'Thank you,' I said, 'so do you!'

'Come on, there's more champagne in the car, let's get going.'

I slid on to the expensive leather and we sped off into the night.

It was the most divine weekend. Very bad news. I was falling for him, hooker, liner and sinker. The worst was I could tell he was falling for me too, but he was so clever, it was like shadow boxing with his emotions. He treated me with exactly the right amount of affection to keep me in a permanent state of stomach-turning, silly-smile land, but without being soppy and maudlin, which I can't bear. Tantalizing sentences that were nearly declarations of love, but not quite. I was never bored for a minute; I could happily have just sat and watched him read the *Financial Times*. In fact I think I did catch myself staring at him on a couple of occasions and had to snap myself out of it. Every meal was a delight as he ordered unbelievably good wine to go with mouth-wateringly delicious food. We got completely pissed on vodka martinis on Saturday night and giggled like teenagers over completely stupid things. We watched old movies in bed in the afternoon, went for walks in the pelting rain and then shared a bath together to warm up. I gave him a foot massage – which is a real affection barometer as I loathe feet – and he gave me a back rub. And, of course, we had sex, a lot. But it was really different with him, sometimes it was passionate and intense and raw, other times it was sweet and gentle and emotional and felt like I was making love, not just having sex. It was a first and completely unhinged me. I had absolutely no idea where I stood with him and kept reminding myself of the troubling aspect of the geography.

What I really wanted to know were all the things I couldn't ask. When would I see him again? Were we 'going out'? Where was all this leading? What was he thinking? Did he love me?

'I sincerely hope you didn't ask all those questions,' said Bumble, when I arrived back, starry-eyed and exhausted on Sunday.

'No, of course I didn't. Although I had to light a cigarette each time the question formed on my lips to stop myself from blurting it out. It's just so ironic. The one thing I said I was going to avoid, I've gone and done all over again. I've fallen for an unsuitable, married, foreigner, who hardly spends any time here – he's off again on Tuesday.'

'Oh, just enjoy it and stop trying to make everything so serious too quickly. You really must allow things to take their own time.'

'But that's my point, Bumble, they don't. The pressure is we don't have much time. Whenever I say hallo to him, I'm preparing myself to say goodbye.'

'Look, stop stressing about this. It'll work, or it won't. It's quite simple. You'll see him again, sometime, there's no reason for you not to. Keep him in the background, while you do a bit more trawling over here. You're so soppy once you've slept with someone – didn't that Steffan teach you anything?'

'Different type of lesson,' I muttered, feeling I needed a very strong vodka.

'Well, it's all lessons. Even when you're married, you never stop learning. Don't give up, silly. Think of him as an add-on.'

'More like a turn-on. He's just wonderful in bed, Bumble. I'll never find anyone as good.'

'Ahh,' said Bumble, 'maybe he isn't and you are. Maybe now you've done the *Karma Sutra* Swedish style, anyone would be good in bed, given a bit of direction. Can't tell you how much Gareth has improved since I employed the Steffan technique. Better get out and test the theory. Come on, dinner and *Dynasty* tonight, take your mind off that gorgeous Bill. Oops!' she clamped a hand over her mouth, 'don't want to encourage you.'

28

Funny how things happen when you least expect them to. The weeks had flown by, work was good. I'd moved everyone to Milton Keynes and was engaged on the redecoration of the offices downstairs, which I was surprised to find I really liked. Bill was in New York, contact intermittent. I missed him hugely, but tried hard not to obsess about him. Johnnie and I had a regular little lunch most Fridays and even I had to admit to myself he was reasonably good company. He still seemed to be shagging half of London, but was always utterly 'correct' with me. My parents had separately popped into the offices and the boys had been charming to them. My father was gearing up to get married in some hideous, *Hello*-style ceremony in Barbados; my mother was hot and heavy with the man from Penang, who turned out to be quite nice, although, of course, like every other apparently suitable man he had a flaw. Not the bit about him being a Northerner, much worse – he too was married! Although, according to my mother, it was an open marriage – 'all very French', as she said – the idea of my mother being someone's bit on the side was deeply weird; but I was glad she had someone to think about while daddy was banging on about his wedding. You want your parents to be happy, but I didn't want to be involved in the details of their love lives, particularly as I didn't have one. On top of it all, Samantha informed us she had met some wonderful man at her new gym and was 'doing domesticity' somewhere in south London.

As I was lolling in a bath one evening at Altonative Towers, the bathroom door was flung open by a seriously over-excited Bumble.

'You will never guess who's on the phone' she shrieked in a most un-Bumble-like way, adding in a dramatically lowered tone, '*Carlo!*'

I sat bolt upright, splashing water everywhere. Carlo is famous among my friends for being – Carlo. My nemesis.

If there was ever to be an antidote to Bill, it would be him, because there are some people in life so irresistible they can never be out of your life, let alone your system, not matter how hard you try to avoid them. People you are so physically attracted to it is inevitable you will end up in bed with them whatever the circumstances. The sex will be passionate, extreme and intense. No matter how long since you last saw each other or how deeply all thought of them has lain dormant or how firmly you'd convinced yourself you were over that person, one look sends you right back. And if you were alone in a room with them it would be cataclysmic and a matter of seconds before your mouths were clamped together.

And, of course, they're often the most unsuitable person for you. For all sorts of reasons, but principally because they reduce you to a quivering, mindless, obsessive creature who bears little resemblance to your normal self. You have absolutely nothing in common with them except lust. Carlo. I've been avoiding him for years.

'Oh, my God!' I said slowly, disbelievingly. 'What on earth does he want?'

'To talk to you, silly,' snapped Bumble.

I hadn't spoken to him for so long I felt quite sick. I put on a bathrobe and raced downstairs. I stopped by the phone. Should I talk to him? What was I unleashing? Then I thought how stupid, just because I had no immunity in my system, didn't mean he felt anything ongoing for me. Anyway, I had some immunity, there was always Bill lurking in the background.

Carlo had been really angry with me the last time we spoke, which was years ago, when I was in France. In retrospect I suppose I had run off with Mats in a desperate attempt to get him out of my life. I knew he was no good for me long term. We'd been going out for a year when I discovered he was five years younger than me! I'd never have got involved with him in the first place had I known (well possibly I would, as he was irresistible). I discovered his passport in a drawer and freaked out, my views on toy-boys being well documented. I was twenty-four and discovered I was going out with a *teenager*! Apart from being deeply embarrassing, it was definitely the most ageing experience of my life. I felt old at twenty-four. How decrepit would I feel at thirty? It didn't bear thinking about. I'd have been forever worrying about my wrinkles and flabby stomach, feeling neurotic about flawless-complexioned, toned-abs, raven-haired, younger Italian girls. On top of which, no one in their right mind would want to be an Italian wife, least of all someone English. Italian men are the most fantastic boyfriends, but lousy husbands. They revert immediately to type. You're whisked into the kitchen and there you remain, usually with their mother, who miraculously materializes the instant you're married, moves in and spends her days criticizing you. Your purpose in life becomes an attempt to emulate her fantastic cooking and to produce hordes of little sloe-eyed children that, incredibly, don't even belong to you. You and your children are your husband's property. You can't leave if you want to and even if you manage it, you never see your children again.

The men, naturally, don't change their lifestyle at all. Indeed, it seems, once they're married, it's almost compulsory for them immediately to take on a girlfriend, or two, or three. It wasn't a life I wanted. So, mad as I was about Carlo, I knew I had to leave him somehow. Mats appeared at the right time and being a blond Adonis and a contrast to Carlo's dark beauty he'd seemed the most brilliant way for me to move on.

I tried to think more rationally. Perhaps this call was important; maybe one of our mutual friends in Capri was ill, or getting married. It couldn't possibly be anything more, it was so long ago. 'Hallo,' I said slowly.

'Ciao, Polita,' said the hideously familiar, deep Italian voice, using his old nickname for me.

Oh shit! It might just as well have been heroin, because I knew in a moment I was still hooked.

'Carlo!' I said slowly, trying to stop my heart racing. 'How incredible, how are you? Where are you?' My Italian came flooding back as quickly as my resistance melted.

'I'm in London for three months to study English. Would you like to have dinner with me tonight?'

No one else would presume I had no plans that night, or that if I did I'd drop them.

'Um, yes, I'd love to.' The words were out, he was like a magnet.

We arranged to meet at a restaurant near his hotel and I fled upstairs to think about clothing.

'Bumble!' I shrieked from my bedroom, 'please come up and help me, I don't know what to wear. Help, help, help!'

'Oh, for heaven's sake,' she muttered, climbing the stairs, 'it doesn't matter. Here,' she handed me a large glass of clear liquid, clinking with ice. 'Ciggie?'

'No thanks, he doesn't smoke and I don't want to reek – and what do you mean "doesn't matter"? Are you mad? Last time I saw him I had a tan, I was in Italy and I was four years younger.' I took a gulp of my drink and spluttered. 'God, that's strong.'

'Medicinal,' said Bumble matter of factly, settling herself down on my bed, glass and cigarette in either hand. 'It doesn't matter, because if you find someone attractive it never goes away, no matter how much time passes. Think about it. You're in a complete tizz because you're seeing him. I bet he's feeling the same way, why else would he ring?'

'Probably because he doesn't know anyone but me in London. Anyway, men don't think the same as women.' I was chucking clothes out of my wardrobe in a desperate fashion.

'Well, that's where I think you're wrong,' Bumble said, lighting her cigarette, clearly poised to give another lecture. 'Who set the rule? Women. Men can be just as messed up, but because we vocalize everything, it appears to affect us more. They internalize, we externalize, the opposite from the way it is with our body parts.' She giggled and then continued.

'It couldn't matter less what you wear, he'll still fancy you. And you,' she looked at me closely, 'will definitely fancy the pants off him.'

'Yes, well, this is what worries me. I'll be swooning over him and he'll be sitting there thinking how badly I've gone downhill. I'm going to have to cover up. I've put on a shed-load of weight since I've been living with you and he's bound to notice.'

'At least you've got your tits back,' Bumble retorted.

'Thank you, but I could do without this bottom.'

'Another bloody myth. Men like shapes and they love bottoms. We only diet for other women, you know, and occasionally ourselves. Unless you're completely messed up with anorexia, in which case you're doing it because you probably hate your mother or you feel your life is out of control, but essentially it's about anger and nothing to do with what you look like. Anyway, attraction isn't to do with looks, it's a sort of essence from within.'

'God, Bumble, you make it sound like BO. Do you think I should have another bath?' I wondered if I had time.

'Don't be silly, you're deliberately misinterpreting. You really can be very dim. Your olfactory sense is your primary one. If someone doesn't smell right to you, you don't fancy them. Simple really. When someone smells wonderful it's an animal instinct kicking in. Some people's BO is attractive to you while to others it's a complete turn-off.'

'You see, you do think I smell.' I tentatively sniffed the air near my armpit. 'How on earth can BO be attractive?'

'Polly, shut up, you're making me digress and I'm trying to make an important point here. Attraction is an aura. Sure you can see a good-looking man and think you fancy him, but when you meet someone, get talking to them, a whole heap of other factors get loaded in.'

'What? Like "she's got a great personality", you mean? I've always thought that was a euphemism for "meet my new girl-friend, she looks like a dog but she's a fantastic shag".'

I still couldn't find anything to wear.

'Bloody hell, you're making this difficult.' Bumble sighed irritably. 'Humour, for a start, is a real turn-on. Confidence is another, without being big-headed, of course. Power, definitely. But generally it's something indefinable. If you're asked, "Why do you love me?" and you start listing the reasons it's a dodgy area. "Because you're tall, short, blonde or brunette," it's ridiculous. Those are not reasons. I think the real answer should be, "I just do." What does Shakespeare say in *Romeo and Juliet*? "There's beggary in love that can be defined." You could find some man attractive and everyone may wonder what on earth you see in him. Equally, you can see a woman whom every man in the room is prowling round and not understand why. We girls have no idea what men find attractive, because we think it's all in the packaging and it's not. Some people actually like brown-paper wrapping. Which sort of brings me back to my original point, if he found you attractive before, he still will, because it's not about looks or weight, it's about *you*. And in that respect, you haven't changed.' She paused for a moment, adding with an evil grin, 'Even if you have put on half a stone!'

I picked up a shirt from the now very large pile of clothes on the floor and threw it at her. 'Most enlightening, thank you. You are telling me I am a smelly, fat, brown-paper bag. You are indeed my best friend. However, I've decided what I'm going to wear: black trouser suit, no shirt – might as well show a bit of cleavage now I have one – and very high heels. Not too much make-up, hair down. Pass?'

'Pass,' replied Bumble.

I got dressed quickly.

'Don't wait up, I might be late.'

'If you come home at all,' said Bumble, in a challenging fashion.

'Don't be ridiculous. I may be fat, but I'm not completely stupid.'

I rushed out of the house.

He was waiting at the table when I arrived and my stomach

lurched. He looked even better than I remembered. Like a 1940s' matinée idol.

Carlo is very tall, with thick, black, wavy hair. He has a permanent light-coffee-coloured complexion. His eyes are black, like coal on a snowman, but drooping slightly at each corner, giving him a sleepy, sexy air. His lashes are thick, his lips are lush, his nose is strong and straight, his shoulders broad, his bottom tight, his legs endlessly long, his hands are beautiful, he even has nice feet. Oh bloody hell, why did he want to see me?

'Polita.' He held out both his arms. 'Vene qui. Diame un bachio.'

I went over and gave him a kiss on both cheeks, he smelled divine. Bumble may be right on the olfactory thing and a good smell allied with drop-dead good looks is a devastating combination.

'Carlo, it's wonderful to see you.'

I thought my voice sounded a bit shaky, certainly my legs were all over the place. I sat down quickly.

'And you, and you,' he said, in his melodic Italian voice. 'Here,' he poured me a glass of wine, 'your favourite Pinot Grigio.'

Clever bastard I thought, what on earth is he playing at?

'Tell me again, why are you in London?' I sipped my wine, fighting the urge to gulp in down in nervous swigs.

'I've finished university and thought it was time to learn English, so I'm staying here for three months and then travelling to the States.'

'What are you going to do there?' I was surprised, Carlo was so – well, Italian. I was amazed he wanted ever to leave the country, let alone speak another language.

'Not sure, just take a holiday and maybe work a bit.'

'Work? That's a new concept for you!' I laughed.

Carlo came from a fabulously wealthy family, who at one time had owned practically all of Capri, so he scarcely needed to work. Not a plus from my point of view, as I was English and was always going to be an outsider in a close-knit, titled Italian family.

'Polita, Polita, always with the jokes. I have to think about my future. What I'm going to do.'

This really was novel. Carlo had always been the live-for-the-moment type, another reason he hadn't been suitable.

'You must be getting old at last, Carlo. Don't tell me you've hit your twenties now.'

He had the grace to look a little shamefaced. 'Don't be angry at me. I want to be friends. I'm not angry with you, even though you left me for a Swiss man.'

'He was Swedish and I'm not angry. At the time I was more sad than anything else.'

'Why sad?'

'Because I realized our relationship could have no future. At twenty-four I wanted to make plans, and you were still a baby, with no idea what you wanted to do but it certainly wasn't going to be settling down.'

'You're right. I'm sorry. I was too young. But,' he continued, 'we can be friends, yes?'

I wondered if I could possibly be friends with this man, but I smiled at him. 'Friends would be nice. We'll have some fun in London, I've got lots of people to introduce you to. You'd better start to learn English fast.'

'And you will introduce me to some nice English girls?' He looked slyly at me from under his black lashes. 'Young ones?'

'You absolute bugger, Carlo,' I said in English, laughing. 'I thought you liked older women! You can find your own young ones.'

'Bugger?' He looked at me questioningly.

'Forget it, that can't be your first English word.' Although there'd been a lot of it about since Roman times in Capri!

We ended up having a really fun evening, and as he gave me a huge, brotherly-type hug goodbye, I thought to myself for once Bumble had been entirely wrong. Clearly he didn't fancy me any longer. It was going to be perfectly possible to be friends.

29

'Polly, I want to have a party for the office.' The whirlwind that was still Johnnie erupted into my office. 'Can you organize it?'

'Yes, of course, Johnnie. What kind of party? When and where?' I looked up from my desk.

'Three weeks' time, beginning of July, before everyone goes on holiday. What on earth are all those papers lying on your d-desk?' He looked aghast at the piles of work.

'Just things I have to do,' I replied, mildly irritated. After all, not everyone actually wanted a desktop which looked like an empty shelf at a supermarket.

'Well, clear it up, it looks a mess. You can't possibly find anything, I certainly couldn't.'

'What do you mean, you couldn't? Have you been rummaging through my desk?' I was most put out.

'Um, well, yes, there was something I needed and it was quite impossible to locate. I'm asking Merry to send a memo to everyone to say their desks must be cleared every evening. You need a filing system.'

'Johnnie, this is my filing system. I know where everything is, and if you want something, ask me. This is my desk and my system. You can't go ferreting about in other people's desks! I'm sure it's an invasion of privacy. I might have all sorts of personal things there.'

'Well, you shouldn't. This is an office, your personal things stay at home.'

I was getting more and more annoyed. Sometimes he could be so nice, and here he was, being all despotic again. He must have had a bad weekend.

'What? Even tampons and lip gloss?' I asked, challengingly. 'Surely you don't want us to keep them in the loos everyone uses?'

'It appears some of you already do. Now the work is nearly completed downstairs, I want one loo for women and one for men. It's quite disgusting to have to see female paraphernalia all over the place.'

'I see,' I said, coldly, 'and would you like me to have a condom-dispenser installed in the new, sanitized gents?'

'D—don't be absurd, Polly. Just try and keep your desk organized.'

'It is organized.' God, he was infuriating. I took a deep breath. 'So, about this party.'

'Yes,' he changed tack, 'don't mind what you do. All the staff, with partners, food, wine, dancing, but an unusual venue. Bill and Freddie will be coming over, so make sure it's good.' He turned and marched out of my office.

I was thrilled Bill was coming and decided I'd bring Carlo as my partner. I'd seen him a few times since we had had dinner. I still found him incredibly attractive, but had managed to control myself. I'd only get stung again if I slept with him. Not that he was offering, mind you. But he was so good-looking I thought it would be good for Bill to see me with someone else, especially as Carlo was a platonic friend.

I spent the next few days having a happy time trawling London for venues which had never held parties before and stumbled, almost literally, on a disused underground air-raid shelter. It had a couple of large rooms for eating and dancing and then lots of little cave-like rooms leading off, perfect for snogging, although I wondered if anyone would dare with Johnnie around! The party-planners, Bartholomew's, whisked into action.

A few mornings later, Johnnie came striding into my office, which was now incredibly tidy. (It was very easy, I discovered. Just put all the piles of paper which had previously sat on top of the desk into the drawers below. Hey presto! Tidy office.)

'How's it all going?' he asked, rather snappily.

'Fine, thank you, everything under control. Nice, neat desk, don't you think?'

'Yes, well done, looks much better. Where's the party? What's happening?'

I looked him in the eye.

'Johnnie, it's under control. I'm having the proof of the invitation done as we speak, everything's organized. You'll see when you get your invitation. You know the date and the time – you told me to get on with it, so I did.'

'What do you mean? I haven't even checked the wording, let alone the spelling.' He looked appalled.

'Johnnie, I'll give you the proof to read. But can I just ask, do the words "don't mind what you do" ring a bell? What's the point of asking someone to do something and then checking up on them all the time? Can't you delegate anything? You and Hugo must have something much more important to do. Like taking over another company.'

We seemed to be going through one of our mutually antagonistic periods again.

'Sorry.' He suddenly changed demeanour and looked rather downcast. I felt I might have been a bit harsh with him; I'm a sucker for a lost puppy. 'It's just . . . ' He trailed off, as if he wasn't sure what to say next. Then, 'Look, would you d–do me an enormous favour?' He paused again, looking very uncomfortable.

'Probably, if you're nice. What is it?'

'My, er, wife, at the last minute, cannot come to the d–dinner I'm hosting tonight for some rather important clients. They're all b–bringing their wives; unfortunately mine doesn't seem to have any interest in my business.' His voice sounded bitter and slightly sad at the same time. 'Clearly the children are more important. Anyway, she's just c–called to say she can't come up, and I'd be so grateful – ' again he paused – 'if you d–don't mind that is, if you could come in her place, as the hostess. I know it's a Friday night and you've p–probably got plans, but if you were free . . . I really didn't know who else to ask who would be, er . . . appropriate,' he ended lamely, stammering more than usual.

I was glad he hadn't seen the Pantheress as being appropriate.

'Of course I can, Johnnie.' I made a mental note to call Frank to say I wouldn't be coming to the pub this evening.

'Thank you very much indeed. Apologies if I've been a bit abrupt recently, but things are, well, it's p–personal so I shouldn't b–bother you with it, but things are not easy at home at the moment.'

'I'm sorry.' I replied, feeling rather uncomfortable with the conversation.

'Well, I'm sure it's my fault. Anyway, thank you. Shall I pick you up from where you live at seven? Dinner is at eight at the Connaught, but we can have a drink before and I'll give you all the information you need to know about the guests.'

He turned around and left the office as abruptly as he had come in. I dragged Merry to the wine bar with me at lunchtime to discuss it.

'So?' I asked her, 'what do you think?'

'Well, it's obvious he fancies you – ' I started to protest, but she continued, 'after all, he fancies anything in a skirt.'

At which point I decided to shut up.

'And I think his wife is a fool. She's falling into the classic situation of ignoring a high-maintenance man and busying herself with children, buried in the country. It's a recipe for disaster. My mother has already had *endless* conversations with me about it. Such a bore, these men. It's one thing to catch them, but then you have to *keep* them. I mean, it would be *bliss* just to live in a nice house in the country, have lots of babies and lunches with girlfriends all day, but husbands have this *irritating* habit of requiring a bit of input from you, not to mention wanting to input you when they feel like it, although I would never object to *that*.' She gave a dirty chuckle.

'You sound like Bumble,' I said.

'Well, she's right. I'm afraid it's a fact. If Belinda isn't prepared to come and support him at work, which after all, is what provides her with her nice lifestyle, she's only herself to blame when it all goes wrong, and believe me, it will. Sooner or later. And it'll be hideous, always is. Rule number one, put your husband first, especially before the children. Or at the very least, make it seem so. If the old Hunter-Gatherer thinks he is being taken for granted, then he's going to start stalking other prey.' She took another sip of wine, before adding, 'Be careful – you don't want to get involved in a messy situation.'

'Merry, I'm not even remotely interested in Johnnie. I'm a safe date, that's why he asked me. If there is a messy situation, it'll be nothing to do with me. I'd never go out with a married man, let alone be responsible for breaking up a marriage. This is their problem and I don't want to get involved. I'm not mad about Belinda, she hardly deigns to talk to me and refers to me as Johnnie's secretary, but I'm not after her husband. I just wanted to get your view on the situation. As far as I'm concerned, this is just a boring work dinner, with a number of other wives who probably don't want to be there either.'

'Ah, but they are there, that's the point. *Nothing* is for nothing in life. It's the one big downside to not having your own career. If you're financially dependent on a man, he'll feel he has the right to ask for his pound of flesh. There again, financial independence brings along another set of issues.'

'I don't even want to hear about it. I'd just like to find someone, anyone, to have these problems with.'

'Oh dear me, I have been *most* unsuccessful in that department for you. I *must* arrange another dinner party for you. Michael has got *loads* more eligibles in his address book.'

I tried to look happy at the prospect. 'Thank you, now we'd better get back to the office.'

30

Johnnie's car pulled up outside Altonative Towers at five to seven. He had to be the only person in the world who arrived early for dinner.

'You're lucky I was ready,' I said as I slid into his rather nice BMW.

'You look very nice,' he commented, without appearing to look at me. I was dressed soberly in my ubiquitous black trouser suit, with a white shirt underneath.

'Thank you,' I replied rather formally, a little unsure of myself.

He smiled. 'You're being very proper tonight. I'd better get you a glass of champagne so you can relax a bit.'

The doorman at the Connaught greeted Johnnie and took his car away; we walked into the bar.

'Good-evening, Mr Lyle,' said the barman.

'They all seem to know you rather well here,' I commented.

'I only go to places where people know me. I like to be greeted by name. I make a habit of going to a few places often, then I feel quite at home. The service is better and I'm looked after really well.'

Merry was right about high-maintenance men, I thought to myself.

'Two glasses of champagne, please, Edward. Could I have some of your canapés as well, but no nuts. We'll sit over there.' He shepherded me over to a corner table.

Being with Johnnie was rather nice, in the way he took control of every situation and one just sort of glided along in his slipstream.

He raised his glass at me, after Edward had served us. 'Thank you for joining me.'

'You're welcome,' I replied, taking a sip. 'Why no nuts?'

'Polly, are you serious? Highest germ rate of any foodstuff. Think about it. Numerous strangers putting their fingers into the same bowl and then into their mouths.'

'God, how horrible! I'd never thought about it, and me a hygiene freak. Yuk. That's me off public nuts. So, tell me about these people.'

'Very formal, very successful, American bankers with career wives.'

'What are career wives? Sounds like a contradiction in terms.'

'Not at all. These are women who know every detail of their husbands' jobs. They are fully supportive. At a party they work a room, knowing whom they should talk to and about what. They host business dinners at home for their husbands, take the other wives out to lunch. They are discreet, bright and the bedrock of their husbands' lives. They see what they do as a career, as important in its own way as what their husbands do.'

'Help, they sound terrifying.' I took a large swig of champagne.

'They are. Belinda can't cope with them at all. They don't understand someone who wants to stay at home with babies and doesn't really have a clue what their husband does all day. She in turn doesn't understand why on earth they'd leave their children to go and discuss business all night. In her world you leave the office at the front door of your home. My mother was a career wife, my father wouldn't have been nearly as successful as he was without her. And she managed to run a farm as well.'

His mother sounded somewhat formidable too.

'I can't wait to meet these women,' I said rather sarcastically, 'I'm sure we'll have tons in common. My mother didn't get out of bed until eleven and never discussed what my father did, other than to make darkly muttered insinuations that he was either seducing his secretary or cavorting with ministerial aides.'

Just then three of the most immaculately clad women I

have ever seen walked over to us, followed by three squeaky-clean-looking men. All six were in suits. Each woman looked like a cross between a school matron and Barbie's mother. Each power hair-do had been set within an inch of its life, scarcely any movement registered. Their manicured nails matched their lipstick, which matched their bags and shoes. They wore skirt suits that if not actually Chanel were at least Chanel-style, all brass buttons and bouclé. Big pearl-and-gold earrings and 'important' diamond solitaires flashed on ears and fingers. They were very grown up, the type of women who don't seem capable of a normal bodily function.

Johnnie was busy shaking hands with the men while their wives looked at me with curiosity.

'Hallo,' I extended an unvarnished hand to them one by one. 'I'm Polly, I work with Johnnie. I'm afraid his wife's unwell so I'm standing in for her. Would you like something to drink?'

My attempt to defrost them was not a success.

'Oh no, thank you, dear,' said one of them, 'just some wadder. Do they have Purriay here?'

'I'll get some for you,' I replied. 'Perrier for all of you?'

'I'll take Evian, thank you,' replied another one. 'Ellen, do you not know that carbonated drinks give you cellulite?'

I thought I might giggle and made a mental note to check my thighs when I got home. I kept wondering over dinner if this was the type of woman Bill was used to, this immaculate 'career wife'. They were a foreign species to me, in one way so old-fashioned, like 1950s' housewives (or should that be 'homemakers'?) who puts their husbands in the 'Master and Man of the House' role, and yet they'd all been to university and were clearly not stupid. They were also ferociously com-petitive with one another. Not only about their husbands' careers, but their children were glittering high achievers too; they talked so much about them I felt I was intimately acquainted with each child. I couldn't imagine when the poor little things had time to sleep, with all the extra activities and talents they had. And as for the amount of charity work these women did, well, it made rattling a tin can outside the tube station on Lifeboat Day look completely pathetic. They talked in terms of gala dinners at a thousand dollars a plate.

It was a whole new world and I was mentally relegating Bill farther and farther into Unsuitable territory. It had been one thing living in Sweden, which you expected to be different, but I realized that even though they spoke a version of English there, America was just as foreign, in a different way.

The men were really quite human by comparison. A bit on the dull side and terribly clean-looking. But very charming, in an anodyne, not flirty or sexy, kind of way. Married to those women, you couldn't imagine they were ever allowed to have sex, unless it was to produce yet another astonishing offspring. It was as if all trace of sexuality had been disinfected out of them. They talked about work, their children and, inevitably, how marvellous their wives were. God, it was boring.

'I need a drink,' said Johnnie, as we walked out of the hotel.

'So do I! I hardly dared touch a drop of wine with those women watching me with such disapproval. Anyone would think it was illegal.'

'Immoral, certainly. The Americans have a very puritanical streak running through them, well the women do at least. The husbands are much more fun on their own. In the summer the wives decamp to their summer houses and the husbands run riot for eight weeks in town on their own, visiting the family for weekends. Listen, let's go to Annabel's for a quick drink to unwind, we can walk from here.'

He took my arm and we strolled down the street into Berkeley Square. It was an early summer night and I don't believe there's anywhere lovelier than London when the weather's good. We stepped down into the familiar club. A chorus of, 'Good-evening, Mr Lyle, good-evening, madam,' followed us to the bar.

'John, I need one of your best caipirinhas, please, and Polly will have a caipiroska.' He turned to me, 'I think you'll like that, it's vodka based.'

I had no idea how he knew I drank vodka.

We sat at the bar, momentarily quiet, having our drinks. It felt a bit strange being on my own with Johnnie in a night-club. I took out a cigarette to calm my nerves a bit.

'Do you mind if I have a cigarette?' I asked.

'Not at all,' he replied, reaching for a box of matches and lighting it for me. 'Do you smoke much?'

'Hardly at all and particularly not in front of my father, who is rabidly anti-smoking *and* he's bloody Health Minister at the moment! I smoke socially, when I'm having a good time.' (And when I'm nervous, I thought.)

'I'm glad you're having a good time then,' Johnnie smiled at me and we fell silent again. It was all a bit weird.

'Would you like to dance?' asked Johnnie, polishing off his funny-looking drink. Mine was so strong I was trying to sip it slowly. The music was pounding through from the swing doors leading to the restaurant and dance floor.

'OK,' I replied, finishing my cigarette.

Johnnie was a very good dancer and we twirled around to a couple of numbers before heading back to the bar, where he ordered two more drinks.

'Where did you learn to dance?' he asked me.

'Learn to dance!' I laughed, 'you must be joking, my dancing is a legacy of too many long nights in dodgy Italian nightclubs. I can't dance at all, but I can clear a dance floor in a couple of very inelegant moves.'

He asked me what I'd been doing in Italy and I told him I used to work as a rep. I realized he knew very little about me.

'A what?' he sounded puzzled.

'You know, silly uniform, foreign airport, placard, follow me to your coach, which hotel are you staying at? That sort of thing.'

'Why on earth did you do it?' He seemed genuinely amazed.

'Well, it was fun.'

'Fun? I really didn't check your CV at all well.' He was, at least, looking amused.

'Well,' I paused, 'it wouldn't have made much difference, I made most of it up.'

I looked at Johnnie, who was holding his hands over his ears. 'I'm not listening any more. I just pray you don't have a criminal record.' He took his hands down.

'Nearly, but not quite,' I laughed. 'It was only supposed to be a stop-gap for a year, but then I ended up living in Sweden.'

'And what did you do there?'

'I taught English as a foreign language,' I replied.

'Did you have some sort of training to do that?'

'None whatsoever; it was another fake CV moment, I'm afraid; but I managed to slip through and ended up, if you can believe this, teaching business English to executives at the Volvo headquarters.'

'For someone who doesn't know the difference between debit and credit in their own language, that must have presented something of a challenge.'

He was referring to a rather embarrassing episode I had had a while back with our payroll people, when I thought my salary had been taken out of my account and not paid in.

'Very funny. And I taught conversation in the evenings at the British Institute. My classes were the most popular, I will have you know. Particularly the advanced class. I took them on all sorts of adventures: we went to wine bars, the cinema, I even took them shoplifting, but it rather backfired.'

'You took your students shoplifting! Were you completely mad?'

'Well, probably. It was just that getting these rather taciturn Swedes to speak was a bit of a challenge, so I told them to chuck away their books. They all spoke much better English than I spoke Swedish at the time, they just didn't treat it as a means of communication, merely as a subject. And Swedes are painfully shy. So in my second lesson I took them to a wine bar and told them to pretend to be students from Ireland, to go over to someone in the room, chat them up and then come over to me and introduce the other person, telling me who they were and what they did. Worked a treat, they were gabbling away like native English speakers after the first glass of wine. So we didn't spend an enormous amount of time in the classroom after that. It was only when I took them into a shop and told them to pretend to steal something and then explain in English it had been a mistake that it went a bit wrong.'

I finished my second delicious drink and pressed on.

'Seems they thought I really meant them to steal something. Just as I was thinking we'd cracked the language problem! Anyway, it all got sorted out; my Swedish improved no end down at the police station, you can imagine. I think the police decided I must just be some sort of eccentric Englishwoman and I was let off. It's the closest I've come to being a criminal. The British Institute weren't thrilled and I was back to teaching beginners for a while.'

'Why did you come back?' Johnnie asked.

I wasn't sure if he was genuinely interested or merely trying to focus his mind and stay on his bar stool. I explained that I hadn't wanted to spend the rest of my life in Sweden and thought I'd better get out while I could and come back to London to start again, which was how I ended up working for him.

'I think I need another drink. John, same again, please.' Johnnie turned to me. 'And how's that working out for you?'

'All right so far. Thanks to you I've got a good job with, mostly, nice people, although you can be a complete pain on occasions, wonderful friends and my own car. All I need now is to buy a flat, but I'm not hurrying that yet. I rather enjoy being at Bumble's.'

Johnnie reached for his drink. 'How many is this, John?' he asked.

'Only the third, Mr Lyle,' replied John with a smile. 'You've a way to go before you can catch Mr Birley up; I believe his record is six.'

'That's all right then.' He took a large gulp, remarking to me, 'They make the best caipirinhas here. What do you think of yours?'

'It's delicious. What is it exactly?' I peered at the mound of crushed ice in my glass.

'Not a clue, but I think mine's a special kind of rum, limes and some sweet syrup. Yours must have vodka instead of rum. John, can you make me another one? Actually, make it one of each, they don't seem to last very long.'

'Are they very strong?' I asked.

'No, not at all,' said Johnnie, downing his third in two gulps, 'come on, let's go and dance.'

I swigged back the remains in my glass and followed Johnnie to the dance floor, where the music had slowed down considerably.

I started doing that sort of swaying thing you do when the music is slow but you don't want to look presumptuous and grab your partner, but he pulled me to him and put his arms round me. I tentatively moved in closer, feeling a bit unsteady. His breath on my cheek was sweet and limey.

'You dance just as well when the music is slow,' muttered Johnnie into my hair.

'Thank you.' I turned to look at him and the next thing I knew he was kissing me!

Wow! He certainly could kiss.

I was completely thrown. I genuinely hadn't been expecting this. But somehow my mouth stayed clamped on his and we just kissed and kissed for three songs. I eventually pulled away, muttering, 'I think I need my caipiwotsit now.'

My head was spinning, confusing thoughts swirling round. Bugger. Bugger. Bugger. First I was going to marry him, then I loathed him, then we had a sort of *détente* and got on as colleagues, friends even, and now he had to go and ruin it all by kissing me. At every possible twist and turn of my life, fate conspired against me to throw just about the exact thing I didn't want my way. It was extraordinary.

He sat down beside me and I grabbed my drink.

'Not only a great dancer, but one of the best kissers. Thank you, that was a memorable dance.' He had a huge grin on his face.

Hell! Now he was making it sound like I kissed him, when it was the other way round. Oh my God.

'Three dances in fact,' I said, trying to regain my composure.

'Really?' he said slowly. 'They all sort of rolled into one somehow.'

He was looking at me intently, his green eyes twinkling. I shivered. I was absolutely *not* going to fall for this man. This serial-seducer, married, horrid boss. I opened my mouth to say something along those lines but he interrupted me.

'Come on, finish your drink, I'll take you home.'

He downed his fourth caipirinha as I struggled to finish my drink. It seemed awfully strong to me.

We staggered up the stairs and the cold night air made me feel incredibly dizzy. I had to hold on to Johnnie's arm for support – not that he was much steadier – and we both weaved our way in the direction of the car.

There were a number of traffic cones in the road. 'Look at those. Woops!' said Johnnie, as he tripped over one. 'Not neat, I'm going to rearrange them.'

He tottered into the road, lurching from one cone to another, carefully placing them so that any passing car – had there been one at the time, he'd have been run over – was going to find itself turning full circle back to Grosvenor Square, in the wrong direction down a one-way street! Stiff, pompous and rude Johnnie Lyle had transmuted into a maverick with a sense of fun whose stammer had disappeared. There was hope for him after all; alcohol certainly released a better side. Job done, he precariously balanced one of the cones on his head and turned to me, swaying. 'Whatd'ya think?'

'Nice hat. Now get out of the road before you get killed, you silly man.'

He reluctantly put the cone down and wobbled over to me,

grabbing on to my arm. 'You're a wunnerful girl . . . always thought so, pain in the arse but . . . ' He trailed off.

'Er, thank you.' I didn't want to say too much, I was feeling very confused, not to mention a bit blurry and possibly slightly sick. 'It was a good evening. Educational.'

He laughed. 'And a funny girl.'

'You're the funny one,' I replied, still smiling at his antics.

'Now,' he hiccuped, 'where's my car?'

I steered him back in the direction of the Connaught. 'You left it with the doorman at the hotel. Are you OK to drive?'

'Absolutely,' he said seriously. 'Never been pissed in my life; hollow legs.'

'Well, that explains why they can't hold you up properly then. The hotel's just there.'

We went up to the doorman, who retrieved the car. I slid into the passenger seat as Johnnie fidgeted with his seat-belt.

'Bloody thing,' he muttered, 'oh s'all right, f'gerrit.'

'Johnnie, you have to put your belt on. Here, let me do it.' I reached over to put his belt on and he gave another little hiccup. Oh God, my head started spinning when it went below my shoulders. I leant back in the seat hoping Johnnie felt better than me.

'S'fine. Less go.' He sounded a bit strange.

He pulled into Park Lane. 'Can't see anything,' he muttered.

'What!' I said, alarmed. 'What do you mean you can't see anything?'

'S'all blurry, hang on, thass better.' I looked round at him: he had one hand on the steering wheel and the other clamped over an eye.

'Bloody hell, Johnnie, you can't drive like that,' I exclaimed.

'Can't drive any other way, at least this way I can see.' He started to giggle and the car swerved into another lane.

'Slow down, you fool, you'll get stopped by the police.'

I seemed to be the one with hollow legs now, and a hollow stomach, but I was giggling with frantic nerves.

'They only stop you if you drive too slow. See!' He put his

foot on the accelerator and we sped round the corner and back up the other side of Park Lane. Thank God there was very little traffic. How he negotiated the rest of the journey remains a mystery; the effects of my caipiroskas were definitely kicking in and I was feeling really dizzy. I just relaxed in my seat and thought, well, if I'm going to die in a car crash, at least it will be when I'm so drunk I probably won't feel anything, and at least I kissed Johnnie Lyle. Or did he kiss me?

31

I *hated* Johnnie Lyle and I was *never* going to drink a caipiwotsit *ever* again. It took me all weekend to get over my hangover and the subsequent week at work was horrendous.

I hadn't spoken a word of what happened to anyone – I was incapable of speech for the first twenty-four hours anyway. I was confused enough, without having to think about it again and hear Bumble's or anyone else's opinion. I'd been dreading going into work on Monday, with justification, as it turned out. Johnnie all but ignored me. On top of which it seemed like half the female population of London was having lunch or dinner with him that week. After two six-thirty sessions with the Pantheress hair-tossing all over the office, demanding glasses of wine, sitting at my desk using my phone or wrapping herself around Johnnie in his office in the manner of some well-shod octopus, I was reaching saturation point. It wasn't that I wanted him, it was just that being cold-shouldered was so infuriating. We'd been a bit pissed, it happened, it was just a kiss, we could move on from there. Mistakes happen, but it wasn't my fault and I didn't see why I had to suffer.

'Do you want to have lunch with me today?' Johnnie strode into my office and shut the door.

'I beg your pardon?' I replied frostily.

'It's Friday, it's been a long week and I wondered if you would like to have lunch with me.'

'Good Lord, Johnnie, are you sure you have time in your hectic social timetable?' I asked sarcastically.

'Look, please give me a break. I want to t–talk to you, about – well, you know, there are some things we need to discuss.'

'Fine,' I snapped, 'I'll book the Caprice. Anything else?'

'No, no, I'll see you there at one.' He sped out of the door.

'What on earth is going on with you two?' Samantha appeared in my doorway.

'Absolutely nothing. Why?' I was startled to see her.

'Well, it's been very weird round here this week, and Merry and I think something's going on.'

'I'm delighted that you and Merry are so interested, but I assure you, nothing's going on; he was just being his usual ghastly self and is no doubt taking me out to lunch to apologize, again.'

'You're going out to lunch with him?' She sounded surprised.

'Yes, I often have lunch with him on Fridays, you know that. We generally discuss work, it's not very interesting and he usually apologizes for being an arsehole all week, we part friends, have a nice weekend and he returns on Monday in Gestapo mode and we start all over again. It's the pattern.'

'I see, well Merry and I think . . . '

I held up my hand. 'Sam, darling, please. I don't want to know what you both think, it's just work.'

'All right, have it your own way,' she said rather huffily, 'but something's going on and when you want to talk about it, we're here for you.'

She walked out and I felt rotten not telling them. But what was there to tell? Apart from a rather embarrassing, drunken moment, which clearly meant nothing to anyone.

We sat at our usual place at the bar and Johnnie ordered a bottle of white wine. 'Look, I have to apologize for what happened last Friday,' he started.

'It's fine, Johnnie, honestly. It's not your fault, we were both a bit pissed; you lied by the way about how strong those bloody drinks were, and it just happened. I'm OK about it. However, I am not OK about how unbelievably rude you've been to me this week.'

'That's what I wanted to explain.' He poured us both a glass of wine. 'I spent the weekend thinking about my life and what I was doing. And what happened with you made me realize that everything was getting out of control, or rather I was and my life was. There are too many people in it already – '

'You can say that again,' I interrupted him rather grumpily.

'Will you let me finish, you exasperating woman!' I waited as he continued – 'starting with my wife and children.'

'Well, that's a first,' I said, immediately breaking my silence.

'Polly, if you're going to make this even more difficult for me, we can just forget it.'

'No, no, sorry, carry on.' I grabbed my glass and told myself to shut up.

'And my life is ridiculous. I stand to lose everything I thought I wanted, everything I've worked so hard to achieve, by fooling around. There might be mitigating circumstances, the old "my wife doesn't understand me/support me" line, but the point is, I really feel I must give it a go.'

'And what does kissing me have to do with all of this?' I enquired.

'Exactly, I really like you and I'm in no position to do that,' he said.

'And what about that Pantheress and all the others?' I asked.

'Who?' He looked very puzzled.

'Dora, your girlfriend, and the hordes of other women you talk to on the phone and take out.'

'Pantheress!' he laughed, 'well, I can see why you call her that. Got names for the others too?'

'Sadly not, but I'm sure I could think of some. Anyway, carry on, I'm all ears.' I took a large gulp of wine, wondering where this was leading.

'So, I decided it was time I sorted myself out and I've had a very difficult week, disentangling myself from my various, er, attachments. Which has not been easy; the Pantheress, as you call her, put up a most unseemly fight about the whole thing – tears, the lot.' He shivered. 'It was awful.'

'What, am I supposed to feel sorry for you now? Give me a break, Johnnie. I suppose this is another kiss off?'

'No, no, don't put it like that. You were the final straw, or perhaps I could word that better.' He looked hastily at my unamused face. 'You were a light that illuminated what I was doing. There I was with someone whom I really like and respect' (yeah right . . .) 'and I was fooling around again. You're worth much more than that. It just made me think. I don't want my life to be like this any more. That's what I'm trying to tell you. I want to start over again with B—Belinda and the children. Really give it a go. I can't have you or anyone else in the background, as a sort of opt-out clause if it doesn't work. I want home cooking, no more outside catering.'

We sat in silence for a while as I thought over what he'd said. If he really was going to give his marriage a proper go, then who was I to say anything negative. It wasn't as if I wanted him anyway, so I relented.

'Listen, if that's what you're going to do, then I fully support you. I think it's a brilliant idea. You and me, we're fine. We work together and can be friends, probably. Just don't ever give me one of those drinks again, and you'd better stay off them yourself too!' I raised my glass to him. 'Here's to you and your family. I hope you decide you like eating in.'

'Thank you, you're being very understanding.'

We fell silent again until I asked him if he had said anything to Belinda.

'Well, I haven't confessed all, if that's what you mean. But I did sit down on Saturday and say I wanted to spend more time with her. Instead of staying in London during the week, unless it's really late, I'm going to try and get back home.'

'And was she pleased?' I asked.

'Yes, I think she was. We had a nice weekend. I bought a puppy, which she's been wanting for ages. I'm going to make a real effort. I know I'm not easy to live with and, God knows, having two tiny children puts a strain on most marriages. I'm a tidiness fanatic' (understatement of the century, I thought) 'and all those nappies and toys lying about everywhere drive me wild. But we're getting a live-in nanny, which I've resisted up until now, so Belinda can spend more time with me in the evenings. It's difficult when you've been working all hours to come back to some frazzled, un-made-up wife who smells of sick and is too tired to talk. All you want to do is unwind, have a glass of wine and share your day.'

'God, I hope you didn't tell her she looked rough and smelled of sick. I can't imagine that would have gone down well.'

I was making mental notes to myself to ensure that I would always be immaculate and fragrant when my husband returned home at the end of the day. Assuming I ever got a husband.

'Of course not. Now, let's eat, I'm starving.'

The rest of lunch was very jolly. Johnnie and I seemed to have turned yet another corner in our rather strange relationship. We started to discuss the up-coming party.

'So presumably Belinda's coming to the party? I asked him.

'She is indeed. I am taking her shopping for a new outfit, which I really enjoy.' He smiled.

'You enjoy shopping?' I was astonished. 'Most men loathe it.'

'I love it. In another life I'd like to have been a dress designer. I love clothes. When I'm on a business trip, I unwind by going shopping.'

'Blimey, a man who likes shopping. You really are unique and so in touch with your feminine side, Johnnie Lyle, I'm most impressed. Do you try them on for size?'

'Don't be funny. I'm not gay in any way.'

That much about him was pretty obvious, I thought.

'I just like to see women well dressed. Who are you bringing, by the way. I've never asked about your private life. I assume you have one.' He chuckled.

'Well, just about, thank you,' I replied. 'I'm bringing my ex-boyfriend, Carlo.'

'Ex?' he raised one eyebrow at me.

'Yes, ex, but we get on very well. He's Italian and he's come to England to learn English.'

'I hope you are giving him lots of lessons.' Johnnie had an irritating grin on his face.

'I'm teaching him nothing, we're just good friends now.'

I was finding it increasingly difficult to remain 'just good friends' with Carlo, but wasn't going to share that information with Mr Curious at the table.

'Is there anyone else in your life, no other boyfriend, ex or otherwise? Stop me if I'm overstepping the mark, by the way.'

'No, that's fine. I'm still sort of getting over my relationship with Mats and I don't want to repeat my past mistakes, so I'm being cautious.' I looked up at him, smiling, 'Except of course when I get pissed in nightclubs with extremely unsuitable married men.' I was most definitely not going to tell him about Bill, but I was wondering how it would be when I saw him at the party.

'But you're OK about that?' He looked anxiously at me.

'Don't worry, I'm fine. We should both just forget about it. Honestly, it was a fun evening, despite those ghastly American women, although, in their own way, they were highly entertaining, without meaning to be. Wow, I could never live in America, I don't have either the right wardrobe or attitude.'

'Well, I'm sure you won't have to. I should get Belinda to organize a dinner party so you can meet some of our eligible bachelor friends.'

I groaned. 'Please don't. I'm not sure I could cope with another corduroy boy.' I explained about the disastrous match-making attempts by Merry, which had him crying with laughter.

'OK, we'll find a man in a suit for you.'

I silently thought that most ironic. 'Listen, I think we'd better get back to the office, in case they start talking,' I said. 'But before we go, I just want to say that I really hope it works out for you. I mean it. And if you ever need a little pep talk to keep you on the straight and narrow, I'm here.'

He leant across the table and held my hand and looked at me intently. 'Thank you. You've no idea what that means to me.'

A little shiver went down my spine, and I drew my hand away slowly.

32

It was the office-party night. The whole event had been organized and I was feeling on top of everything – except, of course, fashion-crisis loomed, as I had nothing to wear.

'For God's sake, stop whingeing and go and buy something new,' said Bumble, irritably. 'You earn enough money to treat yourself every now and then.'

'I know, but I'm supposed to be saving for a flat. My father is nagging me all the time to buy something, but it terrifies me; suppose I get fired and then can't pay the mortgage?'

'For someone so normally upbeat, your cup is definitely half-empty when it comes to your job.'

'Well, I'm constantly worried they're going to see through me and realize I'm qualified for nothing.'

'You're completely mad,' sniffed Bumble, with the super-cilious air of a kept woman. 'You've never been qualified for anything, but you're doing a great job for them. Ciggie?'

'Er, no thanks. Look, Bumble, you don't even know what I do, I don't know what I do, and after the offices in London have been decorated, I don't think there's anything left for me to do. Hugo suggested I take some exams to become the company secretary, which sounded awful, loads of work and all figures and boring stuff. They're just trying to find something for me, which is nice, but we all know, unless the situation changes, in a few months I'll be out of a job. Anyway, you're right, I'll go and buy something sexy for this evening.'

'Is Bill going to be there?' asked Bumble in a casual-sounding voice.

'Well, supposedly, but I haven't heard from him for ages and I can hardly ask the boys without arousing their suspicions. Johnnie is particularly interested in my social life all of a sudden.'

'Well, I can't imagine why that would be,' said Bumble in an irony-laden voice.

It was impossible to keep anything from her.

'Don't be like that,' I said, 'we're just friends. He's trying so hard at home. Goes back every night, talks about the children, it's sweet. He's even nice round the office; everyone likes him. He seems much happier as well. So don't look at me so cynically. It's bad enough having to field calls from that wretched Dora, who appears to think I'm single-handedly preventing her from speaking to him. Johnnie told me to not put her calls through, but I'm running out of excuses as to why he's never there. I tell you, that woman never gives up.'

'Whatever you say,' Bumble replied, airily. 'Go on, go shopping and stop wittering.'

At lunchtime, in desperation, I phoned my mother.

'Mummeeee, help! I can't find anything to wear to the office party tonight. What can I do?'

'Darling,' she cooed down the phone, 'where are you?'

'I'm standing in a telephone booth in Harvey Nichols, having spent nothing except futile hours looking for something sexy to buy – and THERE'S NOTHING!'

'I have the perfect solution for you, darling. What size are you at the moment?'

'Thank you, mother; getting bigger every day, living at Bumble's. What's your solution?' I was already regretting the phone call.

'My black lace outfit. I haven't worn it for ages, it hangs off me, but I'm sure it will fit you. It's an absolute killer, results guaranteed.'

'What is this garment, mother?' I asked. 'I don't seem to recall it in your vast wardrobe.'

'Well, darling, I never wasted it on your father.' She laughed, tinkling down the phone. 'It would be perfect for you.'

'Thank you, but there is one problem, it's there and I'm here.'

'Oh, darling, you do worry so about geography. Get in your

car, I'll meet you halfway, we can have a drink in Oxford. Won't that be fun?'

'Mum, are you mad? Drive to Oxford to get a dress I haven't even seen?'

'If you have a better solution, my darling, let me know. In the meantime, it will only take you an hour to get there, and you could easily spend twice the amount of time in that horrid store and still not find anything. Come on, get in the car, it'll be fun. I know you'll love the dress.'

If it had been anyone other than my mother, I would never have done this. But, I had to confess, she did have a really good eye for clothes, and frankly anything was better than getting depressed by not being able to wriggle into a slinky size twelve (Italian). Anyway, I could do with a dose of my mother's *joie de vivre*.

So I sped down to Oxford and walked into Brown's to find her sitting with a bottle of wine on the table and a large black bin-bag at her feet.

'Darling!' she enveloped me in a perfumed hug, kissing me three times (like the Swiss, she said, so much more advanced than the French). 'You look wonderful. Just look at your bosoms.'

'Shh, mum, everyone will hear.' I looked ruefully at my now rather impressive *embonpoint*. 'Do you have to talk about my breasts as though I'd brought them in on a lead like a pair of chihuahuas.'

'More like great danes, darling,' she laughed.

'And don't mention Scandinavia either,' I snapped, before giggling myself. 'I don't know why you like me fat, must be some latent maternal nurturing thing. Either that, or you're a scheming, competitive mother, who wishes to remain thinner and more beautiful than her daughter.'

'Oh, darling, don't be silly,' replied my mother, running a hand over her very flat stomach. 'I really do think you look better that way. Now, we digress, have a glass of wine, it's quite delicious, that gorgeous waiter thoroughly recommended it, and take a look at what I've brought for you, shoes and all. So don't you dare say I don't care what you look like.' She pulled out a pair of shiny black stilettos, followed by two rather crumpled-looking pieces of lace.

'What on earth are those?' I was horrified. I appeared to have driven fifty miles to collect some sort of hooker's fancy-dress outfit.

'Well,' said my mother, eyeing them as if for the first time, 'they look much better on.'

'Mum,' I started to unravel the lace, 'this blouse is virtually see-through and the skirt definitely is.'

'I told you it was a killer outfit,' my mother replied, sounding very pleased.

'I can't wear this! God knows what message I'll be giving off. Bill the big boss is going to be there, and I'm taking Carlo as my date. He'll get totally the wrong impression.'

'You don't mean that gorgeous boy from Capri?' gasped my mother, 'all black wavy hair and black eyes, and those shoulders. Oh,' she gave a shudder of what I assumed was delight, 'I'll *never* forget seeing him on the beach all those years ago.'

'Yes, him, mummy. The one I lived with in Naples, remember?'

'I didn't know you were living with him in Naples, darling. I'd have come over to visit.'

'Mummy,' I sighed, 'I sometimes wonder if you ever know what I'm doing!'

'Oh, darling, I don't need to know the details, just as long as I know which country you're in and that you're happy. That's enough for me.' She smiled and poured herself another glass of wine. 'You know, my mother was terribly interfering, quite inhibited me. You and your brother must be free. It's very unselfish of me you know, most mothers cling to their children like limpets, poor things. Very important to have your own life.'

I wasn't sure whose life she was talking about at this point, I was back to wondering what on earth I could put on under this ensemble that would make it less revealing. I definitely had no more time to go shopping.

'Now, tell me, how are those nice boys you work with? Any little romance there?'

'You remember them?' I was amazed, and slightly disconcerted; my mother's perception was indeed finely tuned. She was, after all, the seventh daughter of the seventh daughter, supposedly making her a witch, in Spook World.

'Oh yes, darling, of course, that nice Windsor boy, and the other one, with the curly-wurly smile.'

'They're fine, and no romance there, sorry to say.'

'Ah well, never mind. I'd find it so useful booking tables.'

'What do you mean?' I asked, confused.

'Mrs Windsor,' she said, as if stating the obvious.

'I think you are a little too old for Hugo, mummy,' I said, laughing at the thought.

'Not me, you, silly,' said my mother.

'Er, no, I don't think that's an option. But I do quite like their boss.' I was hesitant about saying too much.

'Ooh,' she squeaked, 'tell me more. Have another glass of wine.'

I took a deep breath and slightly against my better judgement told her about Bill.

'Darling,' she said, when I had finished, 'he sounds *divine!*'

'Well, he is, but it's pretty improbable that anything will come of it. He's too old, he doesn't live here, and after what I've seen of American women, I can't imagine living there. Anyway, I've already lived abroad and now I want to stay in England.'

'Oh, don't be so rigid, darling. Life is full of opportunity; you must never close a door before you've looked behind it. And if you do shut it, you can give me the key – he sounds just my type!'

'Mummy, you're impossible, what's happened to the man from Penang?'

'Oh, he's still around, but you know, he's married and,' she lowered her voice dramatically, 'he's a Northerner.'

'So now who's being rigid?' I teased. 'Anyway, it's disgusting, the idea of a mother and daughter having the same man.'

'I'm not suggesting at the same time, darling, that really would be disgusting. He sounds lovely that's all. I'm so pleased you're going to be wearing my dress.'

'Well, I'd better get going if I want to make the party. Thank you so much,' I bent down to give her a hug, 'it was lovely to see you. Are you coming?'

'No, not yet, I think I might just have one more glass of wine. Could you ask that nice waiter to come over? He's from Italy, you know. We were having a lovely chat about Capri before you came.'

'Mum, you're amazing. I only hope I have half your zest for life when I'm your age.' I hugged her again and sped off back to London.

33

'Good Lord!' Gareth spluttered as I walked into the drawing-room. 'Are you planning to keep that on for long?'

'Polleeee!' William the Lodger gave a long whistle, 'that'll get them all going.'

'Pol–li, it's wery sexy. I like dat outfid,' said Pia.

'Killer dress, your mother's right,' observed Bumble, disapprovingly.

'You look like a scary witch,' said Minnie.

'Thank you, everyone, for your comments. I'm extremely nervous about this dress, but sadly I have nothing else to wear. Can someone please give me a drink.'

I fiddled about with the lace self-consciously. It really left very little to the imagination.

Bumble handed me one of her vodka concoctions. 'You OK?' she looked at me enquiringly.

'Sort of. I just got a call from Bill saying that he wasn't going to be able to make the party, which is a real piss-off. Here I am, dressed up to the nines, with only my ex-boyfriend to appreciate it, and the rest of the office will probably think I'm out to steal all their men, it's so bloody revealing. I dread to think what my mother got up to in it. I hope it's been cleaned.'

'I'm looking forward to Carlo's reaction,' Bumble said, as the doorbell rang, 'most entertaining. No doubt that's him now.'

'I'll get it!' said Minnie, racing to the front door. 'Hallo, come in. Are you Carlo? My name is Minnie.' She looked tiny standing in front of him looking up. 'You have lots of black hair. Are you Polly's new boyfriend? She has a witch's dress on, you know, and you can see her boobies, nearly all of them.'

I was grateful his English wasn't good.

'Pollita,' said Carlo, entering the room, 'Dio mio, che vestito!' He stood stock still in the doorway. 'Incredibili!'

'Thank you, Carlo.' I tried to keep a straight face as everyone else in the room fell about laughing. 'I'll just get my coat. Gareth, will you give Carlo a drink, I think he needs one.'

'Poor bloody bloke, I expect he does,' said Gareth. 'Carlo, what – would – you – like – to – drink?' he spoke very slowly, waving his hand back and forth in the manner of someone drinking from an imaginary glass.

'I take a wine, please,' replied Carlo, in his best, newly acquired English.

'What – you – think – of – Polly's – dress? Good?'

Gareth handed Carlo a glass of wine.

'Dress?' Carlo looked confused.

'Quite right old chap, hardly a dress at all. Kay – la – fa – pensa – di – ves–ti–to del Polly? Bonneetoe?' Gareth was very proud of his Italian.

Carlo laughed. 'Si, si, molto bene. Is very nice, I like a lot.'

'Looks like you're in for a good evening,' whispered William to me as I returned.

'Shut up,' I whispered back. 'We're just friends.'

'Won't last long, not in that outfit.' He smirked at me.

We finished our drinks and I thought it was time to go.

'Carlo, andiamo. Let's go. Bye, everyone.'

'Bye,' they chorused, grins fixed to every face. 'Have fun.'

When we arrived at the party, there were only a few people there. Johnnie and Belinda came up to us as I was taking off my coat.

'Polly,' Johnnie kissed me on each cheek, 'good-evening.' He paused as he saw my dress and gave a funny sort of gasp, then gathered his composure and introduced himself and Belinda to Carlo.

'Carlo di Luca Morgano. My pleasure.'

Carlo shook Johnnie's hand and then turned to Belinda, and with a little half-bow, raised her hand to his lips and kissed it. 'Mio piacere. A more pleasure.'

Belinda turned a rather fetching shade of pink. She regarded me with a distinctly frosty stare and said, 'Good-evening, Polly, you're certainly going to drag attention to yourself in that get-up.' She sounded very disapproving.

I was rather irritated by this. I deserved no snide comments from her, considering I was the one encouraging her husband to stay on the straight and narrow (drunken kisses in nightclubs excluded). I suggested to Carlo that we go and get a drink.

We stood at the bar and watched the other people arrive. Samantha came racing up, with her new man in tow, who was almost a clone of Hugo. Very sweet and cherubic-looking, all pink cheeks and floppy blond hair.

She momentarily forgot her not-so-single status when she laid eyes on Carlo and went into her squirmy, sex-kitten mode, until I kicked her.

'Blimey, Poll, he's gorgeous, no wonder you're wearing such a fuck-me dress,' she hissed.

'It's my mother's,' I hissed back at her. 'And we're just friends.'

'Yeah, right. I've seen starving lions look less interested in flesh. You watch out, girl, it's a bit of "spic dick" for you tonight and no mistaking.'

'You are quite revolting, Sam, what the hell is spic dick?' I laughed.

'Spic is short for Hispanic, and dick, well I know it's been a long time, Poll, but I'm sure you'll remember one when you see it.' She giggled and I couldn't be bothered to remind her he was Italian.

Merry had brought Michael, who polished his glasses ferociously when he saw my dress and proceeded to give me a kiss on the cheek and a squeeze on the bottom at the same time.

'*What* a dress!' chortled Merry, as she came up beside me, and then lowered her voice to a dramatic stage whisper, 'and *what* a dish! Yummee. Lucky my Michael is here, otherwise I might not be able to control myself.'

'Control your pants, you mean,' corrected Samantha.

'Excuse me, the pair of you,' I interrupted their banter. 'He's an ex and not on the agenda, you know that. Do I have to go over it all again?' I had to admit, however, that Carlo was looking divine, and attracting all sorts of stares as people came into the party.

'Doesn't count with an ex,' said Merry with an air of great authority.

'I agree,' said Samantha. The pair of them had formed a most unlikely alliance over the months we'd worked together.

'Right then, I'll remember that when I'm back at Altonative Towers tonight, on my own. I'm going to circulate.'

'Well, you'd better take Carlo with you, because I guarantee he won't be here when you get back if you leave him alone,' said Samantha.

I'd done seating arrangements for dinner and followed my mother's 'placement' advice – 'Darling, always put the bores next to each other' – her theory being that everyone makes the mistake of putting their best, chatty guest beside the 'placement from hell', the bore. To her way of thinking, this is quite wrong, on the basis bores don't know they're boring, in fact quite often they believe themselves to be rather interesting, so sit them together and they can bore the pants of each other. And one's lively guests deserve to meet like-minded souls and have fun. I put all the shy ones together as well, that way they could save themselves the horror of having to talk to anyone at all! Naturally, I had Samantha, Merry, Jayne, Rohan and their respectives. I'd scattered Johnnie and Hugo to host other tables.

As the dancing started I felt Carlo, who was sitting beside me, put his hand on my thigh. I turned to him and he smiled, then leaning towards me he whispered, 'Mi stai caldo. You making me hot.'

'Carlo, really!' I smiled, removing his hand. 'It was probably the soup.'

'Is not soup, is you,' he said emphatically.

'Well, thank you,' I replied with a smile, 'flattery will get you everywhere.'

'Ees true.' He leant over to me, placing both his hands round my waist, 'I want to be everywhere.'

He made it sound like, 'I want to pee everywhere,' and I started to laugh.

'Why is funny?'

'Nothing,' I said hastily. Italian men are very proud. 'Do you want to dance?'

'Naturalmente.' He rose from his chair and took me on to the dance floor, where we joined a number of the others. He pulled me in close and started to move slowly. It was disconcertingly familiar being this near to him, his breath was hot on my neck. His black hair brushed my cheek. Oof, it was hard. To resist him, that is. Thoughts of Bill were drifting away as we moved round the floor. I was in ecstasy as our bodies moulded more closely into each other with each song. Belinda and Johnnie came up beside us on the dance floor and Johnnie asked if we would like to change partners. Belinda slipped into Carlo's arms with indecent haste and a smile on her face. Johnnie propelled me masterfully over to the other side of the room.

'Good party,' he stated

'Thank you,' I replied. 'Are you enjoying it?'

'I like this bit of it,' he said, looking right into my eyes.

God, the man was incorrigible, and I told him to behave.

'It's a party,' he said, 'don't be so grumpy, come and have a drink.' He led me towards the bar.

'What about Belinda?' I asked

'I think she's in very good hands, wouldn't you say?' He looked across the dance floor to where Belinda and Carlo were doing a very professional *le rock* type dance, all synchronized movements. I felt slightly jealous that Carlo was having a good time with someone else.

'So, have you and Carlo been going out for long?' he asked, affecting a disinterested air.

I thought for a moment before replying; he'd either for-gotten I'd told him he was an ex, or was being nosy. I reiterated that we were 'just good friends', in a manner I hoped could be interpreted either way. I felt I needed a bit of distance from Johnnie.

'I see.' He sounded strange and we lapsed into an uncomfortable silence. I was happy when Carlo delivered Belinda back to Johnnie and whisked me on to the dance floor again.

He put his lips to my ear and his hot breath made my neck coil with desire as he whispered, 'We can soon go, yes?'

I looked around, the party seemed to be in full swing and I wondered if I'd be missed; the temptation of slipping away unnoticed was too great and Carlo and I stepped out into the night air and hailed a cab. I asked the driver to take us to Fulham and before I even had time to sit back in my seat Carlo pulled me towards him and started to kiss me. I thought my knickers were going to burst into flames.

Every point of my body was electrified by lust. I was instantly transported back four years to our steamy, unendingly sexual time in Italy and knew that once again I was in the grip of an overwhelming passion which had simply been lying dormant all these years. If I could have welded him on to my body it wouldn't have been close enough. God knows what the poor taxi driver thought as Carlo's hands grabbed me everywhere. With one hand he twisted my bra fastening until it snapped open and with a groan he left my mouth where he had been previously ferociously busy and buried his head in my breasts, his fingers probing under my pants, inserting themselves inside me. I nearly came on the spot.

'Carlo, my God, what are you doing?' I managed to gasp.

'You wear this dress,' he reverted to Italian, 'and you expect me to do nothing? Are you crazy? It's impossible to resist.'

Mother was right, as usual, and as Carlo resumed his passionate attentions, I silently thanked her.

As the taxi drew up outside Altonative Towers, we managed to pull ourselves apart.

'Blimey mate,' said the taxi driver. 'You been banged up or summat, 'cos it don't look like you've seen a bit of skirt for a while?'

I tried to smooth down my hair and clothes and fervently hoped no one was awake. We were in luck, the house was quiet. It seemed weirdly normal that Carlo would just follow me to my bedroom. Or perhaps just inevitable.

The moment the door shut, he pulled me towards him, picked me up and carried me over to the bed. In absolute silence he slowly peeled off my clothes, saying nothing but breathing deeply. Once I was naked, he stood back and stared at me; without removing his gaze he slowly took off his shirt, each button revealing another inch of thick black chest hair (he must have been putting Baby-Bio on himself, I didn't remember quite such a forest there before). Once his white shirt was off, revealing his muscled, tanned upper body, he kicked off his shoes and undid his trousers, which slid to the floor, leaving him naked too. He never wore underpants. I couldn't contain myself any longer and stood up in front of him and pressed our bodies together. I dug my fingers into the flesh of his back while he grabbed my hair and pulled my head back, exposing my throat, which he started biting; the pain sent tremors to my groin and my knees buckled. I grabbed hold of his hair with one hand to pull myself up and bit his shoulder as he started to run his tongue up my neck and into my ear, then over my eyes and down my nose until it reached my mouth again. I wanted him inside me so badly. My back arched as I pressed myself to him, feeling him hard like a rod against me. He pushed me on to the bed, still like a clamp on my mouth, and with one swift movement was inside me, fast and furiously pumping with an animal intensity. I couldn't breathe. I threw my head back and gasped then stifled a scream as uncontrollable waves of pleasure crashed through my body. His back tensed and his breathing grew faster and with a final shove he made a noise as if all the air inside him was being punched out. The sight and feeling of him having so much pleasure started me off again and unbelievably I climaxed for a second time, more intensely, as though my insides were being dragged out of me. We remained joined, hot and sweaty, wordless. I was in trouble and I didn't care. The absolute exquisiteness of such heightened passion buried logic and reason, leaving me with stupid fantasies. A tear trickled down my cheek, I felt completely out of control of all my emotions. It was so strange to be lying in Carlo's arms again; I was jelly, physically and emotionally.

'Che cosa c'é, tesoro,' asked Carlo gently, wiping away my tear.

'Niente. Nothing. I'm OK, it was just a bit . . . '

'Lo so, I know, for me too.' He kissed me gently and stroked my face. 'Always with you is incredible. I never forget.'

34

'Polly, I'm going to force you to take either a plumbing or a topiary course, your gorgeous boyfriend moults more than my mother's spaniel.' Bumble was semi-serious. 'Please don't get me wrong, we all love Carlo and feel he has added a wonderful international, not to say garlicky, ingredient to the household, but every time I emerge from my bath I am covered in black hair, which is very alarming. On top of which, the water never drains. I've spent more time getting to know the local plumbers than I care to calculate. Do you think we could drug him one night and shave it all off?' She giggled.

'You just want to see him naked, you old pervert, and I can't say I blame you, he has the most incredible body – and I've never seen so much hair on someone's chest in my life.'

I still hadn't quite come to terms with any of the developments of the last few weeks. After my night of passion with Carlo, I assumed that would be it. I certainly rather hoped it would be because it stirred up all sorts of conflicting emotions. Carlo, however, appeared to want to carry on from where we had left off, as if nothing (other than his chest, of course) had changed. It was lovely, but very confusing. It was also weird being back with someone after a gap of four years. In some ways it's like a time warp, as though the experiences and knowledge you gained in the interim are irrelevant and you're just the same person you were before. You can't be, of course, but it feels like you are. Relationships are unique to the people involved and I think that once the terms and balances are worked out, they don't change. If you were insecure before, you will be again. If one of you was dominant and the other subservient, it doesn't change. You fall right back into the same old groove. Perhaps professional help can shift the dynamics, but I'm not sure. Anyway, even after a long time apart, Carlo and I still had the same relationship we had before.

On the one hand that was fantastic, we had such fun together and let's be honest, no one wants one of the greatest shags of their life to remain anything but that! However, none of my previous concerns about why the relationship wouldn't work had gone away. He was still five years younger than me, with no intention of settling down. There seemed no hope of a future for us and even if there was, I didn't want to be a Italian wife, living a completely restricted life in a country where women are decidedly second-class citizens and the men are universally unfaithful. He was so not part of the Plan, as Bumble was quick to remind me. And there was Bill. Out of sight, but not out of mind. It was all wrong and not what I'd planned.

I decided I had no choice but to give up.

The summer was upon us and it was hot. Six months had passed since I returned from Sweden, and although it seemed that as far as the Plan had gone, I'd spectacularly failed, everything else in my life was working well. So much so, that my once precarious financial position had changed to the degree that I was contemplating buying a flat. It was obvious that you just can't have it all in life and there seemed little point in continuing the search. Fate was either going to throw the right person at me or not, but in the meantime, I was going to have a thoroughly good time with my highly unsuitable boyfriend while working up the courage to tell Bumble I was planning on moving out sometime in the near future.

35

'Happy autumn, everyone,' trilled Merry as she sauntered into the office, 'how are we all? Not late am I?' It was a rhetorical question as Merry had never been in on time, but it highlighted the fact that Johnnie still hadn't arrived, which was strange.

'No, you're in luck, Johnnie isn't in yet,' I replied, smiling at the look of shock on her face.

The office had been shut for a two-week summer break, so we were all madly catching up. Hugo and Samantha were engrossed in his office. I looked at them, thinking what a difference six months can make. Samantha had got engaged to her nice accountant on holiday. She was blissfully content, all thoughts of snaring Hugo well behind her. I'm not sure if he had ever realized he'd been the object of quite such interest to her, but if he had he was far too gentlemanly to make any reference to it.

Merry's summer had been my idea of complete hell, marooned up in the farthest flung, remotest and coldest part of Scotland in a huge draughty castle, stalking. But she had loved it and went into graphic detail about these poor stags' deaths. How she'd crawled through bushes, waited behind rocks till her hands went blue, etc., etc. Hardly surprising she'd been able to catch a man, they sounded easy by comparison!

I spent the holiday in Capri with Carlo. Capri, as I've said before, is like my second home. A tiny island rising sharply out of the sea; houses crammed together cheek by jowl, covered in ivy and flowers, deceptively large and cool on the inside, in a charming old town teeming with beautiful people; a myriad of tiny beaches beside an aquamarine sea; little restaurants and bars, where the owners would greet us like long-lost friends, never querying the fact we were back together. The Italians are very civilized like that. I suppose people's relationships are so 'fluid', for want of a better word; they merely accept what's going on at face value. There's none of the gossipy curiosity of the English. The scenery is stunning inland, the food is incredible and there's no crime – the island is run by just three or four very controlling families, one of them Carlo's. On a clear day you can see the island of Ischia in the distance. Shops sell the latest fashions, the smell of the lemon groves is omnipresent. Carlo's home was in Anacapri – a huge rambling old castle, which we had to ourselves as his family were on the mainland, finding the tourist invasion too much in August. Friends came and went. There was a concert in Tiberius' old castle, at the highest point of the island, from where he ruled the Roman Empire all those years ago. We spent our days on Carlo's boat, going to remote beaches that had no road access, fishing, sunbathing and having copious sex. We passed the nights at dinner, at bars and in bed, having more sex. I was exhausted and almost pleased to be back in the office. I needed a break from Carlo, it was possible to have too much of a good thing.

I walked over to Hugo's office, tapped on the door and went in. 'Any idea where Johnnie is? There's quite a lot of stuff he needs to look at and I need his signature on a couple of large cheques.'

Hugo looked up from his desk, running a hand through his hair. 'Polly, you know as well as I, despite the fact I completely disapprove, you can forge Johnnie's signature perfectly and have done so on many occasions. Why you suddenly feel the need for the genuine article is beyond me, other than as a ruse to find out why he's late. In which case, I cannot help you. I'm as in the dark as you. However, no doubt all will be revealed.'

As if on cue Johnnie walked in looking like I'd never seen him before; he was almost dishevelled. He looked like he hadn't slept for a week, or if he had it was in a car – he was crumpled, both literally and metaphorically. He sat down at his desk, and buried his head in his hands; it was quite shocking.

I was the first to break the silence. 'Er, Johnnie, can I get you some coffee, you look a little . . . ' I couldn't quite think what to say, 'you look like you could do with something.'

He shook his head, 'No it's fine. Samantha, could you leave us for a moment, I need to talk to Hugo and Polly.'

I looked at Hugo, who appeared equally concerned. We went over to his desk, taking two chairs, and sat down expectantly in front of him. I couldn't begin to think what had brought about this awful change in him; maybe someone had died, but then why would he come to work?

He raised his head and looked at us, and his eyes were so sad I couldn't bear it. I reached over and put my hand on one of his. 'What is it, Johnnie?' I asked gently. 'What on earth's happened?'

'It's B–Belinda, she's thrown me out. Someone told her about Theodora.' He put his head back in his hands. 'It happened just before the holidays.'

'Oh shit,' said Hugo, most uncharacteristically. 'What a bad scene. But surely she'll come round?'

'I don't think so,' Johnnie replied. 'She said I could stay for a couple of days to get myself sorted out but after that I should move out. At first, of course, I tried to deny it, but it was no use. Whoever told her did a good job with facts I couldn't refute. So I confessed and said I was sorry, that I would do anything to make it up to her, even have another baby, which shows how desperate I was. I told her Dora and I had broken up a while ago because I really wanted to make a go of it with her and the children. Which is true. She seemed to be relenting a bit and we limped through a few more days while she "thought about things". I was getting my hopes up a tiny bit, when it all went crashing back down, worse than before.'

'What went wrong?' I ventured, hating to hear and see so much pain afflicting anyone, let alone such a hitherto iron-clad man.

'I rang Dora.'

'Oh you fool!' I couldn't stop myself from blurting out. 'Why on earth did you do that?'

'Oh, it's pathetic, I promised I'd phone her on her birthday. It was emotional blackmail I know, but she said she could cope with not seeing me, if only she could hear my voice. I also wanted to tell her what had happened at home, what with Belinda finding out, I thought she ought to know.'

'Most probably she was the one who told Belinda,' muttered Hugo.

I silently agreed with him. She still tried to get hold of Johnnie sporadically at the office, not with much luck when I was there, but who knows, she could phone when I or any of the other girls had gone.

'I don't think so, she sounded genuinely horrified when I told her; but anyway, Belinda came in while I was on the phone to her, took one look at my face and guessed who I was talking to. And that was that. Belinda went absolutely berserk and told me to get out right then and there. Said she'd be contacting the lawyers as soon as their offices opened and I could expect not only to lose the shirt off my back, but she'd make sure I saw as little of the children as possible and that they'd be under no illusions as to what a cheating, lying, disgusting man I was. I believe those were her words. So I packed up some of my things and moved to the flat in London. The reason I'm late is I've just come from my solicitor, who has not filled me with much hope. I can't sleep, I can't eat. She won't speak to me, and worst of all, she won't let me talk to the children. Her parents rang my parents, who are horrified. Half of Hampshire is avoiding me, she's been on the phone to everyone. I just don't know what to do.'

With that, to my absolute horror, he burst into tears. Poor Hugo was so thrown by all of this he was at a total loss; he got up and starting pacing the room.

'Hugo,' I said, 'stop marching up and down; go and get the bottle of vodka from the freezer and bring a glass. It's a tried and tested Swedish remedy for all things traumatic.'

'Ah, right-oh, Polly; better bring three glasses then.' He practically ran out of the office, crashing straight into Merry and Samantha, who'd been listening outside the door. He adjusted himself and tried to walk with more composure to the kitchen.

I got up and went round to squat beside Johnnie and put my arm round him. 'Johnnie, listen, I know you're devastated, but it can't get any worse. Try and think of it in a positive way. The slate's really clean now. Just breaking up with Theodora wasn't going to do it. You were obviously still in touch with her, you may actually have seen her, but even if you weren't or hadn't, it would always be there in the background. That big secret you could never tell, hanging over your marriage like a cloud. I'm not saying this to give you false hope, because Belinda sounds pretty pissed off right now, but for your relationship ever really to work, it has to be on a level playing field. No secrets, everything out in the open. At least this way the truth is out. It's not nice, but it's better than living a lie or deceiving someone for the rest of your life.'

Johnnie raised his head to look at me, a haunted look on his face. 'Deception felt a whole lot better than this,' he said.

'But it wouldn't have done in the long run, believe me. I cheated on Mats and it was dreadful. I felt terrible. Sometimes we cheat on people because it's the only way we have to sort a relationship out. It's pretty desperate and often a cry for help. A big wake-up call. In my case it showed me I was in the wrong relationship. For you, it's shown you just how much you cared about Belinda and the kids. Give her time. Show her how much you really want to be with her. Actions always speak louder than words.'

'I agree,' said Hugo, reappearing with the vodka. 'Drink this, old bean, and look to the future; it can only be better than the all-time low you're at today.'

'You sound like Polly,' said Johnnie, gulping the vodka in one go and proffering his glass for a refill. 'OK then, on her terms be it. Let's drink to my uncertain future.'

36

'If he was a stag we'd shoot him and put him out of his misery,' Merry commented at the end of a long week. We all knew it was Johnnie she was talking about.

'Just as well he bloody isn't then, mate,' replied Samantha, 'because you'd be out of a job and up for manslaughter. He'll get over it; I always thought she was a bit of a bore myself. He could do much better.'

We were sitting in the pub having a quick drink before the weekend. 'He's going to his parents for the weekend and hoping to see her, or at least the children, although I don't hold out much hope. Belinda isn't budging. Poor man is completely in bits. I hope she was nicer to her ponies.'

Our conversation during the past couple of weeks had been dominated by the Johnnie/Belinda situation, which was unfolding like some dreadful soap. Belinda was refusing to talk to him and Johnnie was becoming increasingly desperate. It was lucky there wasn't much to do in the way of mergers and acquisitions in the office because I'm not sure how sharp Johnnie would have been. Hugo was pretty much holding the fort, and I spent a large part of the week at Rowley's restaurant pouring bottles of wine down Johnnie, trying to encourage him to eat a mouthful of steak or nibble a chip. But most of the time I just sat and listened as he poured his heart – what was left of it – out. At the end of the day I even had to drive him home as he was completely incapable of driving. It was pretty sad. Belinda was one tough madam when she was cross.

Bumble, on the other hand, was completely on her side. 'What on earth do you expect?' she said with some irritation. 'That man's hand has been in so many cookie jars it's his just desserts. And some desserts are jolly unpalatable.'

'Well, you haven't seen him, Bumble; I've never known anyone so full of remorse. He won't be putting his hand or anything else near a cookie jar for a very long time, if ever. If Belinda was sensible she'd take him back and have him as a slave for the rest of her life.'

'It wouldn't last. Men don't change; he'd slip back into his old ways soon enough. Look at what you were saying about Carlo, you went straight back into the same old relationship. Although how you have the energy four years later I've no idea!' she giggled.

'Don't change the subject,' I snapped, 'I'm not that over the hill . . . Anyway, to get back to the point, maybe a huge trauma like this can make a change, but it doesn't matter anyway, Belinda's clearly never going to forgive him. I hope she knows what a tough life she'll have as a single mother.'

'Tough life?' Bumble snorted, 'don't be ridiculous. She won't have to lift a finger for years. I don't have much sympathy for Johnnie, but he's going to pay through the nose for his mistakes. Trust me, there won't be many girls queuing up outside his impoverished door for a very long while. Once he gets over the heartache, which he will, it'll come down to what divorce is really about – money. The man who strays is the man who pays. That woman has got it made.'

I pointed this out to the girls; none of us had really thought about that particular aspect.

'If I caught my Michael cheating on me, I'd flay him alive, but I'm not sure I'd divorce him. Although I would make certain he suffered for the rest of his life,' Merry chortled.

'I bet you wouldn't. If you love someone, the idea of them being with another person is just about intolerable,' said Samantha rather sadly.

'Well,' I said, 'I think men are entirely different from women. They don't understand all this fuss about fidelity. Not all men, obviously,' I added hastily, looking at their nervous faces. 'But it's not morals that keep men on the straight and narrow, it's fear.'

'Well, whoever gets Johnnie Lyle next won't have a wandering willy problem with him, I think he's learnt his lesson the hard way. Oops, no pun intended!'

We all laughed. I left them in the pub to go and meet Carlo. I was in a bit of a dilemma. Bill had telephoned to let me know he was coming to London for a few days and wanted to see me. We'd spoken occasionally over the summer, but I hadn't told him about Carlo. Equally, I didn't enquire about his sex life. If he had one I didn't want to know about it and I felt very confused. Carlo was practically living at Bumble's and I have real moral tussles about sleeping with two people at the same time – well not at exactly the same time, that would just be wrong, not to mention exhausting. I didn't want to have to choose between them, yet neither held out any hope of a future for me, so what could it matter? Why *not* have both? I adored Bill, I was crazy about Carlo. Then, in the weird way that fate works, Carlo resolved it.

'Tesoro mio, vene qui. I have something to tell you. Next week I go to America.'

We were sitting in a little tapas bar in Mayfair and suddenly I wasn't hungry any more. 'What did you say?' I managed.

He repeated that he was leaving for America. Apparently his parents had arranged for him to go to New York to work in some big bank now that his English was so improved. Now, in fact, he could actually speak English! I took some credit for this, but was regretting being such a good teacher. He reached over the little table and held my hand, which I was trying to keep steady. It's ironic that it takes the losing of something to show you how much you want it. It was almost a case of Bill who?

Carlo continued to speak softly. 'Never I will forget this time with you. Always I carry you in my heart. But now, is time to go. Sorry.'

I looked at him with tears in my eyes. God, life is shit sometimes. The worst of it was that I knew it was the right thing. He had to go and I had to get back on track. No more

274

mission drift. It was always going to end sometime, and better before I was thirty and only slightly desperate, rather than in my mid-thirties, hallucinating with the fear of spinsterdom.

'I understand, Carlo. You will always have a place in my heart too. Who knows, in ten or fifteen years' time, maybe we'll meet up in Capri with our families and our children will play together.' I gave a wry smile.

'You be OK,' he said. 'Your *capo*, he take care of you.'

'My boss?' I was confused, he couldn't possibly know about Bill.

'Si, si. I see him with you. I very clever, I know this.'

I realized he must mean Johnnie. I shook my head, 'I don't think so, Carlo.'

'You see. Allora, beviamo un drink. To my special girlfriend. I have something for you.' He pulled out a photograph of himself, in a silver frame, looking drop-dead gorgeous.

On it he had written: *To remind you of the happy times we had together. With all the love in the world, Carlo.*

I burst into tears.

37

'Oh, bloody hell, Polly, will you just snap out of it.' Bumble sounded uncharacteristically brusque. 'You knew it was never going to last and that lovely Bill is not going to like you with puffy eyes.'

It was Sunday afternoon. Carlo had left in the morning to finish his packing at the flat he'd scarcely used, refusing to let me take him to the airport. Bill was landing any minute now.

'Bumble, I'm fine. I may look as though I'm suffering, but I'm not. I'm wallowing. I know we'll always be friends and I'll see him again. We'll probably always have some kind of sexual connection, just like you said. I doubt I'll ever be able to trust myself alone in a room with him, but it's not our destiny to be together. I'm merely mourning the passing of a phase. These are maudlin tears, not misery ones.' I buried my face back in the sofa cushion.

'Well, in that case you can get up right this minute, you've been on the sofa quite long enough. Go and have a long bath. I've brought you some cucumber slices for your eyes, which are minuscule and red. Get dressed in something that's fun and come down here and have a large vodka and a cigarette. Bill will be here shortly and you must be on good form when you see him. All these break-ups are having a very bad effect on you. Bill is just the tonic you need. However, for what it's worth I don't think you should sleep with him, it's just too quick. I'm sure he'll understand.'

I removed the cushion from my face. 'Don't be silly, Bumble, I've never met an understanding man with a hard-on. But you don't need to worry on that score anyway, I happen to be at the tail end of the wrong time of the month. He's of a generation that is still a bit squeamish about that sort of thing.'

'Eugh, enough.' Bumble pulled a disgusted-looking face. 'Get up to the bathroom *now*.'

Of course, I had a wonderful time with Bill. I loved seeing him again. It's funny the different emotions you can feel for people. I suppose Carlo was principally about an incredible animal attraction. After our time together in London our relationship had moved to a different stage, we acknowledged our feelings for each other yet knew we would not be together. For the first time since I'd met him I felt as though I had a degree of control over – or at least, understanding of – our relationship.

I could not say that about Bill. I hadn't had years of familiarity, quite the opposite, and he was so different from any other person I'd gone out with. Sophisticated, erudite, successful, grown-up, self-contained, intellectually stimulating as well as physically attractive, he was scary for me; a completely unknown commodity. I didn't know where I was with him and that made me hold back.

Whether it was a sixth sense on his part, or the fact he was simply a gentleman, he didn't even try to get me into bed. There again, he hadn't seen me for a few months and I'd have been appalled at his presumption had he tried. He collected me from Bumble's, took me to the Waterside for dinner and dropped me at the door again. I was almost disappointed.

'There's absolutely no pleasing you at the moment,' sighed Bumble when I got back. 'How long is he over for?'

'A week.'

'And when are you seeing him again?'

'Tomorrow in the office obviously, and then he wants to go to the theatre with me in the evening.'

'Well, I don't know what you're complaining about. Go to bed and stop whingeing.'

Monday morning dawned and an apparently revitalized Johnnie marched into the office, his brusque step almost as firm as ever.

'Morning, everyone,' he said cheerily. 'Polly, come into my office, please – and, Merry, two cups of coffee.'

The girls and I were momentarily stunned into silence by this transformation.

'Do you think he's taking a prescription drug?' asked Merry. 'My friend's mother went nearly suicidal during her menopause and they put her on an antidepressant that made her very peculiar.'

'I don't think the menopause is what's troubling Johnnie,' I said.

'Maybe he's on something stronger than antidepressants,' suggested Samantha, 'like mescaline. He could have swallowed the worm and is hallucinating that his life is fine.'

'You're both mad. Merry, can you get his coffee. I'm going in to find out what's happening. I sincerely doubt it's a worm, even if he has just come back from the country.'

I scarcely had time to set foot in his office before he started gabbling away. 'Polly, I've come to a decision. These last two weeks have been without doubt the worst of my life – other than when my dachshund died' (my thoughts turned to the mescaline theory), 'and I cannot go on like this for ever. If Belinda wants to play hard ball, well so be it. I will not let my life be over because of her. I will fight to see the children, I shall probably be broke, but I'm going to have dinner parties.'

I stared at him, wondering where all this was leading.

'I need to create a social life for myself here in London, one that's not just taking women out for dinner and sex.' (My God, men! Is that all they think about over a meal?) 'No one in Hampshire is speaking to me, which is utterly hypocritical. I know at least three other couples where the husband is playing away, but luckily for them they haven't got caught. I'm a nasty reminder of how bad it can get. Belinda has painted such a black picture of me to her women friends they virtually spit in the street when they see me. Not that I care much, they're so bloody boring, always talking about babies, nanny problems and husbands who won't change nappies. So I'm taking your advice, Polly, I am starting a new life, clean slate and all.'

I was struggling to remember recommending quite such drastic action.

'Quite right too, Johnnie,' said Merry from behind me, putting down the cups of coffee. She'd obviously been ear-wigging. 'I have *lots* of single girls for you, they'd absolutely *adore* to meet you. Even if you will be poor.'

Johnnie looked very surprised. 'Oh no, Merry, not that. I'm not going to date. I'm still hanging on to the last shred of hope Belinda will take me back. I have to behave. I want Polly to be my safe date.' He turned to look at me. 'No one would give it a second thought if I was out with you. Please say you will.'

The man had the sensitivity of a tractor. From Office It to Safe Date, how demoralizing! Particularly as I'd started to think we were getting on better – not to mention that kiss at Annabel's, which now burnt ferociously in my memory. Had he forgotten? He must have been absolutely pissed. I didn't want to be a safe date and I was appalled that people thought I could be. I was never going to wear a sensible skirt again in my life. I opened my mouth to say something, but he continued, 'You will do it, won't you, Polly? Please? You can come into work a couple of hours late each morning if you like. You're not too busy at the moment, are you?'

I gathered my thoughts. Johnnie looked expectantly at me, Merry could hardly contain herself. 'Johnnie, the only reason I'm not walking out of your office in the strop that I feel I deserve to be in is because I believe you are clearly in some sort of deranged, delusional state of trauma. There can be no other explanation for such extraordinary insensitivity and rudeness. And if there is, I don't want to hear it. So, in response to your proposal, although it is almost the reverse, yes, I will be your "safe date". However, I will not come into work late, I will not do the cooking nor the washing-up and I will do this only for a short time. I would like to make very clear that I'm saying yes out of pity. And in the desperate hope that you might have some eligible male friends to introduce me to – who, because of my fundamentally optimistic nature, I tell myself must have a good chance of being more courteous than you and definitely less insane. Now will you excuse me while I go to the kitchen and break a plate on the floor. It's my mother's recipe for releasing terminal frustration.'

I got up and marched out of the room, but not without overhearing Johnnie say to Merry, 'Good Lord, I didn't know her mother was Greek.'

38

It was a really weird week. On Monday evening I went to a musical with Bill in the West End. Afterwards we had dinner at Joe Allen, which was guaranteed to put me in a good mood. A couple of bottles of wine later I ended up at 47 Park Street with him, where I spent a delicious night, remembering all the things about sex with an older man that I liked. I didn't want to compare him with Carlo, but it was inevitable because, to my shame, there hadn't been much of a gap between the two.

The differences between them were even more highlighted in bed. With Carlo it was all about passion, lust, youth and energy, not to mention lots of black hair. With Bill it was more intense, but less hasty, more considerate and somehow more emotional. It seemed more real and, dare I say, more about love than sex?

It was altogether more serious and I realized I'd been hiding from myself for a while that he was someone I could really fall in love with, given time and the correct geography.

The following night was the first of Johnnie's dinner parties. We were eight. To my slight discomfort he'd invited Bill as well, placing him between two very vivacious brunettes, and I found myself feeling distinctly jealous. As the 'safe date', I had Johnnie on one side and a rather good-looking man who turned out to be Hugo's flatmate on the other. Had Bill not been there, I would have been most interested in him as he was perfect Plan A material, but as it was, all I could think about was how much fun Bill seemed to be having with the other two girls. Hugo and Jenny made up the table. The food was delicious, the cook I had hired from Blue's was excellent and Johnnie poured copious amounts of wine. He was an extremely gracious host and I thought that things boded well for him if this first dinner was anything to go by. Bill very publicly offered me a lift home, as his driver was outside, so my feelings of murderous jealousy were snuffed out immediately, particularly as the instant the car was out of sight of Johnnie's flat, Bill grabbed me and kissed me all the way back to his hotel. Johnnie and Hugo made no mention of Bill's having given me a lift, clearly they thought that no one could possibly be interested in me!

As the week progressed and I saw Bill every night I was finding it increasingly hard to play cool. He never volunteered his feelings for me, so I was reluctant to tell him mine for him. I wasn't completely sure of them myself, in fact I was trying hard not to think about them at all. His life seemed so remote from mine I couldn't see where I fitted in. I thought he really liked me, but I didn't want to be one of those gooey-eyed deluded people who imagine other people's affection for them, reading positive signs into the slightest gesture because they're so infatuated they project their own emotions.

It wasn't just the glamour of his wealth and power; going to the cinema with him and eating hot dogs in Leicester Square was just as much fun as dinner at the Waterside.

He even survived Friday dinner at Bumble and Gareth's, where the eclectic group consisted of us, them, William and Pia, who were still completely loved-up, Kevina and yet another new boyfriend, Troy and Girl Friday, and Frank, on his own as usual.

'I like your gay friends,' commented Bill as we left the house. 'But I'm not so sure about that Troy, he couldn't take his eyes off you. I nearly thumped him.'

How very gratifying, I thought. I quite like a healthy dose of possessiveness, it makes you feel wanted. 'Oh, don't worry about him, it's congenital for him to eye-up women. I'm way past even noticing now. I'm glad you like the boys though. Kevina was on particularly good form.'

'Tryin' to impress that Frank. I haven't seen such flagrant flirtin' since my college days.'

'Oh really?' I queried. 'I don't think he was flirting, why would he do that to someone straight?'

Bill let out a loud guffaw. 'Straight?! Frank? Darlin', that man is as bent as a two-dollar bill, make no mistake.'

'He most certainly is not,' I replied angrily. 'Why on earth do you think he could be?'

'Answer these questions and I'll tell you why. Does he have a girlfriend? No. Has he ever had a girl? Probably not. Does he have lots of women friends? Yes. Does he get depressed sometimes? Black moods descending? Does he drink too much? Does he take risks – drive too fast, skydive or go rock-climbing without a harness? You bet he does. Why the hell do you think he's a shrink?'

'I thought I was going to answer the questions,' I said grumpily, although I realized I would have responded the same. 'Anyway, I still don't believe you; apart from anything else, he'd tell me. And for the record, he's a psychiatrist, not a shrink.'

'All the more reason. Listen, honey, that man can hardly tell himself what he is, let alone you. I don't expect he does anything about it, probably just the reverse, tries to have sex with women to prove he isn't driving along the Herschey Highway.'

'Eugh, Bill, what a disgusting expression. He told me he has sex with prostitutes.' I felt really bad telling him, but poor old Frank needed defending.

'Ha!' exclaimed Bill, 'just proves my point. What better way to deny your sexuality than by reducing the act of love to a financial transaction that involves no emotion and no commitment. Merely a physical release, if you can get up in the first place. Men who have sex with hookers don't love women, they hate themselves.'

Blimey, I was stunned. 'But no one who knows him would ever have guessed. I mean he's hardly camp or anything. He's not like any gay person I know.' I was beginning to sound increasingly naïve, even to myself.

'Well, Kevina can tell. Ask him next time you see him. It's called gaydar, they can home in on a queen from miles.'

I was finding it hard to come to terms with this, not because of any homophobia obviously, but because it seemed so sad for Frank. It's one thing to be gay and OK about it, but it's an entirely different matter to be in denial. And he was a psychiatrist. Maybe having your own demons enabled you to help others. Bloody annoying that Samantha had spotted it before me as well. I was silent for a while as the car drove back to the hotel.

'So, darlin'. What do you want to do this weekend?' Bill turned to me in bed on Saturday morning. 'London or the country? I'm on the Sunday flight back to New York, I'm all yours till then.'

'I don't mind at all. I have a good time with you wherever.' I stopped short, I didn't want to reveal too much.

'Do you think you'd have a good time in New York?' he looked at me intently. It was a leading question but I kept my tone light.

'Of course, like I said, anywhere's a good time with you.' I got out of bed, willing myself not to add, 'Why?'

'Next time you get a holiday, you should come over. See how we live over on the other side of the ocean.'

It wasn't exactly the invitation I'd been hoping for, but it was a start. 'I'd love to, thanks.' I walked over to the window and opened the curtains, the sun streamed through. 'Oh, it's such a beautiful day, Bill. Why don't we go to the country? The sun always seems brighter outside London. There's a wonderful hotel in Gloucestershire, called the Lords of the Manor; my mother's always raving about it; we could go there. The food is delicious and the countryside is heaven.'

Bill got on to the concierge and arranged it immediately. The car purred off down the M40 about an hour later.

'Where's your mother live, darlin'?' asked Bill.

'Oh God, don't say you want to meet my mother.' I half

laughed, half groaned. She actually lived very close to the hotel.

'Sure, why not. Call her up and ask her to join us for dinner. She can't be all that bad if she has you for a daughter.'

'Flattery may get you the phone call to my mother, but be warned, she can be quite a handful on occasions. She'll adore you and vice versa, no doubt. It's a while since I saw her, which makes me wonder what the mad old thing is up to.'

'Darling!' shrieked my mother down the car phone, her voice echoing wildly round the car. 'Where are you? You sound like you are at the bottom of a biscuit tin.'

'I'm calling you from a car, mummy.'

'A car?' she sounded perplexed. 'What did you do, dig up a telephone box and take it with you?'

'Mum, some cars have their own phones now.' My mother has always been something of a technophobe.

'Oh, how dreadful, what will they think of next? Phones where you can see each other, no doubt. I should rather die. I'd have to have my make-up on permanently. Now, darling, what did you want?'

I explained that I was going to stay at the Lords of the Manor with a friend and would she like to join us for dinner?

'I'd absolutely love to, darling. Who is this friend?'

The idea of mother cross-questioning me on a telephone that offered no privacy was not an option. 'No one you've met, mummy, but I'm sure you'll like him. He's American.'

'Oh!' squeaked my mother, 'the one – '

I interrupted her before she could embarrass me by revealing I'd discussed Bill with her already. 'Mum, the line's gone really bad, see you at seven-thirty. Love you lots, Byeee.'

I hung up. Bill had a smile on his face.

'So, you discussed me with your mother?'

'Well, I may have mentioned you in passing,' I said lamely. 'She's frightfully nosy, wants to know everything that goes on. Anyway, for God's sake don't give her too much to drink, she'll never stop talking.'

Mother swept into the hotel looking as glamorous as ever. The post-divorce diet was clearly still working, but to my astonishment she'd dyed her hair blonde and was carrying a very small, scruffy dog under her arm.

'You must be Polly's younger sister,' said Bill, taking her hand and kissing it. I nearly stamped on his foot, she needed little encouragement. The dog growled menacingly.

'Oh, you gorgeous man,' she simpered. 'Shush, Snippet.' She stroked the little dog's head and then turned back to Bill. 'Please tell me you have an older brother. In fact, please tell me everything about you. My naughty daughter has kept very quiet about you.' She turned and gave me a theatrical wink which I prayed Bill didn't see.

'Come into the bar, I've got a bottle of Krug on ice waiting for us.'

My mother looked as though she had died and gone to heaven.

'Mum, what have you done to your hair?' I hissed at her as Bill went on ahead, 'and what's with the dog?'

'Oh, darling, one thing at a time. I think I may have had a teeny-weeny depression. All because of that dreadful man from Penang – too much Northern gloom you know. And he was tight. I can't bear mean men. Mean of wallet, mean of spirit, that's what I say. Look at this lovely chap opening champagne, I'd be lucky to get a glass of warm house white with Arthur. And that was another problem. How could I possibly have a friend called Arthur? No, no, darling, it was too bad, he had to go. And along with him went my hair colour. I'm starting afresh.' She sounded a bit like Johnnie.

'And the dog?' I asked.

'Isn't he adorable?' she cooed.

My mother loves animals, believes she can converse with them almost, even goldfish. I won one years ago at a fairground and she put him in a soup tureen and called him Person. He lived for years in the kitchen, sustained by fish food, toast crumbs and the occasional drop of gin in his bowl.

I have no idea how he survived. When, one morning, she found him floating lifeless on the top of the tureen we had to take him to a large pond near where we lived to 'bury' him. Blow me if he didn't suddenly revive and swim away.

'Reincarnation, darling,' said my mother, tears pouring down her cheeks. 'Be happy, Person,'

'Mother, it can't be reincarnation, he's still a fish,' I pointed out.

'Oh, silly me, darling, I meant Resurrection. What a spiritual moment this is.' She sighed dramatically. 'Almost biblical.'

'Mother, this is a fish.'

'Darling, you're too prosaic. Where is your imagination? Gosh, sometimes I wonder if it's possible for me to have had a child so different from me.'

'Mother, I hate to point out that absolutely everyone is different from you.'

'I know,' she smiled happily, 'how sad.'

I emerged from my momentary reverie as mother plonked the dog in my arms. 'He's called Snippet and I'm looking after him for my neighbours. He says he needs a little tinkle. Would you be a darling and take him outside, I'm absolutely gasping for a glass of champagne.' She disappeared into the bar as I took the dog outside.

There were a couple of black labradors basking in the evening sun by the door, so I took Snippet to a bit of grass away from them. He was beginning to wriggle a bit and I put him down quickly, without realizing he didn't have a lead on. In an instant he raced back to where the other dogs were and leaping on one started to hump like a little hairy maniac. He looked like the drummer in *The Muppet Show* called Animal. It was quite a picture and I started to laugh, but the labrador was not amused and got up with a menacing growl. Snippet was quite undeterred, by either the growl or the disparity of size, and clung on like mad to the dog's back. The other labrador got up and started to bark loudly, which set the other one off.

A very worried-looking man came out. 'I say,' he politely remonstrated, 'do you think you could get your dog off my bitch, she's in season and I really can't have any illegits – she's a Sandringham pedigree. And her husband is not enjoying this performance at all.'

Snippet was beginning to slide down the labrador's leg, still rhythmically rocking to and fro, while the second labrador, obviously the husband, was barking insanely.

'It's not my dog,' I said, stifling a threatened attack of giggles as I tried to work out how to get even remotely close enough to remove Snippet without being attacked myself.

'I don't care,' said the man, his voice rising, 'if it's the Queen of England's dog! – which in fact I know it isn't, because Betty is. Now please, get him off before Rex does.'

Mother and Bill appeared at the doorway.

'Darling!' shrieked my mother, 'stop Snippet doing that, it's disgusting.'

'Mother, how exactly do you suggest I do that? He's like some demented wind-up toy.'

Bill turned to the irate man. 'Can you get some pepper, ground pepper? If I throw it at the dogs it should work.'

The man raced inside and came out a few moments later with a pot. The commotion was getting louder and more and more people appeared. Mother hopped from one foot to the other, in an agitated fashion, saying, 'Oh, be careful, poor little Snippet, he won't like that pepper in his nose.'

'He'll be lucky if I don't put it up his backside. Dirty little tike,' said the owner, becoming increasingly agitated.

'Really, language,' said my mother haughtily.

Bill liberally dispersed the pepper over the dogs, who instantly stopped barking and started sneezing. Snippet fell off Betty and mother raced to scoop him up in her arms.

'Oh, you poor little baby, come inside with me.'

The owner of the labradors was inspecting Betty, gingerly lifting up her tail. 'You're lucky, she's intact,' he pronounced, getting to his feet.

'I have to say I think it would have been pretty impossible to have achieved anything,' I said.

'Never underestimate the power of optimism and testosterone in the face of the insurmountable,' said Bill, with a smile on his face. 'My goodness, darlin', I think I'd better take you in, all this excitement seems to have had an effect on Rex.'

I turned round to see Rex humping away on the bitch.

'What?' said the owner, turning too. 'Good Lord! At long bloody last. That's the idea, Rex old boy.'

It was all getting a bit much. There really isn't anything visually attractive about two dogs coupling.

'I owe you a large bottle of champagne,' said the man, all smiles now. 'I couldn't get dear old Rex interested Betty, and what do you know, a little stiffy competition and he's off!'

'At least now I understand Snippet's name, he must drive his poor owners mad with his uncontrollable lust. I expect he gets threatened with the snip constantly.' I started laughing. 'Honestly, my bloody mother! Where is she, by the way?'

Bill and I went back to the bar and found mother with a very odd look on her face.

'Darling,' she hissed, 'ask Bill quickly if he has a handkerchief I can borrow, Snippet's just peed all over the bar. I told you he needed the loo.'

39

Bill had been gone a month, it was most unsatisfactory. He stayed in touch, but it was always a light-hearted chat, a snatched moment in his busy life. I realized that for as long as we lived in different countries I was never going to have the kind of relationship with him I really wanted. It saddened me but I couldn't see a way round it at the moment. Maybe it was how he wanted to keep things, but with the lack of anyone else in my life, it seemed pointless to end it.

My social life seemed to be reduced to Johnnie's dinner parties and the usual crowd at Altonative Towers. I was clearly never going to find a husband. I had a long conversation with Bumble about Frank, repeating what Bill had said.

She was as surprised as me. 'But if he is gay, we must do something about it,' she exclaimed.

'I think we're the last people able to do anything about it; we're the wrong gender for a start,' I replied.

'I don't mean like that. I meant, we should help him come out.'

'But what if he doesn't want to?' I asked. 'I'm not sure. Perhaps I should have a chat with Kevina and see what *he* says.'

I arranged to meet Kevina at the gay bar in Soho where he occasionally moonlighted as a cocktail 'waiteresse', as he so quaintly put it. More like waiting for cock, judging by the amount of beautiful young men with overly plucked eyebrows wafting about the place in very tight-fitting trousers.

'I love it here,' he said, gazing wistfully at all the bottoms, some of which were jigging away to the strains of the Village People playing in the background.

'I'm not surprised,' I said, feeling very dull and unadventurous. Even though heterosexuality wasn't working for me at the moment, I wasn't yet prepared to develop a Sapphic side. I was just going to have to weather the lull. Anyway, my mind was focusing on Frank at the moment. I asked Kevina if he thought he was gay.

'Darling, of course he is. He either knows it and is terrified, or is in such denial that he's psychobabbled himself into believing he's not. Either way, he's fucked, or rather, not, as the case may be. Why do you ask? Do you want me to seduce him? It would be my pleasure; I love breaking in new boys.'

'Spare me the details, please.' I held up my hands. 'No, I don't want you to. I'm not really comfortable having this conversation about such a good friend in the first place, let alone on a topic I know next to nothing about. I just wanted to know what you thought.'

Kevina paused for a moment, before replying in a more serious voice. 'Coming out is never easy, even with the most tolerant of parents. With his background, I expect his family would have a fit, so first he has to contend with that. Secondly, despite the more *laissez-faire* attitude of the general public these days, there's still a feeling of "us" and "them", and you have to be really sure that you're strong enough to deal with that. It can be lonely, unless you find the right partner. You have to face the fact you may never have your own children. The gay world is rampantly promiscuous and you have to be careful of not getting some infection. And once you're out, you can never go back in. At best you will be for ever bi, not sure if you're a Martha or an Arthur. So it's a big decision. And that's just the tip of the iceberg, sweetie. Not that I've ever had one of those up my arse!' He lightened-up again. 'So my advice would be to leave him be. There's nothing you can do except be his friend, same as always. Something will happen in its own time, and tempting as it is to turn him, I think even I might give this one a miss. Oh, my dear,' his head swivelled and his tone suddenly rose a couple of decibels, 'did you see that gorgeous hunk just glide by? Excuse me while I go and powder my nose.' He got up to leave me.

'What happened to the guy from last week?' I asked.

'Last week?' Kevina wrinkled up his little nose, '*soo* yesterday. This one has all the promise of tomorrow. See you soon, my darling, I'm off hunting.'

Two weeks later Frank rang me. 'Miss P, I have something to tell you.' He sounded very serious.

'Good news or bad news?' I asked curiously.

'Good, I think.' He paused. 'I'm getting married.'

I nearly dropped the phone. 'What!' I yelled. 'Ohmygod! Who to?' I prayed it wasn't a man.

'To a wonderful person called Jamie.'

Oh, dear Lord, it was a man.

'Frank darling, when did all this happen? It's only a few weeks since I saw you and you were single and now you're getting married? I mean, is it even legal or are you going to Holland?'

'Holland?' he sounded puzzled. 'Why would I go to Holland? Jamie's not Dutch, she's from Huddersfield too, I've known her all my life.'

I came down off my plateau of hysteria a little at the mention of the word 'she' and then got all worried again that 'she' might be a 'he/she', like a transsexual or something terrifying in drag.

'Well, you might at least congratulate me,' said Frank rather grumpily. 'You're the first person I've told, after my family, and I was hoping for a slightly more positive reaction.'

I rubbed my temples; it didn't seem possible that as recently as two weeks ago I'd been discussing the possibility of Frank's being gay and now here he was telling me he was marrying, of all things, the girl next door. Just as I was getting to think he may not be the marrying kind, I was being jet-propelled into the exact opposite position. And this was the man who'd never had a girlfriend before, the man for whom sex with women was a commercial transaction. It felt all wrong, but if this was more denial, then the least I could do was wish him happiness. I composed myself and took a deep breath. 'I'm so sorry, it's just a shock, that's all. And so sudden. But of course I'm happy for you. And I can't wait to meet Jamie – when are you getting married?'

'In a couple of months, no point in hanging around. My parents are delirious, if that's possible for down-to-earth Northerners. They know her family really well, so they're having a high old time planning the nuptials, as they call them. When would you like to meet her?'

A sudden thought struck me. 'You're not free tomorrow are you? Both of you? It's one of Johnnie's dinner-party nights and a couple have just cancelled. You two could come instead; you can meet the crazy guy from my office at long last.'

'We'd love to. Thanks. I'll get the address off you tomorrow, but I've got a thousand phone calls to make if I'm to spread the good news.' With that he hung up.

It was weird hearing him say 'we'; the whole thing felt weird, it must be the suddenness of it. Although, as Bumble said, rather unfairly I thought, when I told her, it was hardly surprising; how could I expect to be joyful when I was not only losing my best male friend to another woman but having my own lack of success in that department painfully high-lighted. And for the record, she had never thought he was gay anyway. Great.

The following day I made my way round to Johnnie's having told him I'd invited Frank and his new fiancée to make up numbers. Recently I'd started adding some of my friends to the guest list and it worked really well, he was enjoying meeting new people. I made sure everything was ready and we waited for the first arrivals.

The doorbell rang and I went to answer it. Outside stood a rather flushed Frank and, by his side, someone I knew must be his chosen bride.

'Come in,' I said, giving Frank a hug and holding out my hand to introduce myself to Jamie.

'Nice to meet you too,' she said. 'Our Frank's told me that much about you, I'm quite nervous.'

I ushered them in and introduced them to Johnnie. As he

poured them a drink, I studied Jamie. Her accent was a little broader than Frank's and unmistakably Northern. She didn't look like a transsexual, or transvestite, in fact she looked exactly the opposite. She was pretty, much younger than I expected, with a sweet, open face – pink cheeks and a cute little nose. She was the sort of girl whom, if she had a different accent, Hugo might have liked. Very natural. She was about as far removed from a prostitute as possible, in every way. I had a freakish thought for a moment, wondering if she was a lesbian and she and Frank had come to some arrangement. But even in my addled mind it seemed a bit far-fetched and anyway I was completely hopeless at spotting lesbians. Bumble was no doubt right, I was upset by Frank's deserting me on the lonely shelf.

The other guests started to arrive. Naughty Steven from Hugo's party came with his absolutely stunning wife. He was much better behaved when she was around, although he did manage to give my backside a little squeeze when he kissed me hallo and spent most of dinner playing footsie under the table.

Halfway through dinner I decided Frank was being a bit strange. It was as though he didn't want to look me in the eye. I wasn't imagining things, he looked shifty. He was also drinking heavily.

As the last guests left, I realized I'd also drunk a little too much. I tottered back from the front door to find Johnnie in the sitting-room.

'One for the road?' he asked cheerfully.

'Absolutely not, I don't think I can even drive home, Johnnie. I'd better call a cab.'

'Nonsense, have a nightcap. You didn't drink that much. I want a party post-mortem. It was great by the way, thank you. I don't know what I would have done without you these last few weeks, Polly.'

Johnnie had mellowed considerably since his break-up, and now he could be really nice sometimes. He was still down about his wife but was managing to put on a brave face, and certainly his social life was busier than ever with so many return invitations to dinner.

'You're welcome, but I really had better get going. Work tomorrow and all that.'

'Stay for a nightcap, please. It's still quite early.' He handed me a small glass of something that was not wine.

'What's this?' I asked

He looked frightfully pleased with himself. 'It's a caipiroska, I made it myself.'

'Oh no, not one of those, look at the trouble we got into last time.' I put my glass down.

'Don't be silly, it's just one and I want you to tell me about this Frank chap. Looked rather miserable for someone who's just about to get married.'

The creep! He knew it was a subject I could be drawn on. I sat down and told him the whole story.

'Wow,' said Johnnie, 'that's pretty complicated stuff. You're right, it doesn't add up at all. She seemed like a sweet little thing. I do hope she knows what she's getting herself into, or maybe I hope she doesn't. There are times, you know, when ignorance is bliss.' He sounded a little wistful.

I stood up to go and felt a little dizzy. I looked at my glass and saw it was empty. Bugger, I'd obviously been sipping it while I was talking. I must have stumbled because Johnnie grabbed my arm to steady me. 'Oops,' I said. 'Bloody hell, I've definitely had too much to drink.'

'Why don't you stay?' asked Johnnie, still holding my arm, his voice low.

I turned to look at him as he put his other hand behind my head and drew my face towards his. I opened my mouth to say something but before I knew what was happening he was kissing me. The room was really spinning now as the kiss seemed to go on and on. This couldn't be happening again.

'Johnnie, stop.' I managed to pull away.

'No, not this time,' he said and started to kiss me again.

I could feel myself weakening. He started to move back-wards, pulling me with him towards the bedroom, his mouth still firmly clamped on mine. My heart started pounding, my head spun, I was clearly suffering from oxygen starvation; my last coherent thought was, 'This is a very bad idea.'

40

'Good-morning,' said a very cheery, slightly familiar voice.

I groaned. My head was thumping, I opened my eyes. Where the hell was I?

'Owringe juice?'

I woke with a start, there was only one person who spoke like that! Shit, how on earth had I ended up in his bed? I surreptitiously checked under the sheet: I was naked, not even a pair of knickers on. That could only mean one thing. And, ohmygod, Johnnie was naked too! And he was proffering a glass of orange juice. Johnnie, whom I'd only ever seen in an immaculate suit. Whom I worked for. Whom I was going to see at the office in, I checked my watch, three hours. Three hours? It was five-thirty in the morning! What was he doing up and about, with a smile on his face and apparently hangoverless, at this godforsaken hour? It was more usually a time to go to bed, not a time to wake up. How could this have happened.? I started to pray to God, making all sorts of vows of sobriety and chastity if He could just turn back the clock twenty-four hours. What on earth was I going to do? I pulled the sheet over my head.

'Move over,' he said, getting back into bed.

Oh no, it was too embarrassing. I was in bed with Johnnie, who was naked, and unless I was very much mistaken, there was a hard-on poking into my back. I lay very still, not sure what to do.

'Last night was amazing, Polly,' he said, seductively.

Was it? Glad he could remember. There again, maybe I wasn't. He started to stroke my back. It felt really nice. He rubbed my neck and ran his fingers through my hair. I started to feel a little squirmy, getting warm between my legs. Hangovers make me horny enough even when there isn't someone lying beside me, I could feel my resistance sliding, again. Oh well, what the hell, I could hardly protect my integrity at this stage, I might as well try and enjoy it.

Going into the office an hour after Johnnie and pretending nothing had happened was easier than I had anticipated. I managed to race home, shower and change and be at the office before the girls arrived. Bumble raised an eyebrow at me as I came through the front door, but I didn't have time to explain.

The day was slightly surreal, there was not a hint of innuendo, or covert flirting, it was business as usual. By six o'clock I was beginning to feel tired. Johnnie came into my office and shut the door behind him.

'I think we need to talk. Can you meet me at the flat later this evening, Polly?' His face gave no indication of what kind of talk this would be. If it was going to be one of those 'last night was fun, but we can't do it again' type of conversations, I decided I would hand in my notice, it was too shameful.

We arranged to meet at his flat at seven-thirty, I was dreading it. I felt so bad I couldn't even tell Bumble and said I was meeting Samantha.

There was no reply when I rang the bell of his flat and I couldn't see Johnnie's car. Charming, I thought, stood-up before I could even be given the brush-off. As I waited outside I noticed a small brown-paper package by the door. I picked it up, it reeked of scent. How peculiar, I thought. It was soft and not particularly well wrapped, so I pulled a bit of the paper back to see what was inside. It was something pink and lacy. Curiosity got the better of me and with a quick look around to make sure Johnnie wasn't coming down the street I opened it up. Inside was a pair of rather exotic knickers. Attached to them a note in flowery handwriting: *Miss you taking them off. Please return in person. All my love, always, Dora xxx*. That bloody woman never gave up. I stuffed them back into the package and then shoved them into my handbag. If I wasn't going to have him, she certainly wasn't. She'd caused enough trouble already.

Two minutes later Johnnie came racing round the corner apologizing profusely. 'My car broke down, I'm so sorry, Polly. I hate being late.'

I followed him into his flat, feeling uncertain, trepidacious, my stomach doing sick-making cartwheels.

As he closed the door he pulled me towards him and kissed me. I was completely taken aback.

'God,' he said after what seemed like ages, 'I've wanted to do that all day. It was torture having you in the office, but not having you.'

Of all the things I'd been expecting, it wasn't this.

'You haven't said anything,' he observed.

'I couldn't, my mouth was full,' I managed to joke weakly.

'Very funny. Let's have a drink.'

I sat on the sofa while he opened a bottle of wine. I was definitely not going to drink too much, look where it got me last night!

'It seems to me I have no choice,' began Johnnie. 'I do not approve of office romances – '

I held my breath . . .

' – so I have to fire you.'

I couldn't believe my ears. I practically spilled my drink. 'I beg your pardon, you have to what? Fire me?' I was incensed. 'You have the temerity to seduce me when I'm in no fit state to repel you, twice I might add, and having taken enormous advantage of me you then turn round and fire me. Johnnie Lyle, you have done some pretty appalling things in the time I've known you, but this is the worst. The most hypocritical, double-standard, double-dealing, low-down – '

'Polly, please, don't interrupt me. I hadn't finished.' He was laughing, the bastard. I was going to kill him. 'I have to fire you, because I want to keep seeing you. I've tried everything in my power to resist you but from the moment you walked into my life in that red coat of yours, I've been driven completely mad by you.'

'Yes, well, not in a good way, you were jolly rude to me

sometimes,' I muttered, utterly confused.

'I know, I'm sorry. You can be the most infuriating person on occasions.' He smiled at me. 'But every night when I leave the office and come back here, I realize how much I miss you. That's been even more forcefully brought home to me since we've been doing the dinner parties together. They're the highlight of my week. I have this pathetic little fantasy about us being a real couple. I knew you'd never agree to do it unless I asked you as a safe date. You were deservedly cross about that by the way. But I thought with time you might start to realize how I felt about you.' He stopped. He looked adorable, his green eyes all beseeching, his hands trembling slightly.

Dear God, I thought, it never rains, but it pours. What is it about me that attracts utterly unsuitable men? Troy – serial womaniser; Henry – insane; Carlo – too young, too foreign; Bill – too far away, too married. And now Johnnie, emotionally traumatized, going through a horrible divorce, about to be broke and my employer, or rather apparently no longer my employer. Where are all the normal people? And why can't I meet them? I can't go out with Johnnie. It's madness. What would Merry and Samantha think? Hugo would have a fit. Bumble, well it didn't bear thinking about. Frank was too busy with his nuptials to have a view. I put my fingers on either side of my temples and rubbed hard. I could not believe this was happening.

'Say something, for God's sake,' said Johnnie, again. 'The suspense is killing me.'

I looked up at him. Oh what the hell, I thought . . . why change the habit of a lifetime? 'Get me another drink, Johnnie, and let's give it a try. You never know, I might end up falling for you after all.'

41

So I stayed the night, and the next, and the next. The following week I moved my stuff in. Being with Johnnie was like the most normal thing in the world, we just clicked into place. It was quite extraordinary. Perhaps it was because there was no artifice in our relationship, after all you get to know someone pretty well when you work together, particularly if you're not trying to seduce them. There had been none of the game-playing of a 'normal' romance. He was so familiar that after the initial hurdle of intimacy (for me) had been got over it felt like we'd been together for years.

After I left I was in almost daily contact with Merry and Samantha. I missed them enormously. I'd worked out my month's notice and told everyone I was leaving to set up my own company, doing interior design, which they all seemed to accept. It had been Johnnie's idea and he wanted me to start straight away on renovating somewhere for him, or rather us. Us was a concept I was still getting used to. My leaving party had been a rather sombre drinks affair in Green's, with Johnnie giving a formal, stilted speech and then leaving early, only to meet up with me later to take me to dinner at Annabel's. I hated deceiving the girls, but Johnnie and I had decided we'd wait a month or so before announcing we were going out.

Eight weeks later I was pregnant.

'Immaculate timing,' sniffed Bumble, sarcastically, with more than a hint of disapproval in her voice.

'Rather the reverse, I'm afraid. And that's the least of my problems.'

'I can hardly imagine how,' said Bumble, bluntly – she still hadn't really forgiven me for moving out – 'from where I am your situation looks about as bad as it gets. Let's run through this: you are unemployed, pregnant and living with a man who is legally still married to his first wife and whom you are seeing in secret and have been for only the briefest of moments. How much worse can it be?'

'Please don't bother to sugar-coat it for me, Bumble. I'll tell you exactly how much worse it can be. Whose baby do you think this is?'

'Oh my dear God in Heaven,' groaned Bumble, slowly, annunciating every word, 'you cannot be serious.'

'Deadly serious. I am ashamed to admit there wasn't much of a cross-over time between Bill and Johnnie. At least I can strike Carlo off the list. I'm not at all proud of this rather "busy" period of my life. I just wish there was a period, I'm normally so regular. Everything was really intense with Johnnie in the beginning, I didn't even notice I was late. Then I started to feel a bit queasy in the mornings, so I did a couple of those pee tests, but they were all negative. I thought it must be too many hangovers. When I got passed the date of my second period and still nothing, I went to my doctor to get a blood test. Hey presto – preggers. What the fuck am I going to do?'

'Aren't you on the Pill.'

'No, it really disagrees with me. I've had a cap for years. It's always been fine.'

'Well, who's it more likely to be?'

I shrugged my shoulders helplessly.

'OK, so we need to be practical. Although I must say it would have been much easier if at least one of the potential fathers was single.'

I threw a cushion at her. 'Thank you, I feel so much better.'

'So, here's what we do . . . ' She paused. 'Go and see your mother.'

'My mother? What planet are you on? At least you didn't suggest my father – overseeing all those government experiments have made him even more peculiar about sex.'

'Trust me, your mother will have a solution. Only someone

302

as – ' once again Bumble struggled for a word, 'unique as your mother will be able to sort this out. She doesn't think like other people, which makes her eminently qualified to sort out what is essentially a big fuck up. Oops, no pun intended!'

She actually managed to make me laugh.

'Darling!' exclaimed my mother, wrapping me in a warm hug, 'what huge excitement.' Only my mother could view my calamitous circumstances so positively. 'Come in, have a large glass of wine, forget those boring doctors for the moment and let's make some plans. Now, I'm assuming you're keeping this baby?'

I nodded. I had momentarily thought of having an abortion and dismissed the idea immediately. There was no way I could do it.

'Thought so, I remember all those budgerigars you used to breed, you're a natural.'

That was surreal – a natural mother or a natural bird breeder?

'Mother, please get to the point.'

'I think you should go to America.'

'Um well, it's not quite so straightforward. When I rang to tell you I was pregnant, I omitted to tell you a teensy-weensy other detail. I'm not sure who the father is.' I paused, feeling appalled.

'Oh, darling, what a busy little pollinating bee you have been. Who might the other lucky candidate be?'

I told her. She clapped her hands together. 'Oh, darling, I love him too!' The one thing about my mother is that she is not judgemental.

'Yes, so do I now, but that still doesn't solve my dilemma. And by the way, currently neither of them knows.'

'Well,' said my mother, pouring us both another huge glass of wine, 'you have two choices. The first is you tell neither and move in with me. I have plenty of room, you can have this adorable baby, I will look after her – it will be a girl, of course,

I always know – and you can work here in the country. You'd be snapped up, there are so few people with your talents here.' (I wondered what talents she was talking about, but anyway . . .) 'It would be such fun, darling. I adore babies. So that's option one, you don't need to rely on anyone. Which leads you to option two in a position of greater strength, because, darling, you're not desperate. Option two is this. You must tell them. You'll know from their reaction immediately which one to stay with. Trust me, it will be that simple, because – '

I interrupted her, 'But mother, Bill is in America, and I have no idea what he'll say. I'm living in London with Johnnie, who is going through a hideous divorce. A baby is the last thing on their minds.'

'Darling, you never listen. I didn't say tell them you're pregnant. I hadn't finished. Tell them you want to break up, say it isn't working out or something, and eventually, and I do mean after at least half an hour, you let them worm the truth out of you. Then you'll see. And don't forget, you have a fall-back position. I doubt you'll need it, but think of yourself as a lucky girl with three options.'

Bumble was right, again, only my mother could turn calamities into opportunities.

'Which one first?'

'Bill, of course, first come, first served.' She giggled. 'Go and see him. Tell Johnnie you're going away with me for a long weekend, get on a plane, go see him. This is absolutely not what you do on a phone.'

'Mum, there's one thing we haven't discussed. In the unlikely event that this insane plan of yours works and one of these men turns round and says, good, let's be together, etc., etc., suppose it's the wrong father?'

'Darling, really!' my mother sounded quite cross suddenly. 'There has to be some penance for your foolhardiness, but it's for you to suffer, not the men, not the child, no one else must ever know. If one of them had been black, it would have been much more tricky.'

So I rang Bill, who was delighted when I said I wanted to come and see him; he even said he'd pay for my ticket, which I refused – very impractical, said my mother, I might need the money for a cot. I told Johnnie I was going to Capri with my mother – which was half true, as she was going. But I realized, sadly, that for someone who prided themselves on telling the truth and despised duplicity, my life from now on was going to be marred by the shadow of the one huge secret I could tell no one, ever.

Bill greeted me at the airport looking gorgeous as always. How is it possible, I wondered to myself, that I can love two men – albeit very differently. I'd surprised myself by how quickly I'd come to love Johnnie. Perhaps the fact I'd seen him virtually every day for what was coming up to a year helped. But it felt right, as though we were meant to be together. If Bill wasn't around to throw an emotional spanner in the works, I'd have no doubts whatsoever. But here he was in front of me and all my feelings for him came rushing back as he flung his arms around me.

'Darlin', it's good to see you on my side of the ocean. I'm taking you to the farm, it's my special place.'

We drove for a couple of hours, making idle conversation, until his car turned into a long drive off the main road. On either side were tall trees lining the way. There was a huge lake in front of a elegant white house with green shutters. In front of the house was a covered porch, complete with a couple of rocking chairs, and leading down to the lake was a path bordered by the most lavish array of colourful flower-beds. Behind the house was a forest, not dark and menacing, but light, with little tracks disappearing into it. It was breath-takingly beautiful and so peaceful.

'This place is incredible, how can you bear to leave it?' I asked.

'Gets a bit lonely just me on my own,' said Bill, 'so I don't come down as often as I should. It's a family home really, and since my daughter lives with her mother, place seems kinda big for just me.'

He put my bag down in the hallway and I followed him into the kitchen, where he got out a bottle of champagne and a couple of glasses. 'Let's go sit by the lake so we can talk,' he said.

It was almost as if he knew. I was shaking with nerves.

We sat down on a bench by the lake. He popped the cork of the champagne, which he managed to make fly in an arc into the water. He filled our glasses and raised his to me.

'Cheers, darlin'. Welcome to America. Now, what is it you want to tell me? Because, overjoyed as I am to see you, I know this trip ain't without a purpose.'

I tried to pull myself together. While I hadn't imagined this was going to be easy, I hadn't realized quite how impossibly difficult it was going to be. Mother had made it sound so simple. I wished she could have been there.

I twisted the stem of my champagne glass round and round in my hands. My lips were having trouble shaping the words I knew had to come out. I couldn't speak.

'Look darlin', if it's about you and Lyle it's fine, I know already.'

I nearly dropped my glass. 'What?' I exclaimed.

'Not much that I don't know. I blame myself entirely. Leaving a gorgeous thing like you alone. Not being able to give you the commitment you want. I was a fool, I know. But I've been a bachelor for a long time and I never planned to settle down with anyone. Kinda liked my own company. Hiding behind my wife and daughter, having my cookie and eating someone else's as well. Turns out, now I've met you, I don't want that no more. You remember the dog with your mother? Well its just the same for me: now that you're with someone else, I know just how much I want you to be with me. You beat me to it. I was about to get on a plane to London and declare myself to you. I even bought you a ring.' He paused, I held my breath. 'Polly, will you marry me?'

With that he dug into his pocket and brought out a little box.

'Oh God, Bill, wait . . . ' I had tears pouring down my face. I held on to his hand, shaking. 'You don't know everything.' I swallowed hard, trying to compose myself. 'I'm pregnant.' Mother's advice had flown out of the window.

He put the box down and took both my hands.

'Who's baby is it?'

'I don't know. I'm so sorry.' I couldn't stop crying. I buried my head in his shoulder while he held me close, patting me on the back.

'There, there honey. Stop these tears now. It ain't the end of the world. How can life be the end? It's the beginning. You just gotta decide what you want to do. Look at me.' He raised my head in his hands. 'My offer still stands. It's you I want, and if the package is you and a baby, well that's fine by me too. I love you, I love everything about you and if there's just a bit more of you than before, well, lucky me.'

I couldn't believe what I was hearing. I flung my arms around Bill. 'I love you too. I can't believe you love me, that you would take me, baby and all.'

'Well, it might be my baby, but I doubt it. My wife had a lot of trouble getting pregnant and she always blamed me, said her family had a fertility track-record going back to the *Mayflower*. She talked like they populated half of America. Chances are it's Lyle's. You told him?'

I shook my head.

'Well, honey, here's what we're going to do. We are not goin' to discuss this any more. You and me are going to have a wonderful weekend together here, then you'll get on that plane and tell your story to Lyle and I shall hope and pray that you come straight back, collect this ring and accept my offer.'

42

'Polly!' Johnnie opened the door to the flat with a flourish, 'welcome back. How was Italy?'

'Fine,' I lied. 'How was Hampshire?'

'Parents were well, children were adorable, Belinda was a cow. Nightmare woman let them stay with me for the absolute minimum amount of time I'm allowed by law. I miss them so much. I can't wait for you to meet them. I spoke to my lawyer about you, by the way. I asked him when we could go public; even though you were not the cause of our break-up I really don't want your name dragged through the courts. Belinda tried to cite Dora. When I told her, Dora sounded quite capable of murdering her. I managed to persuade Belinda it was not a good idea. Dora's family have some scary connections.'

'Oh,' I said, my curiosity piqued, 'when did you speak to Dora?'

Johnnie went a bit pink. 'I, er, had to speak to her about this citing business. That was all.' He looked decidedly shifty.

During the time we'd been living together I'd been amazed at the persistence of the woman. Initially, she wrote to him most days – I used to bin the letters before Johnnie could see them – and as she clearly didn't realize I was living there, little presents would be left on the doorstep. A jumper, a shepherd's pie, a book of love poems. I wore the jumper, ate the pie and gave the book to Johnnie with the inscription on the first page carefully torn out. Well, a girl has to protect her man from himself after all! My getting pregnant was going to throw a spanner in her works!

'So what did he say?'

'Who?' said Johnnie, distractedly.

'The lawyer.'

'Oh, yes, sorry, he said whenever we wanted to. I thought I

might take you to dinner at Annabel's and plan our next course of action, but not before I ravish you in the bedroom. Come here, I missed you.'

He made a move towards me and I side-stepped him. 'Johnnie, can we have a drink first, I need to talk to you about something.'

'Oh dear, you sound serious. OK then, I'll pour us some wine.'

I went into the sitting-room and waited for him to bring the drinks. He settled himself opposite me.

'Well – ' I started, then paused. 'I think we should break up.' There, I said it.

'What!' yelled Johnnie, leaping up from his chair. 'What the hell are you talking about? Why? What on earth did you mother say to you? I don't believe you.' He went on ranting for a while longer until he finally ran out of steam.

'Johnnie, I'm serious, it's not going to work.' I started to give a list of spurious reasons, but he interrupted me.

'No, there's more, something else, someone else. Fuck, there's someone else, who is it? I'll kill him.' He started pacing the room in a frantic fashion.

This wasn't as easy as I had hoped. I assured him there was no one else, but he simply refused to accept it, said it had to be the only reason, otherwise he wouldn't believe I really wanted to go. This went on for what seemed like ages. I checked my watch, it was only fifteen minutes. I wondered if I could fast-forward mother's half-hour, I couldn't take much more.

'OK, OK, Johnnie, you win,' I said, wearily. 'It is something else. I think you should sit down.'

'I'm perfectly fine standing up, thank you,' he snapped.

'I have to leave you because I'm pregnant.'

There was a long silence.

'Pregnant?' he said quietly.

Bloody hell I thought, what kind of life do I have where I'm telling two different men within the space of one week that I'm pregnant. What kind of person am I? No wonder I can't meet normal guys, there's nothing remotely normal about me.

'Well, that changes everything,' he said quietly.

Oh shit, well I guess mother was right, the decision would be made for me.

'Absolutely everything,' he repeated, almost to himself. He looked up at me. 'Come here, Polly.' I got up and walked over to him, not knowing what to expect. He took hold of my hand. 'You cannot know how what you have just said makes me feel. If you think there's any chance in the world now that I'd let you leave, you're completely misguided. You're stuck with me now, through thick and thin. It isn't exactly the most convenient of timing and God knows what people will think, but these things happen for a reason and perhaps this is to show me just how much I want to spend the rest of my life with you. Darling Polly, I've lost two children already, if you think I'm going to let a third, not to mention you, out of my life, think again.'

43

So that was two proposals in a week, both from men who were married to someone else. It was a result of sorts, I suppose. I was sitting in mother's garden, trying to work out what to do. Maybe I should just stay with her.

I loved Bill and Johnnie in such different ways.

Mother had said something really strange to me and I was mulling it over.

'Darling, you must marry people for their faults.'

Only my mother, right?

She continued, 'There's no point in marrying someone for their good points. We all have good points, and they're easy to live with. When you get married, what you end up living with is someone's faults; are they faults you can live with, that you don't mind?'

I knew Johnnie well and I certainly knew his faults. I'd seen them day in and day out. Bill was an unknown quantity. The idea of travelling halfway across the world to live with a man I didn't really know that well, who'd been a bachelor for a long time, with a reputation for womanizing and drinking, was very daunting. Far more of a risk than to stay with Johnnie, in my own country, with my family and friends. Added to which, there was a greater probability the baby was Johnnie's and we seemed such a perfect match, our backgrounds so similar.

I sighed.

'I have something for you.' My mother came out into the garden. She handed me a sealed envelope.

'What is it?' I asked, lost in my thoughts.

'Your father gave it to me when you were in America.' I had no idea my parents were in touch. 'Well, I felt he ought to know what was going on. However, it was most irritating; he came rushing round here and told me to give you this envelope. He says he put something in it the day he came to your office for the first time and sealed it. He thinks the time has come for you to open it.'

I opened the envelope and inside was a slip of paper on which something was written in my father's distinctive hand:

There are occasional moments in my life when I have strong premonitions. I write them down and put them in sealed envelopes to be opened after the event. Today I believe I have met the man my daughter will marry. Johnnie Lyle.

I gasped. It was dated six months ago. 'Mum, did you know what was in this?'

Mother was looking inscrutable. 'Well yes, he told me. I thought I was supposed to be the psychic one. So annoying.'

'He's not making this up?'

'Darling, your father isn't a scientist, he's a politician, he doesn't invent things.' She almost managed to say that without irony. She came and sat down beside me and took my hand. 'My baby, it's a wonderful privilege to have choices, but as you go through life you will realize that with choice comes loss. It's as inevitable as life and death, you cannot have one without the other. You can't have both these men. The one you choose will set you on a new path. The other will disappear. Take your time, you'll know in . . . THE END.'